GW00707544

VIRTUAL SEXSTASY

Roxy winked at Alice, and closed the door as she left the room. Alice fitted the sensors into place, then put on the headset, took a deep breath, and pressed 'enter' . . .

She was sitting on the sofa between them. Two equally handsome men, both around six feet tall, both with mid-brown hair and hazel eyes. Both of them wore faded jeans, tight enough to reveal shapely buttocks and firm thighs, teamed with a black round-neck cotton sweater. Alice shivered. By some standards, she would call this greedy. But tonight, she considered herself very lucky indeed.

One of them had his arm thrown negligently round her shoulders; the other had one hand resting very lightly on her inner thigh. She could feel the warmth of his hand through her thin leggings, and she could imagine that hand drifting higher, touching her more intimately . . .

Also by Evelyn D'Arcy in New English Library paperback

Midnight Blue
Interlover

NEW ENGLISH LIBRARY
Hodder and Stoughton

Dangerous Passions

Evelyn D'Arcy

NEW ENGLISH LIBRARY
Hodder and Stoughton

Copyright © 1997 by Evelyn D'Arcy

First published in 1997 by Hodder and Stoughton
A division of Hodder Headline PLC

A New English Library paperback

The right of Evelyn D'Arcy to be identified as the Author of
the Work has been asserted by her in accordance with the
Copyright, Designs and Patents Act 1988.

10 9 8 7 6 5 4 3 2 1

All rights reserved. No part of this publication may be
reproduced, stored in a retrieval system, or transmitted,
in any form or by any means without the prior written
permission of the publisher, nor be otherwise circulated
in any form of binding or cover other than that in which
it is published and without a similar condition being
imposed on the subsequent purchaser.

All characters in this publication are fictitious
and any resemblance to real persons, living or dead,
is purely coincidental.

British Library Cataloguing in Publication Data

A CIP catalogue record for this title is available
from the British Library

ISBN 0 340 68266 3

Typeset by Palimpsest Book Production Limited,
Polmont, Stirlingshire
Printed and bound in Great Britain by
Mackays of Chatham PLC, Chatham, Kent

Hodder and Stoughton
A division of Hodder Headline PLC
338 Euston Road
London NW1 3BH

For Valerie and Keith

PART I

ONE

'Roxy, are you home?' Alice called, closing the door with a well-aimed thrust of her bottom.

'In here,' Roxy called.

Alice dumped her briefcase on a chair and the rest of her shopping in the kitchen before walking into her flatmate's bedroom. Roxy was sitting at the small pine table in the corner of the room, tapping codes into her computer. Alice stood with her hands on her hips and a frown on her face, looking at her. Typical Roxy. She was a workaholic, and the only time she wasn't glued to her computer was when Alice brought a good film home from the local video rental shop and persuaded her flatmate to watch it and share a bottle of wine with her. Even then, Roxy's mind was usually half elsewhere, working on some computer program or other.

'You know, if that thing was human,' Alice said, nodding at the computer, 'you'd be having a full-blooded affair with it.'

Roxy rolled her eyes, still facing the screen. 'Oh, Al, don't be so melodramatic.'

'You spend more time with it than you do with anything else,' Alice continued, raking her red-gold hair back from her face. 'I mean, when was the last time you went out with a man, let alone went to bed with one?'

Roxy shrugged. 'I don't know. And to be honest, I don't really care.'

'Well, I do. It's not good for you, Roxy, to spend so much

time glued to that thing. I mean, you do enough programming at work, without bringing it home as well.'

Roxy laughed then, her serious face folding into prettiness. 'Come the Revolution . . .' she quipped.

'You and your Technology Revolution,' Alice grumbled half-heartedly. 'Virtual reality, shopping and working and doing everything else from a computer screen – I mean, it's a nice dream, but that's about it.'

'It'll happen in the next couple of years,' Roxy said earnestly, twisting round to look at her friend over the rim of her glasses. 'It's going to be mind-blowing, Al. Half the world's problems will be halved at a stroke. Just think, there'll be no more rush-hour congestion or pollution, because most people will be able to work from home and they can hold meetings by video-conference. Crime will drop, because everyone's genetic code will be on a central computer – and any unauthorized access will be read by alarm systems in houses and cars and whatever. Burglars will be picked up in seconds.'

Alice shivered. 'It sounds more like Big Brother to me. Anyway, what about your social life? You can't do that by technology.'

'Simple. You use electronic mail and videophones.' Roxy's hazel eyes gleamed. 'So you can contact whoever you want, whenever you want.'

'But you can't replace sex,' Alice said.

Roxy grinned. 'Oh, can't you? What about virtual reality?'

'Nah. That's just souped-up computer games, isn't it? People driving fast cars round a simulated track or fighting dinosaurs or being picked up by pterodactyls and dropped off a castle wall.'

Roxy rubbed a hand along her jaw. 'Not necessarily.'

'Then what?' Alice was interested. She'd known Roxy for

nearly ten years, and the signs were unmistakable. Roxy's eyes were more green than brown, and there was a tiny dimpled furrow almost in the middle of her forehead, just above her left eyebrow. It meant that she was plotting something big.

Roxy removed her glasses. 'Imagine owning a virtual-reality sex programme. You can have sex whenever you like, with whoever you like – and the best thing is, it'll be perfectly safe, with no risk of Aids or pregnancy or some yucky STD. And you're guaranteed an orgasm every time. There'll be no faking it to soothe your man's ego, or lying there feeling frustrated when he's finished and you're just getting started.'

'So I could have Kenneth Branagh on Mondays, Keanu Reeves on Tuesdays, Antonio Banderas on Wednesdays, and David Duchovny for a very, very, very long weekend . . .' Alice smiled. 'Mm. I wish. Come the Revolution, eh?'

'Come the Revolution.' Roxy's eyes glittered. 'Or even before that.'

Alice eyed her suspiciously. 'What are you up to, exactly?'

'Working on one of my boring programs.' Roxy grinned. 'Or maybe it's not so boring, after all.'

Alice made the connection immediately. Her jaw dropped. 'You mean you're working on a VR sex program?'

'Yup.' Roxy leaned back in her chair.

'No wonder it's been impossible to drag you away from that thing, lately!' Alice's laugh faded. 'Roxy, are you teasing me, or is that what you're really doing?'

Roxy shrugged. 'There's only one way to prove it. Why don't you try it out?'

Alice was suddenly nervous. 'It's not going to hurt, is it?'

'No, of course it isn't. This is only the prototype – it's basically a headset connected to the computer, plus a few sensors placed in strategic positions.'

Alice's eyes narrowed suspiciously. '*How* strategic?'

Roxy laughed. 'Nowhere painful, I promise. Tell you what – let's have a glass of wine first. It'll relax you. Then I'll hook you up to the program, and you can try it out. It'd really help if you could tell me what you think of it, so far.'

Alice still felt slightly dubious about the idea of making love with a machine, but Roxy was her best friend – which meant that she owed it to her to help. Eventually, she nodded. 'All right.'

They went into the kitchen, and Roxy extracted a bottle of Chardonnay from the fridge. She uncorked it deftly, poured two glasses, and handed one to her flatmate. 'To the Technology Revolution,' she said, lifting her glass.

'You really think it's going to happen, then?' Alice sipped her wine thoughtfully. 'They've been talking about it for years, Roxy. Home shopping, cash cards, the lot. There was all this talk about the Information Superhighway, and how it was going to change everyone's lives – but we don't seem any further forward than we were five years ago.'

'Give it another eighteen months,' Roxy predicted confidently. 'The quality of the graphics and video interfaces are improving daily. Processors are faster, and modems can handle bigger and bigger chunks of data, faster.'

'Which means, in English?'

Roxy shrugged. 'It means that it costs less. You know yourself how cheap CD players and videos are, compared to when they first came out; and a lot of people have more than one in the house, nowadays. As soon as the equipment's available at an affordable price, technology will really rocket. Believe me.' She looked calculatingly at her friend. 'You could do a great article on it.'

'In *Home Matters*?' Alice scoffed. 'Nah. My readers aren't

interested in anything you can't plant, cook or restore to its former glory.'

'I bet most of them own computers, or at least use them at work. To own the sort of houses they do, you need money – and that's in technology, nowadays.'

'Nice try, Roxy, but no.'

Roxy shrugged. 'Fair enough. So, are you ready to give the program a whirl?'

Alice drained her glass. 'All right.'

They returned to Roxy's room; Roxy gestured to her friend to sit down. Alice watched her, fascinated, as she deftly pressed a few keys, then began to manipulate the small grey space-ball on the stand beside the computer.

'What are you doing?'

'Setting it up.' Roxy smiled. 'We'll start with your ideal man. And I don't mean someone famous,' she added hastily, 'so you can't have Antonio or Keanu or Ken. Like I said, it's only a prototype. I haven't scanned in that many faces yet.'

'You mean you can scan in a picture of anyone you like?' Alice was surprised.

'More or less, yes. At least, that's the intention. Then you can fantasize about your lover, your boss, a movie star – even Alexander the Great or Napoleon, if that's what turns you on.' Roxy paused. 'Anyway, describe your ideal man.'

'I think I'll go for the bog-standard fantasy,' Alice said. 'Tall, dark and handsome, with cornflower-blue eyes. Oh, and perhaps a pair of little round glasses, to make him look a bit intellectual.'

'Thin, medium or well-built?'

'Broad shoulders, narrow hips.'

Roxy nodded, and selected various options on the screen. 'Situation, next.' Her lips twitched. 'It's a bit limited, at the moment. You can have sex after dinner at his flat, or sex after dinner at his flat.'

Alice laughed. 'What a choice! Sex after dinner at his flat, I think.'

'Clothes?'

'Armani suit, crisp white cotton shirt, understated silk tie.'

'Hm.' Roxy looked over the edge of her glasses. 'How about a shirt and dark trousers?'

'Any colour Ford you like, as long as it's black?' Alice quipped, laughing.

'Something like that. I did tell you that it's only a prototype. It's just as well that you chose dark hair, blue eyes and glasses, too, or I'd have had to do a lot of persuading.' Roxy fiddled with a few more buttons, and patted the computer invitingly. 'Welcome to . . .' She tipped her head slightly to one side, her fair hair half covering her face. 'The man of your dreams, I suppose.'

Alice sat down. 'What do I have to do?'

Roxy handed her a headset. 'You put this on, for starters. It's audio and visual. I'm still working on the olfactory side of things.'

'So he might not have bathed for days, but I could still think he smells of Armani?' Alice grinned.

'Something like that,' Roxy laughed back. 'Actually, I was planning to link in some kind of aromatherapy, ylang-ylang and sandalwood or whatever – you know, the sensuous oils. Just to get you in the mood.'

'And that's all there is to it?' Alice asked, serious again. 'What about those sensors you were talking about?'

'Well, I was considering a complete body suit – but it's not really workable, because everyone's a different shape. You couldn't manufacture suits at a commercially viable price. So I thought I'd concentrate on the most important parts.'

'You mean I'm going to wear pants with a built-in vibrator and a pair of nipple clips?'

'Nope.' Roxy handed her a pair of thin gloves. 'These will do your finger-tips. I'm afraid there are wires attached at the moment, but eventually they'll work on radio waves or infra red.' She rummaged in her desk drawer and brought out a set of small plastic patches, again with thin wires attached. 'You place these on your erogenous zones – like I said, everyone's different. Put them on the back of your neck, your shoulders, wherever you really like being touched. Or if you just want a quickie demo, your nipples and clitoris will do.'

'Wow.' Alice was impressed. 'You've really thought this out, haven't you?'

Roxy nodded. 'You arty types don't have the monopoly on dreams, you know! But better than that, we science boffins can make them reality – well, *virtual* reality, anyway,' she amended.

'Mm.' Alice slid one hand under her ankle-length pleated skirt, and pulled the gusset of her knickers aside so that she could place one of the little plastic patches on her clitoris. She placed two more on her nipples, in accordance with Roxy's instructions, pulled on the gloves, and sat down. 'This is it, then,' she said, taking a deep breath and sliding on the headset.

'I'll leave you to it. Just press "enter", and it'll start. If you want to move, use the space-ball. It works more or less the same way as the mouse you use with your word processor, just in three dimensions instead of two,' Roxy said, patting her friend on the shoulder and leaving the room quietly.

Alice paused for a moment. Roxy was far too serious to be

a practical joker. On the other hand, this was too fantastic to be real.

There was only one way to find out. She pressed the "enter" key.

She was sitting at a narrow table, a fine porcelain cup of coffee in front of her. Opposite her sat one of the most gorgeous men she had ever seen. His hair was thick and dark and slightly wavy, brushed back from his face, and his eyes were a rich cornflower blue, framed by unfairly long and thick lashes and a small round pair of glasses which gave him an intellectual air. His lips were well-shaped, and his high cheekbones gave him a slightly Slavic look.

He smiled at her, and reached across the narrow table to take her hand, curling his fingers round hers. It was the most devastating come-to-bed look Alice had ever seen and made a shiver run down her spine.

They didn't need to say anything. Both of them knew exactly what was going to happen. He stood up, leading her away from the table, and turned her to face him. He slid his hands down her sides, hooking his thumbs under her silk top and brushing the skin on her midriff. She tipped her head back slightly, and he kissed her, his tongue sliding along her lower lip. He burrowed further under her top, unclipping her bra and cupping her breasts with his hands.

His thumbs rubbed gently across her nipples, circling the areolae until her breasts began to swell, the nipples hardening into peaks. He broke the kiss then, pulling the soft material of her top over her head and discarding her bra. He cupped her breasts and rubbed his cheeks against them. He had obviously shaved recently, because his skin felt soft and satiny, no trace of stubble to drag against her skin. She closed her eyes in bliss as he breathed on her nipples, the warmth of his mouth a sharp contrast to the cool air.

She unbuttoned his shirt, sliding her fingers through the crisp hair on his chest. Her hands drifted lower, unbuckling his belt and unzipping his trousers. The bulge in his underpants was gratifyingly large, and she smiled, the curve of her lips full of promise.

He kissed her again, and the next thing she knew, they were lying on the floor, naked, and he was stroking her body, feathering caresses over her thighs. Her legs parted automatically, and his hand cupped her quim, feeling her moist heat pulsing under his fingers. He kissed her lightly on the lips, then his head drifted slowly southwards.

He paused over her breasts, licking her nipples and nipping them very gently between his lips so that she arched up towards him. He tracked a path over her abdomen; by the time he reached her solar plexus, Alice was longing to feel him explore the folds and crevices of her quim with his tongue. She couldn't help lifting her hips slightly, impatient; and, at last, she felt his hands settle on her hips and the brush of his cheeks against her thighs as he traced the length of her quim with his tongue.

She tangled her hands in his hair, the pads of her fingers digging slightly into his scalp; he began to work his tongue along her moist quim, circling her clitoris then flicking his tongue across it at speed until she cried out, the pressure of her fingers increasing as her arousal grew.

A rolling warmth spread through her, pooling in her solar plexus; she cried out again, her internal muscles convulsing sharply. Her last thought as she came was that she wanted it to go on for ever ...

*   *   *

Alice leaned back against the chair, slightly shaken. It had been a computer simulation, she knew that – and yet it had felt so *real*. Her nipples were sharply defined through their thin plastic coverings, and her quim was decidedly throbbing, her internal muscles flexing at the end of her orgasm.

When she'd finally calmed down, she removed the sensors, gloves and headset, and went through to the living room to join Roxy, who was lying on the floor reading a scientific journal, her legs kicked back behind her and her chin propped on her hands.

Roxy looked up as she heard footsteps. 'Well?'

'It's one hell of a program. How did you *do* it?'

Roxy grinned and sat up, throwing the journal to one side. 'Have you got a spare few weeks for me to explain it in layman's terms?'

Alice smiled. 'Trade secret, eh?'

'Just very technical, and utterly boring to anyone working outside that particular field. It's what you would term Anorakese.' Roxy looked slightly apprehensive. 'Did you think that it was any good, then?'

'Mm.' Alice bit her lip. 'I was expecting something more – well – more like a computer game. You know, me in the flesh bonking Superman from the comic book. This was almost like starring in my own private film.'

'Video,' Roxy confirmed. 'It's a full multimedia program. Or it will be, by the time I've finished with it.'

'You mean that there's more?'

'Oh, definitely.' Roxy nodded. 'I want to make several different scenarios. You know, adding a bit of choice to it. Replaying the same fantasy over and over again – well, it's too limited. I want to work up from straight programmed scenarios to situations where people's minds can just run free ... though I think that that one's a bit out of my reach, just yet.'

'Well,' Alice said, 'when you get to the next test stage, if you're looking for volunteers, and all your virtual hunks are as gorgeous as he was, I'm game.'

'Cheers.' Roxy grinned. 'You're on.'

'You know, I think I'm going to enjoy being a guinea pig.' Alice paused. 'That man's really something. Who is he?'

Roxy flushed. 'No one in particular,' she mumbled.

'Come on, Roxy. Tell me. Who is he?'

Roxy sighed. 'All right. If you really must know, his name's Tim Fraser. He works for Comco, and I met him at the Visicom exhibition a few weeks ago.'

'And?'

'That's all there is to it.' Roxy hugged her knees, refusing to look her flatmate in the eye.

'Apart from the fact that you fancy him like mad.'

'I do *not*.'

'Roxy, I've known you for nearly ten years,' Alice reminded her. 'I'm your best friend. You can't keep secrets from me.'

'Okay, so I find him attractive. But that's in the same way that I and about six million other women find David Duchovny as Fox Mulder attractive. There's no more to it than that.' Roxy spread her hands. 'What's the big deal?'

'Is he single?'

Roxy looked blank. 'I've no idea.'

'Well, ask the man out for a drink. You'll soon find out.'

'I can't do that!' Roxy shook her head. 'Look, I met him once. He probably won't even remember me. Anyway, I shouldn't think that I'm his type.'

'Meaning?'

'Al, you know what I mean. I'm not exactly a glamour-puss,

am I? I'm a dull, frumpy scientist who wears glasses; I could
do with losing a couple of stone; and you couldn't describe me
as pretty, let alone the drop-dead gorgeous supermodel type
he'd go for.' Roxy took a deep breath. 'Anyway, I'm too busy
to start chasing men.'

Alice topped up their glasses. 'Let's revisit that, shall we?
First of all, you're not dull – you're good company, and you
know it. You're not frumpy, either: you just happen to wear
fairly understated clothes. If you want glamour, all you have
to do is go down Oxford Street with me and let me loose with
your credit card. You won't recognize yourself by the time I've
finished with you.'

'Hm.' Roxy, knowing Alice's penchant for designer clothes,
mentally crossed that out as a potentially bankrupting experience.

'Secondly, glasses suit you.' Roxy's were large, not quite
rounded, and perfectly suited to the shape of her face. 'And
don't forget how much men love taking off a woman's
glasses. It's the same as unpinning long hair – it really
turns them on.'

'If you say so.' Roxy wasn't convinced.

'Thirdly, as for losing a couple of stone, if you went to a
couple of exercise classes every week instead of being glued
to that bloody computer every minute of the day, you'd soon
tone up; besides, men like women with curves.'

Roxy was silent.

'And finally, as for you not being pretty – come on, you've
got gorgeous eyes, your lips are a perfect Cupid's bow, and
most women would dye and perm their hair to get it looking
like yours. A bit of make-up would highlight all your good
points; and, of course, you could always smile, instead of
scowling.'

'I do *not* scowl.'

'You do when you're concentrating. This Tim was probably too scared to come over and ask you out, in case you bit his head off.'

Roxy took a sip of wine. 'That's all pure speculation, Al. Anyway, who says that I want to get involved with him?'

Alice laughed. 'You've put the man in a virtual-reality sex fantasy program, and you're trying to tell me that you don't want to get involved with him?'

Roxy's smile was rueful. 'And since when have I ever been able to hide anything from you, anyway?'

'Exactly what I said. Just ask the guy out for a drink. If he's married, he's out of reach anyway. If he's single, and turns out to be a complete jerk, you don't have to see him again. Though if his personality's as good as his looks, then bingo!' Alice snapped her fingers.

Roxy rubbed her jaw. 'Supposing I ask him out, and he says yes ... What am I going to talk to him about?'

'You said that he works for Comco, and you met him at an exhibition. He's probably as obsessed with computers as you are. You can chat about it, two anoraks together.' Alice rolled her eyes. 'Roxy, don't make such a big deal out of it. It's an evening out, that's all.'

'Mm. I'll think about it.'

Alice was exasperated. She knew that look. It meant that Roxy might *think* about it, but had no intention of *doing* anything. If Roxy and Tim Fraser were ever to get together, they'd need a skilful helping hand. And Alice was just the person to supply it.

A couple of evenings later, they were talking in the kitchen as Roxy cooked dinner. Alice leaned back against the worktop.

'This dating by e-mail business you were talking about, the other day . . .'

'What about it?' Roxy continued chopping mushrooms.

'Do you really think that it'll catch on in Britain? I mean, writing to someone you've never met . . .' Alice wrinkled her nose. 'Isn't it a bit awkward?'

'No more awkward than being a pen-pal. Better, in fact, because you don't have to wait for the post. You can have interactive conversations.'

'What's that, in English?'

Roxy groaned. 'You're a journalist, Al. I can't believe you're not using e-mail already.'

'Only the tecchies in the office have it. And they're . . .' Alice spread her hands. 'Well, they're not very approachable. Whereas you are. And you can at least speak in English, if someone reminds you.'

'Okay.' Roxy grinned at her friend's backhanded compliment. 'It means, if you send me a message, I can send a reply as soon as I've read it – and then you can reply back when you've read my reply. It's a bit like a phone call, but on screen. They do it all the time, in the States. They go a bit further, actually, and chat "on line" – which means that it really *is* like having a phone call.'

'Yeah, but that's the States. It's not the same, in Britain – it couldn't be, even if local phone calls were free, like they are in the States.'

'Give it a year or two, and a lot more people will be using it. Like I said, as soon as the technology's cheap enough, people will use it.' Roxy's lips twitched. 'Actually, I reckon you'd be a terrible e-mail junkie. If you had it here, our phone bill would rocket. Unless we get free local calls, that is.'

Alice ignored the comment. 'Anyway, this e-mail dating

business. You still wouldn't know what the other person looked like.'

'Yes, you would,' Roxy explained patiently. 'The first contact would be on a floppy disk or a CD-ROM, with a video of you talking. If you have a multi-media system, you can use sound and video and graphics – so if you were sending directions to a place where you were going to meet, you could put a map on the screen, highlight the route and talk the other person through it at the same time – and then they could print out the map as a reference for later.'

Alice nodded. 'It sounds like something out of a science fiction movie. *Blade Runner*, but nicer.'

'The technology's there now. I've seen a demo of it, and it works very well. It just isn't cheap enough for mass market yet.' Roxy melted some butter in a pan, and added the mushrooms. 'Why the sudden interest, anyway? I thought you said you couldn't get an article out of it?'

'Not for *Home Matters*, but I can always write something for another magazine, as a freelance.' Alice looked sidelong at her friend. 'So how would you find out someone's e-mail ID?'

'It depends. If it's within a company, there's usually a directory on the internal system. If you want to contact someone else, you can try looking it up on the network directory, though that assumes they've put their ID on the directory. If they haven't, you can always ring them up and ask for it.'

'But it's easy to find an ID?'

'On the network I use, yes.' Roxy nodded. 'It sounds like you're in bloodhound journo mode. It's just as easy as using a word processor, believe me. I'll show you after dinner, if you like.' She grinned. 'In return for you doing the washing up.'

'Done.' Alice smiled. Roxy had fallen for it beautifully. All she had to do was find out Tim Fraser's ID, and then send him a suitable message, supposedly from Roxy.

Roxy was as good as her word, talking Alice through the e-mail program and showing her how the directory worked.

'So you can find anyone?' Alice was impressed.

'As long as you know their name and company, and they've entered their details in the directory, yes.' Roxy typed in a couple of lines. 'Supposing you wanted to know my ID: all you do is call up the standard directory enquiry form, type "Winters" in the surname field, "R" in the first name field, and "Visicom" in the company field, and send it off.'

She pressed the "send" key; ten seconds later, her machine bleeped. She smiled. 'That's the response.' She selected the message. 'And there you have it. My full name, my ID, and my telephone number.'

'Wow. It's quicker than looking someone up in a phone book.'

'I know. I use it a lot, for business contacts.' Roxy stretched. 'So, what else do you need for your article?'

'I'm not sure, really. I need to plan it out properly first.' Alice looked slightly embarrassed. 'This is all going a little bit quicker than I expected. I need time to think about it.'

'Fair enough.' Roxy yawned. 'Well, I'm going to have a bath.'

'Can I play that new patience game of yours for a while?' Alice asked.

'Of course.' Roxy smiled at her friend. 'You know how to get into it, don't you?'

'I'm not *that* computer-illiterate, you know,' Alice retorted with a grin. 'I do use a computer at work.'

'"Use", in the loosest possible sense of the word,' Roxy teased.

'Okay, so I don't write programs – but I'm a damn sight better with the word-processing program than the blokes in the office next door.'

'Most programmers don't need to use word-processing programs,' Roxy reminded her, laughing.

'You science boffins don't have a complete monopoly on brain cells, Roxy.'

'No?'

'No!' Alice stuck out her tongue.

She waited until the bathroom door had closed and the sound of running water had stopped before flipping back to Roxy's electronic mailbox. It was a few seconds' work to look up Tim Fraser at Comco; and a few seconds more to type a message on the screen. She paused for a moment to re-read the message, then smiled and sent it. This was going to solve all Roxy's problems with shyness. And just to make sure that Roxy couldn't recall the message before Tim Fraser had a chance to read it, Alice deleted the record.

'Mail,' the electronic voice said softly.

Tim flipped into his mailbox. Sure enough, there was a message. He frowned, not recognizing the ID. It wasn't anyone from Comco; he could tell that much. Intrigued, he called up the message.

'Data interchange with the woman of your dreams.' Tim's frown deepened. What the hell was this – some kind of electronic junk mail? 'If you want to know more, call me.' There was a telephone number at the bottom, and it was signed "Roxana Winters".

Roxana Winters. He knew the name from somewhere, though he couldn't quite place it. He drummed his fingers on his desk. The woman of his dreams . . . He smiled. Whoever she was, she sounded a damn sight more interesting than most of the women he'd met recently. He'd call her first thing in the morning.

The phone shrilled; Roxy picked it up and answered it on autopilot, keeping most of her attention on the program on her screen. 'Good morning, Visicom Development.'

'Could I speak to Roxana Winters, please?'

'Speaking.'

'It's Tim Fraser.'

Roxy almost dropped the receiver. Why the hell was Tim Fraser ringing her? She swallowed, and put on her best professional voice. 'How can I help?'

'It's about your e-mail.'

'I'm sorry?' Roxy frowned.

'Your e-mail. The one you sent me last night.'

'I'm sorry, there must be some mistake.' Roxy was coolly polite. 'I haven't sent you an e-mail.'

'It was signed Roxana Winters.' He rattled off her ID number. 'That's you, isn't it?'

'Yes, but—' She stopped dead. She'd left the electronic mail package running while Alice had been playing games . . . Her mouth went dry. Surely Alice wouldn't have done that to her?

'You mentioned data interchange with the woman of my dreams – and to call you if I wanted to know more.'

Roxy groaned. 'Look, Mr Fraser, there's been some kind of mistake. I think we're both the victims of a practical joke.'

'Oh?'

A muscle in her jaw twitched. Alice had better have a good explanation for this . . . 'I'm sorry that your time's been wasted.'

'That's all right.' He sounded faintly amused. 'Though I was rather looking forward to meeting the woman of my dreams.'

Roxy squirmed. There was no way she could avoid explaining, now. 'I'm afraid it's my flatmate's idea of a joke. She's a journalist, and she's writing this article about dating via electronic mail. I left my mailbox open, and it sounds like she decided to try a practical example.'

Tim liked the sound of her voice. Quiet, serious, and yet with a sensual undertone as exotic as her name. He wondered what Roxana Winters was like in the flesh. Tall, curvy and red-haired, with green eyes and skin like porcelain. 'Perhaps we ought to meet,' he suggested. 'Just to test the theory, of course.'

Roxy was stunned. 'I . . .'

'That is, if your husband won't mind?'

'I'm not married,' she said.

'Neither am I.' He paused. 'Do you like pasta?'

'Yes.'

'Then how about we meet for dinner on Friday night to discuss it?'

Roxy was stunned into silence.

'Roxana? Are you still there?'

'Yes.'

'Are you free on Friday evening?'

'Yes.' She winced. It sounded like she was a robot, with only one word in her vocabulary.

'There's a little pasta place just off Shaftesbury Avenue. I'll meet you there at eight.'

'Fine. I'll see you then.'

She replaced the receiver, feeling slightly shaky. This time, Alice had gone too far. She quickly dialled her friend's number.

'Southern Publishing,' a bored voice said.

'Alice Jamieson, please.'

The line crackled for a moment; then the extension was connected and Alice's voice came through. 'Good morning, *Home Matters* Editorial.'

'You,' Roxy hissed, 'are going to die very, very slowly, when I get home.'

Alice coughed as she recognized the voice. 'Oh. You've had an e-mail from Tim Fraser, then?'

'A phone call, actually.' Roxy paused. 'The woman of his dreams, indeed! What the hell did you say that for?'

'Well, you might be.' Alice's curiosity got the better of her. 'What did he say?'

'Not much.'

'Oh, come on, Roxy, don't leave me in suspense.'

Roxy laughed, and hung up. Then she placed her phone on "divert". Alice could sweat it out for the rest of the day. She turned back to her computer, and began working on her program again.

The living room door opened a crack, and a slightly battered white tissue was waved up and down very slowly.

Roxy burst out laughing. 'Oh, Al, honestly!'

Alice came into the room, looking slightly shamefaced. 'Well, you did say that you were going to kill me, very slowly.'

'I felt like it this morning, believe me.' Roxy's lips twitched.

'So what did he say?'

'Not much.'

'Roxy, don't be mean. Tell me.'

Roxy said nothing.

Alice came to sit on the arm of her friend's chair. 'Come on, tell your Auntie Al what happened.'

Roxy just smiled.

'Roxy!'

'You don't deserve to be told anything, after that little stunt,' Roxy said sweetly.

'Well, it was the only way to get you to talk to the man!' Alice's blue eyes sparkled. 'Did you ask him?'

'What?'

'To go out for a drink, of course!'

Roxy shook her head.

Alice rolled her eyes. 'You're hopeless.'

'I know.'

'It was the perfect set-up.' Alice sighed. 'Now I've got to think of another plan.'

Roxy decided to be kind. '*He* asked *me* out to dinner.'

'It'll take me ages to think up a good – hang on, did you just say he asked you out to dinner?'

'On Friday night,' Roxy confirmed.

'I hope you said yes.'

'It was about all I could say,' Roxy admitted. 'We're going to a little pasta café.' She suddenly sobered. 'Al – what am I going to wear? What am I going to say to him?'

Alice smiled. 'Leave what you look like to me. I'll sort something out of your wardrobe, and do your make-up. As for what you're going to say to him – just talk about computers, and take it from there.'

Roxy's lips twitched. 'You make me sound like a trainspotter. Perhaps I should wear an anorak or a duffle coat.'

Alice laughed. 'Well, once you computer boffins start jabbering about bytes and RAM . . .'

Roxy threw a cushion at her. 'I'm not that bad.'

'Yeah, yeah.' Alice pulled a face. 'Well – Friday night's going to be a damn sight more interesting this week than it

has been for months. It's a shame I'm away for the weekend.'
She twirled the ends of her hair round her fingers. 'I suppose
I could always cancel it.'

Roxy groaned. 'Don't you dare!'

'On condition,' Alice said, 'that you tell me everything, later.
And I mean, *everything* . . .'

TWO

Roxy swiftly put the sensors in place, pulled on the thin gloves, and donned the headset. She tapped the "enter" key, then curved her fingers round the space-ball.

Tim Fraser smiled at her. She reached up to touch his face, sliding her fingers over his jaw. It felt slightly rough, with the beginnings of stubble. She traced the outline of his lower lip, and he sucked her finger, his eyes warm and full of promise. Smiling, she reached up with her free hand to remove his glasses.

He slid his hands down to span her waist, and lowered his face to hers. He rubbed his nose against hers, and then she felt the warmth of his lips nibbling hers, teasing, tormenting kisses that made her push urgently against him.

At once, Tim's mouth became more demanding, his tongue outlining her lips, then, as her mouth opened under his, sliding in against her own. His hands caressed her buttocks, squeezing them gently; then he began to pull up her calf-length pleated skirt, bunching the material in one hand until he had bared her thighs.

He gave a murmur of delight when he saw her black lace-topped stockings, and slid one hand down to caress the creamy-white flesh visible above the welts. Roxy arched against him, widening the gap between her thighs so that his fingers could curl round to cup her quim; through the black silk of her knickers, she felt warm and moist.

Her chin tilted back as he moved the thin gusset aside and began stroking her quim, his fingers dabbling in her moistness and then coming back to flicker over her clitoris. She gasped, and the pressure and speed of his strokes increased, tantalizing her and bringing her close to the edge of orgasm.

She reached out to undo his trousers, curling her fingers round his thick shaft and squeezing it slightly. He laughed and pushed his trousers downwards, removing his pants in the same lithe movement. As the garments fell to the floor, he kicked them aside and pulled her back into his arms. His cock was hot and hard against her belly; she pushed against him, liking the feel of it, and he groaned.

He kissed her again, hard, and lifted her; she wound her arms round his neck for balance. His cock nudged against her pubis, and she pulled the gusset of her knickers to one side to give him access. He slid his cock into her spongy wet depths and she wrapped her legs round his waist, gripping him to pull him deeper. He felt so good, long and thick and filling her to the hilt; she flexed her internal muscles, and he groaned at the feel of her soft velvety flesh fluttering round his cock.

Tim walked very slowly across the room until they reached the wall, supporting her back against it; then he began to thrust hard, his balls slapping against the lips of her quim. Roxy slid her hands into his hair, the pads of her fingers digging into his scalp; she pulled his mouth onto hers again, kissing him hard.

He murmured something against her mouth, something that she couldn't catch; then he curved his fingers round the neck of her shirt, and tugged at it until the buttons gave and the opening parted, revealing her breasts. He eased his fingers under the cups of her bra and pulled the material down, releasing her breasts; she groaned as he began to play with her already hardened nipples, arousing her even more.

Pleasure began to pool in her solar plexus, radiating through her body; she gave a cry, and her internal muscles convulsed sharply around his thick hard cock. It was enough to tip him over the edge into his own orgasm, and his cock throbbed hotly inside her, deepening her pleasure . . .

Roxy stared at the computer screen. Tomorrow night wouldn't be anything like that. They'd have dinner, talk a little; but that would be it. Everything would be on neutral ground, with as little intimacy as possible. There was no way a man like Tim Fraser could possibly fancy her. And yet she couldn't help wondering what it would be like, if by some mad freak of fate they did end up in bed together. Would he live up to the simulation?

With a sigh, she switched off the machine. Maybe he would, maybe he wouldn't. Not that she'd have the chance to find out. She might as well stop dreaming, use the experience of dinner to improve the program a little, and forget it.

Tim Fraser was waiting by the little restaurant, leaning against the wall with one foot crossed casually in front of the other. Roxy's stomach turned to water as she reached the corner of the street and realized that it was him. She'd only seen him in a suit before; in black jeans and a black cotton polo-neck sweater, he looked absolutely stunning.

She was half tempted to walk past him, pretending that she was someone else: though she knew that Alice would never let her get away with it. Besides, Tim might have seen her picture in some corporate brochure or other. If she tried to walk past him and he recognized her, calling her by name, she'd feel even more stupid and embarrassed than she did now.

She took a deep breath and walked up to him. 'Tim Fraser?'

'Yes.'

She smiled at him, and held out her hand. 'Hello. I'm Roxana Winters. Though everyone calls me Roxy.'

'Pleased to meet you, Roxy.' Tim shook her hand. She was neither the leggy redhead he'd expected nor an exotic semi-Eastern beauty with dark glossy hair and dark eyes. Roxana Winters was quite ordinary, with fair curly hair cut in a jaw-length bob and held back from her face by a navy Alice band, warm hazel eyes, and a slightly studious look on her face. The academic air was emphasized by her dress: a navy calf-length pleated skirt, a cream silk vest-top and a jade green shirt thrown casually on the top to act as a jacket.

There was nothing special about her, at first glance. And yet there *was* something about her that made his solar plexus tighten, almost as though she'd run her fingers over his cock, stroking him intimately. There was something in her smile that promised more than an evening of academic chat about technology, and it did indeed make his cock stir.

'Shall we go in?' he asked.

'Fine.' Roxy's legs felt like jelly. He was even more gorgeous in the flesh than he was on her VR program, and it made her nervous. She was bound to trip over, or spill her drink over him, or knock something flying . . . *God, Al, I wish I had some of your confidence*, she thought ruefully. *I'm just about to make the worst mistake of my life, and I don't know how I can stop everything going wrong*.

He chose a corner table; when they'd ordered food and

agreed to share a bottle of red wine, he turned his full attention to her. 'This e-mail dating business.'

'Come the Revolution,' Roxy said automatically.

'Revolution?' He was lost.

Roxy winced, suddenly realizing what she'd said. God, he must think her such a weirdo. 'Sorry. It's a long-standing joke between Alice and me. The Technology Revolution – I think it's going to have an even greater effect than the Industrial Revolution. Al says we've all been talking about it for so long, it'll never happen. So whenever either of us mentions something about technology, the other one says "Come the Revolution".' She wrinkled her nose. 'I know, it sounds incredibly feeble.'

'But it's funny when it's the two of you,' Tim said unexpectedly. 'In-jokes between friends are always like that.'

'Mm.' Roxy's voice was rueful. 'But this time Al took it a bit too far.'

'Effective, though.' He smiled. 'When my PC said "mail", I wasn't expecting anything like that!'

'Hang on – your PC talks to you?' Her eyes widened.

He flushed. 'It's only a sound file. I programmed the soundcard to say "mail" instead of beeping or playing the first couple of bars of *Stairway to Heaven* when an e-mail hits my mailbox.'

She laughed.

'What's so funny?'

'I told Alice that I wouldn't have a clue what to say to you tonight. She said that you'd be as much of a computer boffin as I am, and we could talk PCs all evening. Two anoraks together, was how she put it. "Anorak" being her favourite term of abuse for anyone remotely connected with science, that is.'

'I see.' He tipped his head slightly to one side. 'Just out of interest, why did she pick me?'

It was Roxy's turn to flush. How could she tell him about the VR program? 'I – er – mentioned to her that I'd met you at the Visicom exhibition, last month.'

So *that* was why her name was familiar. 'You were on one of the stands, weren't you?'

'Yes. I'm on the Shopping Mall project.' She bit her lip. 'Look, Tim, I'm really sorry about Alice's e-mail. Still, I suppose it'll teach me to keep my mailbox secure in future.'

'Alice is your flatmate?' he asked.

'And my best friend – though sometimes I wonder why!' Roxy confirmed. 'We were on the same corridor in our first year at university. Even though she was reading English and I was reading computer studies, we had so much in common – music, films, books and whatever – that we became good friends. We both moved to London after graduation, and it was the obvious thing to share a flat.'

'She's a journalist, isn't she?'

'Mm. The deputy editor of *Home Matters*, to be precise.'

'Not into computers, then?'

'Apart from word processing and patience games, no.' Roxy sighed. 'I should have guessed that she was up to something, when she started asking me about e-mail. She said that she was researching an article. E-mail doesn't exactly have a lot to do with rag-rolling your walls, or stripping furniture.'

'I don't know – it's plausible enough. There's a multimedia decorating service on the Shopping Mall project, isn't there?'

Roxy nodded. 'Everything you could wish for, on your own TV or PC.' She grinned. 'Except a dating agency, that is.'

'I should think your friend Alice could handle that on her own!' Tim smiled at her.

'Mm.' Roxy was uncomfortable. If she wasn't careful, she'd end up blurting out the rest of it – telling him about the virtual-reality sex program, and the fact that she'd scanned-in his face. That would ruin everything.

To her relief, the waitress arrived with their pasta, and she steered the conversation onto a safer subject. She discovered that she and Tim had a great deal in common, and that his personality was even nicer than his looks. He was witty, but sensitive at the same time; plus he could talk seriously to her as well, showing interest in her ideas and her thoughts without putting her down or trying to cap everything she said. It was a heady combination: and, combined with his incredibly blue eyes and a slightly vulnerable and sexy mouth, it made a pulse start beating hard between Roxy's legs.

Part of her wanted to throw caution to the wind – forget all the other people in the restaurant and show him how attractive she found him. If she'd had Alice's confidence, she would have leaned over the table and kissed him, hard. But she didn't have Alice's confidence – and she didn't want him knowing how much she lusted after him. She couldn't bear the shame of him knowing how she felt about him when he didn't feel the same way about her. Sure that her eyes would give her away, she made sure that she kept her gaze fixed to the table. She didn't want to put him off before they'd even had a chance to get to know each other.

If he noticed, or guessed at the reason for her shyness, he didn't say anything. He was perfect company, and she found herself relaxing, enjoying herself and chatting easily to him.

After their third cup of coffee, she nudged him. 'I think that the waiter wants to clear our table.'

He looked up at the waiter, who was trying to suppress an impatient look, and smiled. 'I think you might be right.' He glanced at his watch, and widened his eyes in surprise. 'My God. Would you believe that it's gone eleven?'

'Never.' Roxy had been enjoying herself too much to notice how quickly the time had passed. 'I'd better be getting home,' she said, her voice full of regret, 'or I'll be asleep at my desk, tomorrow morning.'

'You work on Saturdays?' He sounded faintly surprised.

'At the moment, yes.' She shrugged. 'There's a lot to do, so it's all hands on deck, as much as possible.'

'I'll see you home,' Tim offered.

'It's very sweet of you, but Islington isn't exactly on the way to Hampstead. There's no need to go out of your way.' She smiled. 'I can see myself home.'

He grinned. 'Well, I'm a male chauvinist pig. I'm seeing you home, Roxy, and that's that.'

'If you insist. *But* if you're a chauvinist, I'm a virulent feminist, so I'm definitely paying my half of the bill,' Roxy said firmly.

Tim shook his head. 'It was my invitation, so I'm paying.'

'But—'

'You can pay next time,' he added, silencing her.

So there was going to be a next time. Roxy had a sudden delicious feeling that she was going to find out just how accurate her program was – and soon.

He paid the bill, and took her hand as they left the café. Roxy's pulse quickened. The way his fingers were curved round hers . . . and was it her imagination, or was his thumb rubbing against her palm?

Her breathing became shallow. It was the age-old gesture of sexual interest . . . and the worst thing was, she could imagine it all too easily. Lying with Tim, belly to belly and breast to breast, his hands stroking the length of her back and squeezing her buttocks. His cock pressing hard against her, hard and hot. And then, oh, bliss, his mouth moving down her body, arousing her to fever pitch, before he changed their position and gently guided her down onto his cock . . .

She couldn't bring herself to speak, knowing that her voice would be croaky and slightly breathless. Either he sensed it or he felt the same, because he didn't say anything, either. He just held her hand, all the way to her flat: and, from a brief glance at his face, she had a feeling that he was affected in the same way that she was.

'Would you like a coffee?' she asked politely as they reached her flat.

He paused. 'I ought to say no, because you have to go to work in the morning.'

She tipped her head on one side. 'But?'

'This is going to sound terribly corny.'

She grinned. 'As Al would say, you're a scientist – so nobody expects you to come out with great lines.'

He grinned back. 'Here's looking at you, kid.'

Roxy laughed. 'That's cheating! And it's a quote, so it doesn't count.'

'In that case – I've enjoyed your company,' he said honestly, 'and I don't want this evening to end, just yet.'

'Then come in for a coffee.'

He smiled acceptance, and allowed her to usher him into the flat. 'It's a nice flat,' he said, as she closed the door behind them.

'That's all thanks to Al and her contacts at the magazine. It was a real hole when we moved in – woodchip paper everywhere, covered in turquoise gloss paint. It was a Seventies reject, really. Anyway, Al persuaded one of the editors to use the flat as a makeover piece – something about ways of decorating your Victorian house in period style, without paying period prices. Marcie Ellerby took the job, and she's become a good friend of ours – and she sometimes tries out her experiments on us. So I suppose we're pretty lucky, really.'

'Mm. It would cost a fortune to have my place done up like this.' Roxy had already learned that he had a Georgian townhouse in West Hampstead, which he shared with Marcus, his friend and colleague.

'You can always have a word with Al, and she might chat up Marcie for you. Alice loves playing Ms Fix-it,' she said with a grin as she walked into the kitchen and switched the kettle on. 'Not to mention organizing other people!'

'I might just take you up on that.' Tim leaned against one of the worktops, watching her bend over to take some ground coffee from the fridge. The curve of her buttocks made him itch to touch her.

As she straightened up again, he walked over to her and caught her wrist. 'Roxy.'

'Mm?'

She was five or six inches shorter than he was, and had to tip her head back slightly to look at him. He smiled, and dipped his head to kiss her, biting gently at her lower lip and then sliding his tongue along it until she opened her mouth to kiss him back.

His hands slid down to span her waist, resting on the curve of her hip; slowly, he eased his fingers under the hem of her top so that he could stroke her lower back. Roxy arched her back in pleasure, and he rubbed his nose against hers. 'God, you feel nice.'

'So do you.' She slid her hands round his neck, her fingers tangling in his dark wavy hair.

His fingertips brushed her skin very lightly, moving round

to her midriff and then upwards until his hands cupped her breasts. He brushed her already erect nipples with the pads of his thumbs, circling her areolae through the lace of her bra, and he nudged one thigh between hers.

'Oh, Roxy,' he murmured, nuzzling her cheek then kissing the sensitive spot at the side of her neck, licking her skin then breathing on it, to make her shiver. He continued playing with her nipples with one hand; the other sought the clasp of her bra, undoing it deftly. With a murmur of pleasure, he let his hand slide round to her front again, and pushed her bra up slightly so that he could cup her breasts in his hands, squeezing them and lifting them.

She shuddered, and he let his hands drop, taking a step backwards. He raked his fingers through his hair. 'I'm sorry. I didn't mean to go quite this far, the first time I met you,' he said, flushing.

'It's okay.' Roxy swallowed. Her VR program had done him an injustice. The real thing was a hell of a lot better than the simulation, she thought. 'I should have pushed you away.'

Her lips were reddened and slightly swollen from his kisses; he had to force himself to stand still, though he itched to drag her back into his arms and kiss her again. 'I don't usually behave like this.'

'Neither do I. It's been a long time since I've been out with someone, let alone anything like this,' Roxy admitted. 'Things have been too frantic at Visicom – though Al says that I'm a workaholic who's permanently attached to my computer.'

Tim gave in to the temptation to stroke her face. 'That's pretty much what my friends say about me, too.' He traced her lower lip with his forefinger, and she drew it into her mouth, sucking it gently.

He felt a jolt in his loins. 'Roxy.'

She released his finger, and tipped her head on one side. 'Yes?'

'Do you really have to work tomorrow?'

'Yes.' She paused. 'But I have a modem.'

His eyes glittered as he realized what she meant – that she didn't have to go into the office. If she dialled up to the network, she could work from home. He cupped her chin. 'In that case . . .' He smiled, and lowered his mouth to hers again.

He felt her body quivering beneath him, and suddenly realized that she was laughing. He tore his mouth from hers. 'What's so funny?'

'Aren't we too old for this?'

'For what?'

'Necking in the kitchen.'

He grinned. 'Probably. Do you have any better ideas?'

'Mm. If we're going to do this, we might as well do it in comfort – don't you think?' The words were out before she could stop them, and the sensible part of her was horrified. What the hell did she think she was doing, inviting Tim into her bed on the first night they'd gone out together? In this day and age, it was too much of a risk. Stupid. And yet she couldn't help herself. The need to feel his body against hers, skin to skin, was greater than her need to be sensible.

'Comfort. Yes.' His eyes glittered. 'Take me to bed, Roxy.' He tipped his head on one side, looking appealing and vulnerable and incredibly sexy, all at the same time. 'Make love to me.'

Part of her brain told her that this couldn't possibly be happening, that she was hooked up to the VR simulation. And yet she hadn't programmed that particular speech into the virtual situations. Tim was talking to her, saying words that she definitely hadn't put in his mouth. It had to be real – didn't it?

She held out her hand, he took it, and followed her down the corridor to her bedroom. She switched on the bedside lamp and drew the curtains.

Tim looked at her double bed, a smile spreading across his face. 'Thank God we don't have to revert to student days, squeezing into a single.'

Roxy grinned. 'A narrow single, at that.'

Tim rolled his eyes. 'Pure hell. You either ended up with your bum against a burning radiator, or fell onto the floor in the middle of the night.'

'That can still be arranged,' Roxy teased.

Tim laughed, and pulled her to him. 'Thanks, but no thanks. I have something else in mind.'

'Such as?'

He kissed her lingeringly, and slid her shirt from her shoulders, followed by the silk vest top. 'Your friend Alice doesn't know you too well, does she?'

'How do you mean?'

He drew his finger down the valley between her breasts; the lacy material of her bra revealed more than it covered, and although the bra was unclasped, the underwiring still pushed her breasts together and upwards, deepening her cleavage. 'A workaholic doesn't wear stuff like this.'

She grinned. 'That's stereotyping me.'

'I suppose so.' He continued looking at her breasts. 'Alice was right about you being the woman of my dreams, though. All lush curves.' He traced the outline of her breasts, lingering over her erect nipples and gently outlining her areolae through the lace. 'Roxy. You're so very, very beautiful.' He unzipped her skirt. It fell, rustling, to the floor, and she stepped out of it. Tim's eyes widened as he realized that she was wearing matching suspenders, tiny silk-and-lace briefs, and lace-topped stockings. 'Wow. If I'd known you were wearing this under-neath, I don't think I'd have lingered so long in the restaurant.'

'Oh, really?'

'Mm.' His smile broadened. 'That, or I'd have been fantasizing about you so much, you wouldn't have got a sensible conver-sation out of me.'

Roxy blushed, not sure what to say. This couldn't be happening – not really. No way could Tim feel the same way about her, the same heart-thumpingly mad lustful feelings that engulfed her at his lightest touch . . .

He pushed her bra from her shoulders, letting the garment fall to the floor, then cupped her breasts in his hands, lifting them slightly. 'Mm. I could touch and kiss your breasts all night,' he said, pushing his face into them and nuzzling them gently. She smelt faintly of roses, a soft powdery scent, and he inhaled deeply before letting his hands slide down to her waist and kissing her again.

Roxy slid her hands under his cotton sweater. His body was firm, with a light covering of hair on his chest; his stomach was flat, too. Obviously he was a man who looked after himself and didn't live purely on sandwiches and coffee, she thought – unlike most of the scientists she knew, including herself. She ran a finger lightly up his spine, and he pulled back from her with a shiver, his eyes darkening with arousal.

'Christ, Roxy. When you touch me like that, it makes me want more. Much more. I want you to stroke my skin, bring me to fever pitch with your hands and your mouth.'

She smiled at him. 'I will. When you're wearing a bit less, that is.'

'Your wish is my command.' He pulled off his sweater, smiling invitingly at her; she tipped her head to one side, just watching him. He looked as good as he'd felt; suddenly, she itched to touch him some more. She stepped forward again, undoing his belt and the button at the top of his jeans. Then she slowly pulled the zipper downwards. Tim kicked off his shoes, then helped her slide the denim down his thighs before stepping out of his jeans. His cock was rigid, clearly outlined by the soft cotton of his underpants; Roxy licked her suddenly dry lips as she realized just how big he was.

Gently, Tim cupped her face. 'Changed your mind?'

'No,' she hedged.

'But?'

Roxy couldn't put her thoughts into words; he smiled at her, and took her hand, kissing her fingertips. 'If it makes you feel any better, there's a crowd of butterflies having a major fight in my stomach,' he told her softly.

Roxy smiled wryly. Little did he know it, but she'd already made love to him several times, through virtual reality. She didn't think he'd have much of a problem living up to his computer simulation.

'I'll take that smile as a "Let's go for it",' Tim said, kissing her lightly, then guiding her hands to help him remove the rest of his clothing.

She could hardly take her eyes off him. Naked, he was beautiful, she thought. Had she been artistic, she would have sculpted him, recreating the clean pure lines of his body with her hands. As it was, she would have to revise her program, make his shoulders a little broader and his pecs a little more developed. Not to mention increasing the length and girth of his cock, which sprang up against his belly.

She was about to remove her suspenders and stockings, when he stopped her. 'It might be a bit kinky,' he said softly, 'but I love the idea of making love to you in those.'

Roxy reached out a hand to stroke his cock. 'So I notice.'

She gave him a mischievous look through her lashes; Tim pulled her into his arms, sliding one hand under her hair at the nape of her neck and smoothing the curve of her spine with his other hand, pulling her body tightly against his so that she could feel the hardness of his torso.

He lowered his head, brushing his lips lightly against hers; as she opened her mouth, he slid his tongue along her lower lip before plunging it deep into her mouth, the stabbing movement of his tongue echoing what he wanted to do to her with his cock. His free hand slid between her thighs, the hard base of his thumb nudging against her sex. She shifted her position slightly, widening the gap between her thighs, and Tim began to move his hand back and forth, rubbing her quim through the thin material of her knickers.

Roxy arched against him, and he pushed the gusset of her knickers aside, his fingers seeking her clitoris. She gave a sharp intake of breath as he found the hard nub of flesh, and began to massage it, his fingers working in a rhythm almost as familiar as her own hand. Her flesh was warm and wet with arousal; that, together with the hardness of her nipples, told him that she was more than ready for him. Still kissing her hard, he walked her backwards to the edge of the bed, guiding her down gently so that she lay on top of the duvet.

He knelt between her thighs, still holding the gusset of her knickers to one side, and rubbed the tip of his cock against her quim; Roxy tilted her hips, pushing up against him, and Tim's cock slid into her warm wet spongy depths. She lifted her legs, wrapping them round his waist so that he penetrated her more deeply, and he began to thrust, using long slow steady strokes that made the tension in her grow tighter. Her fingers dug into his buttocks, urging him to push harder, deeper; then her body went completely rigid for a second, and he felt her internal muscles contract hard around him as she came. The feeling of her quim rippling round him was enough to tip him into his own release; he cried out and came, his cock twitching deep inside her.

Not wanting to withdraw from her, Tim supported his weight on his elbows; Roxy obviously felt the same, as her legs were still locked round his waist. He rubbed his nose against hers. 'God, you felt wonderful.'

Roxy smiled. It was even nicer than she had imagined – or programmed – it to be.

'That coffee you promised me ... Any chance of having it for breakfast?' he asked.

She laughed. 'That was about as direct as they come.'

'Well.' He didn't look in the slightest bit abashed. 'I'd like to stay with you, tonight, Roxy. I want to sleep with you in my arms, and wake up with you curled beside me.'

She stroked his hair back from his face. 'I'd like you to stay, too.' Her smile suddenly faded. 'I hope you don't think that I'm some kind of trollop.'

He pretended to consider it. 'Sending me e-mail messages about the woman of my dreams, then luring me back to your place on the pretext of a coffee which hasn't yet materialized ...'

'Because you dragged me off to my bedroom before I could make you a coffee. Anyway, I didn't send the e-mail,' she pointed out.

'But I didn't know that when I rang you,' he countered. He grinned. 'Oh, Roxy. Of course I don't think that you're a trollop!'

'Good.' She relaxed again.

He was already hardening again inside her. 'Now we've got

that out of the way, Ms Winters, do you think we could change the subject?'

She began moving her internal muscles. 'Like this, you mean?'

'Mm.' His eyes dilated as she massaged his cock. 'That's much better. There's only one thing . . .'

'What's that?'

He gently stroked her legs so that her feet were flat on the mattress, then withdrew from her.

'I thought you—' Roxy began.

'I do. But this time, I want it skin to skin. I want to make this one last, be really good for you,' he said, removing her knickers and the suspender belt, then rolling her stockings down her legs.

Roxy nearly blurted out that she already knew that he was good, that he was one of the best lovers she'd ever had – including his simulation – but just about managed to hold her tongue.

She closed her eyes and sighed with pleasure as Tim slid down the bed, nuzzling her belly, then licking the soft skin of her inner thighs. His breath was warm against her sex-flesh, teasing her with the promise of the pleasures to come, and she pushed her hips up to meet him, urging him on. As his tongue flickered across her clitoris, she tipped her head back among the pillows, her lips parting in a silent groan of pleasure. She shivered when his tongue slid down her quim, parting her labia and scooping out her nectar before moving back to her clitoris and working over it rapidly, bringing her to the edge of orgasm.

Just as she thought she was about to come, he stopped, flipping her gently onto her stomach and guiding her onto her hands and knees. She sighed in bliss as she felt the bulbous head of his cock against the entrance of her vagina, and she slid her hand down to guide his cock into her.

'God, Tim, this is so good,' she moaned as he began to thrust, his balls slapping gently against the lips of her quim.

'Mm. A perfect fit,' he murmured against her ear. 'You feel like warm wet velvet, wrapped tightly around my cock.'

She tipped her head back slightly, rubbing her cheek against his. He took advantage of her position to slide one arm around her waist, his hand drifting up to cup her breasts. He tugged gently at her erect nipple, making her gasp with pleasure, then shifted to work the other one.

He drove deeper into her, filling her to the hilt, and Roxy's breathing became uneven. She dropped her head again, burying her face in the pillow to muffle her groans; the position meant that he could penetrate her even more deeply, bringing her even more pleasure. Her whole body felt fluid and, as pleasure exploded deep inside her, the shudders of orgasm seemed to travel down every nerve-end, making her whole body tremble.

She felt him stiffen slightly, and then his cock twitched deep inside her. He wrapped his arms round her waist, cradling her against him and resting his cheek against her back. Neither of them moved for a long while, unable and unwilling to break the contact between their bodies; finally, Tim slipped out of her and settled down beside her, tucking her into the curve of his body and lacing his fingers through hers.

She rested her face against his chest, feeling the soft thud of his heart under her cheek. 'That,' she said, 'was fantastic.'

'Mm, it'll do for now,' he agreed, chuckling. He ruffled her hair with his free hand. 'You're one hell of a gorgeous woman, Roxana Winters.'

She slid her hand over his body, learning its shape. 'You're not so bad, yourself.'

'Why, thank you, sweetheart,' he quipped.

Roxy nestled closer. *I could get used to this*, she thought. *If only I could find some way to put this feeling into the sensor loop. The VR program would be dynamite.*

Mulling over ways to modify the program, she fell asleep in his arms.

THREE

Roxy woke to the smell of fresh coffee. She stretched, yawned – then sat up and opened her eyes wide as she realized that Alice wasn't due back until the evening. So it had to be someone else in the kitchen. A burglar, maybe, or ... She pulled a mocking face at her fears. 'How melodramatic can you get, Winters?' she asked herself wryly. Of course it wasn't a burglar. Burglars didn't make themselves coffee, for starters. Which meant that whoever was in the kitchen was there with her implicit permission ...

A smile curved her lips as she remembered the previous night, and she settled back down among the pillows, burying her face against the soft cotton covers and breathing deeply as Tim's masculine scent filled her nostrils. It had been one hell of a night. She'd fallen asleep in his arms, but she'd woken in the middle of the night to feel his mouth tracking over her body. They'd made love again and again, hardly able to sate themselves with each other's bodies, until they'd fallen into another exhausted sleep. And now ... Her eyes widened as she caught sight of the time. It was nearly half past ten! And she was always up at seven on a Saturday, especially since she'd had to work such long hours on the Mall project.

A few minutes later, Tim strolled into the bedroom, a towel wrapped loosely round his waist, bearing a tray of coffee, orange juice and toast.

'I hope you don't mind me poking round in your kitchen,' he said, sitting on the edge of the bed.

Roxy smiled at him. 'Actually, it's a nice change not to have to make my own breakfast.'

Tim balanced the tray on the bedside cabinet, pulled off the towel, and slid back under the duvet. 'Mm, you're nice and warm,' he said, moving closer to her.

Roxy yelped and sat up. 'Your feet are freezing!'

He grinned, and handed her a mug of coffee. 'Black, no sugar, isn't it?'

'You have a good memory,' she said, impressed.

He shook his head, laughing. 'Sadly, no. I based it on scientific principle.'

'Oh, yes?'

'Mm. Most scientists I know are too wrapped up in their work to be bothered about milk and sugar, so they'll drink almost anything.'

Roxy laughed back. 'Yes, I suppose you're right. If I'm working, Al could bring me sulphuric acid and I'd drink it.'

'My coffee isn't quite that bad,' he said, pantomiming hurt.

Roxy took a sip. 'Mm. Nice and strong. Don't tell me – scientific principle, again?'

'Yup,' he confirmed. 'It keeps me awake when I need to work late.'

Her lips twitched. 'And you think that I need keeping awake, do you?'

He traced the curve of her face with a forefinger. 'Oh, I've got some much nicer ideas than coffee for keeping you awake. But you said that you had to work this morning.'

'I do. But I never work on an empty stomach.'

Tim grinned. 'I think I can manage to fill you up.'

Roxy caught on to what he meant immediately, and flushed,

which made his grin even broader. 'You're deliciously teasable. I love the way you blush.' His gaze slid down to her breasts. 'Particularly when you do it all over.'

'You,' Roxy said primly, pulling the duvet up to cover her breasts, 'are a complete lecher.'

He laughed, and sipped his coffee. They relaxed into a companionable silence, and he glanced round the room. It was quite feminine, decorated in blue and white floral sprigged fabrics with pine furniture; and yet at the same time, it was obviously a working room. There were no frills, no ornaments. The top of Roxy's dressing table was covered in books and boxes of disks, rather than tubes of make-up.

Her PC sat on a table in a corner of the room; Tim looked quizzically at her. 'How much work do you have to do this morning?'

Roxy wrinkled her nose. 'Not that much. I can do it later.'

'I'm very nosy about other people's PCs.' He gave her a sidelong look.

She nodded. 'Well, it isn't as if I keep any industrial secrets on there. We have the Mall tender, and Comco has the security card tender, so we're not really rivals in the true sense.'

'In fact, we have to work together. There's no point in having all your details on a pin number if it isn't compatible with the services you want to use,' Tim agreed.

She grinned. 'You're just dying to see what sort of games I've installed, aren't you?'

He laughed. 'Is it that obvious?'

'Scientific principle,' she teased.

'You mean that you're just as bad,' he fenced, ruffling her hair.

'Something like that.' She gestured towards the computer with her free hand. 'Go on, then. Help yourself.'

He walked over to her desk and sat down. He tried to switch on the machine, and frowned. 'Roxy, it's locked.'

'Oh, yes.' She put her coffee on the bedside cabinet, scrambled out of bed, pulled on her dressing gown, and went to join him. She rummaged in a small box, then brought out the key and unlocked the PC. 'It's all yours. I haven't password-protected it.'

Tim glanced through the icons. There were several patience games, and a couple of strategy games, more or less as he'd expected. But there was one icon he couldn't work out – something he'd never seen before. 'What's VRX?' he asked.

Roxy flushed. 'Er – it's nothing important.'

To her horror, he clicked on the programme. As the first screen came up, he frowned. 'Is it anything to do with this e-mail dating thing?'

'Not quite. Look, Tim, I really don't think you'll find it that interesting.'

'If it wasn't interesting, Roxy, you wouldn't be panicking.' His blue eyes were very clear.

'No.' She swallowed hard. 'All right. If you must know, it's the prototype for a virtual-reality sex program.'

'A what?' His eyes opened wide in disbelief.

'A virtual-reality sex program. I suppose you could call it the ultimate in safe sex.' Her colour deepened.

'God, that's incredible.' He gave her a sidelong glance. 'Can I try it?'

She shook her head. 'It's from a woman's point of view, at the moment.'

'That's rather sexist of you. What about men's point of view?'

'I haven't got that far.'

He grinned. 'Well, if you fancy having a guinea pig . . .'

Roxy bit her lip. If only he knew it, he was already her guinea pig! She wasn't sure how he'd take it, so she said nothing.

'And then there's the Tiresias factor,' Tim continued.

'The what?' It was Roxy's turn to look surprised.

'Tut, tut. Someone didn't do Classics at school, did she?'

'Maths, physics, and further maths,' she retorted.

'Yeah – me, too. But in the first year, we did Classics. The guy who taught us knew that we wouldn't be interested in learning Latin, or in reading vast tracts of poetry, so he told us all about the Greek myths and legends instead.'

'And you can still remember them? He must have made quite an impression on you.'

'Mm. For a year or so, I thought about being a Classics teacher when I left school,' Tim admitted.

'So who was Tiresias, then?'

'He was a Greek seer, who was turned into a woman after killing some snakes who were coupling on a mountainside. He was turned back into a man again after doing the same thing some years later. Hera and Zeus were arguing about who got the most pleasure out of sex, men or women, and he could tell them first-hand that women did. Which rather annoyed Hera, as you can imagine. I can't actually remember what she did to him, but it was pretty nasty.' Tim looked at her. 'I've always wondered how a woman feels, when she climaxes. If your VR program could let me experience that . . .'

'Mm.' Roxy was thoughtful. 'And women could experience how a man feels. I like the idea.' She shrugged. 'There's only one problem. I can't program it authentically from the male point of view.'

'Unless you have a man to co-develop it.'

Roxy looked straight at him. 'That sounded like an offer.'

'It was.'

She didn't even have to think about it. 'Accepted, with pleasure.'

'Good.' He shook hands with her. 'That's a deal, then.'

'Deal,' she agreed.

'So if I could run the program and see what you've done so far?'

Roxy went crimson. 'Not now, Tim.'

'What are you hiding?'

She winced. 'Tim . . .' How was he going to react? Would he be flattered – or angry? Would he walk out of her life again, when he found out what she'd done?

He narrowed his eyes. 'What?'

'I don't think that you're going to like this very much.' She swallowed. 'The idea is, you can scan in the face of the person you want to make love with.'

'And?'

She swallowed again. 'Oh, hell.'

'You've scanned in some rock god or other?' he guessed, amused. 'A famous actor? Some guy from a perfume ad, all muscles and smouldering looks?'

'No.' She bit her lip. 'Well, you're going to find out sooner or later. It might as well be sooner, I suppose.'

He tipped his head on one side, not understanding why she was so jumpy. 'Roxy, what's the big deal?'

She pressed the "enter" key. Tim's eyes widened as he saw his own face on the screen. 'Bloody hell! It's me!'

She lifted her chin. 'If you want to leave now, I'll understand.'

He shook his head, torn between admiration and amusement. 'It looks like last night was the first time I'd made love with you – but not the first time *you'd* made love with *me.*'

'So you're not angry?'

He slid his arms round her, pulling her onto his lap. 'No. Actually, I'm quite flattered.'

'Really?' She was still wary.

'Really.' He rubbed his nose against hers. 'Does Alice know about this?'

Roxy squirmed. 'Er – yes.'

Tim made the connection immediately. 'And she's tried it out?'

'Er – yes. The other night.'

He nodded thoughtfully. 'Have you scanned in any other faces?'

'Not yet.' Roxy stared miserably at the floor. She'd really blown it, now.

To her surprise, he was laughing. 'So I've already made love to at least two women – one of whom I haven't met, and the other I only met properly yesterday. Have any of your other friends tried it?'

'No.'

'So I'm not such a stud after all.' He wrinkled his nose at her. 'That's a pity. My ego was just inflating to monster proportions.'

'Actually, you're better than the program,' Roxy told him.

He grinned. 'Flatterer.'

'No, seriously. I'm going to have to do some more work on it.' She bit his earlobe. 'Though not when you're around. You'll distract me too much.'

He twisted his face round to kiss her. 'So how does it work? A body suit and headset?'

'Sensor pads, not a body suit. That way, one size fits

everyone. At the moment, the pads are connected by wires, though eventually the connections will be through infrared or radio waves.'

'I like it.' He traced her lower lip with his forefinger. 'So I've landed me a woman with brains as well as looks.'

Roxy scoffed. 'Oh come on, I'm hardly your tall skinny model.'

'Marilyn Monroe wasn't exactly skinny, and she's been the sexual dream of just about every man I know. Particularly me.' He rubbed his nose against hers. 'We could program her face and your body as the prototype for my part of the development. Or your face and her body.'

'This sounds like a fantasy coming true.'

'Isn't that the point of the program?' His eyes glittered. 'Roxy, this is going to be really big.'

She wriggled slightly on his lap, her buttocks rubbing against his erection. 'You mean there's more?' she teased.

'Let's go back to bed,' he said, 'and I'll show you.'

She let him pick her up and carry her to the bed. 'You really do have macho tendencies, Tim Fraser,' she teased him.

'That's because my brain is currently functioning from my cock,' he told her, stroking her face. 'Which is all your fault.'

'Indeed?'

'Wriggling about on my lap like that.' He sat her on the bed and undid the tie to her dressing gown, revealing her breasts. 'Have I told you that I love your breasts? The way they curve.' He cupped one in each hand, lifting them slightly to plump them, and buried his face between them. 'Mm.' He turned his face slightly to one side and began licking her skin, little cat-laps which made her shiver and lift her ribcage.

His mouth wandered over the soft flesh to one nipple; he rolled it round on his tongue and nipped it gently with his lips, teasing it into hardness. The other nipple received the same treatment, and he lifted his face away from her for a moment to study his handiwork. 'Mm. You have perfect breasts, Roxy. Absolutely perfect.'

Roxy squirmed. She'd always thought them too big. Tim caught the distress on her face, and smiled gently. 'Not all men fancy the skinny boyish type, you know. I told you, I'm a Marilyn man. I like proper curves on a woman. Like here.' He touched her breasts. 'And here.' He let his hand glide over her hips. 'And here.' He slid one hand to curve round one buttock, squeezing it gently.

Roxy's face was impassive; Tim tipped his head to one side. 'Oh dear. It looks like I'll have to convince you.' He took her hand, drawing it down to caress his erection. 'Now, if I didn't fancy you, this would be all shrivelled and limp, would it not?'

Roxy, embarrassed, said nothing.

'But the very thought of burying my cock in you . . .' His cock twitched slightly. 'See?' he said softly. 'You turn me on, Roxy, in a big way. Your mind, as well as your body – otherwise I wouldn't be here now. I'd have made my excuses and left last night. In fact, I would have bolted my dinner, conveniently remembered a prior engagement – and probably left you to pay the bill. Whereas I fancied you like mad, and when you invited me in for coffee, I had this overwhelming urge to take you to bed. It was every bit as good as I'd hoped it would be.' He cupped her face tenderly, and kissed her lightly on the lips. 'And right now, I want to make love with you again.'

She relaxed slightly as he pushed her gently down onto the bed, swinging her legs round and parting them so that he could kneel between them. He stroked her thighs, then bent down to travel their length with his lips, licking and nibbling at her skin.

Roxy could feel his breath warm against her flesh, and closed her eyes in blissful anticipation, remembering the night before: she was disappointed when he bypassed the tempting juncture of her thighs and instead began kissing his way slowly down her other leg. At her obvious wriggle of disappointment, he smiled against her skin. 'Don't be so impatient. We have all day.'

'So we do.' The way he was caressing her, Roxy forgot completely about the work she was supposed to be doing.

She tipped her pelvis up slightly; Tim laughed. 'Was that a hint?'

'Mm. A bit.'

Lazily, he kissed his way back up her thigh; Roxy bent her knees to give him better access, and his tongue slid along the length of her quim, exploring its folds and crevices. As he found her clitoris and began to tease it, circling it with his tongue and then flicking rapidly across it, she brought her hands up to grip the rails of the pine headboard.The combination of his warm breath and the expert ministrations of his tongue soon had her thrusting up to meet him, longing for a deeper penetration. Tim had no intention of stopping, just yet, but slid one finger in her to help ease the ache, sliding it back and forth until she began to moan and rock under him.

The familiar warm feeling of orgasm began at the soles of her feet, a buzzing glow that travelled up her legs and pooled in her solar plexus. She gripped the pine rails more tightly as the sensation deepened; Tim's mouth grew more urgent, licking and caressing until she gave a muffled cry and came, her flesh contracting wildly.

She had half expected him to stop there; to her surprise, he slid his cock inside her, its hard length acting as resistance to her internal muscles and lengthening her orgasm. And then he began to move, very slowly, sliding deep inside her and then withdrawing until his cock was almost out of her.

He stroked her face, smiling at her; she relaxed again and smiled back, wrapping her legs round his waist so that he could achieve maximum penetration. She still felt lazy with post-orgasmic indolence, but the rhythm he was setting up as he thrust into her was irresistible, making her thrust back up towards him.

'Oh, Roxy,' he breathed. His cock seemed to swell again, and then she felt him spurt inside her.

He buried his face against her shoulder, and she wrapped her arms round his neck, stroking his hair with one hand.

'You're fantastic,' he murmured against her skin. 'I wish I'd met you a long time ago.'

She smiled. 'Maybe you should have developed your own VR sex machine.'

'Maybe.' He lifted his head and rubbed his cheek affectionately against hers. 'At the moment, I'd much rather have the real thing. I should warn you, you're making me insatiable. I'm becoming addicted to your body.'

'Is that a promise?' she teased.

His voice grew husky. 'Oh, yes. Definitely.'

He refused to come out of her, taking his weight on his knees and elbows to relieve the pressure on her body; they lay together, relaxed and happy. Roxy silently blessed Alice for her well-intentioned interfering. For once, it had worked. Roxy's last thought as she drifted back to sleep was that she needed to do a lot more work on her program, if it was even going to begin to match Tim's skill in bed . . .

* * *

Some time later, Roxy woke in Tim's arms. She stretched, glanced at the clock, and sat up in horror. 'Tim, it's lunchtime!'

'So what?' he said lazily.

'So, isn't it about time we got up?'

He shrugged. 'I could stay in bed with you all day, quite happily.'

'Mm.' She was uncomfortable. 'It doesn't feel right, being in bed at this time of day.'

'It does to me.' He grinned. 'Though, like I told you earlier, I'm rapidly turning into a sex addict.' He drew one hand down her side. 'I can't stop touching you.'

'Tim, it's gone midday!' she protested.

He sighed. 'Okay. We'll get up.' He gave her a sidelong look. 'How about having a shower with me?'

'You can shower on your own,' she said primly.

'Pity. I was having a lovely dream about you and a shower.'

'Dream or fantasy?' she teased.

'Both.' He got out of bed. 'But as you're not going to indulge me now, I'll have to wait.'

Roxy tidied the room while he showered, then showered quickly herself while he dressed. She joined him in the sitting room, clad in her more usual dress of baggy sweater and leggings; he looked up from the magazine he'd been flicking through and smiled at her. 'Do you fancy lunch out?'

She was surprised. 'Well – yes. Please. That'd be nice.'

They were just about to leave when the front door banged shut, and Alice strolled in. 'Well, hello there,' she said with a grin.

At the speculative look on her face, Roxy wished that the ground would open up and swallow her. 'I thought that you weren't coming back until this evening?'

Alice wrinkled her nose. 'It's a journo's privilege to change her mind.' She looked pointedly at Tim, then at Roxy. 'Well, aren't you going to introduce us, Rox?'

Roxy sighed. 'All right. Tim, this is Alice Jamieson, my flatmate. Al, this is Tim Fraser.'

'Nice to meet you,' Alice said politely, holding out her hand.

Tim grinned as he took it. 'In the flesh, that is?'

Her face went scarlet, clashing dramatically with her hair, and she gave Roxy a horrified look. 'Christ, Roxy – you didn't tell him?'

'About the VR program?' Tim's face twitched with amusement.

Alice groaned. 'Yes.'

'I'm very flattered. And grateful to you,' he added. 'If you hadn't played pirate with Roxy's mailbox . . .'

Alice relaxed again. 'Well, someone had to do something. The woman was mooning around over you.'

'I was *not*,' Roxy protested.

'Yes, you were.' Alice had recovered from her earlier embarrassment, and was back on her usual form. 'Are you two off out somewhere?'

'Lunch,' Tim said. 'You're very welcome to join us, if you like.'

Alice smiled. 'It's sweet of you to ask, but I don't want to play gooseberry.'

'You won't be,' Tim answered honestly, sliding his arm round Roxy.

'What he means is that he's going to pump you for all the dirt on me,' Roxy interpreted.

'How did you know?' Tim asked.

'Because men,' Alice said with a grin, 'can be so predictable.

Are you quite sure that I won't be small, round, hairy and greenish?'

'Of course not!' Roxy told her friend. 'Though there might be a small price involved.'

'Oh?'

'An introduction to Marcie – or to someone who does up Georgian townhouses,' Roxy explained.

Alice looked thoughtful. 'Actually, we're always on the lookout for makeover places ... Hang on a minute, did you say Georgian townhouse?'

'In Hampstead,' Tim confirmed.

Alice groaned. 'Roxy, you didn't tell me that he was rich as well as good-looking! You don't happen to have a twin, by any chance, do you?' she asked Tim. 'Or an equally handsome and rich elder brother?'

He laughed. 'I'm afraid not – not even a younger one. Just a very dear great-aunt, who left me the house – and a friend who shares the place with me.'

They went out to a pizza place, and by the time they'd finished lunch Alice had persuaded Tim to give them his complete life story.

'Sorry for the grilling,' she said afterwards, not looking in the least apologetic. 'It must be the journo training.'

'Or the fact that you're incredibly nosy,' Tim fenced, laughing.

Roxy coughed loudly. 'And who was it who poked around my files on the PC?'

Tim was unabashed. 'I did warn you in advance.'

'And Roxy told you that I was a journalist,' Alice reminded him, 'so you had fair warning in advance, too.'

'True.' He smiled at them both. 'What are you both doing this evening?'

Roxy and Alice exchanged a glance. 'It depends what you have in mind,' Alice said cautiously.

Tim burst into laughter. 'Don't tell me you thought that I was going to suggest a threesome!'

Alice flushed. 'Well. You've tried the VRX program, and Roxy's told you that I tried it out, too. What was I supposed to think?'

'What I had in mind,' he explained, amused, 'was dinner at my place. You're very welcome to bring your boyfriend, Al.'

'The invisible man, you mean,' Alice said.

Tim looked thoughtful. 'Well, to make it even numbers, I'll see if Marcus feels like staying in tonight.'

'Marcus?'

'Marcus Blake. The friend who shares the place with me.' Tim rubbed his nose. 'He also happens to work with me, on the ID project.'

Alice groaned. 'You mean, I'll be spending tonight with three anoraks?'

Tim frowned. 'Anoraks?'

'Scientists. The boffin type,' Alice explained. 'Ones who jabber on in Anorakese.'

'Anorakese being scientific jargon?' he guessed.

'Yup. It's completely unintelligible to anyone else in the human race.'

'You can hold your own,' Roxy said with a grin. 'Just think, you'll have three times as many people to harangue for being unliterary philistines.'

Alice smiled back, her doubts fading. 'Well, in that case . . . What time do you want us to arrive, Tim?'

'Seven,' he said, scribbling his address and phone number on a napkin and handing it to Roxy. He kissed her lightly. 'See you later.'

'That man,' Alice said as they walked home, 'is absolutely gorgeous.'

'Regretting your e-mail now?' Roxy teased.

'Not in the slightest. I think he'll do you good.' Alice gave her a sidelong glance. 'I don't know if I dare ask, but—'

'Is he as good in bed as he is in the program?' Roxy asked, laughing.

'Mm.'

'No, he isn't.'

'Pity.' Alice shrugged. 'Well, there had to be something wrong with him.'

Roxy grinned. 'That's not quite what I meant, Al. Actually, he's better.'

Alice groaned. 'I've got more than my share of the seven deadlies, today.'

'What?'

'Envy.' Alice rolled her eyes. 'You philistine.'

'Look, I'm a poor little scientist. How do you expect me to know all your literary allusions?'

'About as much as you expect me to understand Anorakese. I should give up, really,' Alice agreed, laughing. 'Roxy, how did he react when he found out about the VR program?'

'He was quite flattered.' Roxy coughed. 'Actually, we're going to work on it together. We'll add in the Tiresias factor.'

Alice's eyes widened. 'What's that?'

Roxy smiled. 'Now who's the philistine?' She explained Tim's theory.

'I like it,' Alice said. 'I've always wondered what men feel. They'll never tell you, either – if you ask them, all they'll say is "lovely" or "wonderful".'

'What do you expect, a perfectly crafted erotic essay?' Roxy asked, chuckling.

'No. Just a proper description.'

'Well, as soon as we finish the prototype, you can try out the program,' Roxy promised.

'Thanks.' Alice paused. 'He's really nice, Roxy. And he's obviously smitten with you. You can see it in his eyes.'

Roxy made a noncommittal murmur.

'You *can*,' Alice insisted.

'I wonder what this Marcus is like?' Roxy asked, changing the subject.

'Tim said that he's a geneticist. That makes him a prime Anorak.'

Roxy wrinkled her nose. 'I can't see Tim sharing a house with anyone like that.'

'No. Actually, I'm more looking forward to seeing this house than to seeing Marcus. A Georgian townhouse. I bet it's wallpapered in horrible Seventies paper, and there are hundreds of little period details just waiting to be uncovered.'

Roxy laughed. 'Now who's being the workaholic?'

Alice glanced at her watch as she opened the front door. 'At a rough guess, you. We have to leave at six, so I'll call you at five.'

'Five?'

'So you can get ready.' Alice raised an eyebrow. 'After all, you won't be coming back here tonight, will you?'

'Just a minute. Who said that Tim stayed here, last night?'

Alice smiled. 'Your face, Roxy darling, said it all for you!'

Roxy laughed. 'Oh, dear. Do I look that smug?'

'Very smug indeed,' Alice confirmed, hugging her. 'And it's about time, too.'

'You never know,' Roxy said thoughtfully, 'you might fancy the pants off this Marcus Blake.'

Alice wrinkled her nose. 'Now that,' she said, 'would be a bit too much of a coincidence.'

'Well, you *might*.'

'If he looks like Antonio Banderas or Mulder from *The X Files*, maybe.' Alice shrugged. 'He's probably a nice guy, but we'll have nothing in common.'

'Don't dismiss him out of hand.'

'Maybe.' Alice was thoughtful. 'It's a pity you're into virtual reality. If you were into cloning . . .'

'I'd make you Jamieson's Monster. Like Frankenstein – but I'd use all the nice bits, ending up with the most gorgeous man in the world.'

'One who can cook, has a great sense of humour, a good personality – and knows exactly what to do with his cock!' Alice finished, laughing. 'Yeah. Then I'll be Alice in Wonderland.'

Roxy groaned. 'That was terrible. Keep that up, and you'll be working on the tabloids, not a lifestyle magazine!'

'I couldn't resist it. Though seriously, if you do ever come up with a man like that . . .'

'In your dreams, Al. Tonight, you'll just have to make do with Marcus.'

FOUR

Tim's house, as both women expected, was absolutely gorgeous. It was in need of some decoration – being a scientist, Tim was more or less oblivious to his surroundings – but it had incredible potential, not to mention plenty of original features. Alice itched to call one of her designer friends on the spot. Marcie, she knew, would work on this sort of place as a labour of love.

Tim handed them both a glass of wine, then introduced them to his flatmate.

'Marcus, this is Alice Jamieson.'

Marcus Blake wasn't the boring type Alice had expected: he looked more like an actor, she thought, with light brown hair that he wore down to his shoulders, and keen hazel eyes. He had the vulnerable sort of mouth that always appealed to her, too: with a jolt, she suddenly realized who he reminded her of. The actor that she and Roxy had both raved about in a cult science-fiction TV series.

'Hello,' she said, suddenly shy.

Marcus took her hand. 'Delighted to meet you, Alice.'

'And this is Roxana Winters,' Tim said.

Marcus smiled, recognizing the keep-off signals on his friend's face. 'Hello, Roxana.'

'Roxy, to my friends,' she said, smiling back and taking his hands.

'Roxy.'

Conversation was awkward for the first few minutes, with none of them quite sure what to say; with relief, Tim glanced at his watch and announced that dinner was ready.

Marcus showed them through into the dining room, and Tim brought in the food.

'This is gorgeous, Tim,' Roxy said, after her first mouthful of chicken in tarragon and cream sauce.

Marcus grinned, his eyes flecked with dancing golden lights. 'Are you going to tell her, or shall I?'

'What?' Roxy asked.

'He came home, informed me that he was cooking dinner tonight – then dragged me out to the nearest Marks and Spencer's to help him find something you'd both like,' Marcus informed her.

'That figures,' Alice said.

'Meaning?' Tim asked.

'Meaning that scientists can't cook,' Alice said loftily. 'They're so concerned with their experiments that they forget to keep an eye on the food and end up burning it and setting off the smoke alarm – don't they, Rox?'

Roxy laughed. 'Once, it happened. Just *once*. And will this woman ever let me forget it?'

'She has a point, though,' Marcus admitted. 'When I first started work on the project, I became so wrapped up in it that I either forgot to eat, or stuffed my face with junk food.'

'So what do you do, exactly?' Alice asked.

'I'm working with Tim on the ID project,' Marcus explained. 'Basically, we'll be coding people's genetic patterns onto a microchip on the identity card. It's a marketer's dream, really – it gives perfect monitoring of their product's buyers, so products can be tailored to suit their market at a much lower cost. It'll hold all your medical information, too, so if you're involved in an accident, all the doctor has to do is to scan your card to find out if you're allergic to anything, or have a rare blood group. And because everyone's genetic pattern is slightly different, there's no chance of you being mistaken for anyone else.' He shrugged. 'It could save a lot of lives.'

'Crime will drop, too,' Tim added. 'Security systems in people's houses will have a scanner for cards, so all visitors will be recorded as they pass the door.'

'Isn't it a bit Big Brother-ish?' Alice asked, with a grimace.

'In a way, I suppose,' Marcus admitted. 'But the plus side is, any burglar or rapist will be caught within hours. People will be safe on the streets again.'

'At the loss of their individuality,' Alice mused.

'It depends on what sort of freedom you want,' Tim said. 'If you want to be free to break the law, then the card's a threat. If not – you'll be free to go where you want and do what you want, and the card will protect you. There'll be no more unfair curfews, no more fear about going out at night alone because you're a woman. If you want to go for a run at midnight, you can, and no one will attack you.'

'What if someone steals your card?' Alice asked.

'It won't matter that much. It's connected to your genetic pattern, so if someone steals your card and tries to withdraw money—'

'Money?' she interrupted, with a frown. 'Where does money come into it?'

'It's an electronic purse, as well,' Tim explained. 'Like a cash-card account. You top it up instead of withdrawing cash. Anyway, without the right genetic code, any services on your card are automatically locked.'

'So I can't steal Roxy's card and blitz Oxford Street, then,' she said, with a rueful smile.

'Exactly. So there's no point in mugging her.' Tim spread his hands. 'I rest my case.'

'Anyway,' Roxy added, 'you wouldn't have to go to Oxford Street. You can shop from home.'

'That's all very well,' Alice said. 'But half the fun of shopping is actually going there and wandering round.'

'You mean, earwigging on other people's conversations and pinching lines for the novel you haven't had time to write yet,' Roxy corrected, laughing.

'Something like that,' Alice said, unabashed.

'You're a Luddite,' Marcus told her. 'It's going to be an electronic world soon. Everything's going to be virtual reality.' Tim, Alice and Roxy exchanged a loaded glance. Marcus noticed immediately. 'What?' he asked, his eyes narrowing.

'I think that he'd be interested in it,' Tim said.

'And, being a geneticist, he could probably bring something to the project,' Alice suggested.

Roxy nodded. 'You're probably right.'

Marcus was thoroughly confused. 'What's going on?'

'Roxana here,' Tim said, 'has invented a virtual-reality sex program.'

'Really?' Marcus turned to her. 'How does it work?'

'With sensor pads. Currently, I have to use wires; eventually, it'll be infrared or radio waves.' Roxy explained what she was doing, and how she and Tim were going to develop it together.

'I'm impressed,' Marcus said. 'If you ever need a guinea pig, just give me a call.'

'Join the queue,' Tim said, laughing. 'I think that the co-developer should have first go.'

'This is all an academic discussion, anyway,' Roxy reminded them. 'The program's at our flat, not here.'

'And it's very good,' Alice said, with a sidelong look at Tim.

'I should hope so, too!' Tim responded, laughing.

Marcus frowned. 'There's something you're not telling me, isn't there?'

'Roxy scanned Tim's face into it,' Alice told him.

'Which is why Alice hijacked Roxy's electronic mailbox and sent me a message,' Tim explained.

Marcus was thoughtful. 'I see. And – er – you've tried it out?' he asked Alice.

'Yes.' She flushed. 'Though only the computerized version, of course.'

'Of course,' Tim echoed, topping up her glass.

Marcus turned to Roxy. 'So you programmed it entirely from imagination?'

She nodded. 'And in answer to your next question, yes.'

Marcus burst out laughing. 'I suppose it was a pretty obvious thing to ask.'

'Well, most people would want to know whether he lived up to expectations,' Roxy agreed, smiling.

'Though I'd never thought of myself as a stud,' Tim said honestly.

'Mm. He's just your average boring workaholic scientist,' Marcus said.

'I know what you mean,' Alice said. 'I live with one, too. Ms Roxana Anorak Winters.'

Tim coughed, and looked at his flatmate. 'Excuse me. And who has to be dragged out of his lab?'

'But,' Marcus fenced, 'I don't bring work home with me.'

'Mind you, when it's the sort of work I'm doing,' Roxy said, trying to defuse the situation, 'it's more like play than work.'

'I'll drink to that,' Alice said, raising her glass.

The evening was restored to good humour, and the conversation turned to more neutral topics. Marcus was a first-class mimic, and had everyone in stitches with his impressions of various people that both Tim and Roxy knew, plus a few figures in the public eye.

Eventually, Alice found herself yawning and looked at her watch. 'It's half past one!' she said, shocked.

'Never,' Tim said. 'You've hardly been here a few minutes.'

'That's what it feels like.' She sighed. 'Can I borrow your phone, please, to call a taxi?'

Tim shook his head. 'Don't bother. There's plenty of room; why don't you stay? There are loads of towels in the airing cupboard, and there's plenty of hot water, if you want a bath.'

'Thanks. I might take you up on that,' Alice said with a smile.

'You're a bit of a matchmaker at heart, aren't you?' Roxy said in bed that night, stroking Tim's face.

'Obviously I wasn't as subtle as I thought I was,' Tim said ruefully. 'I just thought that they might hit it off.'

'They did.' Roxy smiled. 'Did you know that your spare room door creaks?'

'You mean . . .' His eyes widened.

She nodded, and her smile broadened into a grin.

'Good,' he said. 'That means I won't feel so guilty.'

'About what?'

'Spending the rest of tonight making love with you.'

She kissed him. 'You're insatiable.'

'That's your fault.' He stroked her breasts, letting his hands slide down her midriff. 'And, tomorrow, I want to try out that program.'

'Okay.'

He eased his hand between her thighs. 'And then, I'll try to match what you've done, from a male angle.'

'Tim?'

'Mm?'

'Stop talking.'

He parted her labia, and grinned. 'You'd rather I did something else with my mouth, then . . .'

'Having second thoughts?' Roxy asked as she fitted the sensor pads to Tim's fingertips.

'No,' he lied.

'That's not what your face is saying.'

He smiled ruefully. 'That obvious, is it?'

'Well, yes. Alice was a bit worried about it before she tried it, so I gave her a glass of wine and then she relaxed. Maybe you should have a brandy or something, before *you* start.'

'I'd rather keep a clear head,' Tim said. 'I'm meant to be looking at this with a view to giving you some idea of how a man feels. Except first I have to find out how a woman feels.'

Roxy suddenly realized what was upsetting him. 'It's the thought of hooking up to a machine and making love to a man that makes you feel awkward, isn't it?'

He flushed. 'Yeah. Well.'

She grinned. 'Oh, Tim.'

'Look, I've nothing against gay men.' He lifted his hands defensively. 'I work with one or two, and I don't have a problem with them being gay. I'm not the sort of person who makes stupid cracks about keeping my back to the wall.'

'I know you're not. You're just a hundred per cent heterosexual, and you don't like the idea of pretending you're a woman and letting a man make love to you.' She kissed him lightly. 'Look, just think of it as – oh, I dunno, a special kind of masturbation.'

'Masturbation?' Tim tipped his head on one side. 'How do you mean?'

'Well, I haven't scanned anyone else's face in, yet, so you'll be making love with yourself. Hence, masturbation.'

'Mm.' His lips twitched. 'Though that's something else I haven't done for a while. Not since I met you – and before that, I was too knackered when I got home from work to think about my libido.'

'Maybe we can do something about that, later.' She stroked his face. 'You don't have to go through with this, you know. Not if you don't want to.'

'I do. It's just . . . It's going to be kind of weird, feeling what you feel.' He paused. 'On screen, and what have you – am I going to look female?'

'No.'

Tim's eyes widened. 'So you mean, it *is* going to be like two men together?'

'No.' She fitted pads to his nipples. 'The scenario's dinner at my flat. You're going to be me, and you're going to make love with an extremely good-looking and sexy man. You're going to feel everything I feel, when you make love to me. The only time you'll see bits of me is if you look at yourself. There aren't any mirrors around, so . . . No, you're not going to look female. You're going to be me – which is different. I'm not a female version of you.' She handed him another couple of sensor pads. 'I think it'd be best if you put one on your frenum, and one on your scrotum.'

'Yes, Nursey.' He couldn't help smiling at her. 'How can you be so cool and clinical about it? You're hooking me up to a virtual-reality sex program.'

'Because, my sweet, if I start telling you what's really going on in my mind, it'll affect the experiment.' She nodded at his erection. 'Not to mention meaning that you're going to be very confused as to what you feel and what I would be feeling, if I were you when you're pretending to be me.'

'Point taken.'

'It will be, later.' She licked her lips lasciviously to tease him, and he groaned.

'Rox, you're being unfair.'

'Sorry.' She looked pointedly at the sensors. 'Do you want to get on with this, or not?'

'I think,' he said, 'maybe we ought to come at this from a different angle. I'm already aroused.'

'I can see that.'

'Which means that maybe I'm too excited to use the program properly.'

Roxy chuckled. 'That's the best excuse I've ever heard.'

'For what?'

'For this,' she answered, dropping to her knees in front of his chair. Tim gave a sharp intake of breath as she bent her head, the ends of her hair brushing his thighs and her mouth only millimetres from the end of his cock. She licked her lips and looked up at him, her mouth slightly open and her eyes sparkling. 'I assume that this *is* what you had in mind?'

He tangled his hands in her hair. 'Oh, yesss.'

She smiled then, and bent her head, licking the tiny bead of clear moisture from the eye of his cock. He groaned, and she gently worked her lips over the head of his cock, sucking gently. He closed his eyes as her mouth worked lower down his shaft. One hand came up to cup his balls, while she used the other to stroke his perineum.

Roxy knew exactly the speed and pressure to bring his

orgasm to a rapid boil; as Tim felt the almost unbearable
pressure at his groin, he cried out her name. The next moment,
her mouth was filled with warm salty liquid; she waited until
his cock had stopped throbbing, then swallowed, kissed the
tip of his cock, and lifted her head again. 'Better?' she asked.

His pupils had dilated so that his eyes were almost black.
'Yes,' he said huskily.

'Good.' She stood up again, and kissed him lightly on the
mouth; he could taste his own juices on her lips. 'Now, I'll be
in the sitting room, when you've finished.'

'You mean, you're not going to stay and watch?'

'Nope. I'd be too tempted to interfere with the experiment,'
she told him, her eyes crinkling at the corners. 'If you need
me, just yell.'

'Right.' Tim smiled at her as she walked out of the room,
then pressed the last two sensors in place, fitted on the headset,
and tapped the "enter" key.

Sitting opposite was one of the most attractive men imagina-
ble. His hair was thick and dark and slightly wavy, brushed
back from his face, and his eyes were a rich cornflower blue,
framed by unfairly long and thick lashes and a small round
pair of glasses which gave him an intellectual air. His lips
were well-shaped, and his high cheekbones gave him a slightly
Slavic look.

*Christ, Tim thought. Is this how Roxy sees me? Some kind
of lady-killing scientist?*

He smiled, and reached across the narrow table to curl his
fingers round his partner's. His eyelids drooped slightly in a
devastating come-to-bed look, which made his partner's loins
tingle – and yet it was genuine, not faked.

Tim felt incredibly confused. This was what Roxy saw in

*him – and the effect, through the sensors, made him tingle with
sudden arousal. At the same time, Tim was a man, and this
was a man opposite him – even if it was himself. Tim suddenly
wished that he'd agreed to Roxy's suggestion of a brandy. This
was really doing his head in. He wasn't sure who or what he
was supposed to be. He was Tim – and yet he was also Roxy,
now that he had the sensors plugged in.*

'You look so beautiful,' he said, his voice cracking in
his throat.

*Tim smiled to himself. Yeah, it was exactly what he was
thinking when he saw Roxy. He loved everything about her
that shy smile, her expressive eyes, and those beautiful,
beautiful breasts . . . He could never resist touching them. Roxy
had always teased him, saying that if he were a woman, he'd
be masturbating all day, playing with his breasts. He grinned.
Well, this was his chance to do it. From now on, he was Roxy,
and – his partner in the computer was him. The only difference
was that Roxy had to guess what was going on in his mind,
whereas he actually knew it. And now, he'd find out what
happened in her mind, too. Roxy had said that the program
would do everything for him – it would lead him through it,
but if he wanted to make a few changes, all he had to do was
speak. She'd recently added in voice control.*

'Touch yourself,' he said huskily. 'Touch your breasts.'

She licked her lips. Most men adored the idea of watching
their lovers touch themselves, she knew, and she wanted
to give him that pleasure. Though, at the same time, she
wanted to do it, too, ease the nagging pulse that beat between
her legs.

'Do it,' he coaxed softly. 'Show me.'

Roxy undid her shirt very, very slowly, her fingertips
brushing lightly against the smooth swell of her breasts.

He watched her, his eyes glittering with a mixture of desire and anticipation. She'd never realized how hot blue eyes could look, and the sheer surge of lust in them gave an answering kick in her stomach.

She shrugged her shirt from her shoulders and reached behind her to unfasten her bra. On second thoughts, she gave him a wicked grin and slipped her hands under the lace cup of her bra, pushing the material downwards to reveal one rosy-tipped breast and following suit with the other. Her nipples were already erect, hard; she traced the areolae with her ring fingers, gently flicking at her nipples and teasing them until the sudden ache made her gasp. Then she squeezed her breasts gently, pushing them towards her; she splayed her fingers so that her nipples peeped between them. She caught her nipples between her middle and ring finger, and continued massaging her breasts.

The sensations were incredible; she'd never felt quite like this before. Shooting, darting sensations seemed to flicker from her breasts down to somewhere deep in her loins, and her sex began to grow wet and slippery. He smiled his approval at her and she undid her bra completely.

'Do you want me to go further?' she asked, smiling.

He nodded and sat back in a chair, his hands behind his head, just watching her. She unzipped her skirt, and let it fall to the floor; it was the sort she normally wore, in a pleated silky material that came down to her ankles, and it made a satisfying rustling sound against her half-slip. She pushed that down, too, and stood in front of him wearing only a pair of white silk knickers and a pair of lacy-topped hold-up stockings. Then she smiled at him, sliding one hand into her knickers and resting the heel of her palm against her mons veneris.

The little mound of flesh felt warm; she slid her hand between her thighs, letting her middle finger glide between her labia, and she was surprised at just how hot and wet her intimate flesh felt. Her clitoris was already protruding from its hood; as she touched it she gasped, the sensation she'd felt earlier returning even more powerfully.

He smiled in approval, and she continued to caress herself. She pushed her hand even further into her knickers, sliding one finger deep into her hot wet channel. Her flesh was smooth and slippery and yet, at the same time, it seemed to suck her finger in, welcoming her touch. She added another finger, and another, working her hand so that her fingers pistoned in and out of her while she massaged her clitoris with her thumb.

She felt the slow rolling boil of orgasm starting at the soles of her feet, working up her legs; then, suddenly, it surged through her body, making her legs grow weak and her whole body seem to tingle. She cried out his name, howling frenziedly that she loved him; and then he was beside her, touching her, kissing her breasts. His mouth felt so good against her flesh, his tongue a hard point as he traced her areolae, and then softening again as he drew one engorged nipple into his mouth, sucking with a gentle yet insistent rhythm.

Her orgasm had barely died before it began again, this time taking her to a higher plateau; and then, somehow, he'd taken off his clothes, divested her of the rest of her underwear, and pulled her down so that she was kneeling astride him. The tip of his cock rested at the entrance of her sex: this moment before he entered her was like nothing on earth. It was so good, so right.

She sank down onto him, and she couldn't help shuddering in delight. His hands came round her waist, supporting her, and he urged her to move over him. It felt amazing. Every time she sank down on him, her clitoris was stimulated even further by the root of his cock pressing against her, and there was the incredible sensation of his cock stretching her, filling her to the hilt. She tipped her head back, glorying in it, and began to move over him in small circles, rocking her hips back and forth and from side to side.

She couldn't help touching her breasts, pulling at her nipples so that they were distended and increasing the delicious sensations running riot through her. He slid one hand between their moving bodies, rubbing her clitoris and making her body jerk in spasm after spasm of delight. She came again and again, her internal muscles flexing wildly round his cock – tightening and loosening, tightening and loosening. It was heaven on earth, she decided, and she wanted this to last for ever. She cried out again as she reached a higher plateau, and he lifted his upper body so that he could jam his mouth over hers, kissing her deeply . . .

Tim lifted up the headset and slumped back against the chair. The sensations he'd just experienced were amazing. It was incredible. Roxy's program was unbelievably good. And if that was really the way that he made her feel . . . He wasn't sure if he felt more humbled or proud.

He sat there for a while, trying to take it all in; then, finally, he removed the sensor pads, closed the machine down, and walked into the lounge, not bothering to dress first.

Roxy looked up from her laptop as he walked in; she saved the file and switched off the machine, closing the laptop and putting it down beside her. 'So, what did you think?'

'Christ,' he said. 'It was like nothing on earth. Is that *really* how a woman feels?'

'Yep. All down to the last little bit.'

'That,' he said, drawing her over to the sofa and pulling her down beside him, draping her legs over his lap. 'Was that how I make you feel?'

'Yes.' She stroked his face. 'So, was Tiresias right?'

Tim nodded. 'I think so.'

'This means that you want a sex change, then?' she asked wryly.

He chuckled. 'No way. The sensation of you sliding onto my cock is too good to give up.'

'And how am I supposed to know how *that* feels?' Roxy asked.

'Show me your source code, give me a week, and you'll find out.'

'You're on.'

He looked at her. 'So did you set up that little scenario?'

'What?'

'Well,' he said, 'I thought that he was going to kiss me. I mean, I thought that *he* as me was going to kiss me as *you.*'

Roxy giggled. 'Oh, for God's sake, Tim. That's getting too complicated. Why don't you just call us Roxy and Tim?'

'Okay,' he said. 'As I was saying, I thought that Tim was going to kiss Roxy, but he didn't! He asked her to touch herself.'

Roxy grinned. 'Okay, I admit it. I programmed that one in specially for you.' She gave him a smile. 'I was right, wasn't I?'

'About what?'

'That if you were a woman, you'd spend all your time playing with your breasts.'

Tim chuckled. 'Yeah, I suppose.' He grew sober. 'And that's how you feel when you masturbate?'

'Mostly, yes. Sometimes it's more intense, sometimes less. Why?'

'Well,' he said, 'the way you felt under my fingertips was more or less how you feel when I touch you, but there was no guesswork involved this time. I didn't need to ask you, or just hope that I was doing it right and that you weren't just being polite in not criticizing me. It just felt – natural. Exactly what I'd want to do, if I were a woman.'

'Well, now you know.'

'You know, Rox,' he said thoughtfully, 'it would make a very good therapy tool. It would stop dozens of relationships and marriages breaking up. All you'd need to do would be to program what you wanted and get your partner to try it out. It's a non-threatening environment, so it's not like making a judgement on your partner; it's just giving them the chance to try something new.'

'Maybe,' Roxy said, 'but the prime element in my program is fun. I want people to enjoy themselves, enjoy their sexuality.'

'And that's why you decided to make your VR sex machine?'

'Yes and no,' Roxy said. 'I suppose the real reason why I did it was because I was too busy to have a relationship. I didn't want all the hassle. I wanted something that I knew wouldn't go wrong, that I'd enjoy, and that would make me happy.'

'And it was my face that you programmed into it.' His eyes held hers.

'Yes,' she said simply. 'That was the fantasy element.'

'But you could have programmed anyone's face into it.'

'Such as?'

'Oh, I dunno – Harrison Ford, whoever it is that women really fancy.'

'According to Alice, it's Antonio Banderas and David Duchovny,' Roxy told him with a grin. 'And I have to admit, I agree with her.'

A flicker of jealousy passed over his face. 'I see.'

She blew him a kiss. 'You started this! You're right, Tim. I could have chosen anyone.'

'But you chose me.'

She rubbed her nose against his. 'When you found out, I really thought that it was going to be the end of it. I thought you were going to blow your top.'

'No. Actually, I was flattered.' He looked at her. 'And after this . . . If that's how you really feel about me, Roxy, if that's how I make you feel when I touch you . . .'

'It is,' she confirmed.

'Then,' he said, 'put it this way. I don't think it's something that happens more than once in a lifetime.'

'You're probably right,' she agreed.

'And I have one hell of a task, to match that. To show you how you make me feel.'

She smiled at him. 'Believe me, I'm really looking forward to it.'

FIVE

'Your source code,' Tim said loftily, 'needs tidying up.'

Roxy stuck out her tongue, and returned her attention to the program on her laptop.

'Seriously.' He sat next to her on the sofa, sliding his arm round her shoulder. 'It was bloody complex. It must have taken you months to work it out.'

'From the basics, yes,' she agreed. Her smile faded as she looked up at him. 'Tim – you didn't really change the source code, did you? There were a couple of glitches, so I put some bypasses in to isolate the problems. I was going to work on them later – once I'd decided the best way to deal with them.'

'I promise, I haven't done anything to it. I took a copy of your original program – and I made that crash, half a dozen times, when I tried tidying it up.' He stroked her hair. 'Anyway, I got there in the end. Whenever you want to try it out, it's there for you, on my machine. I've called it VRX2, if you want to take a copy home and try it out there instead.'

'I don't think so.' She smiled at him, saved the file, and flipped out of the program. 'I've been waiting for nearly a month for you to sort this out – I'm certainly not going to wait until I go home tonight to try it out.'

'You're going home tonight?' His eyes widened in a mixture of surprise and hurt. Since the first night they'd spent together,

Roxy had stayed at his place most nights. He'd grown used to waking up with her curled in his arms.

'Well – not unless you want me to. Or unless you want to go home with me, for a change.' She switched off the computer, then leaned forward and kissed him very lightly on the lips. 'I'm looking forward to this: finding out what it really feels like to be you, when you make love with me.'

He smiled wryly. 'I just hope that it lives up to your expectations.'

She spread her hands. 'I'll tell you, when I've tried it and thought about it.'

'Right.' He looked slightly anxious.

'Just relax with the paper, and some good music.' She grinned. 'But *not* Verdi, please!'

He chuckled. Roxy didn't quite share his musical tastes. Like him, she was fond of baroque chamber music, working to the calm and regular influence of Bach and Corelli, but she disliked the opera arias he adored; and he liked the bluesy rock she listened to when she was driving, but not the pop she indulged in when she was with Alice. 'Okay. And I'll keep the volume down, I promise.'

'Good. See you later.' She walked into Tim's study, drew the blind, and switched on the little desk lamp before swiftly peeling off her clothes. She sat down at the computer, which Tim had left switched on for her, and plugged the sensor wires into the back. Then she placed the sensors on her nipples, her clitoris and the back of her neck, and pulled on the gloves.

She paused for a moment before pulling on the headset. She could understand, now, how weird Tim had felt before trying the machine. Making love to someone of the same sex was mind-blowing enough – but when that person was yourself, your virtual clone ... She shook herself, clicked on the icon, and pulled on the headset.

She was sitting on the sofa, her nose in a book and her legs curled up under her. She looked up suddenly, her eyes almost molten gold, and a shy yet enticing smile on her lips. She was beautiful, though it was an unconscious beauty – she didn't have the arrogant bearing of many conventionally attractive women. Her chiffon shirt was slightly see-through in the light, revealing the generous curves of her breasts and the lacy cups of her bra; her feet and ankles, the only other parts of her body visible under her calf-length pleated silk skirt, were dainty and well-shaped.

It would be so, so easy to sit next to her, and slide your hand under her skirt, stroking her calves and letting your hand drift up over her thighs, smoothing them apart. Finding the beautiful warm wet welcoming place between her legs, and letting your fingers sink into her, caressing her and making that beautiful mouth open with desire.

Roxy's eyes widened. So this was how Tim saw her – all curves, lush and sensual. A kind of shy siren, unaware of how attractive she really was.

She patted the sofa next to her, smiling. 'Come and give me a cuddle.'

Roxy smiled to herself. Tim had captured a typical scene. If she wasn't working at her PC, she was curled up on the sofa with her nose in a book. She couldn't be bothered partying all night, nowadays; her idea of a perfect evening was to curl up on the sofa with Tim and a good bottle of wine. Maybe watching a film, maybe just listening to music: just as long as she was in his arms. And then, as the evening progressed, they would make love ... Did Tim, she wondered, feel the same way that she did? Well, from now, she'd find out. Because she was Tim.

'I've got a better idea.' He walked over to the stereo, and changed the Bach CD for one of Roxy's George Michael albums, picking her favourite track and switching it to repeat mode. 'Come and dance with me.'

'Dance?'

She was faintly surprised; it was obvious in the little frown that always creased her forehead when something happened that she wasn't expecting. He grinned to himself. She knew how much he disliked that particular album: but he'd put up with it tonight for her sake. To please her, to have her weaving in his arms, as a prelude to making love. 'Dance with me,' he invited again, holding out his hand. She slid a piece of paper between the pages of her book, and put the book on the floor, standing up and walking over to join him.

As the first few bars of the piano filled the air, followed by a bass guitar and a soft jazz-type percussion, she slid her arms round his waist and began to sway with him. He smiled, resting his cheek on the top of her head. She always said that she was clumsy, and yet she had an instinctively good sense of rhythm – a better one than he did. It was one of the reasons why he rarely danced, feeling scared of making a fool of himself: but, with Roxy in his arms, he always felt that he could conquer the world. That this incredibly bright and sexy woman could fancy him, feel the same way that he did about her . . . It still amazed him. He wasn't sure whether to be thankful to whatever deity brought them together, or to wonder about it.

He could feel her breasts pressing against him; with a murmur of content, he let his hands slide down her back so that he could stroke her buttocks. Then he let one hand drift upwards, burrowing under her chiffon shirt. Her skin was soft and warm and smooth: one touch wasn't enough. He wanted more. He wanted to dance with her, skin to skin, and then lower her gently to the rug, and make love with her. The thought made his cock so hard, it almost hurt.

'Roxy . . .'

She tipped her head back slightly to look at him, and he lowered his face to hers, kissing her lightly. Her lips opened beneath his and his tongue explored her mouth, probing delicately and then suddenly fiercely as need overcame him.

'Oh, Roxy,' he sighed, breaking the kiss and easing one hand between their bodies so that he could unbutton her shirt. The sight of her breasts was enough to make his heart beat faster; he wanted to bury his face in them, lick them, slide his cock between them. His whole body was conscious of hers, and it made him so hard that it hurt.

He pushed her shirt from her shoulders and held her at arm's length; she swayed before him, smiling, and reached behind her, undoing the clasp of her bra. She brought her hands round to cover her breasts, and let the lacy garment fall to the floor; then she splayed her fingers, letting her nipples peep through them.

'God, Roxy . . .' He dropped to his knees in front of her, burying his face in her breasts and breathing in her warm powdery scent. He closed his eyes, concentrating on the way she felt, the softness of her skin, the warmth of her body; then, slowly, he cupped one breast and turned his face so that he could touch the tip of his tongue to her nipple. The erect nub of flesh felt slightly rough against his tongue, the tiny pimples betraying her arousal; he began to suck gently, feeling her sharp intake of breath and the way she tipped her head back, pushing her breasts towards him to encourage him.

He unzipped her skirt; it rustled to the floor, and she stepped neatly out of it. She was wearing lacy white knickers and lace-topped hold-up stockings; he smiled and rolled her stockings down, stroking her inner thighs in a way that made her shiver. She felt so good, so soft and warm. And she was so deliciously responsive to him. Every time he touched her, he knew that he was pleasuring her. He stroked the hollows of her ankles as he removed each stocking in turn, letting his fingers drift back over her calves, over the sensitive spot at the back of her knees, and then finally back between her legs.

She shivered as he cupped her mons veneris, feeling the heat of her quim through the thin silk of her knickers. He pressed one finger against her, rubbing her clitoris gently, and she widened her stance slightly, tipping her head back and opening her mouth; he smiled and gently hooked his thumbs into the waistband of her knickers, pulling them down.

'Oh, Tim,' she murmured, tangling her hands in his hair as she stepped out of her knickers. The pads of her fingers dug into his scalp. 'Touch me. Taste me.'

He couldn't resist a plea like that. The soft husky tone of her voice as she asked him to perform such an intimate service . . . He bent his head, nuzzling her thighs. Not for the first time, he thought how soft her skin was, how good it felt against his. And the scent of her quim, a warm spicy aroma, made his cock twitch and harden even further. He wanted to kiss her, lick her until she came – and then slide his cock into her warm wet depths while her muscles were still contracting. He opened his mouth, pressing his tongue against her inner thigh: she tasted as good as she felt, warm and clean and spicy.

Then, at last, he shifted slightly, and drew his tongue along her quim. It was like the first time for him, exploring her more intimate folds and crevices and discovering what she liked, what made her body react sharply to him. She tasted of seashore and honey and vanilla, with an undertone of spice, and he loved it. He couldn't get enough of her. He began to lap in earnest; her moans of pleasure only served to urge him on.

He drew her clitoris into his mouth, sucking the hard nub of flesh gently, until she began to shiver; then he pushed his tongue deep inside her quim, tasting her honeyed nectar. God, she was so responsive: it was like having a birthday and Christmas all at the same time, the way she reacted to his touch. He felt her body tense for a moment, and then she came, her body shuddering and her internal muscles flexing wildly against his mouth. He didn't stop: he continued licking, licking, licking, his tongue flickering across her pleasure spots to bring her to a higher peak.

At last, she tugged gently on his hair, and he dropped a kiss on her quim before pulling back and standing up. He drew her back into his arms and kissed her, so that she could taste herself on his mouth; she began to unbutton his shirt, and the feel of her fingers against his flesh made him shiver.

She pushed his shirt from his shoulders, sliding her fingers over his skin and kneading the muscles in his back; he submitted happily to her caresses, wanting her to take off the rest of his clothes and touch him more intimately. Her hands slid down to the waistband of his jeans, and she gave him a tantalizing smile, curling her fingers round his cock, through the thickness of the denim. It made him shiver; he yearned for her to touch him properly, skin to skin.

Her smile broadened as she unzipped his jeans, easing the soft denims over his hips. He wriggled out of the jeans removing his socks at the same time; she hooked her thumbs into the waistband of his boxer shorts and drew them down, very slowly. His cock sprang up, twitching in anticipation. She gave him another of those butter-soft smiles, and then knelt before him.

His whole body quivered: he knew what she was going to do next. He knew that she was going to wrap her beautiful, beautiful mouth around his cock, and the knowledge was dizzying. Her lips curved, and then she curled her fingers round the shaft of his cock. His knees felt weak; he reached down to tangle his hands in her hair, steadying himself. All sensation through his body seemed to be concentrated entirely on his cock; he felt her hair brush against the skin of his belly, the soft silky tresses heightening his anticipation even more. And then his heart almost stopped as, finally, she opened her mouth and eased her lips round the tip of his cock.

He almost came at the thought of what she was doing. His feelings were running riot: he felt like he was on fire, where she touched him. She stayed there for a moment, letting him get used to the feel of her mouth around his cock, the warm sweet wetness of it – and then she began to suck. He shivered with the sheer delight of it, loving the way it felt: the pressure of her palate against his glans felt incredible. It was so good, so right.

She brought him almost to the edge, sucking him hard and caressing his balls with her other hand – and then she stopped, squeezing his cock gently, just by the frenum, to delay his orgasm. Then she covered his cock with tiny cat-laps, moving down his cock to his balls and taking them into her mouth, sucking gently. He was almost beside himself, it was so good. The area around his balls and his cock was a zone of pure pleasure.

The pressure began to be almost unbearable; he almost howled out her name, and she shifted position again, wetting her little finger and stroking gently along his perineum, massaging the soft silky crease.

'Yes, do it, do it,' he moaned; then he felt her finger pushing gently against the puckered rosy hole of his anus and finally sliding into him. It felt so good, so incredibly good; but before he had time to think about it, her mouth was working on him again, and she was taking his cock as deeply into her mouth as possible. The pressure building up in his balls was too much. He yelled out her name in a mixture of love and desire and ecstasy, and then he came, his cock throbbing in her mouth, the hot salty liquid pulsing through him as though his whole body were pouring into hers.

Gently, she removed her finger and sat back on her haunches, licking her lips. He knelt down beside her, kissing her, wanting to tell her how much he loved her. The way she made him feel was so good, it was like nothing on earth.

He lay beside her on the thick pile carpet, stroking her body. He traced a path across her midriff with the tip of his nose and his tongue, taking tiny cat-laps at her skin and breathing in her scent. His hand slid between her legs again; she was still as turned on as he was, he realized, as his cock twitched back into life and hardened again. He slid an exploratory finger between her labia: she was wet as well as hot. He smiled at her, rubbing his nose affectionately against hers. 'You feel like a furnace.'

She grinned lazily at him, not bothering to answer, and tipped her head back for a kiss. He kissed her hard, and then, the next thing he knew, he was kneeling between her thighs, the tip of his cock fitting at the entrance of her sex. He savoured the moment. It felt almost like the moment when she'd first put his cock into her mouth, that delicious feeling of anticipated pleasure and actual pleasure merging. Except that, this time, the flesh that slid round his own was somehow tighter, the pressure more intense. He moved very slowly, enjoying the way it felt as his cock slipped into her, right up to the hilt.

It was an incredible feeling. He tried hard to think of a way of describing how it felt – it was like having warm, wet silk wrapped round him, he thought, or maybe velvet. It was like sliding his cock into a sweet, tight passage filled with thick whipped cream. He began to move, and the sensation was indescribable. The way his foreskin was pulled back and forth, as he pushed in and out of her; the way she used her internal muscles to make her whole quim flutter along the length of his cock. This, he decided, was what Paradise was really like. Your body joined to your lover's, fusing the two of you into one.

He felt the almost unbearable pressure begin to build again, and then finally his body poured into hers. Almost at the same time, he felt her ripple round him, her internal muscles clutching madly at him as she, too, came . . .

Roxy pulled off the headset, shivering. Her hands came down to cup her groin; she grinned. God, it had been so real, she was almost convinced that she still had a penis! Tim had done well, she thought. It had really felt like she was a man, that she'd had a cock. And that weird powerful feeling she'd had when she'd – he'd – penetrated his lover, a feeling of power mixed with tenderness and deep need . . . The nearest she'd ever felt like that was when she'd straddled Tim, hungry for his body, and moved over him, her internal muscles moving demandingly round him.

Thoughtfully, she walked back into the living room; Tim was sprawled on the sofa, reading the paper, a Bach cello sonata playing in the background. He looked up as she walked in. 'Okay?'

She nodded.

'Well? What did you think?'

'It was – different. Good – but completely different from the way I feel.'

'So what's the verdict, Mrs Tiresias?'

She sat down next to him on the sofa, teasing the paper from his fingers and curling into his arms. 'I'd rather be a woman.' She stroked his face. 'Though I appreciate the amount of work that went into that. You've made a brilliant job of it.'

'What were you expecting?' he teased. 'A botch-up?'

'No, of course not. I don't know what I was expecting, to be honest. I thought that a man would feel ... well ... Oh, I don't know.' She rubbed her nose against his. 'It's a bit of a power trip for you, though, isn't it? Sinking into me.'

'Yes and no. I feel like I'm possessing you completely – but at the same time, I don't feel that it's my right. It's a privilege – and it's only happening because you want it, too.'

'Very politically correct.'

He cupped one breast, and grinned. 'Politically correct isn't how I feel at all, when I'm with you.'

'No?' she teased.

No.' He rolled her nipple between finger and thumb. 'Roxy.'

'Mm?'

'I've been very patient. I resisted sneaking into my study and watching you while you were using the program.'

She grinned. 'And you think you deserve a reward for all your hard work?'

'Something like that.' He kissed the side of her neck. 'Shall we continue this discussion somewhere a little more comfortable?'

'I thought you'd never ask ...'

Grinning, he stood up, pulling her to his feet, and led her to their bedroom.

'You're really happy, aren't you?' Alice asked, smiling as she watched Roxy dancing round the kitchen.

'Yeah. And I really like this CD.'

Alice chuckled. It was an old George Michael album, which she and Roxy had often played in the days when they were flatmates and which both Marcus and Tim had pronounced dreadful. She turned up the volume. 'Perfect party music. Do you remember our housewarming, in Islington?'

'Do I ever.' Roxy added herbs to the pasta sauce, then topped up her friend's glass of wine. 'You put this on repeat.'

'Mm.' Alice took a swig of wine, then gave herself up to the seductive beat of the music, and began bopping round the kitchen with Roxy. 'That's because it's one of our best joint CDs. You know, that was the worst thing about moving in with Marcus – giving up your half of our CD collection.'

'Me, too. Actually, I miss sharing with you. Evenings like this, when we'd turn the music up loud, open a bottle of wine, and have a good bop while we sorted out dinner.'

'Mm. Tim's a darling, but I can't quite see him doing that.' Alice grinned. 'It's just as well that he and Marcus are working late tonight. I don't think that they'd enjoy this very much.'

'What the hell – *we* will!' Roxy grinned, and they continued bopping round the kitchen until the track had ended.

Alice flopped down by the kitchen table. 'I must be getting old. I don't have the stamina to dance all night nowadays! Anyway.' She tipped her head on one side. 'So how's it going with Tim?'

'It's working out really well. I have to admit, I like living in Hampstead.'

'But it's not just his house that you like so much, is it?'

'Even though Marcie's transformed it completely,' Roxy agreed. Tim's house had featured in *Home Matters* – both as the neglected house with potential that Roxy and Alice had both seen, the first time Tim had invited them over for dinner, and as the stunningly elegant place it was now. Roxy had moved in with Tim, shortly after the house had been redecorated; and Marcus and Alice had found themselves a Victorian terrace in Walthamstow, which Alice's friend Marcie had made into a virtual shrine to William Morris.

'He's a lovely guy,' Alice said warmly. She'd liked Tim Fraser from the first moment she'd met him, on Roxy's computer program. 'Though I still think that you two work too hard.'

'We're fine. And before you start asking when we ever get time to see each other, Visicom and Comco have moved into the same complex, at Canary Wharf. So we see each other at lunchtimes, and we travel back from work together.' She smiled. 'Plus we've been known to have the odd meeting together. The Mall project ties in pretty neatly with the security database and cards.'

'Well, when do I get to hear wedding bells?' Alice teased.

Roxy grinned. 'You'll beat me down the aisle – that's a definite.'

'Shame. Well, when you *do* decide to do it, I expect to be your matron of honour.'

'Yes, Ma'am,' Roxy teased back. 'Mind you, we're happy as we are. And, as the saying goes – if it ain't broke, don't fix it.'

Just as Alice was about to give Roxy a lecture on the joys of marriage, they heard the front door slam. A couple of moments later, Tim put his head round the door. 'Hi, Al. God, that music's awful.'

'Hello, darling, and did you have a good day?' Roxy retorted. He chuckled. 'Until I came home to this, yes!'

'Oh, go and have a shower.' She pulled a face at him, more amused than cross.

Marcus put his head round the door, and echoed Tim's complaint. 'Now, if you'd been playing *Dark Side of the Moon* . . .'

'No chance,' Alice said, laughing. 'Not in here, anyway.'

'In that case, I'm not going to offer to help with dinner.'

Roxy chuckled. 'You're too late for that, anyway. All I have to do now is put the bread in the oven to warm up.'

'Well, the thought was there.' Marcus smiled at her. 'I'll be in the living room, if you change your mind.'

'You know where the stereo is,' Roxy said, returning the smile.

A few minutes later, when the bread was ready and Tim had emerged from the shower, the four of them sat in the dining room.

'Wonderful. If you ever get bored at Visicom, you could always open a restaurant,' Marcus said, after his first forkful of cannelloni.

'A virtual one, perhaps,' Roxy said.

'Mm, talking of virtual . . .' Marcus squeezed Alice's hand under the table. 'I know I promised not to talk shop, tonight, but how's That Program coming on?'

Tim and Roxy exchanged a glance.

'You've added something, haven't you?' Marcus asked, catching their look.

'Mm. It's the Tiresias factor,' Roxy told him.

'Which is?'

Tim smiled. 'Tiresias was a Greek seer. He had a row with a couple of the gods, and was turned into a woman – then back into a man again. He upset the gods even more by telling them that women had a better time, in sex, than men did.'

'Right.' Marcus ate another mouthful of cannelloni. 'So how does that fit in with your program?'

'You can choose whether you want to experience it as a man or a woman,' Roxy told him.

Marcus' jaw dropped. 'What, literally?'

'Yes. If you choose to be a man in the program, you feel as a man does. And if you choose to be a woman, you feel as a woman does,' Roxy confirmed.

'And on screen? If I wanted to feel what a woman does – would it be another man making love to me?'

'Yes, but you'd feel as though you were a woman.'

Marcus shook his head. 'I can't quite get my head round this one.'

Alice gave him a sidelong glance. 'Why don't you try it out?'

'What, now?'

'After dinner,' Roxy said. 'When you're relaxed. And it's your choice whether you want to be a man or a woman.'

'An instant sex change, hm?' Marcus smiled wryly, and took another sip of wine. 'So when are you two going to go public with it?'

'When it's ready,' Roxy said promptly.

Alice laughed. 'Oh, honestly. They say that painters are never happy with their work, always going back to it to add a shadow here, a highlight there. Is this program going to be the same sort of thing?'

'Of course not. But I want to add in the olfactory bits first,' Roxy said seriously. 'And have at least half a dozen scenarios available. Otherwise, it could be boring.'

'Half a dozen scenarios.' Alice licked her lower lip. 'So

what's it going to be? The *Kama Sutra* or the *Joy of Sex*, virtual-reality style?'

Tim chuckled. 'I think it's going to be more like the latter – but we're not necessarily sticking to just one position per fantasy.'

'The mind boggles,' Alice said.

Marcus took her hand. 'Not to mention other parts of the anatomy . . .'

They all laughed, and Tim topped up their glasses. 'Seriously,' Alice said, 'when are you planning to launch it?'

Roxy shook her head. 'I'm not sure. At least a few months, yet. I mean, once we've finished the program, there's all the hassle of having it put onto CD-ROM, and distribution, and promotion, and . . .' She shrugged. 'I'm a scientist, not a marketer. I don't want all the hassle.'

'I know a couple of people who could help you,' Alice said.

'Thanks. I'll take you up on it – but not yet. Not until it's how I want it.'

Alice groaned. 'Listening to you, anyone would say that you were an artist, not a mad scientist!'

Roxy grinned back. 'Simply using a little creative licence, you might say.'

Tim rolled his eyes, and topped up their wine. 'Well. If you can't persuade her to put it on the market, Al, no one can.'

'Oh, I will,' Roxy said. 'Just – not yet.'

PART II

SIX

Alice fished in her handbag. 'Oh, before I forget – have you seen one of these?' She handed Roxy a small leaflet.

'Traditional Values.' Roxy frowned as she read the heading. 'No, I haven't. Where did you get it?'

'It was pushed through our letterbox the other day.' Alice bit her lip. 'There was a march in the park near us on Saturday. It was – well, it unnerved me, a bit.'

Roxy was surprised. Alice had more sang-froid than anyone else she had ever met. For Alice to be spooked by something, it had to be bad. She skim-read the leaflet, and grimaced at the contents. 'They're nutters, Al. And this is just like the leaflets produced by all the other fringe political parties. They all have a bee in their collective bonnet about something or other, and maybe they'll gain a few supporters for their causes – but not anywhere near enough to come to power, or even close to it.'

'Even so.' Alice rubbed a hand along her jaw. 'There are a lot of disgruntled people out there, Roxy. Men who became redundant through technology. People who work fewer hours and earn less, so they can't afford to make the most of their leisure time.'

'Al, that happens with any change in society. The Industrial Revolution did the same thing for factory workers. There was unrest for a while, and then everything settled down again.' Roxy looked thoughtfully at the leaflet. 'I can see the appeal of this lot to men, yes – but women make up at least half the population. No woman in her right mind would vote away her right to work and her right to do whatever she wants!'

'True.'

'There's nothing to worry about. In two or three years' time, the Traditional Values group will be forgotten, just like all the other pressure groups. People will find something else to protest about.'

'Mm.' Yet Alice couldn't help feeling uneasy. There was something hateful about the little manifesto.

'The best place for this,' Roxy said, screwing it into a ball, 'is in the rubbish bin. That's where it belongs.' She tossed the ball into the waste-paper basket. Her labrador promptly retrieved it and chewed it to shreds. Roxy grinned. 'Well, Monty, that showed them!'

Hearing his name, the labrador lifted his head and wagged his tail. Alice smiled. 'That's one spoiled dog.'

The telephone shrilled; Roxy picked up the receiver. 'Hello?'

'Hello, darling.'

'Tim.' She switched on the viewer. 'At last. Are you two coming home now?'

Tim shook his head. 'We've hit a bit of a snag. I think we're going to be a couple of hours.'

Marcus appeared next to him. 'So we thought, rather than make you two wait for dinner, we'd grab a curry or something on the way home.'

'That,' Roxy said, 'is the most pathetic excuse we've ever heard for a boys' night out. Mind you, I suppose it means that we get a girly night in . . .'

Tim smiled at her. 'What a hardship, eh? Gossiping until all hours, drinking wine and stuffing your faces with chocolate.'

She grinned. 'Don't expect us to leave you anything.'

'We won't. See you later.'

She switched off the phone, and realized that Alice was laughing. 'What?'

'I'm not sure who's worse about gadgets, you or Tim!' Alice raised an eyebrow. 'I've seen videophones before – but a *cordless* one?'

Roxy coughed. 'It's a prototype. Tim shares an office with the guy who's developing it, and we're merely helping him by testing it at home.'

'Playing with another new toy, you mean,' Alice teased.

'Yeah, well.' Roxy shrugged.

'Being here's almost like being in an H. G. Wells novel. Every sci-fi gadget you can imagine . . .'

Roxy grinned. 'Just about enough to inspire you to write that science fiction novel you've been talking about for years, Mrs Blake!'

Alice wrinkled her nose. 'I don't get time, what with the baby and writing to deadlines and—'

'Other such excuses,' Roxy cut in.

Alice coughed. 'And this is the woman who's been working on a virtual-reality sex machine for years – and still hasn't put it on the market!'

'Touché.' Roxy smiled back. 'Mind you, we're still trying to sort out the copyright problems of people scanning in photos from magazines or postcards, that sort of thing. You know how long legal matters take.'

'Tell me about it.' Alice rolled her eyes.

'Anyway, as the boys won't be back for ages, how about we get a pizza delivered and crack open a bottle of wine?' Roxy suggested.

'Just like old times,' Alice said happily. 'Good idea.'

'You sort the pizza, then; I'll do the wine.'

Alice tipped her head on one side. 'I don't suppose that you have a normal phone in the house, do you?'

Roxy grinned. 'No, we don't. But you can turn the screen off, if you want.' She showed Alice which button to press, then went into the kitchen to collect a bottle of dry white wine from the fridge, two glasses and a corkscrew. She returned to the sitting room, deftly uncorked the bottle, and filled the glasses, handing one to Alice.

'Cheers,' Alice said, lifting her glass.

'Cheers.'

'Mm, this is gorgeous.'

'Boring old Aussie Chardonnay. But it's unoaked,' Roxy said. 'Tim discovered it.'

'And you have a case or so in the cellar?' Alice guessed, laughing.

'You know Tim.' Roxy smiled. 'So, what did you order?'

'Four cheeses, with extra toppings of avocado and olives, garlic foccaccia, and salad.' Alice spread her hands. 'Just like old times.'

'Mm. Especially as I have a large bar of Swiss chocolate in the fridge, and some of that Italian ice cream we both like in the freezer.' Roxy curled up in a chair with her feet under her. 'Mind you, I think we're both more settled, now.'

'Me, certainly. Husband, baby, and doing very nicely, thank you, as a freelance.' Alice looked at Roxy over the edge of her wine glass. 'What about you, though?'

'I'm fine. Work's better than it's ever been, and I love living here. And before you start nagging me about marrying Tim, we're happy as we are. A bit of paper isn't going to change the way we feel about each other.'

'Okay, okay, no lectures. I promise,' Alice said, holding up one hand in defence.

'Good. And "no lectures",' Roxy added, 'includes not nagging me about VRX.'

'Just as long as you give me the exclusive interview when you finally put it on the market,' Alice said.

'Of course.' Roxy smiled at her. 'You were the first person to use it, besides me; so you have to be the first person to write about it, too.'

They chatted lightly until the pizza arrived; both of them were hungry and ate ravenously. Another bottle of wine later, when they were idly breaking off squares of chocolate, Alice looked curiously at Roxy. 'I know I promised not to lecture—'

Roxy groaned. 'Here we go,' she teased.

'I'm not going to lecture you, Rox. I just wondered . . . well, how much the program's changed since I tried it that time.'

'Quite a lot, actually. You know that Tim's programmed a man's responses into it, so you can pick which sex you want to be. I've added some choices, so you can choose the sort of person you want to make love with and the scenario. You can even choose your scents! I just need to make a few adjustments to the infrared bits now, so you don't have to be wired up to the PC. The way I want it to work, you can have your PC at one end of your bedroom, and you can live out the program on the comfort of your bed, instead of sitting in a chair.'

Alice chuckled. 'Not everyone has a PC in their bedroom, you know!'

'I was thinking about laptops,' Roxy said, lifting her chin.

'Like hell you were. You and Tim have about half a dozen computers in this house – and they're networked, too!'

Roxy scoffed. 'We're not that bad.'

'No? There's one in your study, one in Tim's, one in the kitchen – and you both have a laptop.'

'Which is five, not six. Look, some of the PCs are really ancient. It wasn't worth trading them in for new models, they'd depreciated so much; that's why we decided to keep them,' Roxy protested.

Alice smiled. 'I know. But you're so teasable about your techie habit.'

'Huh.' Roxy refilled their glasses.

'Seriously, Rox, has it changed a lot?'

'Mm. There's more choice,' Roxy said laconically.

Alice licked her lips. 'So I could, if I wanted, make love with Marcus and a certain actor, at the same time?'

Roxy chuckled, knowing exactly who Alice meant – the actor they'd both fancied in a science fiction series a couple of years before. 'Greedy woman. Yes, if you wanted to, you could make love with two men. Even three. Or another woman, if that's what turned you on. But, like I said, there are copyright problems – so it'll be only an approximation of the actor's face. It's a low-resolution scan, so it's not brilliant. It's not as sharp as a photograph or video.'

'Right.'

Roxy's lips twitched. 'I reckon the boys will be at least another hour. So if that's what you want to do . . .'

Alice flushed. 'Oh, dear. Am I that obvious?'

'In a word – yes,' Roxy said, smiling.

'It's not because I don't have good sex with Marcus, or enough of it, because I do. It's just . . .'

'The lure of fantasy,' Roxy finished. 'Yeah. I know. And the best thing about this program is that you can live out your fantasy without upsetting the real world.' She tipped her head on one side. 'Two men, together, eh?'

Alice's flush deepened. 'In fantasy. I don't intend to act it out in real life.'

'But in fantasy, it could be arranged.' Roxy smiled at her friend. 'All I have to do is make a small adjustment to the program.'

'I thought you said that you still had a lot to do on it?'

'Until it's how *I* want it to be, yes. But I think you'll enjoy what there is, so far.'

Alice flushed. 'In a way, I feel a bit – well, disloyal. I mean, I'm married to Marcus, now.'

'It's fantasy. There's nothing wrong with that. And the best thing is, you're not being unfaithful to Marcus, because it's not happening in real life.'

Alice nodded. 'Sorry. I'm being stupid.'

'Not at all.' Roxy smiled at her friend. 'It's completely up to you. If you want to do it, I'm giving you the chance. If you don't, then fine – I'm happy to sit here, sink some more wine, and bop around the sitting room with you.'

'And if I do decide to do it, what will you do?'

'You know me. I've usually got my nose in some kind of book.'

'The book in question being a notebook computer, you mean,' Alice teased. 'Well – okay. Thanks. I'll go for it.'

'This way, Madam.' Roxy ushered Alice through to her study.

'I'm half-surprised that you haven't got a PC in your bedroom,' Alice remarked.

'We did have, but Tim insisted on moving it into the kitchen. He said otherwise, he'd never get my attention away from the machine.' Roxy tipped her head on one side. 'So what do you want? You can see what Marcus feels like when he makes love with you, if you like.'

'I'll take you up on that, some other time,' Alice said. 'But, right now . . .' She stretched, and gave Roxy a very lascivious smile. 'Right now, I feel like being greedy.'

'Okay.'

Alice stripped to her bra and knickers while Roxy set up the program. Roxy gestured to the sensor pads. 'You know what to do,' she said with a smile. 'Just hit "enter", and you're away.'

'Thanks.'

Roxy winked at Alice, and closed the door as she left the room. Alice fitted the sensors into place, then put on the headset, took a deep breath, and pressed "enter".

She was sitting on the sofa between them. Two equally handsome men, both around six feet tall, both with mid-brown hair and hazel eyes. They were even similar facially, with vulnerable mouths – the kind that Alice had always called the "wounded puppy-dog" kind of mouth, and that always made her look twice. The only difference between them was that one had short hair, brushed back from his face, and the other had longer hair which brushed the back of his collar. Both of them wore faded jeans, tight enough to reveal shapely buttocks and firm thighs, teamed with a black round-neck cotton sweater. Alice shivered. By some standards, she would call this greedy. But tonight, she considered herself very lucky indeed.

One of them had his arm thrown negligently round her shoulders; the other had one hand resting very lightly on her inner thigh. She could feel the warmth of his hand through her thin leggings, and she could imagine that hand drifting higher, touching her more intimately. The thought made her catch her breath; almost as if he understood what she was thinking, he smiled, dropped a kiss on her cheek, and let his hand drift up further so that the heel of his palm rested on her sexual mound, and his fingers rested along the gusset of her leggings. She wanted him to press harder, touching her clitoris: she held her breath, and then he was doing it – exactly what she wanted, pressing his hand closer to her so that he could feel her pulsing heat.

The room was in darkness; she knew that neither of them could see what the other one was doing. She also knew that both of them *knew* what the other one was doing. Although the three of them were ostensibly watching some art-house film on the wide-screen television, they all knew that there was another purpose to tonight.

They were both wearing the same aftershave. Not for them the more common fragrances of Aramis, Paco Rabanne or Xcess: it was something a little more expensive, a little more exclusive. The citrus tang, mixed with musk, always turned her on. And now that the three of them were together . . . Her pulse began to beat faster in anticipation of what was going to happen. Any minute now . . .

The heel of his palm pressed against her pubic mound, rubbing her gently; a small hiss of excitement escaped her, and the man who sat with his arm round her lifted his other hand to stroke her cheek. Then he turned his face so that he could kiss her earlobe, licking the sensitive spot at the side of her neck.

She closed her eyes in bliss. It was going to happen – it was going to happen, now.

It was almost as if they were telepathic because, at the same moment, she felt two hands touch the waistband of her leggings. Slowly, they peeled the soft black lycra downwards; she lifted herself from the sofa so that they could pull the leggings over her hips. Then one of them slid off the sofa onto the floor, so that he could remove her leggings completely, while the other turned to undo her loose tunic shirt, his fingers brushing against her breasts as he undid the buttons.

None of them had spoken a word. They didn't need to. They all knew exactly what they were doing. One of them divested her of her leggings while the other slid her shirt from her shoulders. She leaned forward as he slid his hand behind her, deftly unclasping her bra. The black lacy garment fell to the floor, so that she was naked apart from her matching silk-and-lace knickers.

Somehow, she wasn't sure how, they were naked, too; and then there was only this, this last wispy covering of her nakedness. One of them was kneeling on the floor beside her; he smiled, and leaned forward to kiss her. The other shifted slightly, and bent his head so that he could suckle one breast, licking the areola until the nipple became erect, then breathing lightly on it so that the skin tightened in response to his cool breath, her nipple hardening so much that it ached. Then he closed his mouth over the bud of flesh and began to suck, gently and rhythmically.

And then – oh, bliss – she felt two hands sliding over her inner thighs. Again, they were working in perfect time. She thought she was going to come at the very thought of what they were going to do: and then she stopped thinking, just felt, as they slid their fingers under the elastic of her knicker-leg. As a tongue probed her nipple, so a finger rubbed against her clitoris, in exactly the same rhythm; and as a mouth explored hers, another finger slid into the wet tunnel of her vagina, exploring her there.

Alice felt her internal muscles flex hard at the combined stimulus; it was enough to tip the balance, and the two men began to make love to her properly. One of them added a second, a third, and then a fourth finger; as his hand pistoned back and forth, it felt like she was being penetrated by a short and very thick cock. The other man rubbed her clitoris in a figure of eight, faster and faster, his touch just light enough to skate over her skin but hard enough to make her climax quickly.

Her sex contracted sharply round the fingers inside her; she wasn't sure whose they were, Marcus's or the short-haired actor's, but she didn't care. It felt so good. And, even better, she knew that she was going to enjoy both of them, tonight.

'Alice. Sweet Alice . . .' She found herself being lifted and positioned gently on her knees, with one of them sitting on the sofa and the other one kneeling behind her. She trailed her fingers lightly over the thighs of the man who was sitting in front of her; as she found the birth-mark on his inner right thigh, she realized that it was Marcus.

Slowly, she bent her head, letting her hair fall against his belly. He shivered in anticipation, and she could smell the raw musky scent of his arousal. She traced the tip of his cock with the end of her nose, teasing him. Then, slowly, she fitted her mouth over the tip of his cock, sliding down, down, and taking him in as deep as she could. He couldn't help crying out in delight as she began to suck him.

At the same time, she felt her panties being removed, pushed gently down to her knees. She would have lifted each leg in turn, so that the other man could take them off properly, but he stilled her, gently stroking her thighs and her buttocks. Then she felt the tip of his cock press against her sex, and he slid inside her, stretching her. She shuddered in delight as he pushed into her, up to the hilt. He stayed there for a moment, letting her body get used to his, and then began to move in long, slow, steady strokes.

She changed her rhythm, the way she was sucking Marcus,

so that she matched the actor's rhythm exactly as he pushed into her. Marcus had his hands in her hair, while the actor had his hands resting very lightly on her hips, his cheek pressed affectionately against her back. This, Alice thought, was what heaven was made of. She felt Marcus's balls lift and tighten; at the same time, she felt the actor's body tense. As she tasted the first pungent mouthful of Marcus's semen, she felt her other lover's cock throb inside her. And even as she felt them climax, her body seemed to melt, fusing the three of them in one long orgasm.

They stayed locked together for a while, until their cocks slipped out of her. Then, somehow, Marcus was lying on the floor, his body lit by the flickers from the film. His cock was already hardening in anticipation. She smiled and climbed onto him, sliding one hand between their bodies to hold his cock and guide it into her. Then she sank down onto him, feeling the root of his cock pressing against her clitoris.

Meanwhile, her other lover was kneeling by Marcus's shoulders. He stooped to kiss her, not caring that she tasted of Marcus, and then gradually he straightened up so that she could trail her lips down his body and finally find his cock. Again, they resumed their three-way coupling, the actor's hands tangling in her hair as he urged her on, and Marcus's hands playing with her breasts. Their rhythm was in perfect timing, and when they climaxed, it was explosive. Alice almost sobbed as she came, her internal muscles clenching sharply round Marcus's cock.

They waited until the aftershocks of her orgasm had subsided, then gently lifted her off Marcus, smiling at her and stroking her. They sandwiched her between their bodies, holding her protectively and whispering how beautiful she was. They paid homage to her with their lips and hands, bringing her to several more climaxes between them. And then, drained, she fell asleep, cradled in their arms . . .

Alice removed the headset and sat there for a while, stunned. The first time she'd tried Roxy's virtual-reality sex program, it had been good – but this was unbelievable. Her body was still trembling from its series of climaxes when she finally dressed and returned to the living room – where Roxy was, true to form, sitting on the sofa with a laptop computer on her knees and Monty curled up beside her.

Roxy looked up, and tipped her head to one side. 'Did you like it?'

'Like it? Roxy, it was sheer bloody *bliss*! You'll *have* to put this on the market, and soon.'

'It's not ready yet,' Roxy protested. 'And there are legal problems, like I told you. Copyright, that sort of thing.'

'I don't care,' Alice said. 'That was really something.' She narrowed her eyes. 'You said that you'd had difficulty in scanning in the faces of famous people.'

'Yes – that's one of the reasons why it's not on the market, yet.'

'But you'd already scanned in *his* face – and Marcus's.'

'I put Marcus's face in because I knew that you'd want to test it again,' Roxy said. 'And as for the actor – well . . .'

Alice caught on to what her friend meant. 'You've done the same thing, with him and Tim?'

Roxy nodded. 'Yes. That's why I knew what you wanted.'

Alice chuckled. 'God, Roxy, you never cease to amaze me. Does Tim know?'

'Yes.' Roxy flushed, remembering. Tim had watched her: and she'd given him a running commentary of what was happening in the program. The whole thing had ended with

Tim masturbating furiously and his semen spraying her naked body; then he'd removed her headset and the sensor pads, and made furious love to her on the floor of the study.

'Oh, yes?'

Roxy coughed, not wanting to tell Alice about that. 'He's done it, too,' she said.

'With another man?' Alice was faintly shocked.

'No, with me and another woman.'

'Who?'

'Would you believe, Marilyn Monroe?'

Alice grinned. 'I can see the resemblance.'

'Hardly,' Roxy scoffed. 'Still, he enjoyed it.'

'I'm not surprised! Rox, that program is seriously good. You even had the scent working, too – I don't know what that aftershave is, but it's gorgeous.'

'Invention, I'm afraid. Tim and I have both been tinkering with it, over the last few months, and we came up with that one. The woman's fragrance is even nicer – vanilla and chocolate and cinnamon. It's good enough to eat.' Roxy shrugged. 'When the copyright bit is sorted out, it'll be a doddle.' She smiled. 'Anyway, at least it's taken your mind off that Traditional Values mob, whoever they are.'

'Yeah.' Alice smiled ruefully. 'I just got it out of perspective. You're right. They're complete nutters, and no one will vote them into power. No way.'

'Exactly.' Roxy saved the file she was working on and switched off her notebook computer. She stood up and fetched another bottle of wine, filling Alice's glass and her own. 'Well, here's to common sense, good friends – and fantasy.'

Alice echoed the toast, adding, 'And long live the Tiresias factor!'

SEVEN

A couple of weeks later, Roxy was working from home. Visicom had adopted flexible working and, as she was at a difficult stage with one of the programs, she found it easier to work in the peace and quiet of Hampstead than in the bustling Docklands office. She and Tim had installed a second phone line for their computers so that, if there was a problem in the office, their colleagues could ring them without having to wait for them to switch off their computers.

She switched on the modem, and typed in her password to log on to the network; she frowned as the message came up: *You do not have authorization to perform this action.* Thinking that maybe she'd mistyped it, she tried again; still her access was denied. She drummed her fingers on the edge of her desk, thinking. She'd changed her password two days before, and she wouldn't have to change it again for nearly a month – so it couldn't possibly be because her password had expired. Though if there had been some kind of glitch in the program, maybe her old password was still current. Maybe there had been a network problem and no one had thought to tell her about it. She tried her old password. Again, the message flashed up *You do not have authorization to perform this action.*

She rubbed her jaw thoughtfully. Either something was very wrong or it was some kind of elaborate joke by one of her friends in the office and another message would flash up in a couple of seconds, telling her that she'd been "had", and that her access to the network was restored. It didn't, so she tried again, with the new password, and frowned as the system refused her access yet again.

There was only one way to find out what was going on. She picked up the phone and dialled the number of Sara, Visicom's network administrator.

The single beep on the line proclaimed that the number was unobtainable.

Roxy shrugged. Maybe there had been a few problems in the office and Sara hadn't replaced her phone properly and didn't realize that it was off the hook. It had happened, several times in the past when the office had been particularly busy; if you didn't put the phone back on the hook properly, the line would go "dead", after a while. She hung up and tried again, this time ringing Caroline, her partner on the Mall project.

Caroline's phone, too, had the unobtainable signal.

Maybe, Roxy thought, the problem was with *her* phone. She tried Tim's number next; it was engaged, to her mingled irritation and relief. At least the line was working, then. But why couldn't she get through to Sara or Caroline? She suddenly wondered if she'd missed something on the news – some problem at the Wharf. Security was tight, but the most determined terrorists could always find a way through. Maybe some terrorist attack had wiped out the phones at Visicom, or something.

Just as she was about to switch on the television to find out what was going on, the phone rang. It was Alice.

'Roxy?'

'Hi, Al – are you okay?' Roxy asked, concerned at the fact that Alice's voice was shaking slightly. Usually Alice was fazed by nothing and nobody.

'Oh Roxy, thank God that you're all right!'

'What do you mean, all right?' Roxy asked.

'You know the other week, when I came over and showed you that Traditional Values leaflet? Well ...' Alice's voice was almost a sob. 'They've taken over, Rox. I don't know how they hell they managed it, but there's been some kind of military coup.'

'*What?*' Roxy paused. 'Al – this is your idea of a joke, isn't it?'

'I wish it was.' Alice swallowed. 'I'm okay, because I'm married to Marcus, but you ...' She swallowed. 'Roxy, I think you'd better get out of there, and the sooner, the better.'

'No,' Roxy laughed shortly. 'Al, you're having me on.'

'I'm not. Look, Rox, turn on the television – then you'll see what I mean.'

Roxy was using a cordless phone, so it was easy for her to walk into the sitting room and turn on the television without hanging up. She frowned as she saw the picture: a tall, bearded man with burning eyes speaking from the studio. She changed channels, again and again and again; the channels that weren't showing the man's picture were just fuzzy static, closed down.

'What the hell's going on?' Roxy asked Alice, stunned.

'It's in the papers as well, this morning,' Alice said. 'But of course, you and Tim never have them delivered.'

'No, we use an e-mail news browser.' Roxy smiled wryly. 'Though I haven't logged on to read the news yet. What does it say?'

'It's their manifesto – well, not a manifesto, exactly. It's the law, as they see it. They're proclaiming what the new laws are, as from today. No one's exempt. "Procreation, not recreation" is what they say about sex – so you're in deep trouble, Rox, if they find out about—'

'They won't find out about anything,' Roxy cut in, suddenly aware that the phone might be tapped, and not wanting Alice to implicate anyone by talking about the VRX program. 'Look, it's like any other phase in society. Things are too harsh, and there's a liberal backlash; then everyone goes all moralistic; then there's a backlash against the limitations of society; then it becomes too liberal again, and there's another backlash. It's cyclical. We've seen it in the Sixties, the Seventies, the Eighties and the Nineties. It'll all blow over in a few weeks – or maybe even a few months, if they're really determined.'

'I'm not so sure, Rox. There's a whole lot of other new laws, too. Homosexuality's illegal – and that includes lesbianism. Anybody found "betraying their gender", as the Party puts it, will be put straight into the House of Correction.'

'Into the *what*?' Roxy wasn't quite sure that she'd heard her friend correctly.

'The House of Correction.'

Roxy's eyes narrowed. 'Who the hell do these people think they are, telling everyone how they should feel?'

'There's more than that, Rox. Single women must either marry or return home to live with their father. Their property, their money – everything will be transferred to their husbands or fathers, the nearest male next of kin.'

'That's *outrageous*,' Roxy fumed. 'Christ, that's even worse than Victorian times! I suppose you're going to tell me that I can't call you Alice any more, either – you're Mrs Marcus Blake.'

'I don't think they've gone that far,' Alice answered wryly, 'though that's probably the next step.'

Roxy noted with relief that Alice's voice had stopped trembling. 'Al, it's crazy. This is *Britain*, for God's sake, not some shaky banana republic. There's no way that anyone will put up with this.'

'I don't think they have a choice,' Alice said. 'Have you tried to call anyone at work today?'

'Ye-es.'

'How did you get on?'

'I thought that there was a problem with the network. The numbers were unobtainable.'

'Their direct lines, yes. If you'd called the switchboard, they wouldn't have put you through, either.'

Roxy smiled. 'Visicom uses voice recognition, if you dial the switchboard. I don't think that there would be a problem.'

'What about if the Traditional Values people have control of the network?'

'They can't do that.'

'They can, and they have. It's all the networks – media, communications, the lot.'

'Al, that just can't happen.'

Alice ignored the comment. 'The extensions you tried – were they women's extensions, by any chance?'

'Yes.'

'Precisely. You see, women aren't allowed to have jobs any more, either.'

'What? Are you telling me that I don't have the freedom to choose whether to work or stay at home?'

'That's about the strength of it.'

'This just can't happen,' Roxy said. 'There's no way Europe will stand by and put up with this. Or America. Someone will come to help us, and the coup will be smashed.'

'I don't think it's going to be as simple as that,' Alice said. 'Remember the last war? We were the only ones in Europe to escape invasion, apart from neutral countries like Sweden, because we're an island nation.'

'Weapons and the like have advanced since then,' Roxy informed her. 'And there's also the Channel Tunnel.'

'That's easily closed. All the exits from the country are closed – air, sea, the Tunnel – everything.'

'No. I don't believe it.' Roxy paused. 'Look, Al, I just need to do a couple of things here, then I'm coming straight over.'

'Thanks.'

'I'll see you soon. Now, don't worry, okay?'

'Okay. Take care.'

'You too.' Roxy replaced the receiver, then switched her modem off and on again to clear the line. There was one place the Traditional Values people couldn't gain control, she thought – the Internet. But when she dialled up, a message flashed on the screen: *You do not have the privilege to access this information*.

She frowned, and typed in Tim's ID and password. To her relief, it worked; she worked her mouse rapidly to access her e-mail news file. Her face grew grim as she read through the file. Everything Alice had told her was there – and more.

It seemed that the Traditional Values party had achieved a military coup. The new President, John Ferris, had decreed that all exits from the country would be screened. No one could leave or enter the country without permission from the government. 'How do you like that, Brussels?' she muttered wryly.

The country was under martial law – and very different laws from the ones they were used to. Women were not allowed to have jobs: companies who continued to employ women would be taken over by the new government, their profits confiscated, and the management would be sent to prison.

Single women, as Alice had reported, had either to marry

or move back to their father's house. Their property would be transferred to their husband or their father. Any woman who refused would be sent to the House of Correction. All women of childbearing age were to have one child; further children would only be allowed if the family passed a means test.

What about women who couldn't have children? Roxy thought, furious. Several of her friends had had problems conceiving: would they be sent to this House of Correction, for failing to produce the required one child? Or would their husbands be forced to divorce them, and marry a fertile woman?

The next line told her the answer. Divorce was illegal, and any decrees absolute were no longer valid. Second marriages were also not valid.

'My God,' Roxy said, shaking her head in disbelief.

Her eyes glittered as she came to the last page. No sex was allowed outside marriage. Any woman caught in extramarital sex would be sent to the House of Correction, and any man would be immediately demoted to the lowest grade, regardless of his position. Homosexuality and lesbianism were both illegal; and all erotic literature, films and videos were to be burned. Sex was for procreation, not recreation.

'Shit,' she said. It couldn't be real. It couldn't be. She tried accessing the Mall; the screen flashed up, asking for her ID. She typed in her number, and the message flashed up: *Access denied.*

'So women can't even shop now?' Roxy rolled her eyes, and flicked out of the program. A horrible thought struck her, and she picked up the phone, dialling the local supermarket.

'Customer Services. Can I help you?'

It was a man's voice; Roxy was surprised. Customer Services

was usually staffed by women. 'I'd like to place an order, for delivery later today, please.'

'Your card number, please?'

Roxy rattled off her debit card number.

'I'm sorry, that number isn't valid.'

Roxy smiled thinly. She'd been paid three days before. Her card was perfectly valid. If what she suspected was true, her account had been closed and the balance held in suspense – ready to be transferred to her male nearest-of-kin or the government, depending on her choice. 'I have another card, in the joint name of Tim Fraser and Roxana Winters.' Their bill-payment account. She told the shop assistant the number; there was a sigh over the phone. 'I'm sorry, Miss Winters, you're not an authorized card user.'

'I see. Thank you.' Roxy cut the line, and was just about to dial Tim's number when the phone rang. She thought about answering it, but decided to call-screen instead. She wasn't sure who was ringing her – certainly not Alice, this time – and it would be safest to check first, in case it was some kind of trap.

Two rings, and the message clicked into life. 'Hi, this is Tim and Roxy. We can't take your call, right now, but if you'd like to leave your name and number after the tone, we'll call you back as soon as we can.' There was a beep, then a pause, then Tim's voice cut in. 'Roxy—'

She lifted up the receiver immediately. 'Tim, I'm here. I was call-screening.'

'Thank God,' he said. 'You know what's going on?'

'Yes. Alice rang me – and I logged in under your password. I've just been reading the news.'

'Thank God you're all right. I thought they might have taken you.'

'Well, I'm still here. Though I've just found out that I can't log into the network, and I can't buy anything with my card. Or use our joint account – I'm no longer an authorized user.'

'Rox, that's crazy!'

'Yeah.' She took a deep breath. 'Tim, this is probably just a storm in a teacup. It'll last a week – maybe a month, at most. I'm going to keep my head down and work from here; and I'll work from my hard drive. I'll need you to bring a couple of programs home for me.'

'Sure, just let me know what you want.' He paused. 'But, Roxy, I think there's going to be a lot of trouble in the meantime. I think this is going to last for more than a few weeks, from what I've read in the news.'

'I suppose it stops me spending money,' Roxy said drily. 'Though it'll drive Alice spare, not being able to shop when she feels like it.'

'Until it blows over, just tell me what you want, and I'll get it for you,' Tim said. 'You know that. What's mine is yours.'

'Thanks.'

'Roxy . . .' He paused. 'Maybe you ought to hide the VRX program. Encrypt it, or something, just to be safe.'

'If you're that worried, it might be safer to delete it.'

'Delete it? But it's *months* of work.'

'I did it from scratch, the first time; it won't take me so long the second time, because I can remember most of the source code – and most of the glitches.'

'If you're sure.'

'Yes. Once this has all blown over, I can work on it again.' She paused. 'Tim – if it's as bad as you and Alice seem to think, I don't want anything I've done reflecting on you.'

'I'll be okay, Rox – it's you I'm worried about. Look, I'm coming home, now.'

'Don't be so daft. I'm perfectly all right, and you've got work to do.' She smiled. 'I can take care of myself. I'm going to delete the program, then I'm going over to see Alice.'

'Roxy, be careful, won't you?'

'Like I told you, I can take care of myself. I'll be fine.'

'Rox . . .' He paused. 'I love you. Promise me you'll marry me.'

She chuckled. 'What, just to submit to the law?'

'No. I wanted you to marry me, anyway.' He sighed. 'I didn't ask you before, because I didn't want to spoil what we had.'

'A piece of paper,' she said softly, 'will make no difference whatsoever to us.'

'Well, I love you anyway,' Tim said.

'You too. Take care, and I'll see you tonight.'

When she replaced the receiver, she turned back to her computer. Even if she cut VRX into several files, it would take too long to encrypt it – and there was always the chance that the Traditional Values party could crack the encryption code. Deleting it was the only way to make sure that Tim was safe. With a sigh, she flipped into the file manager, highlighted the file and pressed the delete key.

Thirty seconds later, the front door banged open. Four men came through, dressed in a military-type uniform she didn't recognize. Monty was barking in the garden; Roxy suddenly wished that she'd propped the door open properly, or kept the dog inside. He might not have stopped these people breaking in, but he would have given them a scare, at least.

'Roxana Winters?' the leader asked.

'Who wants to know?' she said, lifting her chin.

He smiled thinly. 'You're under arrest.'

'For what?' she asked, standing with her hands defiantly on her hips.

'Breaking the Traditional Laws, on several accounts.'

'And it takes *four* of you to arrest me?' She shook her head in outraged disbelief. 'My God, look at yourselves! Do you really think that this is the way we should live our lives? You break into my house, you tell me that I'm under arrest, and I've done nothing wrong!'

'Oh, but you have.' His eyes flickered dangerously. 'And you, like the rest of your kind, are going to pay.'

'Pay for what?' she demanded.

'Shut up.' He lifted his hand and struck her face.

Furious, Roxy made the mistake of kicking him hard in the shin. The next thing she knew, something hard hit the back of her neck, and the room went black.

Roxy opened her eyes, feeling rather groggy. The room looked slightly blurred; she closed her eyes tightly shut again, and refocused. This time, the room swam into focus properly. It was about twelve foot square, with magnolia-coloured walls, and a small high window flanked with cheap maroon curtains. The carpet was a cheap cord, in a greyish beige colour.

She narrowed her eyes. This looked like the kind of room she'd had when she was a student – except maybe a little bigger. Where was she? Then she became aware that the hard, narrow single bed on which she was lying wasn't the only one in the room. There was another, on the other side of the room, and the occupant was lying on her side, propped up on one elbow with her head resting on her hand. Her red curly hair was swept back from her face, and she was watching Roxy, her green eyes narrowed in concern.

As she realized that Roxy was looking back at her, the woman sat up properly, poured a glass of water from the jug on the table between the beds, and came over to stand next to Roxy. 'Here. This might help you feel better.'

'Thanks.' Roxy took a sip of water and winced as pain flashed through her.

'They must have hit you pretty hard. You've been out cold for the past six hours.'

'Where am I?'

'I believe that this place is known as the House of Correction,' the woman said, her lip curling with disdain. She held out a hand. 'I'm Jessica Holt – Jess, to my friends. Pleased to meet you.'

'You, too.' Roxy took a sip of water. 'Roxana Winters – Roxy.' Her eyes narrowed. 'Why are we here?'

'Because we've transgressed Traditional Law.' Jess smiled wryly. 'Mind you, I suppose I had no defence, when they came to get me.'

'Why?' Roxy tipped her head to one side in puzzlement. Jess looked completely normal – slightly glamorous, maybe, with her long red hair and wide green eyes – so what had she been doing?

'I'm a writer, by trade. If you've read any of the Blue Silk novels, I'm Dana Roswell.'

'Right. And they traced you through your publishers?'

'I don't know how they found me. But when I'm in the middle of a book, I tend to cut off from the outside world. I don't watch the news, read a paper, listen to the radio – I just concentrate on my work. If I want to see a film or a series on TV, I video it and watch it when I'm having a break from the book. I'm in another world. So I had no idea about this Traditional Values thing – until they burst through my door. I was in the middle of a chapter.' She spread her hands. 'And it was a male-on-male scene.'

'Ouch. A real no-no under Traditional Laws,' Roxy said wryly.

'How about you?'

'I'm not sure,' Roxy said. 'It could be any number of reasons. I work – rather, worked – for Visicom. I was working from home, but I couldn't log into the network. I tried to call a couple of women there – my partner, and our network administrator – but their numbers were unobtainable. The same thing's probably happened to them, because we worked for Visicom, and we were responsible for a lot of the technology advances.'

'Or?' Jess saw the doubt in Roxy's face.

'I wasn't married. I was living with Tim Fraser – "in sin", as they'd call it.' Roxy's lips twitched. 'I doubt if they'd approve of that – and, the way they seem to think, the woman rather than the man would get the blame. And Tim and I had developed a recreational program that they'd disapprove of, too.'

Jess was quick to pick up Roxy's reference. 'A sex program, you mean?'

'A virtual-reality sex program, yes.'

Jess was intrigued. 'Tell me more.'

'We were almost ready to go to market with it. Several of our friends knew about it; maybe one of them told the Traditional Values lot. I don't know. It could have been a colleague, or even someone who'd eavesdropped on a conversation I'd had with Tim. Anyone.'

'Bastards.'

Roxy bit her lip. 'I deleted it from my PC, just before they broke into my house. I just hope they didn't know what I was doing and can access some kind of un-delete program. If they find it . . . God knows what'll happen to Tim.'

'I don't know.' Jess squeezed her hand. 'I can't give you any reassurance, and tell you that he'll be okay, that they're just picking on women. They're – well, fanatical. I would have said religious, but it doesn't seem to be that sort of fervour.'

'No.' Roxy drank some more water. 'Do you know what they're going to do with us?'

'A House of Correction, in one of my books, would have been a place where lots of power- and sex-games were played out,' Jess said. 'But here . . . I don't know. I don't know if they're intending brainwashing, or torture, or what. There were a couple of others in the van with me when I was brought here, but we were forbidden to speak. Anyone who tried it was immediately slapped across the face. It hurt enough for you not to try a second time.'

'Were they all women with you?'

'There were a couple of men.' Jess shrugged. 'Presumably gay, or divorced.'

'So what do you think they're going to do with us?' Roxy asked. 'I mean, Traditional Values or whatever, there's no way they'll pay to keep us cooped up in here. Even if all the women have been taken out of employment, men couldn't pay enough taxes to keep us all here. There must be thousands of us. Writers like you, artists, photographers, computer programmers, marketers . . . thousands of us.'

'Mm.' Jess nodded. 'Plus all the therapists, editors, lecturers – even if they didn't put the men here, there's still too many of us for them to keep.'

'They must be planning to "employ" us in some way,' Roxy said thoughtfully.

'Knitting?' Jess suggested. 'Sewing?'

'Mailbags, you mean?' Roxy's smile dimmed. 'I don't know, Jess. And I *want* to know what their plans are.' She grimaced. 'I told Tim that it was a storm in a teacup, and it'd blow over in a week or so. But they've planned this pretty well. I mean, freezing our bank accounts, cutting off our communication channels, and throwing us out of work, all at the same time.'

'In some ways,' Jess said, 'it was easy for them. We all use credit and debit cards. We don't carry cash any more – there's no need.'

'Mm, it would have been more difficult for them if we'd still been using cash and had some in the house.'

Roxy took a sip of water. 'How long have you been here?'

'About five or six hours longer than you have.'

'Have they fed you yet?'

'Yes. That's the other thing that worries me,' Jess said. 'Lunch was a cheese and salad sandwich, on wholemeal bread, with an apple, and a plain bio yoghurt.'

'Healthy, well-balanced nutritionally ... They're definitely up to something. I mean, surely we should be on bread and water, or gruel, or some kind of slop?' Roxy frowned. 'Even starvation?'

'I know they say they support "traditional" values, but that's just a bit too Dickensian,' Jess said.

'Even so, I wouldn't expect properly balanced meals. Maybe they're planning to make us do hard labour, build roads or houses or whatever.'

'I dunno.'

There was a rattle at the door and a guard came in with a tray. The plates were filled with poached chicken, spinach and a jacket potato. There was a basket of fruit containing two bananas and two nectarines, and a fresh jug of water. He handed a plate to Jess and to Roxy; Roxy noticed with bitter amusement that everything had already been cut up, and that they'd been given plastic forks only.

'Thank you. This looks very nice,' she said to the guard.

He ignored her.

'What's your name?' she asked. 'I'm Roxy, and this is Jess.'
Still, he ignored her.

'Perhaps you could take a message for me, then,' Roxy said,
suddenly snapping. If being pleasant wouldn't work, then what
the hell would? 'Perhaps you could tell your boss that I'd like
a word.'

Still no answer; he didn't meet her eyes, and left the room
immediately.

'I think you'll need different tactics,' Jess said, lifting her
fork. 'Assuming that this isn't poisoned, it's good stuff. They're
definitely into the light protein, and five helpings of fruit and
vegetables per day. It's probably the most nutritious nosh I've
eaten for years.'

They ate their meal in companionable silence. When the
guard came in – a different one, this time – Roxy walked up
to him and laid a hand on his arm. He shook her away.

'Please,' she said. 'I need a bath. I feel dirty, and I smell. I
need a bath.'

The guard shook his head, and walked out.

'Damn,' Roxy said.

'Planning escape?' Jess asked.

'Something like that. If I knew the layout of this building,
maybe I could find a way out of here. But . . .' Roxy grimaced.
'I really *could* do with a bath, or a shower.'

'You're not the only one. Maybe they'll let us have one
tomorrow morning,' Jess said.

'Yeah. Maybe.' Roxy swallowed. 'Tim's taking his time. He
must have found out where I am by now. He won't let them
keep me in here.'

'Maybe he just doesn't know where you are,' Jess suggested.
Neither of them met the other's eye, but they both knew that
they were thinking the same thing. Maybe Tim wasn't trying

to get Roxy out because he couldn't – because he was already dead. For all they knew, it could be raging civil war outside. They had no way of finding out what was going on.

Roxy slept badly that night, thinking of Tim – wondering where he was, what was happening to him. Alice and Marcus, too – what had happened to them? Would they be safe under this new regime? Or would Marcus, as a geneticist, be on their blacklist?

She tossed and turned; the next morning, she was surprised to be woken by the door opening. Their breakfast was as healthy as dinner the night before: oat-bran cereal with skimmed milk, half a grapefruit, and wholemeal toast. 'It's almost,' Roxy said to Jess when the guard left, 'as if they're fattening us up for something.' She looked at the herbal tea in distaste. 'My flatmate used to drink this stuff, but I prefer coffee. Proper coffee.'

'Me, too,' Jess said. She gave Roxy a wry smile. 'Though I don't think caffeine is on their agenda.'

'It's probably illegal,' Roxy said with a grin. 'Just imagine, hordes of pre-menstrual women, all on a caffeine high, and deprived of being able to shop . . .' Her smile faded. 'Just what the hell are they planning for us?'

'I don't know, and I'd rather not think about it, just yet,' Jess said.

'Mm.'

They ate their meal in silence. After breakfast, they were taken one at a time to the shower – under the supervision of the guards – and given a change of clothes. While Roxy rubbed the grime from her skin, she was half tempted to test the guard's will-power. He could see her clearly – there was no shower curtain. What if she began caressing her breasts, her thighs? What if she started to masturbate in front of him

– would he crack? Would he let her seduce him into telling her what was going on?

But it was too soon. In a week, a month, maybe; if the guard was unmarried, maybe she could tempt one of them to "sin". In the meantime, if she tried anything it would probably make things worse.

She finished washing her hair, then dressed in the garments provided for her. She noticed with some amusement that the rusty black skirt was ankle-length, designed to hide her curves, and the matching loose cotton round-necked sweater was equally shapeless. The underwear they'd provided, too, was very plain: either they'd measured her when they were out, or they had some stock sizes, but the undergarments were exactly her size.

When Jess returned to their room, she was dressed in the same kind of uniform as Roxy was wearing.

'I feel all Puritan,' Jess said with a grin.

'So what next? A haircut?' Roxy suggested.

'To stop my vanity? Hm. Now you're going all *Jane Eyre* on me,' Jess said lightly. 'Ah, well. At least we're clean.'

'Praise be for small mercies, hm?' Roxy's mood soured again. On her trip to the shower, she hadn't been able to see much of the building. 'Jess, I just wish I knew what was going on. They can't keep us here like this forever.'

'I know, but there's no point in brooding,' Jess said. 'We're going to have to wait for our chance. In the meantime, don't let them grind your spirits down. That's probably what they're waiting for.'

'What do you suggest – that we have some kind of sing-song?' Roxy's tone was acerbic.

'Something practical. You tell me about yourself, I'll tell you about me, and maybe we can pool our skill-set,' Jess said.

Roxy flushed. 'Sorry. I didn't mean to be rude.'

'That's okay. Stress affects us all in different ways.' Jess shrugged. 'I want out of here as much as you do, Roxy.'

'Yes.'

They spent the morning talking, and Roxy learned that Jess was a couple of years younger than she was, unmarried, with no children; she was a devoted aunt of three. She'd been a journalist before she starting writing erotic novels. The three things she really wanted to do were to visit Egypt, go to the moon, and own a red E-type Jaguar. She also shared Roxy's passion for very dry white wine, Dolcelatte and black grapes.

Roxy, in turn, explained more about her career at Visicom, the Mall development, and her virtual-reality sex program.

'When we get out of here,' Jess said, 'and it's a "when", not an "if", I would love to be a guinea pig.'

Roxy chuckled. 'Put it this way, I think it would be good material for you.'

'It certainly would. You could try anything . . .'

For the next week – at least, Jess said it was a week, because she'd scratched tiny marks into the wall with her signet ring – they were cooped up in the little room. The food continued to be healthy, albeit a bit plain; they were allowed one shower a day, but they weren't allowed out of the room to exercise. Jess had a way round that: she had a routine that a personal trainer had devised for her, in the old days, and she taught Roxy the various stretches and floor exercises. Roxy was half-amused, saying that this was probably the healthiest she'd been in years, eating properly and exercising instead of being glued to her computer.

She tried hard not to think about Tim, Alice and Marcus. She didn't want to start imagining what had happened to them. But at nights, Roxy couldn't help dreaming of Tim, the way he'd made love with her ... She always woke with tears on her face, and a grim determination to be avenged.

And then, after breakfast on the tenth day of their captivity, the door banged open. Two guards marched over to them and indicated to Jess that she should stand up. Roxy stood up, too, but she was pushed back down.

'Where are you taking Jess?' she demanded. 'You can't just walk in here and do this!'

The two guards ignored her, and frogmarched Jess out of the room.

EIGHT

Roxy spent the next few hours pacing up and down the small room. She had no idea where Jess had been taken – or even if she was coming back again. For all Roxy knew, the guards could have taken Jess to some dim courtyard and simply shot her. But if the guards were going to shoot their prisoners, why bother feeding them healthy food? Why not save money and starve them – or even shoot them straight off, instead of keeping them locked up?

Another guard brought her lunch, and Roxy tackled him immediately. 'Where's Jess?' she asked. 'What have you done with her? Is she coming back?'

There was no answer, and the guard's face was set in an impassive mask. Roxy wasn't a medical scientist, but common sense told her that he'd been either drugged or brainwashed. There was something in his eyes, some weird kind of blank, as though he didn't recognize her as another human being.

She picked at her lunch. Even though she adored pasta and salad, she wasn't hungry; she felt sick to her stomach, not knowing what was going on and what would happen next. Would Jess come back – and if she did, would she be badly beaten? Would Roxy be the next to be taken? What were they going to do to her?

When the guard came to take her tray away, he stared at the food on the plate, then at Roxy, and shook his head, very slightly. Roxy interpreted it as a warning: if she wanted to be treated well, she had to do what they said and eat what they gave her. She wanted to scream, to shout at him and hit out, slap him and pummel him and force him into giving her an answer – and yet she knew that there was no point. If she was a difficult prisoner, they'd make it difficult for her and she'd lose whatever chance she had to find out what was going on. She had to play it cool, watch and wait for her chance.

She resumed pacing her room, wishing that she had a watch. Even to know the time would be something. From the shadows cast through the high window, it looked like the middle of the afternoon. Though she still had no idea where they were. It was so quiet outside: she could be in the middle of nowhere. Or she could be in the middle of London, a ghostly city with few commuters and no shoppers. Who was there to shop, now that women couldn't have their own money, make their own choices?

Suddenly sick of waiting, she was about to bang on the door and demand to know what was going on when the door opened suddenly and Jess was pushed back in.

'Are you okay?' Roxy asked, hugging her.

'I'll live.' Jess's face was bitter. She raked a hand through her hair and grimaced. 'I think that I know what we're here for now.'

Roxy frowned, releasing Jess and taking a step backwards. 'What?'

'Think of the traditional roles for a woman.' Roxy wasn't quite with her; Jess smiled tightly as she explained. 'I was blindfolded and taken to another place. When the blindfold was removed, I could see it was quite an opulent place, with thick pile carpets, expensive lined curtains, and good wallpaper. Whoever lived there obviously had a lot of money, and a lot of power. I suppose he must be one of the leaders of the

Traditional Values group, and fairly well up in the hierarchy. One of the privileged ones.

'Anyway, I spent the morning cleaning the house – which I assume was their way of making me more humble, scrubbing the kitchen floors of my "betters" – and then I had to make lunch, to a specified menu, for him and myself. All the time, a guard watched me, so I couldn't make a run for it or secrete a knife about me. Not to use on myself, you understand – I don't have that kind of courage. But I could do a hell of a lot of damage to one of them with a knife.'

'Yeah.' Roxy's face was bleak as she took in what Jess was saying. Was this to be her life, from now on – to be a drudge for the privileged?

'And then I served lunch to him.'

'Who was he?'

'I don't know his name.' Jess ground her teeth. 'But he was no different from any other corrupt man in power. Because I wasn't just there for cooking and cleaning, Roxy – I was there for entertainment. Sexual entertainment, to be precise.'

'You mean, he *raped* you?' Roxy was shocked.

'I could have refused, but it was made clear that if I didn't consent ...' Jess let the words trail off. 'It looks like we're the new servant classes. We're here to learn how to behave ourselves, Roxy. So we clean the house, give the master of the house some sexual relief, and go back to meditate on our sins.'

'You're joking.' Roxy was appalled. 'Housework and sex?'

'That's about it. And they don't care if you don't come, either.' She was fuming. 'He even used a condom – as if that made it all right!'

'God, Jess, I'm so sorry.' Roxy hugged her, stroking her hair.

'I've never been so humiliated, ever! It's not like the power games in the SM scene, where you both know what's going on and you both consent to it. This is nothing short of degradation.' She grimaced. 'I need a wash – and they won't let me have a shower. I can still smell him on me, and it makes me sick to my stomach.'

'Look, there's some water in the jug. I know it's cold, and a strip-wash isn't as good as a shower, but it's better than nothing,' Roxy said. 'At least you'll feel clean again.'

'I don't feel like I'll ever be clean again, after having his paws all over me,' Jess said, scowling. 'What made it worse is that I had to wear this little frilly apron while I was cleaning and serving lunch. It was like some travesty of a French maid's outfit, with big baggy knickers and a shapeless skirt, instead of a black miniskirt, a lace g-string and black seamed silk stockings.'

'Oh, Jess.' Roxy squeezed her hand.

Jess' mouth contorted. 'I feel defiled, Rox.'

'Just calm down and have a wash. It'll help,' Roxy advised. 'I'll keep an ear out by the door; if any guards are about to come in, I'll distract them.'

'Thanks.'

Roxy kept a lookout while Jess washed. When the splashing of water stopped, she turned round. Jess was standing by the table, naked, wiping the water from her body with a pillowcase.

'Feeling better?' Roxy asked.

'A bit,' Jess admitted, 'but I can still feel his paws on me.' She grimaced. 'It's not that I don't like men – I do. I enjoy sex, or I wouldn't write what I do. But that ... It was like some kind of ritual humiliation. It wasn't sex for pleasure at all – or even for procreation, as the Traditional Values lot say, otherwise he wouldn't have used a condom. It was to teach me some kind of lesson.'

'Oh, Jess.' Roxy walked over to her and stroked her face. 'I wish there was something I could do to make you feel better.'

There was a long pause, and then Jess's green eyes met Roxy's hazel ones. 'Actually, there is.' Jess turned her face very slightly, so that her lips were touching Roxy's palm.

Roxy knew instinctively what Jess wanted her to do. She wanted Roxy to wipe out the touch of the man who'd pawed her by comforting her with Roxy's own body, her own caresses. Roxy had never made love with a woman before, even with her virtual reality program, and the idea made her feel nervous and gauche. She also felt guilty, as though she were being disloyal to Tim.

But then again, Tim was probably dead. If he'd been alive, he wouldn't have let her languish here – especially if it had become widely known what was happening in the House of Correction. And if Tim was dead, making love with Jess was no betrayal.

Jess tipped her head to one side, watching Roxy's eyes and guessing at her turmoil. 'Don't feel pressured, Roxy. You don't have to do anything.'

'I'm not feeling pressured. I was just thinking.'

'About Tim?' she guessed.

'Yeah.' Roxy sighed. 'I've come to the conclusion that he must be dead, or he'd have found a way to get me out of here.'

'Maybe,' Jess said carefully. 'In that case, we can give each other some comfort.'

Roxy paused. 'Maybe you're right,' she said finally.

Gently, Jess dropped her hands to the hem of Roxy's loose

cotton top; Roxy raised her hands, allowing Jess to remove it. The skirt followed suit, and Roxy's frumpy bra and knickers; when she was naked, Jess held her at arm's length. 'You're beautiful,' she pronounced.

'With a couple of stones of blubber off me, maybe.' Roxy was offhand.

'No. A washboard stomach, knobbly shoulders and a gaunt face wouldn't suit you. You're the soft curvy type, the type men fantasize about and masturbate over.' Jess brushed her cheek with the back of her hand. 'You're lovely, Roxy.'

Roxy flushed, embarrassed, and Jess leaned forward, kissing her lightly on the lips. 'You don't have to do this,' she said softly. 'I'll be okay.'

'No.' Roxy, too, felt that sudden need for comfort: the need to lose herself in her body. 'I think that we both need this, Jess. A way of forgetting.' She slid her hands round Jess's neck, and kissed her lips. Jess opened her mouth, letting Roxy's tongue explore her; at the same time, she let her own hands drift up to caress Roxy's breasts, cupping them and rubbing the hardening nipples with her thumbs.

Roxy felt a pulse starting to beat excitedly in her loins: what they were doing was very new to her. Part of her was shocked, not quite believing that this was happening; the other part of her revelled in it. Making love with someone who cared about her. Gender didn't matter: it was the touch, the taste, the affection that mattered.

Jess gently walked Roxy backwards, still kissing her, until they were at the edge of Jess's bed. With practised ease, she pushed back the covers, then drew Roxy down onto the narrow single bed. 'I want to explore you,' Jess said softly. 'I want to touch and taste you. I want to see your face when you come.'

Roxy's colour deepened with embarrassment at Jess's forthrightness, but she allowed the other woman to guide her onto her back. Jess lay on her side, propped on one elbow, in the same sort of posture in which Roxy had first seen her. She smiled, and leaned over to rub her nose affectionately against Roxy's. 'This is your first time with a woman, isn't it?'

Roxy nodded. 'I'm sorry.'

'Don't be. It's almost like making love with a virgin – and I think we're both going to enjoy this,' she said softly, her voice slightly husky with desire. 'I'm going to enjoy teaching you – and I'm going to enjoy your experience, remembering my own first time.'

'With a woman, you mean?'

Jess nodded. 'She was about five years older than me – a very good friend, someone I'd met at a class somewhere or other. We had the same sense of humour, liked the same things. Chablis and Chardonnay, Dolcelatte and smoked salmon with water biscuits.' Her eyes softened. 'Simone. I'd never thought of her sexually – I mean, this was a woman I'd talked with very intimately, telling her about the men in my life. We'd swapped stories; as far as I knew, Simone liked men as much as I did. And then, one night . . .' She lifted one hand, tracing the outline of Roxy's body with it. 'One night, Simone came over for dinner. I'd had a hell of a day. I'd had a rejection for a novel I really wanted to write; I'd finally split up with the current man in my life, because he decided that I was spending too much time on my career and not enough on him; and when I went out to my car, thinking that a drive out to Hampstead or somewhere might cheer me up, I found that some bastard had hit my car while it was parked, but hadn't had the decency to leave me a note.' She shrugged. 'Anyway, we drank too much wine. I was howling my eyes out, saying that my life was a mess and I just couldn't get it together; she was holding me, giving me a shoulder to cry on. The next thing I knew, we were kissing each other, and she was touching me.

'Part of me wanted to pull away. I mean, I was strictly hetero, and even if I had thought about going to bed with another woman, this was one of my best friends. I didn't want to mess up the relationship with sex. But – somehow – it didn't. Making love with her was . . .' She smiled. 'Incredible. I'd made love before, I'd had a man perform cunnilingus on me and slide his finger into my cunt. I'd had a man use a vibrator on me, too. But with Simone – it was suddenly all new, completely different. We spent the whole night exploring each other's bodies with our hands and our mouths; by the morning, I was completely knackered, but I couldn't stop smiling.

'Afterwards, she told me that she'd honestly not been intending to leap on me – she was just giving me the cuddle I needed. But my perfume was too much for her, and she couldn't resist kissing me; when I kissed her back, her control just snapped.' She shrugged. 'And I'm glad it did.'

'So what happened? Did you and Simone live together?'

Jess shook her head. 'It wasn't that kind of relationship. After that night, most of the time, we went back to being just good friends. It was just occasionally, if one of us was going through a bad patch, that we'd console each other by making love.' She grinned. 'Besides, I didn't want to give up men completely, and neither did she.'

Roxy shook her head. 'You're incredible, Jess.'

'Thank you.' The writer inclined her head slightly, her eyes sparkling. 'But I want to make this as good for you as Simone made it for me, that first time . . .' She smiled, and let her hand drift over Roxy's body again: moulding her breasts, her hips, sliding across the gentle swell of her stomach, then back up to her breasts again. She began caressing Roxy's breasts in earnest then, tracing the areolae with her middle finger and giving a low chuckle of delight as Roxy's nipples hardened and the dark skin of her areolae puckered.

The pulse between Roxy's legs beat harder; she felt the familiar moist heat of arousal slide over her quim. Her nipples ached, and she wanted them to be touched properly; she tipped her head back into the pillows, lifting her ribcage at the same time.

'Mm, you're so delightfully responsive,' Jess commented. Then she bent her head, her long red curls spreading over Roxy's pale skin, and closed her mouth over one nipple. Roxy gasped at the sheer pleasure that began to ricochet through her veins. Jess was very, very good: the rhythmic sucking made Roxy want more and more. She slid her hands into Jess's hair, the pads of her fingertips exerting enough pressure on Jess's scalp to encourage her.

Jess laughed in delight against Roxy's skin. 'Oh, yes, you taste as good as you look,' she murmured. 'And I can't wait to explore you properly.'

'You've done this before, haven't you?' Roxy asked.

'Initiated another woman into the arts of making love, you mean?' Jess nodded. 'Once or twice. And a few more things – I mean, you have to try things out, if you write the kind of things that I do.'

'Two men?' Roxy asked, thinking of the scenario she'd programmed for Alice.

'Yes,' Jess said. 'Several times. As I told you, I like men.' She grinned. 'And I like women – especially responsive ones like you.' She caressed Roxy's breasts, so gently, then shifted back onto her side, wriggling down the bed slightly, and stroked Roxy's belly. The tips of her fingers just brushed

Roxy's mons veneris, and Roxy groaned, parting her legs involuntarily. She wanted Jess to touch her properly now, bring her to a shuddering climax and drain all the tension out of her body.

'Beautiful,' Jess said, sliding one hand between Roxy's thighs. 'You're so warm, so responsive. I love the way you curve, the way your body reacts to me.' She cupped Roxy's mound of Venus, pressing her fingers lightly against Roxy's moistening quim, and Roxy shivered, opening her mouth and licking her lower lip. Jess smiled, and slid her middle finger along Roxy's labia until she came to her clitoris.

Roxy gasped as Jess touched the hard nub of flesh, then began to rub it, teasing the clitoris from its fleshy hood. She tipped her head back even harder against the pillows, this time arching her lower body. She needed to feel Jess's mouth against her, her hands, bringing her to the edge of bliss.

'We have all afternoon. Don't be so impatient,' Jess teased, bending her head to lick the soft undersides of Roxy's breasts.

Roxy shivered. 'Please.' The touch of Jess's mouth had awakened a need to be more than just touched; she wanted Jess to lick her, too, cover her body with kisses and wipe away all the anger of their captivity with her tongue.

Whether Roxy had spoken aloud, or whether Jess had just been able to read her mind, she wasn't sure; but Jess chuckled richly. 'It'll be my pleasure, sweetheart.' Her voice had grown husky with desire, and an answering desire fluttered in Roxy's stomach.

Jess shifted down the bed, her hair trailing over Roxy's skin in a way that made Roxy shiver; as Jess moved, she trailed her tongue over Roxy's midriff, making Roxy arch in pleasure. Finally, she knelt between Roxy's thighs.

Roxy reached up to grip the edge of the iron headboard,

her knuckles whitening. She spread her thighs, lifting her bottom slightly; Jess slid her palms between Roxy's thighs, spreading her legs even wider, and looked at her friend's sex for a moment. Roxy's intimate flesh had darkened with arousal, until it was almost plum-coloured; Jess couldn't resist blowing softly along her quim, and Roxy shuddered. 'Jess,' she said, her voice cracking. 'Please. Please.'

'I know, I've teased you enough.' Jess bent her head; Roxy opened her eyes, and the sight of the other woman's head between her thighs was almost enough on its own to make her come. What they were doing would never have happened, in other circumstances. She'd never felt any sexual urges towards a woman before; the deep affection she felt for Alice was platonic, not sexual, love. If she and Jess had met in another time, in their old lives, Roxy thought that they would have enjoyed each other's company. Alice, too, would have liked Jess, and the three of them would have spent gossipy evenings together, drinking wine and laughing, and watching the sort of films that their men didn't appreciate.

But here and now, this enjoyment of each other's bodies . . . All thought suddenly left her head as Roxy felt the soft stroke of Jess's tongue along her satiny cleft. She squeezed her eyes shut. God, it was almost like the first time Tim had done this to her, the raw excitement and anticipation of a new lover exploring her most intimate flesh in such an intimate way. She groaned, pushing towards Jess's mouth, and Jess responded immediately, the speed and pressure of her tongue increasing over Roxy's clitoris.

'Oh, God, Jess, that's so good,' Roxy moaned. She loosened the grip of one hand on the headboard, bringing it down to caress her friend's head, twining her fingers in Jess's silky tresses. Jess simply smiled, and changed the rhythm of the way she was licking Roxy, making it long and slow until Roxy was writhing under her.

Roxy groaned as Jess pushed her tongue deep inside her, lapping at her nectar; then Jess began building the pressure over her clitoris again until Roxy cried out sharply, her flesh convulsing under Jess's mouth.

When Roxy's breathing had slowed back to normal, Jess lifted her head. 'Better?' she asked softly.

'Thank you. Yes.' Roxy stroked her hair.

'Good. Though I haven't finished yet.' Jess kissed Roxy's inner thighs, her face smooth and soft against Roxy's skin. 'Not by a long way.' She slid one finger into Roxy's hot moist channel, and began to manipulate her clitoris with a knowing thumb.

Roxy shivered as her climax began to build again; Jess added another finger, and began to massage Roxy intimately, pressing on her G-spot and making her body jump sharply. She rubbed her face against Roxy's belly, and continued pistoning her fingers in and out, driving her lover over the edge into a long and gasping climax. Roxy sobbed as she came, her internal muscles flexing hard around Jess's fingers; Jess stayed where she was until the aftershocks of Roxy's orgasm had faded, then shifted up to cuddle her, stroking her face and her back and her buttocks, murmuring soft endearments.

'Okay?' she asked.

Roxy nodded, then leaned over to kiss her lightly on the mouth. 'Thank you. I needed that.'

'Mm. You did feel pretty tense, earlier,' Jess remarked wryly.

Roxy stroked Jess's shoulders, her fingers feeling the knots in Jess's muscles. 'So do you – and I think I can do something about that.' She tipped her head on one side. 'Though I should tell you that I haven't done anything like this before.'

'I know. You were so surprised when I touched you – even if you hadn't told me that you'd never made love with a woman, I'd have known.'

Roxy flushed. 'Now I feel like a teenager.'

'And I feel very privileged that I was the one to . . . well, show you how good it is.' Jess stroked her face. 'You're lovely, Roxy. So warm and soft and sexy: I can hardly wait to feel you use that beautiful sensual mouth on me. Just follow your instincts,' she said softly. 'You can't go wrong.'

Roxy smiled then, and shifted onto her side, moving Jess so that she was on her back. Almost nervously, she began to stroke Jess's breasts, the tips of her fingers tracing the soft undersides in the same way that she liked being touched. She played with Jess's nipples, intrigued by the differences between Jess's breasts and her own: Jess's body was longer and leaner than her own, her breasts smaller, but her nipples were just as sensitive.

Jess's skin was the colour of pure cream ice cream, the translucent sort of skin that sometimes went with red hair. Her nipples were plum-coloured, protuberant: they hardened and lengthened as Roxy caressed them, gently arousing her. Roxy smiled, and dipped her head, making her tongue into a hard point and flicking it over Jess's nipples; Jess groaned with pleasure and tangled her fingers in Roxy's hair, urging her on. 'Please,' she whispered. 'Do it.'

Roxy grazed Jess's nipples with her teeth, just hard enough for pleasure, and Jess gasped. 'Christ, that feels so good! Touch me, Roxy. Go down on me. Lick me. Make me come.'

Roxy, suddenly remembering what had happened to Jess earlier that afternoon, gradually kissed her way down her friend's body. She was going to make Jess forget everything, let the tension drain out of her completely. All she had to do was follow her instincts, give Jess the same type of pleasure that she liked herself. And she did have one experience that she hadn't told Jess about – the experience of making love to herself, as though she were Tim, with the VRX program.

She shifted so that she was kneeling between Jess's thighs; Jess spread her legs more widely, allowing Roxy the access she needed, and Roxy drew a sharp intake of breath at the sight. Jess was beautiful, her sex a rich vermilion shading into plum, fringed by the fiery red of her pubic hair. Jess was a natural redhead, then, and not a bottled one, Roxy thought with amusement.

Roxy traced the folds and crevices of Jess's quim, pulling gently on her labia, and finally pushed one finger, then a second, into Jess's creamy channel. She moved her hand back and forth in the age-old rhythm she'd used herself, on nights when Tim had been away on business and had treated her to an erotic phone call, tempting her to masturbate for him while he did the same for her, miles away.

But there was something just as nice as touch, she thought – taste. And she wanted to taste Jess, use her mouth on her in the same way that Jess had pleasured her. She bent her head to Jess's quim, breathing in the sweet musky scent of her arousal and then blowing lightly on the moist flesh, teasing Jess as Jess had teased her earlier.

'Oh, God,' Jess said, the pressure of her fingers on Roxy's scalp urging her on.

Feeling slightly nervous, excited and bold, all at the same time, Roxy lowered her mouth onto Jess's quim, drawing her tongue along the other woman's intimate topography. As Jess moaned with pleasure, Roxy began to lap in earnest, tasting the sweet nectar pooling in Jess's quim and using her tongue to bring Jess to a higher peak of arousal.

'Oh, yes,' Jess moaned, as Roxy gently sucked on her clitoris, pushing a finger into her moist channel and pistoning it back and forth, using the same rhythm as her mouth as she worked on the small hard nub of flesh.

Jess climaxed, crying out Roxy's name; Roxy lapped up the sweet nectar, and continued her ministrations, pushing Jess up to another shattering climax. Then, as Jess slumped back against the pillows, drained, Roxy shifted up to cuddle Jess. Jess, although taller, curled into Roxy's body, resting her head on her shoulder and curving her hand round one breast.

'Thank you,' she said, dropping a kiss on Roxy's collarbone. 'You've taken the feel of him away.'

'Any time.' Roxy nuzzled her hair. 'Though, Jess, I think maybe we shouldn't stay here too long.'

'In this place? You must be joking. I want to break out as much as you do.'

Roxy smiled. 'I didn't mean that. I mean, if one of the guards came in and found us in the same bed . . .'

'It's every man's fantasy. Two women, making it – then he can come in and prove that men are superior, and his cock can do better things to both of them than they could do to each other,' Jess said.

'A man with a pretty fast recovery rate, then,' Roxy mused.

Jess chuckled. 'Or one using your program, maybe.'

Roxy smiled. 'Yeah. Even Tim admitted that it was the ultimate male fantasy – and programmed it in.' She stroked Jess's shoulder. 'Mind you, I had my revenge. I programmed two men and one woman.'

'It's a shame that it's gone,' Jess said. 'The more I hear about it, the more I want to try it.'

'It's only gone from a computer. It's still up here,' Roxy said, tapping her head. 'Unless they intend to wipe out bits of my memory, I can build it again, when all this is over.'

'And I,' Jess said, 'will be your first customer. And I'll dedicate a book to you.'

'I'll hold you to that,' Roxy said.

NINE

The next morning, it was Roxy's turn to be taken by the guards.

'Good luck,' Jess said, as Roxy left. 'And don't lose your temper.'

Roxy smiled wryly. Until she'd been stuck in the House of Correction, she'd never regarded herself as the sort of woman who lost her temper easily. But being deprived of knowledge, when she was used to having more information at her fingertips than she could ever need, had made her temper much sharper.

'Where am I going?' she asked the guard.

Silence.

'Look,' Roxy said softly. 'I won't tell anybody. I won't tell them what you tell me, or even who told me.' She smiled at him. 'I'd like to know where I'm going. Who he is – who asked for me to be sent to him. It can't do any harm, can it? Just to tell me a little thing like that. All I want to know is who he is.'

The guard seemed to consider it for a while. Roxy thought that he was on the point of telling her, when another guard came. She sighed inwardly. With one of them guarding her, she might have had a chance. She might have persuaded him to talk to her. But with two . . . There was no way.

She was blindfolded, and then helped into the back seat of a car. It was a fairly large car, because the guards were able to sit either side of her without squashing her. She touched the seat experimentally; it was leather. Traditional Values obviously included having the best of everything if you were in power, she thought, torn between disgust and cynical amusement.

The blindfold meant that she was completely disoriented. She didn't know where she was going; and she couldn't tell even the direction in which they were going. The chauffeur, whoever he was, was an expert driver, and the ride was so smooth that she could barely tell when they met a bend, let alone anything else.

At last, the car stopped. The guards helped her out of the car and up some steps. The front door was opened; then they removed the blindfold and left, closing the door behind her.

A man stood in front of her in the narrow hallway, dressed in an expensive-looking grey suit, a white cotton shirt and a very sober tie. Roxy's eyes raked him insolently. He was about the same height as Tim – six foot – with dark hair brushed back from his face and glittering blue eyes. But whereas Tim's eyes were cornflower blue, this man's eyes were a very pale blue, the colour of ice.

'Roxana Winters,' he drawled. His smile wasn't pleasant, and his face repelled her.

'And who are you?' she asked, lifting her chin.

'You don't have the right to ask that.'

'And you're telling me that you have the right to have me dragged here in a blindfold?' Roxy asked quietly.

'Not dragged. Brought in a limo,' was the immediate response.

'What sort of society is this?' she asked.

'One with traditional values,' he said tartly.

'Well, under *traditional* values—' she made the word as insulting as possible '—children were the ones to be seen and not heard. I'm not a child.'

'Ask no questions, you'll hear no lies.'

Roxy decided to try a different tack. 'Aren't you insulting both our intelligence?'

'Touché.' He nodded. 'They told me that you were clever.'

'Who told you?'

'The House of Correction.'

Roxy spread her hands. 'And how would they know? I haven't been subjected to any tests.'

'They have your records.'

'So you know what I was before.'

'A project manager at Visicom. Very well thought of; responsible for the shopping mall project. A woman with excellent organizational skills, but who was sharp enough to keep up to date with developments, and was probably one of the best programmers they ever had.' His lips thinned. 'And I believe that you worked very closely with Comco, too.'

'Comco?' She kept her voice light. Was he going to tell her something about Tim?

'You were close to two other project managers.'

'I knew several people at Comco. Do you mean anyone in particular?'

He smiled nastily at her. 'I'm surprised that you need to ask. You know who I'm talking about.'

'I'm afraid I don't.'

'Tim Fraser and Marcus Blake.'

Roxy's eyes narrowed. 'Where are they? Are they all right?'

'As I said, ask no questions, you'll hear no lies.'

'Tell me. Are they all right?'

He spread his hands. 'That isn't the issue.'

'So ignorance is strength, then?' she said, her lip curling.

He caught her reference immediately: *Nineteen Eighty-four*. 'Well-read, for a scientist. But then, you lived with Alice

Jamieson for a number of years – Mrs Marcus Blake, as she is now.'

Cold fear settled in Roxy's stomach at the thought of her friend. 'Alice. You haven't hurt her? Or the baby? You haven't done to them what you've done to me?'

'Mrs Marcus Blake has a position in our society. A married woman with a child. Roxana Winters . . . Well.' He made a dismissive gesture.

Roxy remembered what Jess had said the previous day. 'A household drudge, I believe.' She shrugged. 'You might as well tell me where the cleaning stuff is, and what needs to be done.'

'Ah. The legendary ability to focus on the demands of her task,' he said mockingly.

'And I'm sure that you'll be satisfied with the result.'

'Not quite.' He stared at her. 'Do you know how many people were put out of work by what you and your company did with the Mall development?'

'And that's why you joined Traditional Values?' Roxy grimaced. 'What we did is called progress. People learn to live with the times.'

'Just as you'll learn now. You went too far. It was time to stop, to go back to the old ways.'

'If you hate technology so much,' Roxy asked, 'then why did you use it?'

'How do you mean?'

'Cutting off our communications, our bank accounts, all at one stroke – to do that, you had to have control of all the databases. Otherwise you couldn't have done it.'

'Don't try to be too clever,' he said, his eyes narrowing. 'Now – the cleaning. This way.'

He marched her down the hall. Roxy noticed the plush pile of the carpet, and the expensive paintings on the walls. Whoever he was, he liked the trappings of status. She guessed that he was someone in the government. To have this many privileges, and to talk to her alone, without a guard – he had to be someone that the Traditional Values party trusted. It was a risk that only someone with a lot of power could afford to take.

He opened the door at the end of the corridor and pushed her into the kitchen. It was a large room, floored with glazed terracotta. He indicated a bowl of water that sat on one of the worktops, together with some detergent and a toothbrush. 'I want this floor gleaming,' he said.

'I beg your pardon?'

'Gleaming,' he repeated. 'So that you can see your face in it.'

Humiliation was his game, was it? And Jess had said, *Keep your temper*. That would rile him more – knowing that he couldn't break her spirit, no matter what he did or said to her. She smiled sweetly at him. 'But of course. That's what I'm here for, after all.' She reached out to take the bowl.

'Wait,' he said, laying a hand on her wrist. 'Your skirt. Take it off.'

'Aren't women supposed to be clothed demurely nowadays?' Roxy asked sweetly.

'Yes – but waste not, want not. We can't afford for you to get your clothes dirty.'

'"Clothes" meaning my skirt?'

'Meaning *all* of it.'

Roxy only just stopped herself laughing at the incongruity of it. Herself, completely naked, scrubbing this man's kitchen floor with a toothbrush ... No doubt he was expecting her to rebel – and that would give him the excuse to touch her. Hurt her, even. There was no point in that. She simply spread her hands and shrugged. 'As you say.' She stripped swiftly, folding her clothes neatly and placing them on the worktop. She removed her shoes, too, placing them upside down on top of her skirt.

'And the rest,' he said.

It wasn't quite like Jess's experience of being a maid, and wearing a little frilly apron on top of her clothes. But this was what the man demanded – and Roxy knew that she had no power to oppose him. Not yet. And there was always the chance that if she did do what he wanted, she could wheedle some information out of him.

She reached behind herself, unclasping the ugly bra. She removed the garment, revealing her generous breasts, and then removed the hated big knickers. He watched her while she was doing it; Roxy was half-tempted to turn a mocking pirouette, but knew that it wouldn't be a good idea. Not if she wanted information. Not if she wanted to find out what had happened to Tim, Alice and Marcus. From what he'd said earlier, she was certain that this man knew what had happened to them.

His blue eyes glittered. 'On your knees,' he said.

'Well, that's how you normally scrub floors, isn't it?' she said cheerfully, taking the bowl and kneeling down.

He stood there watching her, and Roxy was suddenly aware of a change in the atmosphere. The fact that she was kneeling and naked ... it turned him on. *Knowledge is strength*, she thought wryly, deliberately misquoting. *If watching me scrub this floor is what turns you on, sunshine*, she thought, *then let's make it a bit more interesting for you*.

From what Jess had said the previous day, it was obvious what Roxy's other role was to be in this house. A drudge and a call-girl, who had no choice but to fulfil the demands of the privileged classes. The Traditional Values party obviously wasn't free of corruption, people who were happy to abuse their power.

She lifted her buttocks slightly, widening the gap between her thighs to give him a clear view of her quim. She continued scrubbing, every time that she moved making quite sure that he could see either her intimate flesh or her breasts moving. The air grew stiller and stiller, tension filling the room. Roxy waited, still scrubbing the floor: then, at last, she heard the sound she'd been expecting. The rasp of his zip.

He knelt on the floor behind her. She was tempted to ask him if he minded about getting his own clothes dirty, but stopped herself in time. This was going to happen, whether she liked it or not, and she wanted to make sure that she was in control of what happened – so that she could get some information from him.

She felt the tip of his cock press against her sex, and shivered. It reminded her of the time when Tim had done something similar. It had been her turn to clean the bathroom; and she'd just finished shaving her legs, in the bath. She had been wearing only a towel, wrapped round her sarong-style, and Tim had caught her leaning over the bath, cleaning it. He'd been unable to resist the temptation that she presented to him: and he'd slid his body into hers, holding her against the bath and thrusting hard, escalating the pleasure for both of them.

Roxy squeezed her eyes shut, willing the memory to stay back. This man was treating her like a whore. She had to remember where she was, what was happening in this life, and that it definitely wasn't Tim behind her.

Very slowly, he pushed his cock into her. Roxy continued to scrub the floor, assuming that he'd expect her to finish her work, not respond to him. This was, after all, just part of her duties in his house. She scrubbed the terracotta tiles; eventually, he slid his hands down her forearms, stilling her wrists. She remained perfectly still, and he began to thrust.

He slid one hand back over her arm, curving his hand over one breast, stroking and kneading it, playing idly with her nipple. To Roxy's horror, her nipple became erect, her body responding to him; he laughed softly in the back of his throat as he realized what had happened, a sound of triumph. Roxy was mortified. This man was using her body. Abusing it. It was a physical reaction, she knew that. It didn't *mean* anything. But she hated herself for it.

To her relief, he didn't try to kiss her. She didn't think she could have borne the feel of his mouth against the nape of her neck, her shoulders. As it was, she wanted to push him away: but this, this was when she was most likely to get information from him. When his body was taking pleasure from hers, and his mind wasn't at its sharpest.

'Your name?' she asked softly.

'That isn't a privilege for you to know.'

'Maybe,' she said, 'but under traditional values, a woman would know a man's name before he penetrated her body. Unless she was a whore, of course – but you haven't paid me.'

He tensed, as though stung; then sighed. 'Mr Reeve, to you.'

He wasn't going to give her a first name: but at least she knew something. And somehow, some way, she'd find out who he really was. When this nightmare was over, she'd make him pay for every last scrap of humiliation he visited on her.

He continued to push into her body, in long, slow, measured thrusts. Despite herself, Roxy's quim grew slick with arousal, easing his passage into her. His pace quickened; and, at long last, she felt him spurt inside her. Unlike Jess's persecutor, he wasn't wearing a condom. Roxy thought about pointing out to him what a risk he'd taken – that he could have impregnated her – but decided against it. There was no point in antagonizing him. Besides, he'd told her his name. Maybe he could be tempted to tell her more.

When he'd finished, he eased out of her – not caring that she hadn't reached a climax – and stood up again. Roxy stayed still, until she heard the hiss of his zip; then she continued scrubbing the floor, crawling over the tiles and making sure that she cleaned up every scrap of dirt with her toothbrush.

He stood there, watching her, watching the way his semen ran out of her quim and down her inner thighs in a sticky, creamy mess. *One day*, Roxy promised herself, *I'll kill you for this, Reeve*: but she said nothing to him until she'd finished the floor. Then she stood up, ignoring her nakedness, and put her hands on her hips.

'Perhaps you could give me the courtesy of a shower.'

'And what if it isn't on the agenda?'

She smiled wryly. 'It's not so much humiliation, as basic human decency.' She nodded at the floor. 'I think you can see that I've done an adequate job.'

'Yes.'

'Well,' she said, 'you owe me. In recompense.'

'Women,' he reminded her, 'don't have jobs, any more. It's against the law. So I won't be paying you.'

'I'm not asking for money. I'm asking for payment in kind.' She chose the words deliberately, knowing that in another world they could have been interpreted differently. He, too, was aware of the connotation: she could see it in the pale blue eyes as he looked at her. He paused for a while, then nodded. 'All right. Upstairs.'

'After you,' Roxy said, only just holding back a mocking "my lord".

'No, after you.'

'Courtesy, or are you afraid I'll make a run for it? Look, I can hardly run into the street, naked.'

'And even if you were clothed, you wouldn't get very far.'

'How do you mean?' she asked, surprised.

'Well, we can track you easily now. All we need to do is to code your genetic patterns into the computer, and we'll find you.'

'But I thought you despised technology.'

'Not always.'

'The system you were talking about,' Roxy mused, 'was developed by Comco. But it wasn't meant for tracking criminals – it was for burglar alarms, and for gathering statistics. For marketing information.'

'It has other uses now,' he said.

'Then I imagine,' Roxy said carefully, trying not to betray the leap of excitement in her stomach, 'that the team that developed the system must still be working on it, refining it for you.'

'You ask too many questions,' he said roughly.

Roxy hugged the nugget of hope to herself. Marcus, at least, was alive. The ID cards and statistical system had been his baby. His, together with Tim. But then again, Tim . . .. Her mind whirled. He couldn't possibly be alive. There was no way that Tim would allow this to happen to her. If anything, he'd rig the system, and make sure that she was "ordered" by himself, or by one of his friends. Someone who'd treat her well. She swallowed. Unless he thought that she was dead . . . Or if he was dead. She still had no real answers from Reeve. And she had no way of knowing if what he had hinted to her was the truth.

'This way,' he said, leading her to the bottom of the stairs. She walked up the stairs, closely followed by him. 'Turn left,' he said, when they reached the landing.

She opened the door, to discover an extremely luxurious bathroom. The bath and sink were white marble, with old-fashioned brass taps. The carpet was thick pile, in a deep blue, and the colour was echoed in the blue-and-gold border tiles on the walls. The rest of the walls were tiled in white, and there was a large mirror opposite the bath – which was actually a jacuzzi, she realized as she drew nearer.

The shower gel was expensive: it was a brand she recognized from the old days, rich in extracts of seaweed and minerals. It was a far cry from the showers in the House of Correction, which were tiled in ageing white tiles with no borders, and which only worked sporadically, with cool water. The towels in this bathroom were thick and large and fluffy, unlike the small and scratchy towels at the House of Correction.

Roxy turned on the shower and stepped in. It was good to bathe in hot water again, with lots of creamy shower gel; she washed her hair in the shower, too, luxuriating in the feeling of being clean. She washed every trace of Reeve from her body, ignoring the fact that he was watching her closely. She couldn't afford the luxuries of anger or petulance – for now, all that mattered was that he was letting her shower.

When she'd finished, she was about to turn off the water and step out when she was aware of a movement beside her. While she'd cleaned herself, Reeve had stripped off; he stood next to her, now, in the shower.

Roxy swallowed hard as she saw his erection jutting up

against his belly. In hindsight, she should have expected this. As it was, it was a surprise: that he wanted her again. He turned her to face him, and she braced herself, willing him not to kiss her. To her relief, he didn't: he simply gave her a twisted smile. 'You just can't help yourself, can you?' he asked, taking one hardened nipple between his finger and thumb and pinching it.

Roxy flushed, angry and embarrassed. 'I think it's a natural reaction to a shower. As that is,' she said, indicating his erection.

'Really?' he mocked; then he lifted her up, pinning her against the wall.

Roxy's face paled. It was a fantasy she'd once had about Tim, one which he'd acted out for her: making love in the shower. It was corny and old-fashioned, but she'd loved every minute of it – the feel of Tim, lifting her and balancing her weight against the wall, then Tim's cock thrust deep inside her, and her legs wrapped round his waist, the water beating down on them as they made love. This was a travesty – a cruel, evil travesty. It was as if Reeve had tortured Tim, or something, made him tell everything about his sex-life with Roxy . . . and was using it against her.

Reeve said nothing: he simply smiled in triumph, and lowered her until the tip of his cock pressed against her entrance. Then he thrust, hard, pushing deep into her. He slid his left hand down her thigh, moulding it so that she put her leg round his waist for balance; then he rested his left hand on the wall, and did the same with his right hand. When her legs were wrapped round him, he began to thrust properly.

He pushed one hand round the nape of her neck, dragging his face to hers, and opened his mouth over hers. She kept her mouth firmly closed, but he was too strong for her, forcing her lips apart. Her resistance excited him – or maybe the fact that he was stronger than her – and he kissed her deeply, plunging his tongue into her mouth.

Roxy counted inside her head, focusing on something else in an effort to forget what he was doing to her; then, at long last he came, emptying his body into hers. He withdrew, and let her slide down the tiles until her feet were on the floor again. Then he held her hands behind her, with one hand, while he washed himself with the other – and turned the shower off.

Bastard, Roxy thought. *You won't let me wash the traces of you from me, this time*. Steeling herself, she climbed out of the bath. He dried himself, then tossed the damp towel to her; forcing herself not to show her disgust, she scrubbed at her skin with the towel. *I'll kill you, Reeve*, she said inwardly. *One day, I'll kill you*.

He led her downstairs again, and she dressed; a few moments later, the guards came in, blindfolded her again, and took her back to the House of Correction.

When she returned to their room, Jess welcomed her with open arms. 'Roxy, are you okay?'

'I'm fine,' Roxy said through gritted teeth. 'But I swear that, the moment I get out of here, I'll kill Reeve.'

'Reeve? Who's Reeve?'

'The man,' Roxy said roughly, 'who sent for me.'

'You found out his name?'

'And more. I think that Marcus and Alice are all right.' She swallowed. 'I don't know about Tim, but if I can access e-mail, I can send a message to Marcus and Alice. They'll get us out of here.' She gritted her teeth. 'I know something now, that's the main thing.'

'How did you find out?'

'He made me scrub the floor – with a toothbrush, and naked. I think it was meant to give me some kind of humility.'

'Bloody pervert,' Jess said.

'Mm. He took me while I cleaned the floor.' Roxy's jaw clenched. 'Anyway, then I asked him his name. I think he was surprised enough to tell me – his surname, anyway.' She shrugged. 'I asked him for a shower, when I'd finished cleaning. He let me have one.'

'A bit more considerate than the man who ordered me,' Jess said.

Roxy shook her head. 'He let me wash, and wash my hair – then he took me again. He made me dry myself on his wet towel.' Her lips twisted. 'And on such little things, murders are planned.'

'Roxy.' Jess was anxious.

'Don't worry, I won't do anything rash. That's when he told me that even if I tried to make a run for it, it wouldn't work – he can pick me up on computer, through my genetic make-up.'

'I didn't know that sort of technology was around,' Jess said.

'It was meant to help people. Statistical analysis of people's habits, to help with transport plans, and maybe medical help. One quick scan, and you'll know if your unconscious patient is allergic to penicillin or aspirin.' Roxy spread her hands. 'This is a further step – and he as good as told me that the original team was still working on it. Which means that Marcus and Alice are all right.'

'I've learned something, too,' Jess said. 'While you were away, I checked the room.'

'You've found a way out?' Roxy asked.

'No – but I've found something almost as good.' Jess smiled.

'The central heating system's done by warm air. There's a vent under my bed, and there's a vent on the other side of the wall, too. I managed to make contact with the woman on the other side.' Jess spread her hands. 'Her name's Giselle Baines. She used to be a journalist, and she only came here today. I heard it, because she was yelling her head off as they shoved her in the room. Then I heard something knocking – and there she was, talking to me through the air vent.'

'That's fantastic!'

Jess looked at the door. 'I'll guard this. Why don't you introduce yourself to her? If I start singing, you know it's time to get out of there.'

'Thanks.'

'You never know. With what you found out today, and what she knows, you might make some sense out of all this mess.'

Roxy hugged Jess. 'You never know. Well – time to say hello, then.' She crawled under Jess's bed; as Jess had said, there was a heating air duct. She tapped lightly on it, and was rewarded by someone tapping from the other side, echoing the small staccato rhythm.

'Hello?' Roxy asked.

'Hello.' The woman had a slightly west London accent.

'Giselle Baines?'

'Yes. You must be Roxy Winters.'

'Pleased to make your acquaintance,' Roxy said. 'Jess tells me that you were brought in today.'

'Yes.' Giselle's voice was bitter.

'So what's going on out there?'

'The Traditional Values party has taken over. There hasn't been much resistance – I thought it was strange, at first, but I can see why. Women dare not protest, in case their men are taken out and shot, or worse. Married men don't protest, in case their wives are thrown into places like this one. The Traditional Values mob rule by fear.' Giselle coughed. 'The ones who have had the courage to protest – well, you're here, so's Jess, and so am I.'

'So the outside world knows what we're here for?' Roxy was outraged.

'To correct our beliefs – that's the official line. I was expecting solitary, and bread and water if I was lucky.' Giselle's voice was filled with wry amusement. 'What I've eaten, so far, could be sold for a lot of money at a health farm.'

'Yeah, well. They need to keep us fit.'

'So what's the story?' Giselle asked.

'Household drudges to the rich and mighty. Oh, and a bit of sex in between.'

'Bastards.' Giselle ground her teeth. 'They won't get away with it.'

'They're doing okay, at the moment.' Roxy coughed. 'So tell me more about this Traditional Values lot. Who are they?'

'John Ferris is the president. He has about a dozen hand-picked men, looking after various parts of the administration – defence, publicity, transport and the like.'

'Would one of them happen to be called Reeve?' Roxy asked.

'Yes. Malcolm Reeve. He's the Minister for Publicity – he used to work in an advertising agency, but he lost the top-dog slot to a woman. He's never forgiven our sex for it.' Giselle paused. 'Do you know him?'

'I was sent to him, today,' Roxy said. 'For a lesson in humility – or what I'd term being a call-girl for government officials.' She paused. 'Giselle – I need to know. My best friend Alice was a journalist. She's married to a man called Marcus Blake. I know it's a stupid thing to ask – like asking someone you've only just met if they know someone on the other side of London – but do you know if they're okay?'

'Marcus Blake – he's a high-ranking science official, so I think he's safe. I imagine his wife must be, too.' Giselle thought for a moment. 'Hang on. You're not the Roxana Winters from Visicom, are you?'

'Yes.' Roxy frowned. 'Have we met before, then? At a party, or something?'

'No. I was researching an article on electronic mail. You're one of the people I was going to interview.'

'When we get out of here,' Roxy said, 'you can interview me as many times as you like.' She swallowed. 'My partner ... I wish I knew if he was safe.'

'What's his name?'

'Tim. Tim Fraser.'

Breath hissed through Giselle's lips. 'Tim Fraser.'

'You know something about him.' Roxy picked up the uneasy tone of Giselle's voice. 'Is he dead? Did they kill him?'

'No.' Giselle sighed. 'I don't know how to tell you this, Roxy.'

'Tell me what?' Roxy's voice grew urgent. 'Tell me what, Giselle?'

'Tim Fraser is the Head of National Security.'

'He's *what?*'

'He's one of Ferris's top men.'

'He can't be. It can't be Tim. Someone else must have taken his identity – there's no *way* that he would be involved with that lot.'

'Would I be right in saying that he's tall, with dark hair, fairly good-looking, and in his mid-thirties?' Giselle said.

'Yeah.' Roxy choked. 'Christ, I can't believe this, Giselle.'

'I think it's him. Roxy, what did he do before?'

'He worked for Visicom. He was working on the national identity database. He was planning the infrastructure; Marcus worked on the genetic side, but Tim was the programmer and planner.' Roxy's voice faded as she grasped the implications of what Giselle had told her. 'I suppose that ties in with his position, now.' She paused. 'When I get out of here, I'll kill him for betraying me.'

'Roxy, you don't know if it's like that.'

'If he hadn't betrayed me,' Roxy said, 'he'd have got me out of here, by now.'

'Maybe he's working as a double agent,' Giselle said. 'Maybe he's the one we can contact, to get us out of here.'

'I don't think so.' Roxy squeezed her eyes shut. 'Giselle, I'm sorry. I need some time to think about all this. I'll talk to you later, okay?'

'Take care.'

Roxy crawled out from under the bed; Jess's face brightened expectantly. The conversation had taken place in whispers, so Jess hadn't been able to catch it. 'How did it go?' she asked.

'I found out about Reeve, like you said. He's the Minister for Publicity. My friend Alice is safe, and so is Marcus.'

'That's great,' Jess said.

Roxy rubbed her hand across her face. 'But Tim . . . He's the head of National Security.'

'There must have been a mistake,' Jess said. 'The man you told me about – he couldn't possibly be involved with this lot.'

'It's what he was working on – the national security database.'

'Maybe they forced him to do it,' Jess suggested. 'He wouldn't have done it of his own accord, I'm sure.'

'I don't know,' Roxy said. 'But now I need to get out of here – fast. And I'll need your help, Jess.'

'Sure, whatever I can do. Just tell me.'

'Thanks.' Roxy's face tightened.

'Don't brood on it. I'm sure it's not how it looks,' Jess said, stroking Roxy's face.

'Maybe. Maybe not.' Roxy shrugged. 'Give me a day or two, and I'll have our plan worked out.'

TEN

Roxy put her ear to the door, then turned to Jess. 'Ready?'

'Ready, whenever you are,' Jess said.

'I appreciate this, you know.' Roxy said feelingly. 'I owe you one, I really do.'

'Hey, that's what friends are for,' Jess said with a shrug.

Although they'd known each other for only a few short weeks, since their incarceration in the House of Correction they'd become firm friends. Roxy was still faintly surprised by the fact that they were allowed to share a room – she'd always thought that political prisoners would be kept in solitary confinement – or that the room hadn't been bugged. Or maybe the Traditional Values party thought that as Jess and Roxy had no power, it didn't matter what they thought or said. They had no chance of acting on any of their ideas. She smiled wryly. Well, the Party would soon learn their mistake – and they'd learn pretty soon. Starting with Tim.

'Anyway,' Jess said, 'I want to get out of here as much as you do. I don't enjoy being a domestic drudge, or a call-girl for the privileged. I want to go back to my old life.'

'I don't think I do,' Roxy said slowly.

'But – I thought you wanted to get out of here?'

'I do. But after what I know now, I couldn't go back to living with Tim. And to think I almost caved in and married the guy ...' Roxy's mouth twisted. 'I'd rather stick a knife in his heart now. And I want him to know who's twisting that knife – I want him to know that it's me, and why.'

Jess winced. 'Roxy. Don't let yourself turn bitter about him. He isn't worth it.'

Roxy pulled a face. 'Yeah, I know.'

'Anyway, we need to concentrate on this. It's got to work, Roxy.'

Roxy nodded. 'It will. Believe me, it will.' She listened again at the door, then looked at Jess. They'd planned this for weeks – after noticing that there was a pattern to which guards came into their room. Unless there was a very radical change, the man who would open their door in a few seconds was one of the younger guards, the one they thought was most likely to be affected by what they were going to do. 'Now,' Roxy said softly.

Jess nodded, and moved into position. She was lying on the bed, naked, with her knees bent and her feet flat on the mattress. The sheet was pushed back, and she tipped her head back on the pillow as she slid one hand between her thighs. She widened the gap between her legs so that her quim was in full view of whoever opened the door, and slid one finger along her moist satiny cleft.

She began to masturbate, moving her hand back and forth in the age-old familiar rhythm, stroking one finger very gently along her quim, moving from the top to the bottom of her slit in one slow, deliberate movement. As her quim began to grow slick with juices, she began to quicken the rhythm, then thrust her middle finger deep into her warm dark wetness, using the heel of her hand to press against her clitoris.

It made a pretty sight. Roxy would have been tempted to join in ... but she had a slightly more testing agenda. The door opened; the guard stood there, shocked into stillness for a moment. Roxy took a chance, gambling on his surprise, and pulled him inside, closing the door behind him.

'What the – that's illegal,' he said swiftly, his voice almost panicky.

Yet there'd been a note of interest, before he'd slapped it down under the guise of duty. Roxy smiled to herself. She'd definitely chosen the right one.

'Sex is for procreation, not recreation,' he reminded them sharply.

'But that's not how it used to be,' Roxy said, her voice sultry. 'Look at her, lying there, her body ripe and openly inviting. Peaches and cream. Don't you want it? Don't you want to touch her, taste her?'

He swallowed hard. 'No. No. Not this. This can't be happening.'

'Oh, but it is,' Roxy purred. The young guard was attractive: about eighteen or nineteen, she thought. He wasn't quite baby-faced, but nearly so; he had dark curly hair, which was kept short in a regulation cut, but Roxy was convinced that he would have had longer hair, in the old days. He reminded her of one of the arts students that Alice had gone out with, years before. His eyes were a cornflower blue, emphasized by small round glasses, and his mouth was generous, with a sensual curve that belied his job under the Traditional Values party.

At the same time, he wasn't one of the arrogant young men who knew that they were good-looking and played on it. This one was shy, not quite sure of himself. And it was going to be a pleasure to do what she planned to do to him. She glanced at his crotch; with a mixture of desire and amusement, she noticed that his cock was hardening beneath the dark stuff of his trousers. Well, it was working, so far. All she had to do was to keep playing on him – playing on his memories of what used to be good. Because a man who was as attractive as this one, even if he hid his sexuality under a light of studiousness or shyness, couldn't be inexperienced.

'Don't you remember what it was like?' she breathed. 'The scent of an aroused woman, all seashore and honey and musk and vanilla, all mingled together? The taste of her skin as you explored her body with her mouth, and then at last the heavenly taste of her quim, her juices dripping over your lips like nectar as you aroused her, sucking her clitoris and pushing your tongue into her?'

He swallowed hard. 'Shut up. This is heresy!'

Roxy smiled broadly. He was near to cracking, she could tell. 'Just think,' she said. 'Remember what it was like when you touched her breasts, feeling them all warm and soft and heavy in your hands.'

Jess acted out Roxy's words, massaging one breast with her free hand and pulling at the nipple so that it hardened and lengthened. She gave a small sigh of pleasure as she touched herself, and tipped her head back further into the pillows.

'Don't you remember?' Roxy asked softly. 'The way she felt, the way her nipples hardened against your fingers as you touched her?'

He shivered, and Roxy continued. 'Don't you remember what it was like, that first incredible moment when you slid your hands over her belly, feeling her soft curves, and then at last she opened her legs for you, let you look at her and touch her and taste her? And the moment when she first undressed you . . .'

Roxy was standing behind the guard, standing on tiptoe so that she could whisper into his ear; she slid her hands round his waist, undoing the buckle of his belt. He put one hand up, as if to protest, and she nuzzled his shoulder. 'Ah,' she said, 'can't you remember the way it felt, that incredible feeling of anticipation, when she first did this, and you knew that she was going to touch you, that she was going to wrap her fingers round your cock?' She finished undoing the buckle. 'And when she came closer, like this?' She slid the zip down. 'And then, when she did this, teasing you with a promise of what it would be like, skin to skin?' She curled her hand round his cock, through the thin cotton of his underpants.

He shivered, his cock twitching into life; Roxy took advantage of his momentary discomfiture, sliding her fingers under the elastic of his underpants and curling her hand round his cock again, this time skin to skin. 'And don't you remember how it felt, when she did this?' she asked, pushing his underpants down with the heel of her hand, and gently rubbing his foreskin back and forth, until he moaned with pleasure. 'And the first time that she did this?'

She moved swiftly, so that she was kneeling in front of the young guard. 'The way she felt when she was on her knees before you, when she shook her hair back and you knew exactly what she was thinking, what she was going to do next?' She gave him her best come-hither smile. 'And the first moment when her mouth touched you . . .' She closed her eyes, thought of the times when she'd performed such an intimate act with Tim, and grew furiously angry. Tim – he was the reason why she was doing this now, planning to suck the cock of some complete stranger whose name she didn't even know, and whom she didn't care about. For Tim – because she was going to get even with him, no matter what it cost her.

The guard shuddered as Roxy bent her head, taking the tip of his cock into her mouth. He tasted sharp, clean – to her relief – but the tang of his arousal wasn't the same as Tim's. His cock was slightly thicker, slightly shorter than Tim's; it didn't have the familiar weight and shape of Tim's cock. Even so, she was going to do this. She squeezed her eyelids together even more tightly, and began to suck rhythmically, moving her head back and forth and tightening her lips as her mouth slid near to the head of his cock. His breathing changed, becoming harsher as his excitement grew; Roxy's nostrils were filled with the clean musky scent of his arousal. All the time Roxy was sucking him, Jess continued to masturbate, rubbing her breasts with one hand and her quim with the other.

'We shouldn't be doing this,' the guard said, remembering his place despite his pleasure, and panicking. Watching one of them masturbate, while the other one worked her mouth over his cock – if he were caught like this, his trousers round his ankles and the women acting so lewdly, there was no way that the Governor would ever forgive him. He'd be demoted to the lowest possible position, having to work for a mere pittance and never, ever, ever have another chance to prove himself . . .

The next minute, he stopped thinking as Roxy fondled his balls and slid her hand between his thighs, stroking his perineum and moving towards his anus. He cried out softly as she began to massage the puckered rosy hole, then slid her first finger in up to the middle joint. As her head moved back and forth, so did her finger, using exactly the same rhythm. It was too much for him, and he came, his cock throbbing in her mouth.

Roxy swallowed every drop, then sat back on her heels and looked at him, her head on one side and her hazel eyes soft and inviting.

He opened his eyes, and moaned. 'God, I can't believe what we just did.'

'There's more than that,' she said, her voice deliberately

pitched low and husky. 'Other pleasures. Any time you want it, any time you walk into this room, you can have either of us. You can do anything you like with us, anything your imagination allows. You can have both of us at once, your cock sliding deep into one of us while you lick the other's cunt. You can have us individually: touch us, taste us, slide your cock into us. Anything. We'll even perform for you, if you like – if you want to watch us bring each other to orgasm, mouth to cunt, two women loving each other. Anything you like.'

He swallowed, his eyes widening as he took in her words. 'But – what if they find out?'

'They won't find out,' Roxy said confidently. 'They'll never find out, not if you don't tell them. And if they do find out . . . Well, it'll be too late for them, then. This will all be over. It isn't natural – you know that.'

'This?' He stared down, and realized that he was still completely clothed, with just his cock bared.

'It isn't natural, to make us live like this.' Roxy repeated. 'Stopping people having sex for pleasure – how can they? Look at Jess, on the bed.' Jess, by now, was very carried away. Watching Roxy suck the young guard's cock had turned her on even more, and she was masturbating furiously, rubbing hard at her crotch. She brought herself to the point of orgasm and stilled for a moment, lifting herself slightly off the bed, all her muscles stretched to tension point; then she shuddered deeply as her climax overtook her, a small groan passing her lips. A moment later, she slumped back against the mattress, drained, a blissful smile on her face.

'Look at that,' Roxy said softly. 'Look how happy she is – how much she enjoyed doing that. Remember how much you enjoyed watching her, too. And they say that it's wrong, it's harmful.' She looked at him. 'You enjoyed what I did to you, didn't you? You liked my mouth working on your cock. You liked me taking you as deep as I could – and you liked my finger pressing against your arse.'

He said nothing; Roxy smiled. 'Your face gives you away. Your mouth. You'd like me to do it again.'

He flushed deeply.

'It's all right,' Roxy reassured him, standing up and taking his hand, squeezing it. 'Nothing's going to happen. Nothing's going to hurt you.'

'I didn't realize that you'd miss it so much,' he blurted out. 'I'd always thought that women didn't enjoy sex as much as men, that they only did things to please you – not that they did them for their own sake.'

Roxy chuckled. 'Believe you me, they do. Women always enjoy sex, with the right man.' She paused. 'What's your name?'

He shook his head, not willing to betray that much information.

'I'm Roxy,' she said, 'and this is Jess. And you are?'

'Philip.' That soft look on her face made him bold enough to tell her his name. 'Philip,' she said. 'Tell me. Did you enjoy what we just did for you? Because we did it for you, you know – we wouldn't have done it for any of the others.'

He swallowed. 'Yes.'

'And you'd like to do it again?'

'Yes.'

'What would you like to do, in particular?' Roxy continued, her voice still soft and encouraging.

'I want . . .' His words suddenly rushed out, as though they'd been suppressed for months, and had suddenly been freed. The excitement of saying forbidden words to these women was a heady feeling, something that made him feel out of control –

and love every second of it. 'I want to fuck you. I want to slide my cock deep into you. And I want to suck Jess's cunt,' he said, 'at the same time. I want to see you licking her, too, I want your tongue on her clitoris while mine's deep inside her.'

'That can be arranged,' Roxy said. 'Any time you want, we can do that.'

His face betrayed his growing excitement. 'Really?'

'Really.' She paused. 'And, in return, what will you do for us?'

'In return?' His eyes widened in sudden shock. 'But I can't do anything for you. I can't let you out – you know I can't do that.'

'I'm not asking you to do that,' Roxy said. 'Besides, if you let us go, how can we make love with you?'

He nodded thoughtfully. 'What do you want, then?'

'Do they have an e-mail system here?'

He nodded.

'What do they use it for?'

'To send messages. To take orders – so we know who to send where.'

'I thought so,' Roxy said. 'Could you do me a very, very, very big favour, Philip?'

'I can't do anything,' he said, panicking again and doing up his zip, frantically restoring order to his clothes. 'I'll be caught.'

'Let me put this another way,' Roxy said silkily. 'Look under the bed. You might see something interesting.'

'What?'

'Look, and you'll see. Just under where Jess is lying.'

Jess obligingly moved the sheets, and the guard bent down to look under the bed. 'There's a box there,' he said, frowning.'

'Not just a box. A dictaphone. A tape recorder,' Roxy informed him. 'The woman in the cell next door used to be a journalist. For some reason, they didn't take all her things away from her. And under the bed, there's a vent, which leads to next door. We undid the screws, using a fork – and the woman next door did the same. She passed us the tape recorder, and we taped everything that went on, just now.'

'Everything?' he asked, his face draining of colour.

'Everything,' Roxy confirmed. 'You told us your name, you told us that you enjoyed sex – and you told us exactly how you wanted both of us together.' Roxy tipped her head to one side. 'How do you think that the governor of this place would react if we played the tape to him?'

'You couldn't. You wouldn't.'

'I could,' Roxy said. 'The next guard who comes in . . . All I have to do is tell him I have the tape, and play him a tiny section. Just enough to implicate you. Then he'll let me play it to the governor. And that's your career done for. Sex for recreation, sex outside marriage – you know what that means, under Traditional Laws. Demotion to the lowest level. And the woman goes to the House of Correction. Since we're already here . . . Well, the whole burden will fall on you. The shame, the disgrace, the punishment.'

'No!' He looked frightened; Roxy felt almost sorry for him. He was young and, in another life, she would have found him delightful: but she couldn't be sentimental. Not here, not now. She had to do this.

'Well, you know what you have to do. Just one little tiny thing. Then I'll destroy the tape.'

'You promise?'

'I promise.'

'So what do you want me to do?'

'Well,' Roxy said. 'I assume that you learned how to use e-mail, at school.'

'Yes.'

'I need you to send a message for me. Do you have a pen and paper?'

He nodded, and brought out a small pad and pen that was standard issue for the guards. Roxy wrote down Alice's e-mail ID, and a short message. It was only thirteen words long, and didn't even mention her name – but she knew that Alice would know immediately who had sent it.

'And you'll send this for me tonight?'

He nodded.

'Thank you, Philip,' she said softly, standing on tiptoe and pressing her mouth gently to his. 'I'll remember you for this. And any time you want us, you only have to ask.'

He swallowed, and left the room, looking slightly flustered.

'You don't think that he'll give us away, do you?' Jess asked, stretching and opening one eye lazily.

'I doubt it,' Roxy said. 'He'll be too scared – in case I play the tape to the governor.'

'Lucky for us that he didn't look too closely and see it was an old cigarette packet,' Jess said drily. They'd found it at the bottom of one of the cupboards in their room, and it had given Roxy the idea of the threat, in the first place.

'Yeah.' Roxy bit her lip. 'I wish we hadn't had to resort to it.'

'You tried the nice way first. You're not a natural bully.' Jess grinned. 'Though I can see you as a dominatrix, in shiny black thigh-boots and a black leather basque.'

'Balls,' Roxy said, pulling a face at her friend.

'Rox – do you think he'll deliver the message?'

Roxy shrugged. 'We'll soon find out. But I trust him, Jess. He looks more likely to help us than the others – that's why we picked him, remember?'

'Mm – and because you wanted to get your hands in his knickers,' Jess teased.

'And so did you – didn't you?'

'Yes,' Jess said honestly. 'And I quite fancy that little scenario he outlined. Reading that sort of scene would always make me horny – and if I was writing it, it was even worse. I'd end up spending as much time masturbating as I did writing.'

Roxy grinned. 'You would!'

'Well.' Jess shrugged. 'If he delivers that message for us, I'm more than happy to live out his fantasy.'

'Yeah. I know.' Roxy smiled at her. 'And in a week, we'll be out of here.' What she left unsaid, they both knew: then, Roxy would start to plan her revenge on Tim.

For the next three days, Roxy was very quiet. She'd had no word from Alice. But she'd been so sure that Alice would read the message and know it was from her. Unless . . . Her stomach clenched. Unless Alice's e-mail ID had been changed. For all she knew, the Traditional Values party could have reallocated everyone's ID, changed all the phone numbers. They could even have changed people's addresses, moving them from houses they considered unsuitable for their needs.

'Don't worry,' Jess said, squeezing Roxy's hand. 'Maybe he just hasn't had a chance to send the e-mail, yet. He's probably waiting until it's safe.'

'Yes. Probably.' Roxy clung onto the hope. It was the only thing that kept her going through her daily drudgery. She hadn't done any housework since she'd moved in with Tim

– in fact, even before then. When she'd shared the flat with Alice, they'd paid a woman down the road to come and do the bulk of the hoovering a couple of times a week. She and Tim had paid someone to do their ironing, too, on the premise that they both worked full-time, their jobs were demanding, and they'd rather spend their free time together than doing housework.

Roxy had forgotten how incredibly mind-numbing hoovering could be – particularly with an ancient vacuum-cleaner which didn't work very well – and dusting. And then, to be used for the Minister of Publicity's pleasure ... Somehow, she managed to keep her face an impassive mask while he was using her, so he couldn't see her revulsion. And as for him being able to think that she had any pleasure from their coupling: how could she, when he didn't bother arousing her and didn't bother stimulating her to orgasm?

So she kept her mind blank, whenever his body pushed into hers. All she could focus on was the message, and her hope that Alice and Marcus would rescue her. Then, finally, she'd be free to face Tim. And then ... then, at last, he'd pay for his betrayal.

Marcus raised his eyebrows as he saw the message on Alice's mailbox. 'This is odd,' he said. 'Very odd.'

'What?' Alice came over to where her husband was working, rested her arms on his shoulder, and looked at the screen. 'Bored with housework?' she read. 'Looking for the woman of your dreams? Then call me.' There was a phone number there, one she didn't recognize. Her eyes narrowed. 'Marcus – this is from Roxy.'

'Roxy? But she's dead! They took her away, remember? Tim told us, they killed her because she resisted arrest, and because they'd found her files. Remember what a state he was in when he called us? She's dead, Alice. You have to face it.'

'She isn't, Marcus.' Alice shook her head. 'This is definitely Roxy. No one else would send this message to me.'

He frowned. 'I don't understand.'

'Remember when I first met you? Tim told you that I'd e-mailed him from Roxy's ID, saying that if he was looking for the woman of his dreams, he should contact Roxana Winters. This is her way of reminding me, Marcus – only Roxy would know that, and send a message like it to me. And she needs us.'

'If it's really her, then where the hell is she? And why did Tim say that she was dead?'

'I don't know,' Alice said, 'but there's one way to find out. I'm ringing this number.' She picked up the phone – like Roxy and Tim, Marcus and Alice used a separate phone line for his PC – and dialled swiftly. She waited as the phone rang: once, twice, three times. Then, at last, it was picked up.

'Hello?' she asked.

'Who is this?'

The clipped tones sounded, Alice thought, like they belonged to someone in the Traditional Values party. 'Mrs Marcus Blake,' she said, using their preferred form of address.

'And what will you be requiring from us?'

'The usual,' she said quietly. 'A woman.'

'For housework, or extras?'

Alice was shocked. It sounded almost like one of the old-style massage parlours. What kind of place was it? 'I . . . Housework,' she said, remembering Roxy's message. *Bored with housework? Looking for the woman of your dreams?*

'Do you require any particular offender?'

Offender? Alice frowned. *What the hell was this place*? 'Someone,' she said slowly, 'with an upper-class name.'

'A good choice, Mrs Marcus Blake. Someone who needs humbling. I think we have just the person for you.'

'Her name?'

'Justina Merton.'

'No. I want something . . . more unusual.'

There was a cough. 'There is one . . . but the Minister of Publicity usually has her. Though I believe she's free tomorrow, because he has an all-day meeting.'

'Her name?' Alice asked again.

'Roxana Winters.'

'That will do nicely,' Alice said. 'You have the address?'

There was a soft laugh. 'But of course, Mrs Marcus Blake. Your husband worked on the prototype of the National Database, didn't he?'

'Yes.' Alice swallowed. 'Tomorrow, at ten. Don't send her late.'

She cut the receiver and looked at Marcus, tears welling in her eyes. 'It's her. She's there.'

'Where?' Marcus asked.

'I don't know. I think it's some kind of prison – they talked about offenders, people who needed humbling. They asked me if we wanted any extras . . .' Her voice faded. 'God, Marcus, I hate to think what she's been through.'

'It's all right.' He took her into her arms. 'Once she's with us, she'll be safe. For the day, at least. And when we've talked to her, found out what's going on, we can make plans to rescue her properly.'

'What about Tim? Shouldn't we tell him that she's all right?'

Marcus looked thoughtful. 'I don't know, Alice. I mean, I

know he's – *was*,' he corrected himself swiftly, 'my best friend, but he's the Head of National Security.'

'You're employed by the Party, too,' Alice reminded him.

'Even so. I think, for the time being, we should say nothing – until we've heard Roxy's side of the story.'

'You mean, Tim might have known all along?' Alice was outraged.

'Don't jump to conclusions.' He squeezed her hand. 'I'm just saying, I think we should tread very carefully, until we know more about what's happened.'

'Yeah, you're right.' Alice bit her lip. 'We'll play it your way.'

'Don't worry,' Marcus said. 'If there's a way to get her out, we will.'

'And if there isn't?'

'Then we'll find one.'

ELEVEN

That evening was Philip's evening for duty, unless the Governor of the House of Correction had suddenly decided to change the duty roster: though Roxy didn't think that he would. The Traditional Values party officials liked order. They liked people and things to be in defined places, at defined times.

Jess and Roxy were playing cards, with a pack that Jess had managed to steal from the man who usually ordered her. A key rattled in the lock and Jess hurriedly shoved the cards under her pillow, just in case it wasn't Philip.

To their relief, it was; he entered the room bearing a tray of food, and closed the door behind him.

She smiled at him. 'Hello, Philip.'

'Hello, Roxy,' He smiled back at her.

'Did you – um – did you manage to do it?' Roxy asked.

He nodded. 'I'm sorry I haven't told you before. It took me a while; I had to wait until it was safe to do it. I don't usually have access to the system, you see.'

'But you did send it?'

'Yes. And I wiped it from the screen, afterwards, so it can't be traced.'

'Good.' Roxy smiled at him. 'Thank you.'

His face betrayed his longing; Roxy and Jess exchanged a meaningful glance, and then Jess stood up, walked over to Philip, and cupped his face in her hands. She kissed him very lightly on the mouth; his mouth opened in surprise, and she slid her tongue between his lips, exploring his mouth more deeply.

He reacted immediately by sliding his hands round her waist, smoothing them down over her buttocks. Slowly, Jess began to undress him, unbuttoning his uniform.

'I can't do this.' He pulled away.

'What's wrong?' she asked, surprised. 'I thought you wanted to?'

'I do. But not right now,' he said, his voice softening. 'I'm supposed to deliver more meals.'

'Later, then,' Jess suggested. 'When you come to pick up the tray – or whenever would suit you better. I think you deserve your reward, for helping us.'

'Later,' he agreed. He kissed her lingeringly, then tore himself away.

Roxy had brightened at the news that he'd sent her message, and ate her meal almost cheerfully.

'Alice will definitely know that it's you?' Jess asked.

'Yes.' Roxy grinned. 'She's been my best friend for over fifteen years, Jess. We were at university together, and we shared a flat for ten years. She'll know it's me. The phone number, or maybe the e-mail ID, will help her find me. That's why . . .' She swallowed. 'That's why I sent the message I did. If it's intercepted, no one else who reads it will think that it's anything important; but she'll know it's me, and she'll know that I want her to contact me. As long as Philip typed in the right phone number, she'll ring this place, and she'll get me out of here.' She smiled at Jess. 'And you and Giselle, too. I don't know how she'll do it, but she will. Alice is *very* resourceful.'

'Oh, yes?'

Roxy grinned. 'Just ask Giselle. I think that their profession attracts a particular kind of person – and, believe me, Alice is one of the best.'

Later that evening, Philip came to collect their tray. He locked the door from the inside. 'Just a precaution,' he said.

'In case one of us knocks you out, and we run away?' Jess teased.

He shook his head. 'Just in case one of the other guards tries the door. I don't want any of them walking in on us. I'm not even supposed to talk to you, let alone do anything else with you.'

'Right.' Roxy tipped her head on one side. 'Tell me, Philip, are you the only one of the guards who isn't happy with the way things are?'

He wrinkled his nose. 'Yes and no. We're not unhappy with *everything*. I mean, it's good to have a job, and feel that I'm being useful instead of a parasite on society. There were a lot of things wrong with the old days.'

'Such as?'

'All the political correctness. It had all gone way too far. You couldn't even compliment a woman without her thinking that you were trying to come on to her; then she'd complain about you, and I've been thrown out of God knows how many libraries just because I was trying to be friendly to one of the women in the reading room.'

'Friendly, or familiar?' Jess asked.

'If I told you that I liked your hair, what would you say?' Philip asked.

'Thank you,' Jess said.

'Exactly. And you, Roxy, if I said that I was studying the same subject that you were, and would you like to discuss some topic or other over a cup of coffee, would you think that I was trying to chat you up?'

Roxy wrinkled her nose. 'It depends on how you asked me. If you suggested something obscure, something that only someone who really *was* studying it would know, then no, I would think that you were on the level.'

'Exactly.' Philip rolled his eyes. 'It had all gone too far. God, I'm not the sort of guy who'd leap on a woman without knowing her better and knowing that she wanted me, too.'

Jess grinned. 'We know.'

He flushed, realizing what she meant. He'd been shy with them, not taking their caresses as his right. 'Well. It was crazy. And as for homosexuality – don't get me wrong, I had friends who were gay, and I'm not a homophobe. but it just annoyed me how they went on and on and on about how important their sexuality was. I mean, it really doesn't matter whether you prefer the same sex or the opposite sex, or even both at the same time: it's what you are as a person that counts. I was sick of the way that people used their gender or their sexuality or their religion or their colour as an excuse if they didn't achieve what they wanted. If they didn't get a job, or they had a low grade in an assignment, they said that it was because someone was prejudiced against them, not because they weren't the best one for the job or they'd written a crap essay.'

'That's true,' Jess agreed. 'It was getting to the point where merit didn't matter – it was who you were rather than what you could do.'

'But now it's gone too far the other way. There has to be something in between,' Philip said. 'Why can't people just be nice to each other, and treat each other with respect?'

Roxy chuckled. 'How old are you, Philip? Nineteen? Twenty?'

He lifted his chin, nettled. 'Twenty-two, actually.'

She smiled at him. 'When I was your age, I was just as idealistic as you are. I wanted people to be nice to each other, too. I believed that everyone could be happy.'

'And now you don't?'

Roxy shrugged. 'I just haven't seen it, so far. But when I get out of here, I'll work on it. Because, like you, I think that there has to be something in between, a middle ground where people can be happy.'

'That message you sent,' Philip said. 'What's going to happen now? Are you planning some kind of riot?'

'Hardly.' Jess chuckled. 'Women have no power, remember.'

'What, then?'

'Well, you said that people order us.'

'Ye-es.'

'The person you sent it to will realize that it's from me, and she'll ring this place to order me, or e-mail you – whatever it takes to order someone. And she'll get me out of here.'

'That's the other thing.' Philip swallowed. 'The Party motto is "Sex is for procreation, not recreation".'

Roxy's eyes narrowed. 'The people who order us ... are they planning to impregnate us, use us as brood mares?'

'I don't think so,' Philip said. 'But the laws have changed again, recently. You're only allowed to make love on a woman's most fertile days.'

Roxy didn't know whether to laugh or scream. 'That's incredible,' she said finally. 'But what about the rules? I thought that you could only have one child.'

'Unless you can afford to have more. It's means-tested.' Philip shrugged. 'And people like me ... I can't marry until I'm twenty-five. I can't have sex outside marriage. And I can't choose my bride; the Party will do that for me.'

'*What?* Arranged marriages?' Jess asked. 'How do you mean – creating political dynasties, or something?'

'Not exactly. It's more to do with genetics.'

'My God,' Roxy said. 'It's the sort of thing that Hitler did, before the Second World War.'

'I suppose so.' Philip looked slightly gloomy. 'Before they took over, life – well, if you could blank off the fact that you felt useless without a job, life was okay. You could at least enjoy things. Now, it seems that everything people enjoy suddenly becomes illegal. There are rules and regulations for everything, new ones springing up every day.'

'Mm.' Roxy looked thoughtful. 'If you're only allowed to have sex within marriage, just for creating a baby ... how the hell can they stop people doing things on other days?'

'Random tests,' Philip said succinctly.

Jess and Roxy immediately knew what he meant, and pulled a face. 'That's terrible.'

'I know.' He grimaced. 'No doubt they'll pass a law against masturbation soon, too.'

'It sounds like they're trying to stamp out sex completely,' Jess said. 'Which is crazy.'

'You're telling me.' He looked at her. 'I accessed your record, the other day. You're Dana Roswell, aren't you?'

Jess nodded. 'And Elvira Barrie, and a couple of others.'

'I read one of your books, in the old days. Well, my girlfriend read it to me, in bed. ' He flushed. 'I enjoyed it.'

Jess grinned. 'Thanks.'

'I wondered what you'd be like – what sort of woman would have the imagination to write that sort of thing. I thought you'd be tall, with long dark curly hair, and a beautiful mouth painted crimson. Dark sensual eyes that could turn you on with a glance. Oh, and long nails with either black or bright crimson varnish. And lots of jewellery – silver and lapis lazuli and amber.'

'Nearly right,' Roxy teased. 'Though she's not a bottle redhead.'

Philip's lips curved. 'Yeah. I know that.'

'When we get out of here,' Jess said, 'I'll dedicate my next book to you.'

'Really?' His face lit up; then he remembered where they were, and sobered again. 'It's a nice thought, anyway.'

'I have lots of nice thoughts,' Jess said. 'And that little scenario you outlined for me, last time you saw us ... It's definitely something that I would use.'

Philip's breathing suddenly became very shallow. 'In real life?' he asked, 'or in a book?'

'Both,' Jess told him.

He coloured then, and she grinned. 'Now, where were we?' she asked, her voice becoming husky. She walked over to him and slid her hands round his neck, drawing his mouth down to hers. As he kissed her back, she slowly began to undo his uniform. Layer by layer, she removed his clothes, and helped him with the ungainly black garments she wore. His breath hissed through his teeth as Jess's body was revealed, her breasts still generous and inviting, the nipples almost plum-coloured against her creamy skin.

He pulled her back into his arms, kissing her deeply and sliding his hands down her back, kneading her buttocks and delighting in the forbidden feel of her flesh against his fingertips. He pulled back, gasping, and looked at Roxy.

Jess held out one hand, and Roxy walked towards them, taking Jess's hands. Very slowly, Phil and Jess undressed Roxy, discarding her hated black clothes and unglamorous underwear.

'I believe,' Jess said slowly, 'you wanted to feel your cock sheathed in Roxy's cunt. You wanted to bury your cock in her, you said.'

He swallowed, his penis twitching with excitement at the suggestion.

'And that you wanted to watch Roxy lick me,' Jess continued.

'Yes.' His voice cracked in a mixture of desire, excitement and disbelief.

'Then walk this way, my sweet,' she coaxed, drawing him over to the bed and pushing the covers to one side.

He lay on the bed, stretched out. His body was good, firm and well-toned. If, as Roxy suspected, he'd been a student before he'd become a guard, it looked like he'd spent nearly as much time in the gym as he had in the library. He'd kept up the work, too. His body was good; and although his cock wasn't like Tim's, it was very nice indeed. And the best thing, it was going to be used in desire, for mutual pleasure between them – not like her humiliating sessions with Reeve, when she felt that Reeve was making a statement about his power rather than anything else.

She felt her quim moisten at the thought of Philip making love with her – making love, rather than having sex. She was about to climb astride him, when Philip shook his head. 'No,' he said softly. 'I want to look at you, first, Roxy. I want to see you.'

She stood next to the bed, and he stroked her thigh, gently drawing her towards him. She lifted her leg, bent her knee, and put one foot flat on the bed. He twisted, so that he could look into her quim. With one hand, he spread her labia; with the fingertips of the other, he traced her intimate folds and crevices, exploring her and knowing her. By the time he'd finished, Roxy was shivering, her channel moist and ready to receive him.

He grinned, and pushed one finger deep inside her. She gasped, not expecting it, and he smiled, withdrawing his finger again. His flesh glistened faintly with her arousal; keeping his eyes locked on hers, he drew his hand up to his mouth and licked every scrap of nectar from his finger. 'Mm,' he said. 'Do you know how good you taste, Roxy? Almost as good as I think you're going to feel, when your cunt's wrapped round me ...' At that, he pulled her astride him properly.

Roxy lifted herself slightly; he curled his hand round hers, and manoeuvred his cock so that its tip fitted against the entrance of her sex. Very slowly, she sank down on him, enjoying the feel of his penetration, millimetre by millimetre. She gave a small moan of pleasure when he was in her, up to the hilt; he felt so good. Rather than just abusing her body, like Reeve did, Philip cared enough to make sure that she was aroused first.

'God, that's good,' he breathed, his voice husky with desire. 'Your cunt's so beautiful, Roxy, the way it clings to me.' He looked at Jess. 'And I want you, too,' he added. 'I want to touch you, I want to taste you, and I want to watch Roxy tasting you, as well.'

She smiled. 'I thought you'd never ask,' she teased, and knelt on the bed by his shoulders.

He spread her legs a little more widely, so that he could look at her properly; then he sighed in satisfaction. 'That's what I've missed,' he said softly. 'The scent of an aroused woman. The way she feels, the way her flesh changes as she grows more aroused, all soft and slippery,'

A thrill of delight slid down Jess's spine at his words. He smiled, and repeated the action he'd started on Roxy, spreading

Jess's labia apart and exploring her with his hands and his eyes. Then he raised his head from the pillow, stretched out his tongue, and drew it along her quim. Jess gave a small moan and lifted her hands to touch her breasts, cupping them and pinching her nipples.

Roxy was spellbound as she watched her friend and her new lover: the scene in front of her was incredible. Then Philip undulated his hips, and she began to move over him, leaning back slightly to change the angle of his penetration and give them both the most pleasure. She touched her breasts, stroking the soft undersides and pulling gently at her nipples; and she began to use her internal muscles to squeeze his cock as she lifted up, before relaxing again as she slammed back down on him.

He brought Jess to a swift, sharp orgasm on his tongue, then looked at Roxy. 'Remember what I wanted to do?' he asked softly.

'Yes.' Her voice was as husky as his.

'Tell me,' he invited. 'I want to hear you say it.'

And he wanted her to want to do it, too: that much was obvious. Sudden affection softened Roxy's gaze. 'You said,' she informed him, 'that you wanted to see me work on Jess's clitoris with my mouth, while you had your tongue deep inside her.'

'And?'

She grinned. 'I want to do it, too.'

'Sounds good to me, as well,' Jess added.

'Mm. Though I didn't say just *where* my tongue was going to be,' he reminded them.

Jess stiffened, amazed. If he was suggesting what she *thought* he was suggesting . . . He was obviously more sophisticated than she'd credited.

He smiled, tipping his head back and looking at Roxy. 'I want you to kiss me first, Roxy. I want you to taste Jess on my mouth.'

She bent forward; his mouth was shiny with the proof of Jess's climax at the way he'd worked on her, and Roxy outlined his lips with her tongue, licking up every scrap of the aromatic salt-sweet juices. Gently, Philip lifted his hands to adjust Jess over him. Roxy, too, adjusted her position, using only her internal muscles to massage Philip's cock, and bending so that she could reach Jess's quim. She stretched out her tongue, finding Jess's clitoris almost instantly, and began to tease the hard nub of flesh, flickering her tongue over it in a figure-of-eight pattern that had Jess writhing over her.

Jess thought that she could hardly stand it when she felt Philip insert one finger into her quim, then another: and then, finally, she felt his tongue pressing against the puckered rosy hole of her anus – a delightful pressure that was at once hard and soft, and made desire flutter in her stomach.

As Philip and Roxy used their mouths and hands on Jess to bring her to yet another climax, Philip began to pump his hips rapidly. Roxy felt the pressure of her orgasm grow – then, suddenly, she felt the familiar inner sparkling. Her muscles convulsed wildly round the thick hard rod of his cock; at the same instant, she felt his cock throb deep inside her, and Jess's internal muscles convulsed too, rippling round Philip's fingers. Roxy could feel the reverberations against her mouth.

When their breathing had slowed down, Jess climbed off the bed, as did Roxy. 'If this was a double bed,' Jess said, 'we could have curled up together, gone to sleep for a while, and then . . .' She smiled ruefully. 'These single beds are barely big enough for one, let alone three.'

Philip sat up, and stroked her face, kissing her lightly on

the lips. 'One day,' he promised softly, 'one day, we'll do that. And I'll have the pleasure of making love with you both, all night long . . .'

The next morning, the guards came as usual to take Roxy from the cell. They still blindfolded her, although gradually she'd got some idea of where they were going. Somewhere in the west of the city, she was sure. From what she'd seen of the Minister of Publicity's house, it was somewhere like Holland Park – somewhere in the borough of Kensington and Chelsea, anyway.

But today – today, she had the feeling that they were going in another direction. Either Reeve had two homes, she thought in disgust, or . . . she was being taken somewhere else. Her stomach clenched. The opposite direction to usual meant that they were going east. Maybe to East 17 . . . *Oh God, please*, she thought, *let it be Walthamstow*. She said nothing to the guards, not wanting her hopes to be dashed too quickly: she couldn't bear learning that way that she wasn't going to Alice's, that she was going to some other place to drudge for Reeve.

Eventually the car stopped, and the guards helped her out. This house didn't have steps, she discovered. She stumbled over a loose paving stone; memories flickered in her mind. She'd done this before. If she was right, this was a very, very familiar path. It had worked. The message had worked! She strove to keep the sudden joy from her face – at least her experiences with Reeve had taught her how to mask her emotions – and then the blindfold was removed. She looked straight into Alice's face.

'Thank you,' Alice said dismissively to the guards. 'This one will do. Pick her up at the usual time; and make sure you're not late. I don't want to be bothered with her in the evening.'

They waited until the front door had closed behind the guards, and then embraced joyfully.

'My God – Alice, it's really you.'

'It's me,' Alice confirmed, stroking her hair. 'It's me, it's me.'

Roxy was overcome with relief and joy; she simply hugged her friend and let the tears stream unchecked down her face. Alice, too, was crying; they remained locked together for a while, and then Alice pulled back, holding Roxy at arm's length and staring at her.

'What the hell have they been doing to you, Rox?' she asked.

'They've fed me well, before you start worrying about bread and water,' Roxy said. 'It's healthier food than I've lived on for years! And I'm doing regular exercise now.' She sighed. 'God, Al, you don't know how good it is to know that I'm free, even for a couple of hours – and that I don't have to be where I thought I'd be today.'

'Coffee,' Alice said decisively. 'With chocolate hob-nobs. And you can tell me everything that's happened – everything.'

Roxy followed her into the kitchen, leaning against the worktops. Everything around her was so familiar, it almost hurt. It was so good to be back. Even if it was only a temporary respite, it was good to be back.

Alice made proper coffee. 'If you've been given healthy food, it's a fair bet that you've had no coffee, and I don't think that your system could take instant stuff,' she said.

'What an excuse,' Roxy teased. 'Blue Mountain, is it?'

'Yep.'

'Black market?'

'No – coffee hasn't been banned yet.'

'You look well, Al. I bet Marcus does, too, and Eleanor.'

'She's asleep, but I'm sure that she'll be pleased to see her godmother later,' Alice said. 'And, yeah, Marcus looks all right. He's aged a bit, but he works ridiculous hours.'

'He always did.'

'Worse than that,' Alice said with a sigh. 'In the old days, at least he had a bit of choice about it.' Her face twisted. 'He's quite a high-ranking science official now. I hate the whole system, and so does he, but we have to put up with it.'

'For Eleanor's sake,' Roxy guessed.

'Yes.' She swallowed as she ushered Roxy through to the sitting room. 'I've missed you so much, Rox. I thought that you were dead.'

'Dead? Why?' Roxy asked, very quietly.

Alice's eyes widened. 'You tell me what's happened to you, and I'll tell you what's been happening here.' She shoved the tin of biscuits at Roxy. 'Here.'

Roxy took one gratefully. 'Chocolate. I can't remember the last time I had chocolate.'

'It'll probably bring you out in spots,' Alice said with a grin.

'Yeah. So Marcus is at work?' Roxy asked.

'Yes. But he'll be back later.'

'And it's safe to tell you?'

Alice's eyes widened in hurt. 'Rox, I'm your best friend. How can you ask that?'

'I don't mean if it's safe to tell *you*,' Roxy said. 'I'd trust you with my life. I mean, are you sure that there aren't any bugs around here? I don't want you and Marcus to end up in trouble because of me.'

'No, we're fine.' Alice took her hand and squeezed it. 'So tell me. What happened?'

Roxy launched into the story of how she'd been taken to the House of Correction, how she'd shared a room with Jess and spoken to Giselle, next door, through the air-vent. How she and

Jess had seduced Philip into helping them. And, glossing over the more sordid details, what had happened with the Minister for Publicity.

'That's appalling!' Alice said, when her friend had finished. 'I had no idea that this sort of thing was going on.'

'It'd be a great piece of investigative journalism,' Roxy said wryly. 'Giselle would have had a field day on that. I don't think you and Giselle know each other, do you?'

Alice shook her head. 'You tend to know people in the group of magazines or newspapers where you work, people in the same sort of market, and that's about all.'

'You'd like her,' Roxy said. 'And you'd love Jess. I can't wait for the two of you to meet.' Her face sobered. 'So, tell me what happened to you.'

'Not a lot, really,' Alice said. 'I was waiting for you to come over. I thought you might be an hour, at most; I gave it three, and then I thought that something might be wrong. I tried ringing you, but your phone was disconnected. So I rang Tim.'

'Yes, Tim.' Roxy was careful to keep her face impassive. She hated Tim now, as much as she'd loved him – and she wouldn't rest until she'd had her revenge.

'Well, he was okay. He said he'd wanted to go home and make sure you were all right, but you'd told him not to. When I told him that your phone was disconnected, he went straight round to the house.' She swallowed. 'He rang me from his mobile. He said that the front door had been bashed in, and they'd taken you.' She rubbed a hand over her face. 'He rang the police to find out what had been going on. They told him that you'd resisted arrest, and that you were dead.'

'And that's it? He didn't even try to press further, check that they were telling him the truth?'

'No. He believed them. You see, Rox, we know you. We

know how you feel about freedom and justice. You've always been so passionate about them. There was blood all over the place. And . . .' Alice squeezed her eyes shut. 'Several of my friends from work *were* killed. There wasn't a funeral, either, so I couldn't even pay my last respects to them.'

'Maybe they're still alive, too,' Roxy said. 'Maybe they were put in the same sort of place that I was.'

'I – I just don't know what to think.' Alice was near to tears. 'I mourned you, Roxy. I missed you so much.'

'You did, yes.'

Alice ignored the bitterness in Roxy's voice. 'And then we had this e-mail, and I realized that you were alive – that they'd been lying to us all along. From that, it was easy. I just rang the number.' Her eyes narrowed. 'I thought there was something funny going on, when they asked me if I wanted extras.'

Roxy laughed, despite her anger. 'It sounds like something from a sleazy massage parlour!'

'That's what I thought.' Alice winced. 'If it wasn't you, and it was someone I didn't know, I'd think it was funny, in a sick sort of way.'

'Tell me about it,' Roxy said drily. 'You never know. One day, we'll look back on this and laugh.'

'In the meantime, though,' Alice said, 'we need to make a plan. There has to be a way of getting you out of that place, for good. Now I know you're there, I'll order you every day, so at least you won't have to go back to Reeve.'

'Do you know Reeve?' Roxy asked.

Alice shook her head. 'I don't have any contact with the Party officials. I'm a mere woman, remember.'

'And I can imagine how much that must please you.' Alice had been a strident feminist, more vocal than Roxy, when they'd been in their early twenties.

'I'm just biding my time,' Alice said lightly. 'One day, all this will be over. I'm sure we can change it, if we work on the inside – provided we get a high enough position in the Party.'

'We already know someone who's high up in the Party,' Roxy reminded her.

'How do you mean?'

'Tim. He's the Head of National Security, so Giselle tells me.'

'Yes. Tim.' Alice sighed. 'I think they must have drugged him, or brainwashed him, or something. He's not the same, Roxy. He's hardly said a word to us. After they told him that you were dead, that was it. He believed it, and he seemed to shut off – he's barely seen us since then.'

'Do you have access to the computer?' Roxy asked.

Alice shook her head. 'Only Marcus can do that. They've changed the security system; we don't use passwords now. It's done through some genetic thing, and only Marcus can get into the system.'

'I don't want to get Marcus into trouble,' Roxy said, 'but there must be some way of accessing that computer. I'll hack into it, somehow.'

'Wait until Marcus comes home,' Alice said. 'He can tell you more about how the security system works, and then you'll have a better base to work out what to do next.'

'Mm. Good idea.'

Alice smiled, shaking her head. 'I still can't believe that it's you, Rox. I mean, for the past few months, I thought you were—'

'Still me,' Roxy said with a grin. 'Just a little thinner and a little fitter. Jess has been persuading me to do floor exercises every day.'

'I suppose at least one bit of good has come out of this, then.'

'Trust you to look at it that way!' Roxy laughed. 'Well, we're here now. At least I'm not at Reeve's place.'

'So what did he make you do?'

'Apart from scrub his kitchen floor with a toothbrush, endless dusting – which I detest – and ironing? He checked every single item, to make sure I'd ironed it the way he wanted. God, if I could access some poison that worked in contact with the skin, I'd iron it into his bloody shirts,' Roxy said. 'He always found some excuse to get me on my knees, scrubbing. Then he used to—' She shrugged. 'Have me for his pleasure, you might say.'

'After Tim, that must have been hell.'

'Well, Tim, if he'd bothered to look a bit further, could have found out exactly where I was. He's Head of National Security. He must know what's going on in the House of Correction. He must know who's in there. The fact that he hasn't sprung me,' Roxy said, 'means that he didn't want to. And when he and I meet again . . . There'll be a reckoning. He has a hell of a lot of apologies to make.' Her eyes glittered. 'I swear, I'll be even for his betrayal.'

'You don't know that he's betrayed you, Rox,' Alice said. 'Like I told you, Tim's changed. I'm sure they must have done something to him.'

'I don't think so,' Roxy said. 'Tim could be very single-minded, when it suited him.'

'Give the guy a chance. I'll set up some kind of meeting, so you can talk.'

'Give him a *chance*?' Roxy shook her head. 'No way. Leave this to me, Alice – I don't want you going soft on me. He's going to pay for what he's done.' Her mouth twisted. 'And I'm the one who's going to make him pay.'

TWELVE

Later that afternoon, when Marcus came home, he was delighted to see Roxy. He hugged her, kissed her, and hugged her again. 'I'm so glad you're here,' he said.

'Mm. Al said you thought I was dead.' Roxy wrinkled her nose. 'Who was it who said, "The report of my death has been an exaggeration"?'

'I think it was Mark Twain,' Alice said.

'Whoever. It's true for me, too. Here I am.' She spread her hands. 'Marcus, I'll need your help, please.' She updated him on what had happened to her, Jess and Giselle at the House of Correction, and his face darkened.

'That's appalling. There's no way you should be subjected to that – any of you.'

'I need to spring us from that place,' Roxy said. 'I need to get Giselle, Jess and me out of there. I need new identities for all of us – and, more importantly, I need access to a good PC and a modem.'

'What are you planning, Rox?' he asked.

'I've been thinking about it, all the time I've been there. If I can hack into the central computer and delete my record, and put in a new one for my new identity, I can work without any problems.'

'Women can't work,' Marcus reminded her. 'And you won't be able to hack.'

'No?' Roxy was quick to rise to the slur on her abilities.

'If anyone could do it, Rox, I'd put you at the head of the list,' Marcus said, seeing the anger in her face. 'I wasn't saying that you're not good enough. I'm saying that there are so many security layers, it'll be a real minefield.'

'Tim built it. I know the way he works.'

'So do I. I was his partner at work, remember.' Marcus sighed. 'There are a hell of a lot of genetics-based fields that work on recognizing your DNA patterns.'

'In that case,' Roxy said, 'we have two options. I need some way of getting to the people who put codes into the database and persuading them to change mine – or to delete it and give me a completely new identity. A male one. I'll be a man who has enough power to change things.' She tipped her head on one side. 'Which means I'll exchange Tim's record for mine.'

'There's more to it than that,' Marcus said. 'We'll have to give you a female identity, Rox. You'll pass various checkpoints, and they'll verify that you're a woman. If we give you a male identity, they'll realize that something's wrong, and you'll be caught before you can even start to do something.'

'What sort of checkpoints?' Roxy asked.

'There are guards at certain points. When you go into shops, or if you go to a museum or a library, you have to put your hand against a sensor pad. It reads your genetic codes, and the guards verify that the record on the screen matches the person in front of them.'

'Right. Then what we need,' Roxy said, 'is to change my genetic code. Could we put some kind of implant in my finger, to polarize the codes?'

Alice groaned. 'You two are talking Anorakese. I'll fix us something to eat and leave you to it.' She glanced at her watch. 'I'd better phone the House of Correction to get you ordered here for tomorrow.'

'Won't they think something's up,' Roxy asked, 'if you order me every day?'

'Well, Reeve did.'

'He's the Minister of Publicity,' Roxy reminded her gently. 'He has the position to demand that sort of thing.' She sighed. 'We don't want to draw attention to this. Make it twice a week – Tuesdays and Fridays.'

'That means you'll have to go to Reeve for the rest of the time.' Alice was shocked.

'But it means that he won't suspect anything.' Roxy smiled. 'I'm a lot nearer to getting what I need now – so I can put up with him.'

'If you're sure.'

'I'm sure.'

Alice nodded. 'Okay. I'll play it your way.'

'It's a sensible precaution,' Marcus agreed. 'Even though it sickens me to think of it, Roxy's absolutely right.'

While Alice sorted out dinner, Marcus and Roxy began to work out their plan. Marcus would develop a kind of finger-sleeve, which would mask her real data and allow them to put in the new data without making anyone suspicious. At work, Marcus would put in a requisition form, to add her new data to the computer. He'd have it authorized by four other people, within a batch of real requisition forms.

Roxy would secrete the finger-sleeve in her mouth, and the next time she went to Reeve she'd break out of the house, somehow, and put the sleeve on her finger. Alice would be waiting outside Reeve's house in the car, and would take Roxy home.

When Alice came in, Roxy and Marcus were smiling. 'We've cracked it,' Marcus said, and told her of the plans. 'It'll take us a couple of weeks. But we'll do it. And when

Roxy's out, we can spring Jess and Giselle in the same way.'

'Sounds good to me,' Alice said. 'But if you have a new identity, Rox, you'll need to look different.'

'How do you mean?'

'We'll change the colour and cut of your hair. We'll get you coloured contact lenses – I'll forge an optician's form, and then go to a different place to get the lenses. When he checks my records on screen, and says that they're different from normal, I'll explain that I want to surprise my husband. If need be, I'll seduce him into doing it. Violet-blue lenses, I think,' Alice said. 'Then we'll give you a crop – and dye your hair black.'

'Oh, great. I'm going to look like a Goth or a Punk,' Roxy said.

Alice grinned. 'You'll be fine. Make sure you wear make-up, and we'll tell everyone you used to be an actress. Then everyone will expect luvvie-like behaviour from you.'

'Better than that,' Marcus added. 'We'll say that you're my cousin, and you're coming to live with us. We're an approved household.'

'Sounds brilliant,' Roxy said. 'Then I'll hack the computer, and have myself sent to Tim.'

'You can't do that, Roxy.'

'Yes, I can. It's easier than breaking into his house – at least, when he looks at his mailbox he'll see a legitimate order for me. The guards will let me in without any hassle. And I'll be there, waiting for him.' She smiled.

'Roxy, he's changed,' Marcus warned her. 'He's not the Tim we knew. He doesn't have anything to do with me nowadays – and we shared a house for years, worked on the same projects. He's become hard, Roxy. Don't expect too much. He's one of Ferris's right-hand men.'

'He used to oppose everything that Ferris stood for,' Roxy said. 'He believed in freedom, he believed in equality. And I mean true equality, not the politically correct kind: true equality, when you recognize that men and women are different but have equal rights.'

'Roxy, don't do anything rash,' Marcus said.

'Me?' Roxy opened her eyes wide. 'When have you known me to do anything rash?' She smiled wryly. 'I won't do anything that would harm Alice, you or Eleanor. You know that.'

'Yeah. Sorry. I should never have said it, in the first place.'

'It's okay. In your position, I'd do the same,' Roxy said. 'The thought of seeing Tim again, and getting even with him – it's the only thing that's kept me going in the House of Correction. And when we meet again . . .' She smiled, although there was nothing soft or kind in her smile. 'You're right, Alice. I need to look completely different, so he doesn't recognize me – until it's too late.'

Somehow, when the guards came to pick her up, Roxy managed to give the impression that she was sulky and tired of her work as a drudge – much the way that she really felt when she came back from Reeve's house.

When they closed the door of her room behind her, it was another matter. She beamed and Jess, and hugged her.

'So how did it go?' Jess asked.

'Absolutely brilliantly. I don't know how Alice and I managed to pretend, in front of the guards – but it was really her, and she and Marcus and Eleanor are fine.'

'When are you escaping?'

Roxy winced. 'It's going to take a few weeks. The thing is, all the systems have changed. There are all these elaborate security procedures. Marcus and I are going to develop something that's going to help me through them; then we're going to change my name, my identity, the way I look – everything. And then,' she said, 'we'll spring you and Giselle.'

'What about Philip?' Jess asked softly.

'I've been thinking about that. If there's some way that I can change his records, too – give him a promotion, a better life, to say thanks for what he did for us – then I'll do it. But it's not all going to happen at once,' she warned.

'Message received loud and clear,' Jess said wryly. 'So your friends haven't changed, then?'

'Not at all.' Roxy's eyes sparkled with unshed tears. 'It wasn't until I saw them again that I realized how much I missed them. My best friend, her husband, my god-daughter.'

Jess took her hand, squeezing it. 'I hate to ask this, but – what about Tim?'

Roxy's face hardened. 'Alice and Marcus think that the Party's drugged him or brainwashed him, or something, because they say he's not as he was. He doesn't have anything to do with them now – and they were our best friends, Jess. What the hell is he playing at? Did I live with some kind of schizophrenic?'

'I doubt it,' Jess said. 'It's just that different times make people different.' She paused. 'How long do you think it's going to take, to spring you?'

'Three or four weeks, at a rough guess.'

'So you'll go to Alice and Marcus every day until then?'

Roxy shook her head. 'That makes it too obvious – too suspicious. No, I'm going to go there twice a week. Tuesdays and Fridays. The rest of the time, I suppose I'll be at my dear friend Reeve's.'

'And then what?'

Roxy paused. 'I don't know if I should tell you, Jess. It's not that I don't trust you – of course I do – but maybe it would be better if you didn't know. If anything goes wrong, they'll interrogate you and find out what you know. They'll probably start with a lie detector, so if you really don't know anything, you'll be fine.'

Jess' face sobered. 'You have a point.'

Roxy smiled at her. 'I promise you, Jess, I'm not going to leave you in here. As soon as I can, I'll get you out of here.'

'If there's anything I can do,' Jess said, 'just tell me.'

'You've already helped, with Philip,' Roxy said. 'But there may be a point where you'll need to deny that you ever knew me – or even that you shared a cell with anyone.' Because the final part of her plan was to wipe her records from the database – as if she'd never existed.

'Right. The least said, the better,' Jess agreed.

A few weeks later they were all set. Incredibly, Marcus had managed to rig up a device which Roxy could slip along the side of her gum, to hold the finger sleeve with the new data until she was ready to use it. She took it gratefully, hiding it before she returned to the House of Correction.

The next day, she was taken, as usual, to Reeve's house. She submitted to scrubbing his kitchen floor with the toothbrush, and didn't even flinch at the hated indignity of him stripping and violating her body.

And then, right on cue, the moment he'd finished fucking her, the phone shrilled. Reeve made a growl of impatience. 'I'd better take that,' he said. 'It might be important.'

Roxy waited until he'd left the kitchen, then quickly pulled on her top and skirt, not bothering with her underclothes, picked up her shoes, and left the kitchen noiselessly. The study door was open: she paused, frozen, for a moment. If Reeve was facing this way ... But then she heard the clicking of a keyboard. If he was at his computer, he wouldn't notice her. She rushed past his study, quietly opened the front door, and slipped out. She didn't close the door behind her, not wanting to alert him by the sound, and walked quickly down the garden path.

Alice was waiting for her, as they'd agreed. The moment she was in the car, Roxy took the finger-sleeve from her mouth and fitted it over her right index finger. If the car was scanned as they went along, the monitor would show the records of Mrs Marcus Blake and her husband's cousin, Emma Lynn P. Hurst. Those records would show on the scanner of Alice's front door, too. Soon, it would be as if Roxana Winters had never existed.

She kept her head low until they were out of the street, and then Alice drove to Walthamstow – not too quickly, to avoid drawing attention to themselves. Neither of them spoke until they were in Alice's house – and then they turned to each other, embracing.

'I don't believe this, Rox. We've actually done it! We've sprung you!'

'Not quite,' Roxy reminded her. 'We have to finish changing my identity first.'

'Starting now,' Alice said. She looked critically at her friend. 'You're about the same size as me, now, so feel free to borrow any of my clothes. Marcus has rigged a bank account for you, but of course you can't withdraw any money without his authority.'

'Thank God that your husband isn't a miser,' Roxy said feelingly.

'Too true. Come on, let's get this over with.'

They went into the kitchen; Roxy sat on a chair, and Alice cut her hair. Roxy winced as the curls dropped onto the newspaper; Alice saw the look, and smiled. 'It's not that bad, Rox. Okay, so it's not exactly Vidal Sassoon, but it'll do.'

'Mm. And we have to burn the evidence,' Roxy reminded her.

'Don't worry. I'll take care of that, while you dye it. There's a packet of dark brown dye in the bathroom cabinet.'

'Okay. Thanks.' Roxy smiled at her and headed upstairs. She stripped off the hated black garments, washed her hair, and picked up the packet of dye. It was going to change her appearance radically, but ... *Needs must*, she thought, and applied the dye. She waited, rinsed it out, and then dried her hair on her old top. Then, wrapping a towel round herself, she went into Alice's bedroom.

Alice was already there, sorting out clothes. 'They'd better be burned, too,' she said, glancing at the rusty black bundle in Roxy's arms.

'Mm.'

'Here. Take your pick.'

Gratefully, Roxy plumped for a pair of loose navy-and-white striped trousers, and a white shirt. 'I feel better already,' she said.

'You'll look it, too. Once we do your make-up.'

Half an hour later, the transformation was complete. Alice looked critically at her. 'Yeah, you'll do. No one would ever recognize you.'

'Do you have any old photographs anywhere?' Roxy asked.

Alice nodded. 'Downstairs.'

Roxy followed her into the sitting room, and Alice rummaged in a cupboard, producing an album. There was a picture of Roxy, a couple of years before, just after she'd moved in with Tim. Alice handed it to her. 'Go and look at yourself in the mirror.'

Roxy did so, glancing from the photograph to her reflection. Nobody would ever recognize her. The fair curls had gone, replaced by a dramatic dark elfin crop. The teasing hazel eyes had been replaced by piercing violet ones, and even her face seemed to have changed shape, become more angular.

'It's a shame that I can't change my height,' Roxy said.

'Apart from wearing stilettos – which are not approved footwear, according to the Party – you can't,' Alice said. 'You're fine as you are.'

'The test will be if Marcus recognizes me.'

Alice chuckled. 'Well, he's expecting you.'

'If you tell him that it didn't work, that I couldn't leave Reeve's house, and your new neighbour has come visiting . . .'

'All this subterfuge.' Alice wrinkled her nose. 'I really hate it. Look, I'm not lying to Marcus for you.'

'I know. I just need to check that I can't be recognized.'

'Fair enough.' Alice shrugged. 'He'll be home in a couple of hours.'

They spent the rest of the afternoon chatting, drinking coffee and playing with Eleanor. Then they heard the front door close.

Alice went to greet Marcus. He kissed her. 'Hi. Did everything go to plan?'

Alice shook her head. 'Roxy couldn't leave the house. We'll have to try it another day.'

'Oh, God.' Marcus grimaced. 'I'm glad you told me. I was going to wipe her records tonight, and it would have caused problems at the House of Correction. They'd have noticed the change, and Roxy would have been taken off somewhere else where we couldn't find her.'

'We have new neighbours,' Alice said. 'The wife's just dropped over to say hello.'

'Oh?' Marcus was interested.

'Come and say hello to Chloe.'

Marcus put his head round the door. 'Good afternoon, Chloe. I'm Marcus. Nice to meet you.'

Roxy smiled back at him. 'You too, Mr Blake.'

Marcus frowned. 'Hang on. I know that voice.' His face cleared as memory snapped into place. 'I believe I'm speaking to Emma Lynn P. Hurst.'

Roxy grinned. 'You are indeed.'

He came over to her and gave her a hug; then he looked at his wife. 'Al. You lied to me.'

'No. I was teasing.'

'It was my idea,' Roxy explained. 'I needed to be sure that you didn't recognize me.'

'Not until you spoke, anyway.' Marcus frowned. 'Can you adopt some kind of accent? An American drawl would probably do.' Roxy's voice was accentless, classless.

She shook her head. 'I don't think I could sustain that.' A horrible thought struck her. 'You're not using voice recognition in the security systems, are you?'

'No, just the DNA.' He frowned. 'Talking of which, I'd better check our door scanner.' He returned, a couple of minutes later, smiling. 'Yes. A-one perfect. Now, we just have do some work on your record.'

'I imagine that Reeve's already reported me missing,' Roxy said, 'so if you delete it, and they trace the transaction back to you, we're all in trouble.'

'Rox, if we don't delete that record, and anything happens to that sleeve, you're done for.'

Roxy shook her head. 'We'll leave this to the next stage.

There's one person whose word won't be questioned when it comes to security matters.'

'Tim's?'

'Yes. When I can access his ID, I'll delete it myself from the records. It'll show that he's the one who deleted it, so they won't come after you.'

Marcus looked at her. 'You're playing a dangerous game, Rox.'

'No more risk than you're taking. Trust me, Marcus. I told you I wouldn't do anything that would hurt you, Alice or Eleanor, and I meant it.'

Eventually, Marcus nodded. 'I won't bother trying to change your mind. I thought you might feel that way – so I did a little hacking this afternoon.'

'Hacking?' Alice's eyes widened.

'Don't worry, I was careful. I only went through one layer of security.' He shrugged. 'I suppose I could have phoned Mr Fraser's secretary, and asked him which evenings his boss was free, but the question would have been reported back to Tim. I don't trust the guy – there's something slimy about him. Even if I'd explained that Tim and I were old friends, he probably wouldn't have told me the truth. So I hacked into Tim's diary.' He handed Roxy a screen printout.

'Thanks.' Roxy smiled at him. 'That's a hell of a risk you've taken.'

'Not that much.' He shrugged. 'All it tells you are the times when he's "available" – which means that he's at his flat. It doesn't tell you where he is the rest of the time.'

'It's brilliant.' She hugged him. 'Marcus, I appreciate this more than you'll ever know.'

'Well, I hate this regime as much as you do, Rox. If I

can bring it down, without hurting my wife and my daughter, I will.'

Two weeks later, Roxy gave Alice and Marcus a last hug. 'If I fail,' she said, 'please get Jess and Giselle out of that place.'

'We will,' they promised.

'Because if I fail,' Roxy said, 'I don't think they'll send me to the House of Correction again. I think they really will kill me, this time.'

'Roxy.' Alice squeezed her hand. 'I wish that you'd change your mind. I can't bear to think of you taking such a risk.'

Roxy shook her head. 'Not a chance. It has to be done, Al, and I'm the one to do it.' She smiled. 'There's already an appointment in Tim's diary. The Party has sent Emma Lynn P. Hurst to see to his needs.'

'Look, I'll run you over to Tim's place,' Marcus said.

'No,' Roxy insisted. She didn't want to implicate him even more. 'I'll walk to the High Street and get a taxi.'

'Sure?'

'Sure. But thanks, anyway.' She gave them a last smile and walked to the High Street. As she neared the old market place, adrenalin began to pump through her veins. This was going to be the time of reckoning. Her stomach churned. Part of her was very, very, frightened: at the same time, she knew that it had to be done – and that she was the one to do it.

It was easy to find a taxi. She'd memorized Tim's address; it was somewhere in the West End. Thank God, she thought, that he wasn't still living in their house in Hampstead. If he'd still been living there, she couldn't have stood it. Not in the place she'd loved so much. But in a new place, with no memories, it would be easier.

The taxi stopped outside a tall building in the middle of

the West End. Roxy went to the door to the apartments and pressed her index finger onto the security pad. There was a beep and the door opened, allowing her into the reception.

'Yes?' The man at the reception desk was brisk, impersonal. He gave Roxy a look of disdain; she only just managed to choke down her annoyance. He thought that she'd been sent by the Party, to look after Tim's sexual needs – just like all the other women who had probably been there. Well, she was there for other things, too.

She let the hood of her cloak drop to reveal her face, and gave him an equally disdainful stare. 'I'm here for Mr Tim Fraser.'

'Mr Fraser doesn't have visitors,' he said, surprising her. So Tim *hadn't* ordered women, even to do his housework?

'I think,' she said icily, 'if you check his diary, you'll find that I'm expected. Ring his secretary.'

'Wait there.' The guard made a quick phone call, his back to Roxy. She thought about making a bolt for it, but she knew that it would be a mistake. Apart from the fact that she didn't know which one was Tim's apartment, she wanted to make this look like a legitimate situation.

A few moments later, he replaced the receiver and turned back to Roxy. 'The secretary says that it was put in by Mr Fraser himself.'

'Exactly.' Roxy smiled at him. 'It's personal.'

'Mr Fraser isn't back yet. You'll have to wait here for him.'

Roxy shook his head. 'No. I think he'd prefer me to wait in his apartment. Somewhere less' – she paused – 'exposed.'

'I don't know if I can do that,' the guard said.

Roxy studied him for a moment. As the security guard to the block of apartments where someone as important as Tim lived, it was obvious that he was a fully-fledged Party member, believing in everything it stood for. And yet, there had been a flash of interest in his eyes. If only her clothes hadn't been so demure. Then she could have sat in the reception, letting her skirt ride up over her thigh and crossing and uncrossing her legs deliberately. Or maybe leaned forward, treating him to a view of her cleavage. As it was, all she had was her smile – and a very limited amount of patience.

She was so close to seeing Tim; she couldn't bear to be thwarted, now. She leaned over the desk, and took one of his hands. 'Please,' she said softly, 'I need to see Mr Fraser. I won't make any problems for you, I promise – but I would feel much more comfortable if I waited in Mr Fraser's apartment.'

He paused for an agonizingly long while, then nodded. 'It's the penthouse flat. I'll program the system to let you in. All you need to do is press your finger against the keypad, and it'll read you.' He tipped his head to his left. 'The lifts are over there.'

'Thank you.'

The penthouse, Roxy thought as she walked towards the lift. Tim lived in the penthouse of this beautiful building. It was nice, yes – but she couldn't understand how he could have borne to move here, after their place in Hampstead. Or maybe the Party had decided that the house in Hampstead would be better for a family, and had made him move.

Whatever. She stepped into the lift and pressed the button for the top floor. It was very small, and mirrored all the way round; it was the sort you used to see in erotic romantic movies, where the leading man and his lady would end up in some passionate clinch. Though this lift was barely big enough for two people and a sportsbag, she thought wryly.

The lift stopped; she left it, and headed for the glossy navy blue door which led to Tim's apartment. She pressed her finger to the pad at the side of the door; there was a soft click, and then she was inside the flat.

'Now, Tim,' she said. 'Now it's time for the reckoning.'

She glanced at her watch. She'd memorized the diary that Marcus had shown her. Tim wasn't due back for a good half an hour. That gave her plenty of time to find out where he kept his PC, to log into the network – and to hack into the system.

All the doors to the entrance hall were closed. She tried the first one and discovered that it led to the sitting room. It was a large room, comfortable, with large squashy sofas, tall windows, and expensive lined curtains. There were prints of ferns on the pale plain walls – not quite Tim's taste, as she remembered it, but not that offensive, either. Anyway, hadn't Marcus said that he'd changed?

She tried the next door and walked into the kitchen. It, too, was large: gleaming white and chrome, with all the latest labour-saving devices. The guard had said that Tim didn't entertain – did that mean that he didn't have a daily woman from the House of Correction, even to keep his kitchen gleaming? Except, maybe, if the Party told him to.

The bathroom was next. It, too, was large and white and gleaming, with chrome fittings and thick fluffy towels. The bath was sunken – a jacuzzi, Roxy realized, with a mixture of amusement and bitterness. The sort that she and Tim would once have enjoyed.

Tim's bedroom was opposite, containing a king-size bed with a firm mattress, she discovered as she sat on it, and dark wood chests of drawers. The wardrobes were fitted; the whole place had an oddly impersonal air. It could have been anyone's bedroom: there was nothing to link it to Tim, not even a book on the table at the side of the bed.

The last door yielded exactly what she was looking for. His study. There were a few bookshelves, and then a plain table at the end of the room. And there, on the table, was his PC. She smiled, and switched it on. She placed her finger on the sensor pad and, as she'd expected, the words *Unauthorised Access* flashed up on the screen. She knew how Tim's mind worked. Unless he had changed his pattern of work even more drastically than he'd changed the rest of his life, there would be a manual override. All she had to do was type in the right password.

She tried "Roxy". It didn't work. Neither did "Roxana", or "Tiresias". She frowned. She'd been expecting him to use her name, or some classical reference. If not Tiresias, then . . . Of course. The watchman with a thousand eyes. Argus. She typed in "Argus", and it worked.

'Well done, Timmikins,' she said mockingly. She flicked through the machine, and found the e-mail package. She sent Tim a memo to himself, then edited it. As far as he was concerned, someone had just gone in to look at it. It was an old message, from the House of Correction, confirming his special order for that evening.

She had just accessed the national security database when the door slammed open.

THIRTEEN

'What the *hell* . . .?' Tim asked furiously from the open doorway.

She looked up at him, and her stomach lurched. He looked
more or less the same as the last time she'd seen him – except
maybe a little thinner, a little older, a little more tired. He was
still the man she'd fallen in love with on sight, a few years
before. And although she'd told herself that she hated him, she
found that what she felt for him was a lot more complex than
that. Anger, love, hate, desire . . . they were all intermingled.

He marched over to her, and she realized that his eyes had
changed. They were harder than she remembered – as if he
just didn't care about anything any more. 'Who the hell are
you?' he demanded. 'What are you doing there?' He pulled her
away from the PC.

She spread her hands. 'You ordered me.'

'I did nothing of the kind.'

'Go into your e-mail. I think you'll find a confirmation
there.' She shrugged. 'Maybe your secretary read the message
for you.'

He stared at her, and then flipped into his e-mail. He checked
the memo, then looked at her. 'Emma Lynn P. Hurst. That's
you, is it?'

He'd lost his sense of humour, too, Roxy thought. In the
old days, he'd have picked up the reference; he'd have realized at once that "Emma Lynn P. Hurst" was Emmeline

Pankhurst, leader of the Suffragettes, the pioneer who'd fought for women's rights. This was the man who'd sworn he'd love her and look after her. This was the man whose last words to her had been to take care, and that he wanted to marry her. And yet he'd left her to rot in the House of Correction.

Her eyes hardened. 'So, what's the matter, Mr Head of National Security? Something bugging you?'

'I didn't order you,' he said. 'Someone's been hacking into my system.'

'Hacking? I thought that was impossible, with today's security systems,' she mocked.

He was stony-faced. 'I didn't order you.'

'I think you'll find that you did.' She gave him an arch look. 'Or maybe the Party ordered me for you, if you haven't been conforming to what they want.'

'I didn't order you,' he repeated, his voice cold.

She shrugged. 'We both know why I'm here.' *At least, in part*, she thought grimly.

He shook his head. 'No. I've never, ever ordered anyone.'

'Fair enough. I'll go back to where I came from, and tell them that you weren't very co-operative.'

'You can do what the hell you like.'

Mixed emotions seethed through her. He wasn't *that* much of a Party animal, then, if he didn't care what they thought about him. That made his betrayal doubly worse, because it meant that he could have sprung her from the House of Correction from the very first day. And yet, if Tim was telling the truth – and she believed that he was – about never ordering a woman, the way that people like Reeve did . . . then maybe, just maybe, he was keeping faithful to the memory of the woman he'd once loved and thought was dead. After all, Alice and Marcus had believed her dead.

She had to know for sure. Did he still love her? Could he be seduced by a strange woman, by "Emma Lynn P. Hurst"? Slowly, she sashayed over to him, sliding her hands round his neck.

He pushed her away. 'Leave me alone.'

'You ordered me, remember,' she informed him. 'You might as well get it over with.'

'I am *not*,' he said, through gritted teeth, 'having a child with you.'

'Who says that I'm here to conceive a child?'

'Because sex is for procreation, not recreation.'

And you don't believe a word of it, she thought. 'That's for the masses. You know that.'

'I am not going to bed with you.'

'You don't know me,' she pointed out. 'You might even like me, if you got to know me a little better. In the Biblical sense, that is.'

'I doubt that, Miss Hurst.'

She smiled inwardly. It looked like her disguise was so good, he didn't even recognize her. So much the better. She'd disguised her voice by adopting a slightly London accent, so that wouldn't give her away. And there was one way to check that he really believed her to be Emma Lynn P. Hurst. Slowly, she undid the brooch at the neck of her demure white blouse, dropped it on the floor, and unbuttoned her blouse.

Tim stared at her in disbelief. 'What the h—'

'I'm just doing what I have to do,' she cut in quietly, shrugging the blouse from her shoulders. Her breasts were still generous, despite the weight she'd lost, and the lacy bra she'd borrowed from Alice showed them off to their best advantage. She unzipped her skirt, letting it fall to the floor in a rustle of silk, and stood there in her underwear.

Despite himself, Tim couldn't help looking. His eyes travelled down her body, taking in the white lacy bra, the matching knickers and suspenders, the sheer grey silk stockings. A pulse began to beat in his clenched jaw; Roxy noticed it, and gloated inwardly. She reached behind her, unclasping the bra and tossing the lacy garment on the floor.

She crossed the distance between them and slid her arms round his neck again, drawing his head down to hers. She touched her mouth to his, very gently. He didn't respond, and she deepened the pressure on his mouth, taking his lower lip between her teeth and biting it gently. Then she pressed her pelvis against his, rubbing his hardening cock with her mound; Tim couldn't help but be turned on. She wasn't sure whether she was more elated that her plan to seduce him was working or furious with him for being turned on by a complete stranger.

She smoothed her hands down his back and slid them under his black cotton poloneck sweater. He felt good, she thought, so good; she shivered in anticipation of what was going to happen between them. Tim's face was anguished; he wanted to pull away, and yet he couldn't help his body reacting to her.

'Tim,' she said softly.

He closed his eyes. If he didn't know that Roxy was dead, and that this woman – whoever the hell she was – was a complete stranger, he could have sworn that it was Roxy standing by him. The way she said his name . . . It was just like Roxy.

He said nothing, and she tugged at the hem of his sweater. Tim, lost in memories of Roxy, did nothing to stop her removing his sweater. He didn't push her away as she undid his belt, then slid down the zip of his trousers, easing the black chinos over his hips. She curled her fingers round his stiffening cock through his silk boxer shorts; it reminded him so much of the way that Roxy had touched him that he shuddered in pleasure.

Roxy, who had her eyes open and was watching him intently, saw the flicker of pain across his face. Had she not known that he'd betrayed her, she would have been tempted to fall in his arms, tell him who she was, and kiss the pain away. As it was, he would have no mercy from her. She was here to get even with him, and clear her name from the records.

She moved closer to him, kissing him. This time he responded, kissing her hard in return. She didn't speak again, but led him to his bedroom. He pushed the duvet from the bed, then turned to her, deftly gathering her breasts into his hands.

Her nipples hardened at his touch; he massaged her breasts, stroking the soft undersides and rubbing her nipples between his thumb and index finger. He closed his eyes, and dropped to his knees in front of her, rubbing his face against her belly; desire flared deep within her, and she curled her fingers into his hair.

If she could only forget about his betrayal – this was like coming home. Being loved by the man she loved, having him touch her and taste her ... The way he trailed soft kisses across the plains of her belly, at the same time as he unclasped her suspenders, made her shiver.

Tim, lost in a private dream, continued undressing her, unclipping the suspenders from her stockings and rolling the grey silk sheaths down her legs, stroking the sensitive patch at the back of her knees. Roxy leaned against him, urging him on: feeling his breath, warm, so near to her quim. She wanted him, oh, so badly.

She swallowed hard as he hooked his fingers into the sides

of her knickers, drawing them down; she lifted each foot in turn so he could remove the lacy garment completely, and then let him push her thighs wider apart. She shivered as he rubbed his cheeks against her inner thighs: then, at long, long last, she felt the slow stroke of his tongue against her sex.

She almost cried out with the pleasure of it. For all the fact that her mind hated him, her body craved his touch, and it really did feel like coming home again, the way he lapped at her and brought her to a swift and sharp climax, his tongue flicking rapidly over her clitoris. She shuddered, digging her fingers into his scalp, and he drew her closer, resting his head against her thighs until the aftershocks of her orgasm had died away.

He still had his eyes closed as he stood up, pulling her onto the bed with him. He nuzzled her skin, licking and kissing her, making her shiver with desire: and then he was kneeling between her thighs, splaying her legs and fitting the tip of his cock to the heated entrance of her sex. She groaned as he slid inside her and she wrapped her legs round his waist, tipping her pelvis upwards to deepen his penetration.

He began to move then, long slow thrusts that drove her crazy with wanting him; she slid her arms round his neck, drawing his face down to hers and kissing him deeply. He tasted of her, and the familiarity of it made her want to cry.

She pushed up against him and he smiled, drawing his hands along her thighs and gently straightening her legs. Then he sat back on his heels, bringing her body up into a curve, with her thighs resting over his. Roxy shuddered as he began to pump his body against hers, bringing her to another peak. She felt the familiar heat curling around the soles of her feet, moving up through her calves, and finally exploding in her solar plexus; the feel of her quim contracting sharply round his cock was enough to tip him into his own climax.

'Oh Roxy,' he groaned, his cock throbbing deep inside her. 'Roxy, Roxy, Roxy.'

She stiffened. Had he guessed who she was, now? Or was he lost in some dream of the past, calling out the name of the woman he'd once loved? 'Who's Roxy?' she asked, her voice sharp.

He opened his eyes in shock, suddenly remembering where he was, and stared at her in distaste. He withdrew from her, rolling off her and putting as much distance between them on the bed as he could. 'That's nothing to do with you.'

'Isn't it?' She propped herself on one elbow, pulling him onto his back so that she could see his face. 'Who's Roxy?' she repeated.

'No one you know,' he said roughly. 'Now, just go, will you?'

She shook her head. 'The order was for me to stay all night.'

His lip curled. 'You're joking!'

'No. That's the order. Check it, if you like.'

'In that case,' he said, 'you can sleep on the sofa. There's some spare bedding in the airing cupboard.'

Roxy wasn't sure whether to be more outraged or relieved. Outraged, because the Tim she knew had always believed in cuddling her to sleep; then again, he thought that she was a stranger, Emma Lynn P. Hurst. And relieved, because the look on his face proved beyond all doubt that he was still in love with Roxy. He'd made love to a stranger, thinking that the woman he loved was dead – and fantasizing that she was there in his arms, again.

Sleeping on the sofa would suit her fine. Until she and Tim were reconciled – and she was none too sure when that would be, if it happened at all – she had work to do. If she spent the night in bed with him, things would be difficult. In sleep, she'd end up curling into his arms, and maybe she'd betray herself as she woke. Sleeping on the sofa would remove the risk – and she'd also be certain not to disturb him when she crept into his study to finish what she'd started earlier. 'As you wish,' she said coldly, climbing out of the bed and walking out of the room.

Tim watched her leave, hating himself for treating the woman badly. He should never have made love to her in the first place. He should have sent her back where she came from, Party orders or no Party orders. And yet, losing himself in her body, it had felt like making love with Roxy again . . .

She waited for an hour, until she'd judged that he must have fallen asleep, and crept back into his study. She switched on the PC again, overriding the security system as she had before, and going into the database. It didn't take her long to find the record. *Winters, Roxana*. She flicked through the file. It had everything: her date of birth, her height, the colour of her hair and eyes, her qualifications, her employment history . . . Not for long, though.

She flicked up into the menu and was just about to delete the record when Tim's arms came round her, pulling her away. She screamed, and he clamped a hand over her mouth; then he spun her round to face him.

His eyes were cold as he stared at her, his face grim. 'Right. Who are you, and who are you working with?'

'That's none of your business.'

'If you won't tell me, I'll call the guard. He'll get it out of you,' he threatened, 'and he won't ask you as nicely as I have.'

'Why call the guard? Are you too scared to hit me yourself?' she flashed back.

He clenched his jaw. 'Let's start again, from the beginning. Who are you?'

'Emma Lynn P. Hurst.' She kept her gaze fixed on his. Maybe if she spelled it out for him, he might twig. 'Miss Emma Lynn P. A. N. K. Hurst, to be precise.'

He stared at her, his eyes narrowing. 'Okay, so that's your pseudonym. Your fighting name.'

So he'd caught the reference, at last. When would he work out the rest of it? She stared defiantly at him.

'Who are you working with?' he asked.

She shook her head. 'I'm working alone.' That much was true. Marcus, Alice, Jess and Giselle would all be behind her, as much as they could – so, too, would Philip. But this was something that only she could do.

'You can't be.'

'No?'

'No. Women don't have access to the computers without a man's authorizing ID.'

She gave him a contemptuous look, then nodded her head at the computer. 'Maybe your security's just not good enough, Mr Head of National Security.'

'Maybe.' At last, he looked at the screen; he froze as he saw the name on the record. 'What the hell are you playing at?' he demanded, hissing the words through his teeth.

'Just deleting a record that's no longer required.'

He shook her then, anger finally cracking his control. 'You bitch. Tell me what's going on!'

She yelped in pain, and he loosened his hold on her arms; she pulled away and rubbed her bruised skin, scowling at him. 'There's no need to bully me.'

'You get someone to hack into the system and send you to me; you tell me a ridiculous name when I ask you who you are; and you're trying to delete a file.' He counted her actions on his fingers. 'You won't tell me who you really are, or who you're working with – and you say there's no need to bully you, Miss Hurst?'

'What do you do with dead people?' she asked.

He frowned, jolted by her answer. 'What?'

'What do you do with dead people?' she repeated. 'Their records. Do you keep them as live?'

'No. They're deleted.' He suddenly realized what she was getting at. The record on the screen – Roxy's record – hadn't been deleted. Which meant . . . His eyes suddenly blazed with hope. 'You mean, Roxy's alive?'

She folded her arms. 'She might be.'

He swallowed hard. 'Look, Miss Hurst, or whatever your name is. We have to talk.'

'Not on your terms. I don't deal with bullies.'

'All right, I'm sorry. I didn't mean to hurt you.' He sighed. 'Look, I'll make us a coffee. Then can we talk? Please?'

The look on his face, when he'd suddenly realized that Roxy might be alive – the sheer desperation and longing, and the fear that it might turn out to be untrue – melted her. Perhaps he wasn't as far gone as she thought he was. Perhaps he really, really hadn't known that she was alive. Perhaps he hadn't betrayed her . . . 'As long as it's proper coffee. Blue Mountain,' she said. 'Or Royale will do.'

He shot her a glance. 'That's what Roxy drank. You know something about her, don't you?'

She shrugged. 'Coffee. Then we talk.'

'All right, Miss Hurst.' He spread his hands. 'After you.'

'Don't you trust me enough to leave me alone in here?'

'No, I don't.'

She suppressed a smile and headed for the kitchen; Tim

closed the study door behind him and followed her. He made the coffee swiftly and without talking to her; she watched him covertly, her body tingling with memories of the way he'd once made love to her. That night, it had been almost perfunctory, as though she was a substitute for the woman he loved: but her body still surged at his touch.

He handed her a steaming mug.

'Not bad,' she said, after her first sip. 'Though it's not Blue Mountain.'

'No.' He paused. 'Would you like to talk in here, or in the sitting room?'

'In comfort, I think.'

He nodded, and led her into the sitting room. She drank her coffee in silence, watching Tim all the time. He was tense, waiting to hear news of Roxy. *Well*, she thought, *he can damn well wait and wonder. Like I did, in the House of Correction, waiting and wondering if he was safe. Not knowing – that was the worst thing.*

She finished her coffee and he looked at her, his eyes pleading. 'Miss Hurst. Tell me – please – is Roxy alive?'

'Why do you want to know?'

He closed his eyes. 'Please. I need to know.'

She spread her hands. 'You called out her name when you came.'

He swallowed. 'Yes.'

'And yet you still made love to me.'

'No offence, Miss Hurst, but it was a physical reaction. You started it. And you reminded me of her.'

'So she's medium built, with short dark hair and blue eyes?' she tested.

He shook her head. 'No. Roxy was built like a pocket Venus, all lush curves. Her hair was fair – and it was curly, too, not spiked like yours. Her eyes were hazel: they were green when she was happy or excited about something, and brown with orange lights when she was in a bad mood.'

'And when she was in pain?'

He closed his eyes, his face darkening. 'Please – don't tell me that they hurt her.'

'All right. Supposing I do know what happened to her. What will you give me in return?'

He opened his eyes again, met her gaze, and smiled wryly. 'Are you trying to blackmail me, Miss Hurst?'

'No. I'm bartering. You want my knowledge. What will you do for me in return?'

'What do you want?' he parried.

She smiled. 'Knowledge. I want to know what's going on. But you sure as hell don't know, either.'

'I'll find out – whatever you want, I can find it out. I'm the Head of National Security.'

'I know.'

He swallowed. 'Tell me about Roxy.'

'When did you last see her?'

'The morning when the Party took over. I heard about the coup, and I rang her. I said I was coming home, but she said she was okay, that I had work to do and she'd be all right.' He grimaced. 'I wish to hell now that I'd ignored her and come home. I might have been able to save her.'

'I doubt it,' Roxy said. 'Not if you'd had to face the thugs and bully boys. They'd have beaten you senseless if you were in the way.'

'You mean, they beat her?' He was shocked.

'No. They just knocked her out. Then they took her away.'

'Alice rang me, a couple of hours after I'd spoken to Roxy. She said that Roxy was meant to be going over to

Walthamstow, but she hadn't turned up. Roxy was almost never late. Alice had tried ringing her, and our phone was out of order. I tried the other line, the one linked to the PC, and that was out, too. So I went home and found the place smashed up, and blood everywhere.'

'Blood?' Roxy suddenly realized what was wrong. All along, she'd expected Monty to be in the flat. And he wasn't. Either Tim had given him to a good home, or . . . 'Whose blood?' she asked sharply.

He swallowed. 'Some of it was Roxy's. From what you've told me, it could have happened when they knocked her out.'

'And the rest of it?'

He closed his eyes. 'Our dog.'

'They killed Monty?' Roxy squeezed her eyes tightly shut. 'Bastards. Bloody, bloody bastards. He was only a labrador – he had nothing to do with VRX.'

He frowned. 'How do you know about all that? Monty and VRX?'

'I just do,' she said through gritted teeth.

'Yes, then. It was because of bloody VRX. She was going to destroy it – obviously, she didn't have time. And they wrecked the place when they caught her.' He took a deep breath. 'I rang the police. I wanted to know what was going on, where she was. They told me that she was dead – because she resisted them.'

'And you believed that?'

He nodded. 'Roxy believed in freedom. She was the sort who'd go out fighting for her beliefs.'

'And you did nothing?'

'What could I do? They said that if I caused any trouble about it, they'd work on me until I saw their point of view.'

'You mean, they'd hurt you?'

'Or brainwash me – which would be worse, because then I wouldn't know any better. So I did nothing. Then Ferris called me. He said that I was to be his Head of National Security, because of my work for Comco.'

'And you agreed to do it.' Her lip curled. 'You bloody coward, Tim Fraser.'

'Miss Hurst, without Roxy, there was nothing left to fight for. At least this way, I've been able to keep myself busy. Busy enough not to think about her, most of the time.'

'Didn't it occur to you to check the records?'

'No.' He winced. 'Look, I loved her, all right? She was the most important thing in my life. I came home to find the place smashed up and blood everywhere. They killed our dog. Of course I believed it when they told me she was dead too. I didn't look up her record because it hurt too much even to think about her. Besides, I didn't think her record would be there. Like I told you, we erase the records of dead people.'

'You're still a coward.'

A muscle in his jaw flickered at her taunt. 'I've told you what I know. Now, tell me about her. Is she all right?'

'You want to know what happened, after they knocked her out?'

'Yes.'

She paused. 'They took her to the House of Correction.'

'So she's in jail? Where?' His eyes widened. 'If you tell me where she is, I can give orders to have her released.'

'Too late, Mr Fraser. Too late.'

The light in his eyes died. 'So she *is* dead.'

'I didn't say that. Just that she's no longer at the House of Correction. The place where dangerous women are kept, and used as domestic servants and call-girls for the privileged classes.'

'You mean they made her into a whore?' A mixture of shock and fury flooded his face.

'Yes.' She smiled thinly. 'But not any more.'

He smiled then. 'You're working with her. She's your accomplice. She's the only one who would have guessed about the override, and the right password.'

Roxy kept her voice neutral – just. 'I'm sure she'd be flattered to hear your good opinion of her.'

'Miss Hurst . . . Look, I'll do anything you want. Anything. Just tell me where she is, and I can make sure that she's safe.'

She shook her head. 'How do I know that you're not intending to kill her?'

He stared at her in disbelief. 'Kill Roxy? You're joking, aren't you?'

'I'm perfectly serious. For all I know, you might want to be rid of her – be rid of your past.'

He shook his head. 'I can't prove it to you, but I swear I'll make sure that she's safe. I'd never do anything to hurt Roxy, never. God, you're talking about the woman I love. The woman I want to marry, and spend the rest of my life with.'

Roxy shivered inwardly with delight. He still felt the same about her, then . . . She fought to keep her face impassive. 'Okay. Here's what you do. You set up a new record on the database – Chloe Fraser.'

'Chloe Fraser?'

'Mrs Chloe Fraser. Your wife,' Roxy said tartly.

His eyes narrowed. 'And whose data will I be using?'

'Mine, of course.'

'Yours.' He coughed. 'Miss Hurst, I appreciate the fact that you've helped Roxy, but no way can I marry you.'

'Is there a legal bar?'

'A moral one. There's only one woman I could marry.'

'Me. You put me in as your wife, or no deal.'

He thought about it. 'On condition that when I get Roxy back, you divorce me.'

'Divorce is illegal.'

'While the Party is in power, yes.'

She smiled. 'You'd bring down the Party, for Roxy?'

'Not just for her. *With* her.' His face grew animated. 'With Roxy, I can make it work – I can change the system from the inside.'

'Then let's go make that record, Mr Fraser.'

He nodded. 'All right. Though there is another condition.'

She stilled. 'What's that?'

'That the marriage is in name only. I'll give you the protection of my name, but that's all.'

'And supposing I want it otherwise?' she asked softly.

'No deal.'

She smiled to herself. She had a feeling that he'd change his mind as soon as he realized who she was. In fact, she'd stake her life on it. 'All right,' she said.

'Let's go, then.' He led her into his study and closed down the PC. 'It has to be through official channels,' he said, at her frown. 'Mine. If you hack, you'll leave a trace.'

'I will not.'

'Look, Miss Hurst, I don't know your background. But even if you were in the same line of work as Roxy and me, you'd leave a trace on the system. So would I, so would Roxy – even though she's the best programmer I've ever met. It has to be this way.'

She spread her hands. 'How do I know that you're not going to betray me?'

'The same way as I know that you're going to reunite me with Roxy.'

'Which is?'

'I trust you. I have to.' He swallowed. 'We have to trust each other.' He switched the machine back on, used the finger-pad to log in, and went into the security database.

She sat on the edge of his desk as he called up the new form.

'Chloe Fraser,' he typed. 'Age?'

'Thirty-three.'

'Date of birth?'

'Eleventh of February.'

His eyes widened. 'That's *your* birthday?'

'Mm-hm.'

'Height?

'Five foot four. And a half.'

He looked up at her, and suddenly connected. 'The half being important, right?'

She smiled. 'Hello, Tim. You've woken up, then?'

'Nearly.' He pulled her onto his lap, and looked closely at her. 'That's quite a disguise. You've lost weight, your hair's different – even your face looks different.'

'Healthy food and exercise,' she said lightly. 'Amazing what it can do to you. Not to mention a pot of hair dye.'

'And lenses. Coloured contact lenses. I bet that underneath them is a pair of hazel eyes. Probably brown with orange bits, at the moment, because you want to kill me – right?'

'Right.' She noticed the glitter of tears in his eyes, and couldn't help bringing up a hand to cup his face. 'Tim. I hated you, I really did. I wanted to kill you, very, very slowly. When I found out that you were the Head of National Security, I thought that you'd betrayed me. I thought you knew where I was, and you'd left me to rot in that bloody place.'

'Never. If I'd known where you were, I would have done

something about it, believe me.' He held her close. 'Oh, Roxy. I've dreamed about you, and woken like Caliban.'

'Crying to dream again? Very literary, from the man who used to quibble with Alice.' Her face tightened again. 'You do remember our best friends, I suppose? Marcus and Alice?'

'They reminded me too much of you. It hurt, Rox. I couldn't handle it. Seeing them reminded me of the fact that I'd lost you. So I cut off. It was the only way I could deal with the pain. That, and working all the hours I could.'

'Well, you owe them,' she said.

'They got you out?'

'Yes.' Roxy enlightened him as to the true nature of the House of Correction, what had happened with Jess and Giselle and Philip, and how Marcus and Alice had rescued her.

'I'm going to kill Reeve,' he said, when she'd finished.

'That's my privilege,' Roxy said. 'And I think you'd better make his record tamper-proof. I'd be too tempted to give him all sorts of antisocial diseases. Or rabies. I'd like to be the one giving him the inoculations.'

He stroked her hair. 'So you let another man make love to you.'

She nodded. 'And you're not pure and innocent, so don't get heavy with me. There's the small matter of you bedding Miss Emma Lynn P. Hurst.'

He laughed. 'That doesn't count.'

'Oh yes, it does. You didn't know that I was her at the time.'

'No.' He smiled wryly. 'It was a good name.'

'I'm surprised you didn't pick up on it before. I gave you enough chances. In the end, I had to spell it out for you!'

'Mm.' He rubbed his nose against hers. 'I'm sorry.'

'Did they really kill Monty?' she asked. 'I thought he'd be

with you – unless you'd given him to a good home. That's why I didn't ask Alice about him. I thought you'd look after him.'

'I would have done, Rox. If they hadn't got to him first, I would have looked after him. He'd be here with me now.'

'Is that why you moved here? Because of what happened in Hampstead?'

'Mostly. The Party accepted it, because they needed the accommodation for a family. Though I can get the house back if you want me to.'

She shook her head. 'Not yet. Not until it's all over.'

He brushed the tears from her face. 'And we'll have another dog then. We'll call him Monty the Second.'

'There could only be one Monty.'

'I know.' He kissed her lightly. 'Look, hadn't you better phone Alice? She's probably fretting about you, worrying about what I'm doing to you.'

'Yeah. I assume you have a mobile – something that can't be tapped?'

'Digital, of course.' He smiled at her, rummaged in a drawer, and brought out a mobile phone.

'While you're there, you can give a couple of orders. I want Jess Holt and Giselle Baines released, and I want Philip promoted.'

'What's his second name?'

'I don't know,' Roxy admitted, 'but you can damn well find out for me.'

'All right.' He pulled her closer. 'But I'm going to find it hard, calling you Chloe.'

'You'll get used to it.' She kissed the tip of his nose and rang Alice.

'Hello?'

'Mrs Blake? It's Chloe,' Roxy said. 'I just thought you should know that your new next door neighbour has just moved to the West End.'

Alice's relief was obvious in her voice. 'Thank God. Rox – I mean, Chloe – you haven't killed him or done anything drastic, have you?'

'No, she hasn't,' Tim said into the mouthpiece. 'Though she was thinking about it.'

'Now we know that you're alive, perhaps we'll see more of you,' Alice said pointedly.

'Yes. I'm sorry, Al – and I really owe you a lot,' Tim said.

'Don't worry,' Roxy cut in. 'I'll make him pay. Because he, of course, will authorize his wife to spend whatever she wants. And she intends to take her best friend on one hell of a shopping spree, I promise you that.'

'I'll speak to you tomorrow,' Alice said, laughing. 'And I'll keep you to that, as a promise.'

When Roxy cut the line, she looked at Tim. 'I hope that you meant it.'

'About what?'

'Changing the system, from the inside. Because we start tomorrow.'

The forcefulness in her voice made him frown. 'Do I take it that you already have something in mind?'

She nodded. 'I've had long enough to think about it. Hacking into your system was only the start.' She smiled. 'And I suppose that it'll work better, with you on my side – if you meant it, about bringing down the Party.'

'Of course I did.'

'Good. Then this,' she said softly, stroking his face and bending down so that her mouth brushed his ear, 'is what we do . . .'

PART III

FOURTEEN

Tim agreed with her plans, and their counter-revolution started the next morning. Tim, as the Head of National Security, was above suspicion and could requisition what he liked. His first order was for a state-of-the-art PC, that wasn't connected to the security network, so that Roxy could begin to build the VRX program again without any interference from "security". His second order was for Marcus to work full-time with him, on a "special project" to enhance the security cards. And the third order was for two women to work on decorating a run-down house in Holland Park for him and his wife, starting by stripping the walls and the skirting boards.

Naturally, the women were to be accompanied by a guard – they couldn't risk any more of the security slips that had allowed Roxana Winters to escape. 'Luckily,' Tim told the rest of the Government, 'she's been neutralized. She escaped from Reeve's house because he was slack.'

The Minister of Publicity looked at him with dislike; Tim returned the look blandly, although he wanted to beat the man to a pulp for what he'd done to Roxy.

'But the infrastructure of our security system is good. We tracked her through to the High Street, caught her on the edge of Hampstead Heath and neutralized her.' Tim spread his hands. 'All records of her existence have now been deleted.'

Nobody from the security system was there to dispute

that he was telling the truth, and Reeve, embarrassed by the revelation of his incompetence, didn't challenge Tim's version of events. Tim heaved an inward sigh of relief as the meeting turned to other government matters; at last Roxy was safe, in her new identity.

Three days later, Jess, Giselle and Philip came to the house in Holland Park.

'I don't know what's going on,' Giselle muttered to Jess in the back of the car, 'but I've never heard of us going out in pairs before.'

'No. I think we'd better keep quiet,' Jess said.

Giselle took her hand and squeezed it gently, in agreement. The drive seemed to take forever; then, at last, they were let out of the car and Philip led them into the house. He removed their blindfolds quietly.

'So where are we, Philip?' Jess asked, looking round at the run-down house with distaste.

'I don't know.' He smiled tightly. 'I just had orders that I was to bring you both here. I'm to supervise you.'

'Who ordered us?' Giselle asked.

'I did.'

Giselle turned round at the sound of the unfamiliar voice and stared in surprise at the tall, dark-haired, good-looking man standing in the doorway. Then recognition set in. 'I know you,' she said, her lip curling.

He frowned. 'How?'

'I know what you do.' She looked at him in contempt. 'And I know why we're here.'

'Do you, now?' He spread his hands. 'I wonder.'

Jess looked at them both in surprise. The hatred in Giselle's voice was obvious . . . and yet Jess had no idea who the man was. Someone in Giselle's past, perhaps? An ex-lover, or an old enemy?

'Jessica Holt and Giselle Baines. Philip . . .' He tipped his head on one side. 'You're not what I expected.'

Jess frowned. 'Look, who are you?'

'All in good time, Jess. All in good time.' Tim stared at Philip. So this was the man Roxy had made love with. Young, with the sort of face most women would find attractive. A good body, kept fit and taut by working out in a gym. His rival. Then he noticed that Philip was standing just in front of Jess, an air of protectiveness about him . . . and he smiled. Philip, it seemed, had eyes only for Jess. He wasn't missing Roxy and wishing that she was there with him instead of Jess and Giselle.

Giselle simply regarded Tim with hostility, her blue eyes hard, and Jess looked at him in puzzlement.

'What the hell is going on here?' Jess asked, finally.

'I think,' Roxy said, appearing in the doorway behind Tim, 'that it's known in prison circles as springing someone.'

'Roxy!' Jess ran over to her and hugged her. 'Oh, Rox. I can't believe it. You did it!'

'The name's Chloe, for the moment,' Roxy reminded her quietly, hugging her back. 'You've met Tim?'

Giselle tipped her head towards him, the movement short and jerky with contempt. 'The Head of National Security, you mean?'

'Yes. And because of my position, I'm above the law,' Tim said.

'Indeed.' Jess regarded him coolly, now that she knew who he was. 'I'm surprised that you didn't spring Rox – I mean, Chloe – before, if you're so powerful.'

'I would have done,' Tim said. 'But they told me that she was dead. I believed them.'

'And you didn't bother checking?' Giselle asked, her lip curling.

Tim sighed. 'Look, I've been through all that with Chloe. And with Alice.'

'He's telling the truth,' Roxy said. 'I wouldn't be here if he wasn't.'

Tim looked at her, his blue eyes narrowing. 'What would you have done if I really had betrayed you?'

She smiled. 'I would have found somewhere else to go – and another machine I could use to hack into the system. Then I would have destroyed your security database. I'd have allied myself with Reeve, or someone like that, and got some kind of power. And I'd have made your life hell.'

'But – I thought that you hated Reeve,' Jess said.

'Oh, I do,' Roxy said quietly. 'I do. And believe me, when I've finished with him . . .' Her eyes glittered.

'I get the message,' Jess said. She walked over to Tim and held out her hand. 'Jess Holt. Pleased to meet you.'

He smiled at her. 'Tim Fraser. Likewise.'

He turned to look at Giselle; she sighed. 'Okay. If Roxy – I mean, Chloe – says you're straight, then I believe her.'

Tim smiled at her but didn't offer to shake her hand, knowing that she'd refuse.

'Philip Howard.' Philip held out his hand.

Tim took it, still slightly wary of him. 'Philip.'

Philip smiled then, and hugged Roxy. 'And thanks for not forgetting me – Chloe.' He ruffled her hair. 'If it wasn't for your eyes and your voice, I wouldn't have recognized you.'

'Amazing what a pair of scissors and a pot of dye can do for you,' Roxy said, laughing. 'That's why I left the lenses out this time – because I didn't think that you'd know who I was otherwise.'

'So, what's the plan?' Jess asked.

'Tim and I will be working together. I don't want to tell you all the details, because if anything goes wrong and they interrogate you, it's better for you if you don't know anything.'

'Agreed,' Giselle said grimly.

'But, for now, we have you both requisitioned to work on the house, and Philip to look after you – to make sure that you're doing your job properly and that you don't try to escape. After all, we can't afford a repeat of the Roxana Winters episode.' Roxy smiled. 'You'll be pleased to know, Jess, that there's a good supply of decent coffee in the kitchen, plus the finest Swiss chocolate, and the fridge is well stocked.'

'We're getting some furniture sorted at the moment. If there's anything else you want,' Tim added, 'just ask, and we'll get it for you.'

Giselle looked thoughtful. 'It's a nice idea, R— Chloe,' she corrected herself hastily, 'but what if someone comes round to check up, and discovers that nothing's been done to this house?'

'Shit.' Roxy winced. 'I didn't think of that.' She shrugged. 'Maybe I can do some work on it myself, during the evenings or something.'

'Actually,' Jess said, 'I had writer's block once. It was hell. I couldn't work – so I decided to forget about it and start decorating my house instead. It loosened the block.' She grinned. 'And I really enjoyed it – doing something I didn't have to think about, singing along to the radio and slapping paint everywhere.'

'And I worked as a decorator,' Philip said, 'when I was a student in the holidays.'

Giselle grinned. 'Well, I'm game to do it, if you lot are.'

'Hang on,' Roxy said. 'We didn't spring you out of that place to make you slave for us.'

'It won't be slavery,' Jess said. 'Though don't expect the house to be finished *too* quickly.'

'Of course not,' Roxy said. 'It has to be done properly. You might even have to do it three times over, before I'm satisfied.'

They exchanged complicit grins, and hugged each other again.

Tim slipped his arm round Roxy's shoulders. 'Well, it was nice to meet you all,' he said, 'and I'm sure we'll get to know each other a lot better. But I have to go and show my face in official circles, and Chloe here has work to do.' He ruffled her short hair. 'We'd better be going.' He took a pad and paper from his pocket, scribbling a number and handing it to Jess. 'This is my private line. Digital, untappable, and safe. Memorize it and destroy the paper, please.'

'Will do.' Jess smiled at him. 'See you later, then.'

Tim glanced at Roxy as they drove back to the flat. A smile was playing at the corners of her mouth: half mischievous, half amused.

'What?' he asked softly.

'Nothing.'

'You're thinking of something,' he persisted.

'Mm.' She smiled. 'I was thinking about Jess, Giselle and Phil.'

Tim's face darkened. 'I see.'

'It's not what you think.' She laid her hand on his thigh, squeezing it gently. 'What happened between us in the House of Correction – it was circumstances, Tim. First of all, I thought you were dead. I was incredibly miserable, and all I wanted was to get out of that place and be revenged for you. I took some comfort where I could. Then, when I found out that you were alive, and I thought that you'd betrayed me . . .'

'They say that revenge is a dish best served cold,' Tim said wryly.

'As a matter of fact,' Roxy said, 'I was just thinking that Phil seems pretty besotted with Jess. And I imagine that Giselle will step in to fulfil the role that I had.'

'Right.'

'There really is nothing to be jealous about.'

'I know.' He looked at her as he opened the door to the flat. 'Is there anything else you need me to get for you?'

She shook her head. 'I can do all the coding, and you got me a replacement headset.'

'Mm. The original was in pieces when I got home. Like the rest of the PC – totally trashed.'

'Well, this one's more up to date. I'll treat it as a bonus.' She closed the door behind them. 'And, talking of a bonus . . .' She grinned. 'How do you feel like being late for your meeting?'

'No. I have to go – otherwise they'll be suspicious. I'm never late.'

'I see.' She slid her arms round his neck, kissing him lingeringly. As she pressed her pelvis against his, she felt the gratifyingly large bulge of his erection push against her.

Tim groaned, tearing his mouth from hers. 'Rox. You bloody witch. You know I want you – how much I need you. But if I don't go to this meeting, they'll guess that something's up. We can't risk it.'

'As you wish.'

He groaned again, rubbing his cheek against hers. 'As it is, I won't be able to concentrate, thinking about you.'

'Knowing what I'm going to be doing – setting up the

program, as I did before, with you in it. Making love to you, all day, when you're a couple of miles down the road ...' She chuckled, and kissed him lightly on the lips. 'See you later.'

'Mm.' He smiled at her. 'And later, I'll claim my reward. A very prolonged lovemaking session.'

'Tut, tut, Mr Fraser. Sex is for procreation, not recreation, remember ...' Laughing, she escaped to her study.

A few days later, when Jess, Giselle and Phil had settled into a routine at the house in Holland Park, Roxy decided that it was time to introduce them to Alice. She drove over to Alice's and Marcus's house, saying that they were off on a minor mystery tour.

'Where exactly are we going?' Alice asked as she strapped Eleanor into the baby seat in the back of the car and climbed into the front seat.

'My new house,' Roxy said. 'Rather, it will be, in a few months.'

'What are you plotting?' Alice asked. Even though Roxy was using the lenses, so Alice couldn't use her old method of telling Roxy's mood from the colour of her eyes, the mischief on Roxy's face was a dead giveaway. 'Seriously, Rox – where are we going?'

'Like I told you, to my new house,' Roxy repeated. 'And the name's Chloe.'

'Chloe.' Alice rolled her eyes. 'I'll never get used to calling you that.'

'You will.' Roxy smiled at her. 'And the reason we're off to Holland Park isn't because I want to show off, it's because there's someone I want you to meet. Well, three people, actually.'

Alice's eyes widened as she made the connection. 'You mean, you managed to spring Jess and Giselle?'

'I did indeed.' Roxy grinned. 'They're working for Mrs Tim Fraser, right now, doing up her new house.'

'Working for you? And who's the third person?'

'Their guard, Philip.'

'You mean – the guard that you – er—'

'Made love with?' Roxy supplied, laughing. 'Yes. Nowadays, all working prisoners have to be guarded. We can't risk another of these dangerous women escaping, can we?'

Alice laughed back. 'You wicked woman! What's really happening?'

'Actually, they really are doing up the house for me. They're enjoying it, would you believe?' She pulled a face. 'God only knows why. I hate the smell of paint.'

'You hate doing anything,' Alice said, 'that doesn't involve your computer.'

'Well.' Roxy didn't look abashed.

Eventually, they pulled up outside the house. 'Wow,' Alice said. 'Talk about the trappings of power!'

Roxy flinched. 'It's not like that.'

'I know.' Alice squeezed her hand. 'I was teasing you. And I think you picked the best possible way to get them out.' She paused. 'Have you had any contact with Reeve yet?'

Roxy shook her head. 'We'll be inviting some of the Ministers over to dinner, one by one, but Reeve won't be among them. It's too much of a risk. If he recognizes me . . .' She shrugged. 'Anyway, come in. I want you to meet them all.'

As Roxy had predicted, Alice, Giselle, Jess and Phil took to each other immediately. Giselle and Alice discovered that they had friends in common, although they'd never actually met, and Jess appreciated Alice's easy humour and quick wit.

Philip liked her, too, responding to her warm smile and pretty face. He seemed to have changed over the past few weeks, from the surly and taciturn guard that Jess and Roxy had first met to an articulate, friendly and fun-loving young man – more and more like the art students that Alice used to go out with, at university. Philip had eventually told them that he was an English graduate, and Roxy had groaned, saying that now she had *four* people to tell her what a philistine she was. Alice, Jess, Giselle and Philip.

Alice could see exactly what had attracted Roxy to Philip, and smiled to herself. He reminded her very much of a younger Tim Fraser, with those incredible blue eyes, small round glasses, and a mouth that was made for kissing. Not that Roxy would ever admit it; but Alice was amused and touched, at the same time.

Roxy smiled at them all. 'I hope you don't think that I'm neglecting you,' she said. 'But . . .'

Alice rolled her eyes. 'Don't tell me. You have some work to do.'

Roxy was surprised. 'How did you know that I was going to say that?'

'Because,' Alice said, 'I shared a flat with you for years. I bet I can guess what kind of work it is, too.'

Roxy nodded. 'I don't want to talk about it, though. The less you all know about it, the better it will be for you if anything goes wrong.'

'Just be careful.' Giselle said.

Roxy smiled. 'I don't need to be careful. Tim's the Head of National Security, so no one questions what he does.'

'Yes, but you're not Tim,' Jess reminded her.

'I'm Mrs Tim Fraser, which is the next best thing.' Roxy spread her hands. 'And under this government's laws, what can a mere woman like me do?' She winked, and left them, heading back to the flat to work on the code for VRX.

She worked surely and rapidly, not even stopping for a cup of coffee. When the alarm on her PC beeped at her, her eyes widened in surprise and she looked at her watch, checking that it really was half past four. Time to pick up Alice, and for Jess and Giselle to be escorted back to the House of Correction by Philip.

Roxy always made a point of being there when the guards came to pick up the prisoners and when they were dropped off in the morning. Although it cut into her working time, she thought that it was best to keep up appearances, and Tim backed her on that. They were doing so well; it was stupid to risk ruining everything for the sake of a couple of hours' work.

Once the official car had come to pick up Jess and Giselle, Roxy took Alice home. 'I hope you're coming in for a coffee,' Alice said.

Roxy smiled regretfully. 'Sorry, Al. Not today. I'm in the middle of a difficult patch.'

'You're working too hard,' Alice said. 'You've got shadows under your eyes. You've been working late at night, too, haven't you?'

Roxy nodded. 'But Tim's been helping. When he can, that is. Though he made the program crash again last night.'

Alice bit her lip. 'You don't think that Tim's . . .' She winced. 'No, forget it.'

'That Tim's what?'

'That he's . . .' Alice took a deep breath. 'Rox, don't be angry, but I can't help wondering if maybe he's deliberately sabotaging you? Setting you up?'

'A double agent, you mean?' Roxy's stomach lurched. She'd

been trying to keep that thought out of her mind, thinking that her experiences in the House of Correction had made her paranoid. Now that Alice had voiced it, too ... She tried to sound bright. 'I don't think so. We kept making the last version crash, too, when we developed it; we just need to remember what the glitches are. You're talking about thousands and thousands of lines of code, Al – and although my memory's pretty good, it's not photographic.'

'Do you trust him?'

Roxy's face was bleak. 'I want to. What he's told me – it's all plausible, but there's something deep inside me that wonders. I don't understand why he believed them when they said that I was dead – why he didn't check, and get me out of that place.' She looked Alice straight in the eye. 'You don't trust him, and I'm not a hundred per cent sure. What does Marcus think?'

Alice spread her hands. 'Marcus trusts him – and don't forget, Marcus has known Tim for a lot longer than we have.'

'Well, I'll trust Marcus's instincts, then. We're just being paranoid, now that we're second-class citizens.' Roxy gave her friend a hug. 'See you later, Al. Take care.'

'You too. And don't work too hard.'

Roxy grinned. 'Moi?' she teased, as she walked back to the car.

Alice rolled her eyes. 'You never change!'

Roxy drove home again; she was still working on the program when Tim came in. He came into the study, resting his hands on her shoulders; she tipped her head back, looking at him. He leaned forward and kissed her lightly. 'Good day?'

'Yeah. I'm at a critical bit, at the moment.'

'You work too hard.'

'I'm working,' Roxy reminded him, 'to a deadline. That

is, if you did manage to get an invitation for one of the ministers?'

He nodded. 'Next Wednesday night.'

'Well, then. There's still a lot to do.'

'I can help, if you like.'

'So far you've been more of a hindrance.' The words were out before she could stop them.

Tim had been massaging her shoulders; he stilled his hands, and spun the chair round so that Roxy was facing him. 'Roxana.'

She was surprised. He hardly ever used her full name, except when they were having a row. 'What?'

'We need to talk.'

'About what?'

'About us. You and me.' He swallowed. 'Save the file, Rox. I need to talk to you.'

'I'm busy, Tim.'

'This is more important than that damned program. If you don't save it, I'll switch it off anyway.'

Her lip curled. 'That'd be clever, wouldn't it? Wiping out everything I've done today?' She remembered that uneasy conversation with Alice, and her eyes narrowed. Maybe Alice had a point. She had to know the truth. 'Sometimes, Tim, I wonder if you're trying to sabotage what I'm doing.'

'Sabotage?'

He looked shocked: yet it could all be an act. She shrugged. 'Well, whenever you've worked on the program, you've crashed it.'

'Which is exactly what happened the first time round. I'm sorry.'

'Are you?' She saved her work, backed it up onto a disk, and switched off the machine. 'How sorry?'

'If you want me to show you ...' He took her hand, and turned it over. He drew her wrist up to his mouth and kissed the sensitive skin of her inner wrist, his tongue stroking her pulse point.

Roxy shivered, despite herself. Part of her was angry with Tim – and yet part of her couldn't resist him. She didn't pull back when he led her to the bathroom and undressed her swiftly; he switched on the shower, letting the water heat up, then stripped swiftly and lifted her into the warm jets.

'God, you're so lovely,' he breathed, taking a bar of soap and lathering her skin. He played with her nipples, teasing them into hardness, and then bent his head to suckle them gently. Roxy groaned, sliding her hands into his hair and urging him on. He laughed against her skin, and then lifted her slightly, pushing her against the wall. He was already hard, and she gave a shudder of pleasure as he fitted the tip of his cock to her sex and entered her.

He thrust hard, fast, needing the release as much as she did; Roxy cried out as she came, her internal muscles flexing hard around his cock. It was enough to tip him into his own climax; he stayed there for a moment, just holding her close, then gently withdrew from her, letting her slide back down his body until her feet were on the floor again.

He washed her gently, lovingly, in silence; then he switched off the shower, picked her up, and carried her into the bedroom, not bothering to dry either of them first. He pushed the duvet aside and lowered Roxy onto the bed, then moved her so that her knees were bent and her legs parted, her feet flat on the mattress. He knelt between her legs and paused there for a moment, looking at her.

Roxy met his eyes; his eyes were very dark, very serious. He seemed to be pleading with her – to trust him, to believe in him. She wanted to: and yet, there was still that niggling fear.

She made an effort, and reached up to touch his face. 'Tim.'

'Yes?' His voice was very controlled, and yet she could hear the longing in it.

'Make me forget it all,' she commanded, her voice husky; his face filled with relief and he leaned forward to kiss her, his tongue sliding between her lips. He caressed her breasts, his touch light yet sure, and she found herself arching up towards him, desire snaking within her.

He slid his hands down her thighs, gently lifting and straightening her legs; then he pushed just the tip of his cock inside her. Roxy groaned, and he began to move, moving just his prick-end rapidly in and out of her.

It felt good, so good: she cried out, pushing up against him, wanting to feel him completely sheathed inside her. And yet he held back, still pumping the tip of his cock back and forth, teasing her, until her quim was liquid and throbbing, her internal muscles contracting sharply with her climax. Then, and only then, did he allow himself to sink into her properly, up to the hilt, so that the aftershocks of her orgasm rippled over his cock.

Roxy moaned, and Tim continued to thrust, lifting her buttocks slightly to increase his penetration; as the second wave of her climax pulsed over her, he, too, came, his cock throbbing deep within her. He held her close, his head against her shoulder, and Roxy was shocked to feel moisture against her skin. He was crying.

She said nothing, not knowing quite what to say: in the end, she just held him close and stroked his hair, soothing him.

At last, he lifted his head and looked at her. 'Roxy,' he said softly, his voice catching. 'I know that this isn't a good time – but I don't think that any time would be good. We have to talk.'

She'd taken her lenses out earlier; her eyes were very green as she looked at him. 'Talk?'

'About you and me.' He paused. 'I don't think you trust me.' She was silent, and he sighed. 'You accused me of sabotage this evening.'

'I was tired, Tim. I've been overdoing it, trying to sort the program as quickly as I can. I just got a bit snappy with you.' She bit her lip.' I'm sorry.'

He withdrew from her, and rolled onto his side. 'But you've also passworded some of your files so I can't get into them.'

She shrugged. 'Force of habit.'

'You never used to password your files when we worked together before – not unless you were using a password we both knew, or could guess. So why this? Why now?'

'I don't know, Tim.' She rubbed her hand across her eyes. 'Tim, just leave it, will you? I'm tired, and I don't want to row with you.'

'But it's important, Rox. I don't want it to go wrong. Now I've got you back, I don't want to lose you again. And if you don't trust me, I'll lose you.'

'I do trust you.' Her voice was flat.

He shook his head. 'No. There's still a reserve between us. Even when we make love, sometimes I think you're holding back.'

She sighed, closing her eyes and resting her forehead against his chest. 'Look, Tim, I've been through a hell of a lot. I was in the House of Correction; I was forced to go to Reeve every day – drudging for him, being used. It's going to take me a long time to forget it.'

'I know, and every time I see Reeve I want to kill him for what he did to you.'

'No,' Roxy said quickly. 'If you give him any chance to suspect us, we're done for. Leave it. Besides,' she said, 'I want to be the one to bring him down. I want to see his face, and I want him to know that I'm the one who's the cause of his downfall.'

'And you don't trust me,' Tim said softly.

'I want to.'

'But?'

'Tim, I had a lot of thinking time, in the House of Correction. First of all, I thought you were dead – I was sure that if there was any way, you'd have sprung me from that bloody place.'

'Rox, we've been through this. I swear, if I'd known that you were there, I *would* have got you out. Believe me.'

'But you thought that I was dead.'

'I've already told you that.'

'And yet you didn't think to check, to make sure?'

'I had no reason to think that they'd lie to me.'

'Didn't you? Tim, you're the Head of National Security. You must have known about the House of Correction. You must have known what they were doing there.'

Tim held her closer. 'What they told me was that the House of Correction was a place for women who resisted the new order. It would be like a training school, where women would be taught the reasons behind the new regime. Learning through kindness.'

'And you believed that?' Roxy said. 'Christ, the name itself should have given you a clue. It's all about power games, ritual humiliation. Except that the woman who's been cast in the role of a submissive doesn't want to be in that role. It wasn't a mutual game, Tim – it was hell.'

'They told me that there would be no pain.'

Roxy thought about it. 'I was never hit – not after the first time, when they knocked me out.'

'So they didn't lie to me about that.'

'No.' Her face tightened. 'Though I still don't know whether you're just naive or stupid.'

'Thanks a lot. And what would you have done, in my position?'

'If you'd been taken?' Roxy thought about it. 'Well, fighting the system would have been pointless – then I'd have been thrown into jail, too, and I wouldn't have had a chance to do anything useful. The best way to find out what was going on would be to be part of the government, and work from the inside to bring it down.'

'Which is exactly what I did – what I'm doing now.'

'But I would have gone further than you did,' Roxy said. 'I would have checked the database, to see if they were telling me the truth. I would have found out what was really happening, and done something about it. Tim, you just buried your head in the sand!'

'In my work, actually,' he corrected tightly. 'It was the only way I could cope with losing you. People have different ways of coping – like the way you coped, in the House of Correction. I wouldn't have done that.'

'You mean, if you'd been sharing a cell with another man – a man you liked, someone you thought would become a good friend – and he'd been abused, the way that Jess had been abused . . . You wouldn't have taken the pain and shame away, by giving him affection?'

'Not sexual affection, no,' Tim said. He buried his face in her hair. 'Rox. I love you. I just wish you'd learn to trust me again.'

'Like I said, I've been through a lot.' She didn't respond to his caresses. 'I won't forget it in a hurry.'

'I know. And I'm sorry for what happened. Believe me, if I could change it, I would. But I can't turn back the clock, Roxy. All I can do is be here for you, now, help you as much as I can. I got the PC for you, and the rest of the equipment. I'm arranging the small and intimate dinner parties you wanted. What else can I do?'

She took a deep breath. 'If I don't trust you, then they've won – they've destroyed what we had.'

'Exactly.'

She nodded. 'All right. But, Tim – if I ever find out that you've lied to me . . .'

He cupped her chin, turning her face so that she could see his eyes. 'I'm not lying to you now, Rox. And I never will.'

'Good.' Her eyes were very intense.

'Now, Madam, if you'll tell me your password, I'll link up your code with mine.' He smiled. 'And then, we get the first minister on our side.'

She smiled back. Whatever she'd been through – it wasn't Tim's fault. He loved her; his body had proved that much to her. She had to forget the past – or, at least, put it to the back of her mind when he was around. 'In a moment. I think we have something more important to do first.'

'Oh?'

She slid her hands down his body, curling her fingers round his stiffening cock, and smiled. 'Like this . . .'

FIFTEEN

Roxy had butterflies in her stomach. Supposing that it didn't work? Supposing that the minister either refused to try the program, or blew the whistle on Tim? If Tim went to jail, she'd be without protection – and, even worse, she'd be sent back to Reeve . . .

She swallowed hard and clenched her fists, trying to calm herself. Of course it would work. They'd researched the database thoroughly, and Roxy had compiled a dossier on each of the ministers, with Tim's help. They'd agreed between them which were the most likely to be affected by the program, the ones who were most likely to crack.

Of course it would work. The ministers would try the program. The temptation would be too much – they wouldn't be able to help themselves. And they couldn't go to the President afterwards, exposing Tim's plans, because they'd be implicated themselves. They wouldn't want to risk Ferris's displeasure and being demoted themselves, particularly as Tim could say that he was merely testing out a theory that some of the ministers weren't true Party members.

She took a deep breath, counted to ten – and jumped, as Tim's hands settled on her shoulders. 'Christ, Tim, don't do that!' she said crossly. 'You frightened the life out of me!'

He spun her round to face him, rubbing his nose affectionately against hers. 'Calm down, Rox.'

'Sorry.' She managed a watery smile. 'I was just thinking.'

He read her thoughts accurately. 'About what will happen if it goes wrong tonight, you mean?'

She nodded, not wanting to put her thoughts into words.

He stroked her face with the backs of his fingers. 'Rox, it isn't going to go wrong. Think about it logically.'

'I just have,' she said. 'If they bring you down, they bring themselves down at the same time. Not one of them will do it.'

'Exactly. We've planned this thoroughly, so it can't go wrong. We've built in all the fail-safes.'

'What if the program crashes?'

'It won't. You've tested it. Now, will you stop fretting? I want you to enjoy yourself tonight.'

'I'll try.'

He kissed her lightly. 'This is it, Rox. It's the start. We're going to bring down Ferris, and everything he stands for.'

'You'd better believe it,' she quipped.

A few seconds later, the doorbell rang. Roxy looked at Tim, her eyes wide. 'Just relax,' he said. 'Be yourself – Chloe Fraser.'

'And don't forget to call me Chloe,' she reminded him. 'Not Roxy.'

'How could I forget, with those laser eyes of yours?' He grinned, and went to answer the door. A few moments later, he returned with Alan Sheppard, the Minister of Finance.

'Chloe, this is Alan Sheppard,' Tim said. 'Sheppard, this is my wife – Chloe.'

Sheppard shook her hand. 'Pleased to meet you.'

'And you,' she responded. Sheppard wasn't quite what she'd expected. He didn't look like a finance person. True, he was wearing a dull grey suit, a white shirt and a very sober tie – but he didn't have the cool detachment that Roxy remembered from the finance team at Visicom. His brown eyes were sparkling, and his smile was genuine. Under other circumstances, Roxy thought, she would probably have liked the man.

They kept to small talk throughout the meal. Sheppard complimented Roxy on the avocado-and-bacon salad, followed by sole *bonne femme* with fresh vegetables, and strawberries Romanov; she accepted the compliment with a smile, not meeting his eyes. Wives were meant to be quiet and decorous, under Traditional Values rules: she couldn't afford him to suspect that she was anything different.

Tim made sure that Sheppard's glass was kept filled – first with Chablis, then with Beaumes de Venise. By the time that the meal had finished, Sheppard had drunk twice as much as Tim and Roxy put together. Roxy had hardly touched a drop of alcohol, keeping to her quiet and submissive image, and also being too nervous to drink.

When Tim poured out the brandy, he smiled at Sheppard. 'So,' he said softly. 'My wife and I have a little something we'd like to show you.'

Sheppard was interested. 'A sneak preview of something you're working on for the President?'

'Not exactly,' Tim said. He tipped his head on one side. 'I think that you're the sort of man who'd appreciate this – unlike Ferris.'

'Appreciate what?'

Roxy looked at Tim, her eyes wide. Don't say that they'd miscalculated – that Sheppard wasn't who they thought he was! *Please God*, she begged, *let this work. It* has *to*.

Tim caught the panic in her gaze and shook his head, the movement almost imperceptible. 'It's something very special,' he said softly to Sheppard. 'It's something I think that you'll enjoy. You always liked women, didn't you, Sheppard?'

The older man's eyes narrowed. 'How do you mean?'

'At Cambridge. You had some very interesting discussions with your Classics tutor – on *Lysistrata*.'

Sheppard's voice was carefully neutral. 'That's in the past.'

'But you miss the old days, Sheppard, don't you? You miss the freedom.'

'Is this some kind of test?' Sheppard asked. 'You've got this taped, testing me to see if I'm loyal to the President?'

Tim laughed. 'The room isn't bugged, Sheppard. I'm the Head of National Security.'

'Exactly. How do I know that you're not trying to catch me out?'

'Because I'm offering to show you a program. A very special program.'

Sheppard was torn. On the one hand, he was the Minister for Finance, and Tim Fraser was offering him something that was obviously illegal. He should have nothing to do with it. Anything to do with the old days had to be banned. And yet the reference to Rose Baker, his old Classics tutor, caught his memories. They'd had a wild affair, after that tutorial on *Lysistrata*. Alan could still remember the way she'd felt, the softness of her skin, her sweet powdery perfume, her little cries as she came . . .

He shivered. Quite how Tim had managed to find out about Rose, he had no idea: but that was obviously something to do with being Head of National Security. Tim could find out anything he chose. And yet, in his position, Tim should be trying to stamp out people who thought about the old days, not encourage them. What the hell was he playing at?

Memories of Rose, wakened by the amount of wine and brandy he'd drunk, tipped the balance. 'All right.'

Roxy and Tim exhaled simultaneously; neither of them had

been aware that they'd been holding their breath, waiting for Sheppard's decision.

Tim led Sheppard through to the study. Roxy followed, still feeling nervous, with her heart hammering wildly.

'So where's the program?' Alan asked.

'It's here,' Roxy said, walking over to the machine and switching it on.

'You mean, you're involved in this as well?'

She nodded. 'It's something that Tim and I call the Tiresias factor.'

He frowned. 'The Tiresias factor?'

'Yes. You read Classics at Cambridge, so you know who Tiresias was – and what happened to him,' Tim said.

'Yes – but what does that have to do with a computer program?'

'Try it. You'll find out.' He handed the headset to Sheppard.

'What's this?' Sheppard asked, looking at it.

'You've heard of virtual reality?' Roxy asked.

'Yes.'

'This is the sort of headset you use to work with virtual reality programs. It's a new design, lightweight. And these . . .' She gestured to the sensor pads. 'You put them on your skin, and they connect with the program through infrared waves. It means that you feel things, as well as see them.'

'That's incredible,' Sheppard said. 'And this Tiresias thing . . . are you telling me that you've made a program that will make you switch sex?'

'No – it'll just make you *feel* as though you've switched sex,' Tim said. 'Or you can use it in your own gender. It's up to you.'

'Sex is for procreation, not recreation,' Sheppard reminded him. 'If the President knew about this . . .'

Tim spread his hands. 'He doesn't know about it, Sheppard. It's a secret, between you and us.'

Sheppard was silent for a moment, as if debating whether to leave immediately and tell Ferris what Tim was doing, or whether he should stay and try out the program. In the end, curiosity won. 'I've always wondered what it feels like to be a woman,' he admitted quietly.

'Then now's your chance to find out,' Roxy said.

'How does it work?'

'You put the sensors in place.' She coughed. 'Precisely where is your decision, but I think that Tim can tell you where they work best. Then you choose the option you want from the menu.'

Tim set the program running. 'You can be a man or a woman; you can choose whether you want to make love to a man or a woman, and even how many,' he said. 'It's up to you what they look like. And then you can choose your fantasy, using one of the programmed scenarios, or even a free-format one where your imagination is the only limit.'

Sheppard was stunned. 'My God! In the old days, if you'd produced this you'd have made a fortune.'

'Yeah.' Tim smiled. 'We were stuck with the legal issues. I as a private individual could enjoy making love with Marilyn Monroe, Elizabeth Taylor as Cleopatra, Meg Ryan – or maybe an unknown actress who'd caught my eye. Anyone I chose. But that was a private decision, in a prototype program. If I'd sold it to someone else, marketed it as a way of making love with the stars . . . I would have been in breach of all sorts of legislation.'

'Hm.' Sheppard's mind worked quickly. 'What you would have needed was a good lawyer, someone with experience in copyright and patents.'

'Yeah. We were getting round to it. That, and the finance angle.'

'You mean, you developed it before?'

'Chloe did,' Tim said quietly.

'Your *wife* developed it?' Sheppard was shocked.

'She's the best programmer I've ever met,' Tim said honestly. 'And even though women aren't allowed to have jobs, under Ferris's rule, he can't wipe out her intellect. He can't stop her working on projects like this. Not with my protection.'

Roxy rolled her eyes, half-embarrassed by Tim's praise. 'Look, I'll leave you to it. I'll be in the sitting room.'

Sheppard smiled. 'All right.' When she left the room, he turned to Tim. 'You knew her before, didn't you? The last thing I knew, you weren't married. Then, all of a sudden, you have a wife. I checked it out on the system, and it says that you've been married for five years – and yet she just appeared out of nowhere.'

Tim shrugged. 'A system's only as accurate as the data you input.'

'You mean, you bent it yourself?' Sheppard whistled. 'You're taking a risk, Fraser.'

'A calculated one. And I don't want to talk about my wife.' Tim looked at him. 'So do you want to try this program, or not?'

'Yes.'

'I think you'll enjoy it.'

'Marilyn Monroe,' Sheppard said ruminatively. 'I don't know whether I want to make love to her, or feel what she would feel if I was making love to her.'

'Why not both?' Tim suggested. 'You can be Marilyn – and then change places. Or even clone her, so you're making love to her at the same time as being her.'

Sheppard's eyes widened. 'My God. What a choice!'

'And you don't have to stick to her choices. You don't have to sleep with Arthur Miller, or Joe DiMaggio – you can sleep with anyone you like. Even a woman, feeling what it's like to make love with another woman.' Tim shrugged. 'I'll leave you to it, Sheppard. When you're ready, put the sensor pads in place, choose your options, put on the headset, and press the "enter" key.'

'Mrs Fraser said that you knew where to put the sensors – where they'd be most effective.'

Tim nodded. 'Your perineum, your frenum, the back of your neck, your fingertips, and your nipples. And if you need a shower afterwards, it's the next door on the left.'

He left the room; Sheppard stripped swiftly, and fitted the sensor pads in place, as Tim had suggested. He chose his first option, put on the headset, and pressed the 'enter' key.

She lay on the king-sized bed, her blonde curly hair fanning across the thick feather pillow, and a smile on her face as though she was dreaming something very pleasurable indeed. The black silk sheet over her had slipped down so that one round soft breast was uncovered, the nipple temptingly hard and rosy. A book lay next to her on the bed, as though she'd been reading and had fallen asleep, dropping the book as her eyes had closed.

Sheppard smiled at the scene. She looked so beautiful, that full generous mouth curved like that, the beauty spot over her lip in sharp relief against her creamy skin. He walked over to the bed and picked up the book, his smile broadening as he skim-read the cover. It was an erotic novel, and no doubt that was what had put the smile on her face.

The mattress gave slightly as he sat down next to her. She

made a small murmur of encouragement, moving towards him in her sleep. He stroked her face, and then – very gently – peeled the sheet downwards, revealing her beautiful and lush body.

She was utterly perfect, soft and rounded; her breasts were generous and her hips curvy, teamed with an impossibly narrow waist. The perfect hourglass, he thought happily. Her legs, too, were beautiful, perfectly shaped. Perfectly smooth, too, he discovered, as he ran his hand lightly over one thigh.

She shivered at the light contact of skin on skin, and moved again, her legs parting. He caught the faint aroma of her arousal, vanilla and honey and seashore. It was too much to resist. He slid his hand along her thigh until he cupped her delta, his fingers stretching along her quim. She felt warm, so warm, and he slid one finger between her labia, his fingers skating across the hot damp flesh. She shivered again, and widened the gap between her legs.

Sheppard smiled. He'd brought her a rose, a deep red rose; it was still in bud. When she lay there like that, so warm and soft and inviting, he couldn't resist her. He parted her labia. Inside, she was a deep, deep crimson, the same colour as the rose. He'd once read in a book, somewhere, about a woman's sex looking like a stylised rose. Anaïs Nin, or someone like that. *A rose for a rose*, he thought with a grin, and drew the tip of the bud along her quim. The petals darkened as they absorbed her juices, and he began to stroke the rose rhythmically along her musky divide, brushing her clitoris and making her moan. He continued stroking her. As her excitement grew, so the scent of her arousal grew stronger, and the way he brushed the rose against her made the flower release its scent, too. It was a heady mixture, and one that he found irresistible.

She was still half asleep, enjoying what he was doing to her.

Her hands came up to cup her breasts, and she began to roll her nipples between her forefingers and thumbs, pulling at the hard rosy flesh, and increasing her own pleasure. She made a small noise in the back of her throat; he grinned, working the rose on her, changing the rhythm and the pressure, until at last she stiffened and cried out.

Her quim fluttered under his hand, and the rose was almost drenched with her dew. She opened her eyes then, looking up at him, her pupils hugely expanded. He smiled at her, keeping his eyes locked on hers, and drew the rose up to his face, breathing in the combined perfume of the rose and her arousal.

He brushed his lips with it; the softness of the rose petals reminded him of the way her quim had felt beneath his mouth. Then, very slowly, he licked his lips, tasting her. She tipped her head back into the pillow, arching herself as she watched him; she licked her lips, mimicking him, and gave him a sensual pout.

He smiled at her again, his eyes sensual, and took the rose into his mouth, tasting the soft muskiness of her juices and the sweetness of the rose, sucking the scented moisture from the petals . . .

Sheppard flipped up the visor. *My God*, he thought. Whatever Fraser and his wife put into this thing, it was incredible. It had been so *real*. He could still smell the scent of the rose, and that beautiful woman's arousal – and her perfume, Chanel No. 5. He could feel the softness of her skin under his hands, the velvety sensation of the rose against his mouth . . .

He swallowed hard. The Tiresias factor, they'd called it. So now he could swap places with her, be her as her lover teased her with the rose. He couldn't resist it. He didn't care how long he'd been in the study already: time no longer mattered.

He just wanted to know what it was like to be her, what it felt like . . .

Quickly, he tapped another choice into the computer and slid the headset back in place.

'My God,' Tim said softly, 'Sheppard's got one hell of an imagination. I never even guessed that he would have that in mind.'

'Or something else.' Roxy pressed the pause button of the video recorder as the screen went blank. 'I think we should make him a copy of this tape, Tim.'

'It's too dangerous. We're using it to make sure he keeps on our side, remember?'

'Mm.' She turned to him, her face sensual. 'But I don't think we'll need to. He's one of us, Tim. Someone normal, someone with a good imagination and the guts to use it.'

'Yeah, you're probably right.' Tim nodded at the screen. 'I think he's just about to switch back into the program, by the look of that.'

Roxy glanced at the screen, and pressed the remote control back to "record". 'I'm not sure who's going to enjoy this most,' she said, curling back into Tim's arms as they prepared to watch Sheppard's second fantasy. 'Him, or us . . .'

She lay on the bed, half-dreaming. The sheet covering her was black silk: corny, she knew, but she liked the way that the colour offset the creaminess of her skin, her almost white-blonde hair. The contrasts of colour amused her.

She'd been reading a book, an erotic novel, that had been dedicated to her. She knew the author slightly, and it thrilled her to think that he'd been fantasizing about her as he wrote. The feeling intensified when she'd started reading it, and discovered it to be almost a very personal love-letter to her, describing what he'd like to do with her. She'd grown aroused by it, to the point of needing to masturbate, rubbing her clitoris hard until the familiar feel of pleasure snapping through her veins had brought her release.

Then, idly, she'd fallen asleep, drowsing in the late afternoon. She wasn't sure how long she'd been asleep; then she felt a sheet being pulled very gently down her body. It was one of three people, she thought, smiling to herself and keeping her eyes closed. One of her lovers, who had dropped in unexpectedly.

She lay there, still feigning sleep; when she felt the mattress give slightly, as her lover sat down next to her, she smiled and moved closer, making a small encouraging noise in the back of her throat and widening the gap between her thighs to tempt him . . . or her. She wasn't quite sure who it was yet, and didn't want to peek.

As she felt a small and soft hand sliding up her inner thigh, she stretched and tipped her head back among the pillows, suddenly knowing who it was. Only one of her lovers had hands that small, that smooth, the nails perfectly filed. Elena.

Elena was Greek, and she was still excited by the contrast of Elena's olive skin and dark eyes with her own fair skin and blue eyes. She gave a small moan of pleasure as Elena began to kiss her way down her body, tracking over her collarbone and licking the hollows, then moving down over her breasts. When Elena took one nipple into her mouth, she cried out, tipping her head back into the pillows and thrusting her body upwards. Elena chuckled and moved lower, licking the plains of her belly.

She moaned and widened the gap between her thighs,

willing Elena to move lower. Elena did so, breathing gently on her quim until she moaned again, then, with another chuckle, Elena positioned her just where she wanted her, running her hands up the creamy white thighs and gently straightening her legs. Her buttocks lifted, and Elena bent her head again.

She gave another small moan as she felt Elena's tongue stroke along her quim, starting with her clitoris and moving slowly backwards, dabbling in her folds and hollows. And then, she felt Elena lift her slightly, moving her legs so that the puckered rosebud of her anus was exposed. She felt excitement beat hard in her belly, anticipating what the beautiful Greek was going to do next, and moaned as she felt Elena's tongue probe her.

At the same time, something soft was running along her quim: something that felt very smooth, very soft. It was thicker than a finger, and yet it wasn't a vibrator or dildo. She stiffened, wondering just what it was: then, as the scent of roses filtered up to her, she smiled. Elena was trying something very new, by the feel of it, crushing the velvety petals against her quim.

She wondered idly what it would feel like to have the rose pushed into her – Elena, of course, would have planned this in advance, and chosen a flower with no thorns – and almost at the same time she felt a pressure on her vaginal entrance. It felt something like the tip of a cock pushing into her, smooth and velvety; she shivered in delight. And yet she wanted more, she wanted something bigger and harder.

Again, Elena seemed to read her mind, and the rose was gently and skilfully withdrawn. She felt something brushing her lower lip, and laughed; the soft petals of the rose were soaked with her juices, and the beautiful scent of the rose was mingled with the spicy aroma of her arousal.

She lay there, letting Elena tease her with the rose, opening her mouth and letting Elena brush her lower lip, coating it with her juices; and then she felt a finger insert itself into her warm, wet, slippery depths. She murmured, pushing up against it, and Elena added a second finger, and a third. Elena's thumb was pressed squarely against her clitoris, rubbing it in the same rhythm as her fingers pushed in and out.

Pressure built in her groin, and a warm feeling began at the soles of her feet, travelling up her legs and gathering momentum and pressure until it snaked in her gut, coiling and boiling and finally exploding. She cried out, her internal muscles contracting sharply round Elena's fingers as she reached her climax; Elena waited until her breathing had calmed, and the aftershocks of her orgasm had died away, before shifting up to cuddle her, stroking her skin and telling her how beautiful she was . . .

Sheppard removed the headset, breathing heavily. The program was dynamite. Tim was right about his wife. Chloe Fraser had an incredible brain – firstly, to dream up the virtual-reality sex program, and secondly, to make it real.

He pulled on his shirt to make himself decent, then headed for the shower. The towels were thick and fluffy; it was a luxurious room, perfect for lovemaking. Sheppard could imagine making love in the jacuzzi, in the shower – even on the bathroom floor, on one of the thick fluffy towels which hung over the Victorian-style mahogany towel stand.

What the hell was it, he wondered, about Fraser's flat? Was it the program, still reverberating in his brain; or was it something more subtle? Fraser worked with Marcus Blake, a genetics expert; were they playing around with pheromones, or something? Had they managed to create artificial ones, and were they testing them in Fraser's flat so that anyone who walked in immediately thought of making love?

He showered quickly, then dressed and walked back to the sitting room. Tim and his wife were sitting there, apparently engaged in light conversation: but Sheppard could smell sex in the air. They'd been making love while he'd been using the program. Her face was radiant, glowing, the way a woman always looked after an orgasm. Soft and warm and lovely. He thought about making love with Chloe Fraser, the woman whose mind had dreamed up that incredible program, and shivered. If she could dream up those sort of scenarios – or, at least, give people the germs of the ideas for the scenarios – then what would she be like, skin to skin?

'What did you think?' Tim asked softly.

'I think,' Sheppard said, 'that I ought to report you to Ferris.'

'That's interesting,' Roxy said. 'Maybe you ought to see something first. Just to help you make up your mind.' She nodded to Tim, who switched on the video recorder. He only played a few seconds, but it was enough for Sheppard to see himself, wearing the headset and sensor pads, and hear himself moaning as he neared the point of orgasm.

Tim pressed another button, and the video zoomed in to show the screen of the PC. On it was the scene Sheppard had envisaged: two women, making love.

He flushed, and Tim turned off the machine.

'Seen enough?' Roxy asked.

'My God. You taped it all. Everything that happened.'

'Yes. Chloe here thought that it might be a nice little present for you. But if you're going to see Ferris . . .' Tim spread his hands. 'Maybe Ferris might like to see this instead, and see how his ministers spend their leisure time. Or maybe I can just wire this to one of the press agencies, through the multimedia networks. If this tape hit the news . . .'

Sheppard closed his eyes and sat down, feeling sick. 'So what are you playing at, Fraser?'

'I'm not playing,' Tim said. 'I'm serious.'

'What do you want?'

'I want to know,' Roxy said, 'whose side you're on.'

'How do you mean?'

'Ours, or the Traditional Values Party's,' Tim explained.

Sheppard was silent while he digested the implications. 'You mean,' he said at last, 'you're planning to overthrow the Government?'

'That's precisely what we mean,' Roxy said.

'Either you're with us,' Tim added, 'in which case you can have a copy of this tape and unlimited access to the program. Or you're not.'

'In which case, you show the tape to Ferris, and I can kiss my career goodbye,' Sheppard finished.

'Clever boy,' Roxy said. 'So which is it to be?'

Sheppard sighed. 'Does it matter?'

'Yes, actually. We don't want anyone working with us who isn't really on our side. If you want to work with us, then we'd be pleased to have you on board,' Roxy said.

'And if I don't?'

'If you really believe in Ferris's values, you'd rather die than compromise them,' Tim said. 'From what I've seen in your file, I don't think you do.'

Sheppard sighed. 'No. Some of it, yes – I do think there should be means-testing for families, so children are brought up in decent conditions, and because they're really wanted. But the suppression of women, and sex only for procreation . . .' He spread his hands. 'I'm with you, Fraser.'

Roxy smiled at him. 'Good. I'm glad you feel that way, Alan.'

It was the first time that she'd used his Christian name, and a thrill went through him. God, he could imagine her whispering his name in passion . . . He shook himself. 'What do you want me to do?'

'Firstly,' Roxy said, 'we want names. Names of others you think might be on our side.'

'And the more help I give you now, the better it will be for me when the Traditional Values party is overthrown?'

'Something like that,' Tim agreed.

He smiled. 'If I do this, it's because I want to – not because I'm out to feather my nest.'

'I was hoping that you'd feel that way,' Roxy said, returning his smile.

He nodded. 'I like your program, Mrs Fraser.'

'Chloe.'

'Chloe.' He smiled again. 'And I think it's going to be a pleasure, doing business with you.'

Her answering smile was broad. 'I don't. I *know* it is.'

SIXTEEN

Tim kissed Roxy lingeringly. 'It's working,' he said softly. 'Sheppard's on our side. Roper, the Minister of the Interior, is with us all the way.' He slid his hands down her back, squeezing her buttocks gently. 'Some of the other ministers are interested, too. They say that they've heard that I have some revolutionary new idea.'

Roxy pulled back slightly, looking him straight in the eyes. 'Tim, don't fall too much in love with danger, will you?'

'How do you mean?'

'I mean, it's exciting, knowing that you're doing something that's illegal – something that could have hideous consequences if you're caught. This isn't a game, Tim. It's for real. Don't take risks.'

'I won't,' he told her. 'Don't worry. Nothing's going to go wrong.'

'You don't know that for sure. Don't tempt fate.'

'Okay.' He sobered. 'Rox.'

'What?'

'Reeve approached me today, too.'

Her gaze darkened. 'I hope you told him to piss off.'

'No, I didn't.'

She was shocked. 'You mean, you're going to invite him here?'

'No.'

'Then what?' She glared at him. 'Don't tease me, Tim.'

He grinned at her. 'Keep your hair on. You told me that you'd like to see him brought down – and that you wanted him to know that you were the one who caused it to happen.'

'Tim, we're not ready yet. We don't have enough support!'

'Which is why I simply fobbed him off.' He stroked her hair. 'I told him that it was a very techie solution, then launched into a jargon-intensive ramble.'

'And?'

'What do you think?' Tim chuckled. 'His eyes glazed over, then he muttered something about being very busy in the evenings, but he was sure that he'd get to see it, some time soon.'

'Yeah. And I'll get the chance to see him rot in hell.'

Tim slid his hands under the hem of her chiffon shirt, deftly undoing her bra and sliding his hands round to the front of her body, cupping her generous breasts in his hands. Although since moving back with Tim Roxy had put back on some of the weight she'd lost, it suited her, softening her curves slightly; and Tim, feeling her body so close to his, utterly adored her. 'Roxy,' he murmured throatily.

She rubbed her nose against his. 'I want you, too – but I thought you said that we had another of the ministers coming over tonight?'

'Yes.' He coughed. 'Actually, that's what I wanted to talk to you about.'

She pulled away. 'Tim, if you're going to tell me that Reeve's coming here—'

'No,' he cut in, 'it isn't him.'

'Who is it, then?'

'I don't know if I should tell you.'

She glared at him. 'Tim!'

'Even with those lenses in, I can still tell what colour your eyes are. Full of angry orange sparks.'

'Just bloody tell me, will you?'

'He's the Minister for Correction.'

'You mean, he's the one in charge of the Houses?'

'Exactly. But he's not what you think. He was promoted last week. The original Minister for Correction had a heart attack. Jed doesn't like what he's finding, and I think he'll be very interested in our ideas. He's been picked by Ferris because he did a psychology degree and wrote a brilliant paper on social behaviour. Ferris read it, liked it, and decided to promote him when the post became vacant.'

'I see.'

'Rox, I think you'll like him. Jed Mortimer is a good man.'

Roxy wasn't convinced, but she decided to give Jed Mortimer the benefit of the doubt, for Tim's sake. She let Tim answer the door when the bell rang, and her eyes widened in surprise when Tim led Jed Mortimer through to the sitting room. He was a lot younger than Roxy had expected. She'd been expecting someone of around Sheppard's age, believing that Tim was the youngest member of the government. Jed Mortimer looked·as though he was a couple of years older than her, at the most, and he was unexpectedly attractive.

She'd scanned in the photograph that Tim had given her, in preparation for the evening, but it hadn't been a particularly good likeness. If anything, Roxy had thought it an old photograph from a minister too vain to admit to his age; and it hadn't done him justice. Not at all. She usually fell for men with blue eyes, like Tim, but Jed Mortimer . . . Her mouth went dry. He was almost the double of the actor that she'd programmed into the original VRX program for Alice's enjoyment – the actor that they'd both fallen in lust with, years before.

He was about six feet one, slightly taller than Tim, with dark hair swept back from his forehead, and hazel eyes that were almost green. His face was slightly heart-shaped, with a strong jaw, and there was a mole on his right cheek that Roxy suddenly yearned to reach out and touch. He had a wide mouth, with a slightly vulnerable slant to it, and he was wearing black trousers, black shoes and a black round-necked loose sweater. All he needed, she thought, was a pair of small wire-rimmed glasses and a long black coat ... She shivered.

Tim glanced at Roxy and saw the change on her face. As he'd half-expected, she found Mortimer very, very attractive. Part of him was annoyed – he regarded Roxy as his private property – and yet, although her name, for the moment, was Mrs Chloe Fraser, she wasn't married to him, and he wasn't sure that she ever would be. If anything, he thought, when this was all over, her independent streak would be stronger than ever; and if she did marry him, she wouldn't take his name. She'd still be Roxana Winters.

At the same time, he couldn't help feeling a little turned on. If Jed Mortimer captured Roxy's imagination, no doubt she would bring him into the VRX program in one of her private scenarios. He had a feeling that Roxy was going to enjoy herself very much indeed.

'Jed, this is my wife, Chloe Fraser,' he said.

'Chloe. It's a beautiful name.' Jed looked at her, a smile playing about his lips, and took her hand. Roxy flushed as he drew her hand up to his mouth and kissed the back of her fingers. All of a sudden, she could imagine him using his mouth very pleasurably on other parts of her body, and it made her shiver with longing.

'Chloe – this is Jed Mortimer, the Minister for Correction.'

'Mr Mortimer,' she said demurely. She wanted to snatch

her hand away – and yet, at the same time, she wanted to touch him, much more intimately. 'Can I get you a drink?' she asked.

He smiled at her. 'Actually, I don't drink.'

Her eyes widened, and she glanced at Tim. Had he miscalculated? If Mortimer was sober, there was no way he'd try the program. Then she remembered her initial fears with Sheppard, and how well that evening had gone. She was being ridiculous. Tim wouldn't let her down – he wouldn't do anything stupid. He knew how important it was.

'In that case, how about some mineral water?'

Mortimer smiled at her. 'Thank you. Plain and still will do me nicely; no ice or lemon, thanks.'

Tim had told her that their visitor that evening was a vegetarian, and Roxy had been careful in her choice of menu. He ate the buttered asparagus with obvious enjoyment; she didn't dare look at him as she ate her own, using her fingers, because she knew that it was too suggestive. She was embarrassed, too, because she didn't want to feel like this. Tim was the man in her life. But Jed Mortimer *was* overwhelmingly attractive.

She was silent as she ate the mushroom bake and green salad, and she avoided Mortimer's gaze as she served up the white chocolate mousse with raspberries. It was lucky that she'd chosen this recipe and not Alice's current favourite, an equally creamy concoction that was spiked liberally with Drambuie.

Eventually, after coffee, Mortimer looked at Tim. 'So,' he said. 'This program you were going to show me – the one you thought I might find quite interesting.'

'Yes.' Tim coughed. 'It's very special; but it's not for the narrow-minded.'

Mortimer's eyes flickered. Roxy decided at that moment

that she'd never play poker with this man. She couldn't tell what he was thinking, or what he was feeling. 'What makes you think,' Mortimer said, 'that I'm broad-minded enough to enjoy it?'

'Let's call it a hunch,' Tim said.

Roxy's eyes darted from one to the other. They were verbally circling each other, testing each other. If this went on for much longer, the whole thing would crash down around their ears. She decided to intervene, for safety's sake. She stood up, and laid her hand on top of Mortimer's. 'Tim has a good intuition,' she said softly, 'but he also told me about you, and I've read part of your file.'

Mortimer frowned. 'I didn't think that women had access to the security database.'

She smiled. 'I'm the wife of the Head of National Security. Surely that puts me above reproach?'

'That depends . . .'

She couldn't help rubbing her thumb over the back of his hand. 'I think,' she said softly, 'that you'll enjoy this.'

He stood up. 'All right. Where is it?'

Tim looked at Roxy. 'I think,' he said quietly, 'that you might be better at explaining what the program is, seeing as you developed it.'

She met his eyes, and flushed. Tim knew exactly what she thought about Jed Mortimer. 'I think that you ought to be there, too, Tim,' she said.

'Are you sure?'

She nodded. 'Sure.' She led the way to the study, and explained to Mortimer about the program.

Mortimer's eyes were bright as he looked at her. 'And you developed it all yourself?'

'At first, yes. But I could only program it from a woman's

point of view – which is where Tim came in, and it became a joint project.'

'What would you do,' Mortimer asked idly, 'if I went to Ferris, and told him what you were doing?'

'As Head of National Security,' Tim said, 'I can, of course, test that people are who they say they are, and hold official views in private as well as in public.'

Mortimer nodded. 'And I, as the Minister for Correction, could call your bluff, and say that I was testing you, too.'

Roxy held her breath. What was Tim going to do, now? Was he going to blow this by arguing with Mortimer, wanting to outsmart him?

To her mingled relief and surprise, Tim merely smiled. 'You could,' he acknowledged. 'Which would leave us in stalemate. But—' he paused '—I've read your paper, too. I don't think that the way the government is going is the way that you'd like to see it working.'

'You're right,' Mortimer agreed. 'And you don't need to make a back-up tape for me.'

'How do you mean?' Roxy asked.

'Well, it's fairly obvious. If you tape me trying this program, then I can't denounce you to Ferris. I'd be denouncing myself. But you don't need to do that with me.'

'How do we know that we can trust you?'

His eyes held hers. 'Because,' he said softly, 'if you want to overthrow Ferris's government, you'll have to do it by trusting people. If you "persuade" people onto your side by threats and fears, then you're as bad as Ferris – as much of a despot as he is.'

'You're right,' Roxy said. 'But actually, when we have taped what happens, we've given it to the Ministers concerned as a very personal present.'

'I don't have a video,' he informed her, 'or a television.'

Roxy smiled. 'We don't use ours that much, actually. Just to see the occasional film.' She shrugged. 'Well, it's up to you. If you want to try the program, you're welcome. If you don't, then that's your decision.'

'I think,' he said slowly, 'I'd like to.'

'Fair enough. I'll leave you to it. Tim will show you how it works.' She left the room without meeting his glance again.

Tim went through the basics, as he had with Sheppard and Roper, then went to join Roxy in the sitting room. She had the television on; Tim frowned. 'I thought you said that you weren't going to tape this?'

'I'm not. There isn't a tape in the machine.'

'Then what are you doing?'

'I'm curious. I want to see what he does – who he picks, who he fantasizes about. Some actress, maybe.'

Tim met her gaze. 'You fancy him, don't you?'

Roxy coughed. 'Look, Tim, I'm not going to be unfaithful to you, if that's what you're thinking.'

Tim wasn't convinced. 'It's mutual. And Jed Mortimer is a very clever man – if he wants to go to bed with you, he'll find a way round every argument, every defence, until you end up agreeing with him. He's a psychologist by training, remember.'

Roxy was silent for a long while. 'And if I do end up making love with him?' she asked, finally.

'Then there isn't much I can do about it.' He took her hand, kissing the palm and curling his fingers round it. 'If it makes you happy, and it's only the once, then I won't make a fuss about it.'

She nodded. 'If it happens, it'll be with your consent or ＇ at all.'

'Yeah.' He smiled ruefully. 'You're not my personal property. I don't have the right to tell you what to do.'

'Even though I'm Mrs Chloe Fraser?'

'Especially because.' He squeezed her hand. 'Now – I think Mortimer is about to make his choices.' He pulled her onto the sofa, next to him, and curled one arm around her; with the other hand, he manipulated the remote control to zoom in to the PC screen. His eyes widened as he saw the options that Mortimer had chosen.

Tim had already selected Mortimer's face; Mortimer had flipped rapidly through their library of faces, and selected two more – Tim's and Roxy's. 'What the . . .' Tim's breath hissed through his teeth. 'I don't believe this.'

'He's either teasing us,' Roxy said, 'or he's trying to tell us something. The question is, which?'

They watched Mortimer flick deftly through the other options; then he settled back into the chair, put on the headset, and pressed 'enter'.

They were sitting together in the living room, listening to a Beethoven string quartet. The lights were low, and there was a bottle of champagne standing on the coffee table. There was only one glass, and the three of them were sipping from it in turn.

Tim had one arm round Roxy's shoulders, and Jed had one hand resting lightly on her thigh. She was wearing a very demure pleated skirt, in navy blue, and a loose white shirt. The material was very thin, and Jed could feel the heat of her skin through her skirt. Tim's hand slid down from her shoulders, so that his fingers cupped one breast.

Roxy shivered and arched back against the sofa. The signal was the one that the men had been waiting for: Tim smiled and began unbuttoning her shirt, revealing the white lacy bra they'd glimpsed beneath it. Jed also smiled, and gradually bunched her skirt in his hand, pulling the hem upwards until he could slide his hand beneath it and along the smooth creamy skin of her thighs.

He could feel how excited she was, through the lacy gusset of her knickers; her quim was heated, and she wanted them just as much as they wanted her. Jed brought up his left hand to cup her chin, turning her face towards him and kissing her lingeringly. Her mouth opened beneath his, and he slid his tongue into her mouth, exploring her. She slid one hand round the nape of his neck, massaging it and urging him on.

Meanwhile, Tim had pulled down the lacy cups of her bra to expose her breasts. Her nipples were hard and dark, in sharp contrast to the creaminess of her breasts; he moved slightly, so that he could kneel before her, and buried his face between her breasts, breathing in her soft scent. She made a small sound of pleasure, and his mouth tracked down to one nipple, sucking at the hard nub of flesh and using his teeth just enough to give her an extra *frisson* of pleasure.

Almost as if they could reach each other's minds, Jed broke the kiss, and Tim stopped sucking her breasts. Roxy opened her eyes, surprised; they smiled at her, and Jed stood up, pulling her to her feet. He unzipped her skirt, and the material fell to the floor in a soft silky rustle. She stepped out of the garment, and Tim slipped her shirt from her shoulders, so that she was wearing only the lewdly-positioned bra, matching lace knickers, and navy lace-topped hold-up stockings.

As one, Jed and Tim knelt beside her. Each took one side of her knickers between their fingers, and gently eased the flimsy ꞇ ment down over her hips, over her thighs. She stepped out ꞁ, and then they started on her stockings, each one rolling the silk down towards her feet. She rested her hands on their shoulders for support, and lifted first one foot and then the other, letting them remove the stockings completely. Then, finally, Tim unclasped her bra and let it fall to the floor, cupping her breasts with his hands and pushing them together and upwards, deepening the vee of her cleavage.

He dipped his head to kiss her breasts, and then stood back, looking at her. Roxy's eyes met his, and then they turned to Jed. He lifted his arms, letting them remove his black sweater, and then Roxy dropped to her knees in front of him. She unbuttoned his trousers and drew the zip down, then pushed the soft material over his hips. He stepped out of them, and Roxy removed his socks, at the same time. Then she tipped her head onto one side, looking at him.

He was wearing black silk boxer shorts, and the outline of his erection was visible through the material. She curled her fingers round his cock, squeezing the shaft gently, then hooked her fingers into the sides of the boxer shorts and drew them down. When he was naked, she leaned forward, tracing the tip of his cock with the tip of her nose. He grinned and helped her to her feet, kissing her lightly on the mouth.

Then they turned to Tim, divesting him of his clothes, so that the three of them were naked together. Tim refilled the glass of champagne. They each took a sip, toasting the other two, and then Tim and Jed dropped to the floor, drawing Roxy down with them onto the thick pile carpet. They knelt either side of her; Roxy shivered as each of them cupped a breast, taking her hard nipples into their mouths and rolling them on their tongues, in perfect timing. They nibbled gently at her with their lips, then began to suck rhythmically.

Roxy moaned; she couldn't help opening her legs, wanting them to touch her there, too. She felt them both chuckle against her skin, and then they were kissing down her body, licking the soft undersides of her breasts and nuzzling her ribcage. They moved down over her abdomen; as they rubbed their faces against the plains of her belly, she felt the slight roughness of their stubble, and it made her wet with anticipation.

Then, teasing her, they moved down to her feet as one. They each picked up one leg, caressing her foot and sucking her toes, licking the hollows of her ankle-bone. Their synchronization was so perfect that she could hardly believe that it was the first time they'd done this. And then all thoughts stopped as they moved upwards, kissing the sensitive spot at the back of her knees. She felt them each slide one hand under her buttocks, lifting her slightly; and then, oh, bliss, one of them tongued her clitoris, using his mouth on the hard nub of flesh in a way that made her wriggle with pleasure, while the other made his tongue into a hard point, lapping at the entrance of her vagina. They worked on her skilfully and in such harmony that she climaxed within moments. They didn't stop as they felt her flesh convulse under their mouths but continued, bringing her to a higher peak.

When her breathing had calmed back to normal, Jed lay on the carpet; Tim helped Roxy onto her knees, and she swung a leg over Jed's body in an almost balletic movement, straddling him. He caught her gaze, and smiled at her; he lifted his hands to caress her breasts, rolling her nipples between his fingers and thumbs. Roxy closed her eyes for a moment, revelling in the sensation; then she slid her hand between their bodies, holding his cock in position, and slowly eased herself down onto the rigid column of flesh.

ade a small noise of pleasure as the tip of his cock
' her. It felt like being wrapped in warm wet silk
'ike having his cock caressed and kneaded between

the petals of a perfect orchid. His mouth opened in a gasp of ecstasy as she sank onto him, so that he was in her up to the hilt; then he became aware of Tim kneeling by his shoulders, and looked up.

The other man's cock was large and erect, in similar proportions to his own. Jed was spellbound as he watched Roxy dip her head, cupping Tim's balls with one hand and, making her mouth into an 'O', sliding it over the tip of Tim's cock. As she began to move over Jed, lifting herself until his cock was almost out of her, her head moved down so that she was taking Tim as deeply into her mouth as possible. Then, as she slammed back down onto Jed's cock, so she withdrew from Tim. It was perfect, Jed thought, absolutely perfect, and he closed his eyes tightly as he felt his orgasm rip through him, and his body poured its essence into Roxy's.

He felt her quim flutter round his cock as her internal muscles contracted; and at Tim's low moan, he guessed that Tim, too, had reached a climax. They remained like that for a while, too lazy and sated to move; then, gently, Tim caressed Roxy's face, and lifted her off Jed.

She stayed on her hands and knees; Jed smiled, and handed her the glass of champagne. She drained it in one gulp; he replenished it, and handed it to Tim, then drank some himself. Roxy took the glass again, and patted the floor invitingly in front of her. He nodded, and sat down as she'd indicated, with his legs spread, so that she could kneel in between his legs. Tim knelt behind Roxy this time; his cock was fully erect again, and he pressed its tip against her vagina, sliding easily into her warm wet depths.

Roxy kissed Jed lightly, and pressed one fingertip gently to each eyelid. He closed his eyes, and then he felt her breasts moving against his thighs as she bent down. She curled h fingers round his cock, and he cried out as she opened her mouth over the tip, and he felt something tingling against his skin. Then he realized what it was: she had a mouthful of champagne.

He opened his eyes, and her eyes laughed back at him. He smiled at her, stroking her short dark hair, and she began to fellate him properly, swishing the bubbles against his skin until they tingled, then swallowing the champagne and soothing the sensations with her tongue. She sucked him rhythmically, her movements matching the way that Tim was thrusting into her. Jed cried out as he climaxed again; from the way that Roxy's body stiffened, he knew that they had reached a climax, too . . .

Jed removed the visor and smiled. If, as he suspected, Tim and Chloe Fraser had been watching this, they would have had a lot more than they'd bargained for. He dressed quickly and went through into the sitting room to join them.

Tim's wife, he noticed, couldn't meet his eyes. He smiled, and sat down.

'What did you think?' Tim asked.

'Very interesting,' he said mildly.

Roxy looked at him in surprise; he grinned. 'And what did you think, Chloe?'

She flushed deeply. 'How do you mean?'

'Come on. You were watching what happened.' He paused. 'I would have done the same thing, in your shoes. I would have wanted to know what you were going to do with that mach'

ur deepened even more. 'Put it this way, I wasn't u to choose *those* options.'

'Well – for a start,' she reminded him, 'you don't drink.'

His smile broadened. 'I make an exception for champagne.'

Tim put his hand over Roxy's, squeezing it gently. 'You may be interested to know, Mortimer,' he said softly, 'that we always keep a bottle of champagne in our fridge.'

Jed's eyes met Roxy's. 'I think,' he said quietly, 'that it's for Chloe to decide.'

Roxy swallowed hard. 'I – um – look, I just develop programs.'

Jed stood up and took her other hand, rubbing her palm with his thumb. 'That's a very feeble excuse, Mrs Fraser. Developing things like this,' he said, 'should make you be able to guess the consequences.' He drew her hand up to his lips, and took each of her fingers in turn into his mouth, sucking gently.

Roxy shivered, and he drew back slightly, still smiling at her. 'If you're cold, then I think that Fraser and I can do something to warm you up. And as we've done it in virtual reality, why not make it happen in real life, too?'

Roxy looked at Tim; he looked back at her, torn between jealousy and excitement. They'd just witnessed Jed's fantasy, and now he was offering to let them share it. 'He's right,' Tim said finally. 'Besides, how else can you test whether the program's working as you planned it?'

Roxy licked her lips. 'Well, as a true scientist, I should always do empirical tests, as well as check the theory.'

Tim returned her smile. 'I'll get the champagne.'

SEVENTEEN

The next morning Roxy woke, wondering if she'd just had a very, very vivid dream; then she realized that she was lying on her back, sandwiched between two men, each of whom had one arm thrown over her. One had an arm resting just below her breasts, over her ribcage, and the other had an arm wrapped round her waist.

She couldn't resist moving slightly, curling her fingers round the erect cocks that brushed against her thighs. Tim reacted by nestling closer, shifting his hand upwards to cup her breasts, and Jed slid his hand down to cup her delta. He licked her earlobe. 'So you're thoroughly greedy, as well as beautiful and intelligent, Mrs Fraser?' he whispered, his breath fanning warm against her ear and sending a shiver of desire through her.

She grinned back, and turned her face to one side to kiss him lightly. 'Hello, Jed. I wasn't sure whether I was dreaming, whether I'd been working on that damned program for too long, or whether what happened last night was real.'

'Oh, it was real, all right.' He let one finger lie flat over her labia, not probing her; a pulse began to beat hard between her legs, betraying her anticipation of the moment when he would press a little harder, slide his finger into her sex. 'How do you feel?'

'To be honest,' Roxy admitted, 'delightfully satiated.'

'Good.' He rubbed his nose against hers. 'Though, much as

I'd like to make love with you again, I have to go to work. There are a few things I need to sort out in the office this morning.'

'You're a workaholic, Mortimer,' Tim grumbled, waking enough to hear the last sentence and a half.

'Says the pot calling the kettle black,' Jed quipped. 'How many times have you worked twelve-hour days recently?'

'Yeah. But you're right – there's a lot to do.'

'And a lot to plan,' Jed agreed. 'Who's on our side, already?'

'Sheppard, so that's finance sorted. Ellis, so we can mobilize any transport and do what we like with the ports; Roper, the interior minister; you; me; Marcus Blake.'

'You're dragging Marcus into this?' Roxy interrupted, shocked. 'But he's not in the government.'

'No, but—' Tim stopped. 'I don't want to tell you any more than this, Roxy. You're implicated enough as it is.'

'Oh, come on. I'm part of this. I'm the one who developed the program; I'm the one who planned how we were going to get the ministers onto our side, if you remember. It was all my idea.'

'Yes, but it's too dangerous. I don't want anything happening to you.' Tim's face tightened. 'I thought I'd lost you before, and that was enough.'

'Before?' Jed asked, his gaze narrowing.

Tim sighed. 'Well, after last night, you might as well know the whole truth. Chloe isn't Chloe.'

'Then who are you?' Jed asked, frowning and looking into Roxy's hazel eyes. 'And I thought that you had blue eyes yesterday evening.'

'I did. They're coloured contact lenses,' she said. 'I was – someone else, before the Traditional Values coup.'

'Roxana Winters?'

Roxy was shocked. 'How did you know?'

'An educated guess. I was going through the minutes of some old committee meetings, and Tim mentioned that a Roxana Winters had been neutralized. I checked the database; Tim hadn't changed one of the cross-tabs, and your name came up. Then I checked Tim's record, to find out that he'd been married to Chloe for five years. But the entry didn't tally with the printout I had from some time previously, when it said that Tim was a bachelor.'

'Shit,' Roxy said. 'Tim, I thought you'd checked the cross-tabs?'

'So did I.' Tim frowned. 'I'll go through them again today.'

'I wouldn't bother,' Jed said. 'I did it for you.'

Tim's eyes widened. 'Are you telling me that you had an idea about what we were planning before you came here, last night?'

'Yes – but don't forget, I'm a psychologist. I reckoned that if you'd had nothing to do with Marcus Blake since you came into power, despite the fact that you were partners on the security project, and then decided to annex him onto a new project . . . Well, there had to be something going on. And when you said that you'd had Roxana Winters neutralized . . .' He shrugged. 'It was an easy guess.'

Roxy whistled. 'I'm glad that you're on our side, Jed. You'd be a formidable enemy.'

'Thank you.' He inclined his head. 'It must have been pretty rough, though.'

'Being parted from Rox? Yeah. They told me that she was dead.' Tim sighed. 'When you come home to find the house smashed up and covered in blood, you don't ask for proof. I never want to go through that, ever again.' He looked at Roxy. 'I was thinking about sending you away somewhere, before we act.'

'Don't you dare,' she warned. 'If you do, I'll disguise myself as a man and come back to London, anyway. And I'll be the one with the knife at Ferris's throat.'

Jed grinned. 'I'd love to psychoanalyze you, Mrs Fraser.'

'Huh.' She pulled a face at him.

'Well, you've got the most important ministers on your side. The others will go with whoever they think has the upper hand. What about publicity?' Jed asked.

'Publicity?' Roxy's eyes snapped with anger. 'If you mean that bastard Reeve, then no. He's not part of this.'

'You need publicity, if you want to win a campaign.'

'I'll handle that side of it,' Roxy said. 'My closest friends are writers and journalists – they'll help me.'

'Reeve will be a good ally.'

'Never.' Roxy was vehement.

'Why do you hate him so much?'

Roxy enlightened him, very succinctly, adding in Giselle's comments about Reeve's background.

Jed's face darkened. 'The bastard,' he growled.

Tim put a warning hand on the other man's forearm. 'Don't get any ideas,' he said. 'Reeve will get his come-uppance – but I believe that it will be at a certain woman's hands.'

'Too bloody right, it will,' Roxy spat.

Tim kissed her. 'Calm down, sweetheart. Look, I have to go into the office, or someone will suspect something.'

'Yeah, it's already going to look bad that I came here last night and didn't leave until this morning,' Jed said.

'That's easy,' Roxy said. 'You came over for dinner; then you and Tim started talking shop. The Head of Security and the Minister of Correction have to work together, after all. And you ended up working until the middle of the night; it was so late that you stayed overnight rather than going back to your own place.'

He grinned. 'That's true – we were busy, until the middle of the night. But no one needs to know what we were working on.'

'Or even whom,' Tim added with a grin.

Roxy flushed. It had been a very long night. Both Tim and Jed had made love with her until the early hours; they had re-enacted Jed's fantasy from VRX, adding a couple of interesting variations along the way. Her quim moistened at the memory of where Jed had kissed her – and how. He'd explored her completely with his mouth, licking every scrap of skin, and Tim had followed Jed's mouth with caresses, until Roxy's body had felt as though she were melting.

Tim climbed out of bed. 'See you in a bit. I need a shower,' he said.

While Tim showered, Jed took Roxy back into his arms, holding her close and stroking her hair. 'I think,' he said quietly, 'that last night was a one-off. Much as I'd like to repeat it, I don't think that Tim would be too happy if we did.'

'You're probably right there,' Roxy agreed.

He kissed her lightly on the mouth. 'I'll see you again, socially, and I think that we'll be friends. But I'll never dare drink champagne again near you.'

'No.' Roxy smiled wryly. 'Jed . . . I wish it could have been different.'

'Me, too – but.' He stroked her face. 'This is the one good thing that's come out of Ferris's government: meeting you.'

'I think that there's a lot more good to come, when Ferris is deposed.'

He nodded. 'There are more than enough people who'll side with you and Tim. It's going to work.'

'Yes. I know.' Roxy sighed. 'I just wish that it would be sooner, rather than later.'

'Better to wait until you're ready.'

'I know.' She smiled ruefully. 'I never was the patient sort.'

'I am.' His gaze held hers. 'Roxy.' She was surprised at how easily he slipped into using her real name. 'If it ever does go wrong between you and Tim . . .'

'It won't.'

'But if it ever does – all you have to do is call me.'

'Thank you.' Roxy had her own ideas on that subject; when they overthrew the government, she had an idea that Jess and Philip would set up house together. Which would leave Giselle at pretty much a loose end; and she had the feeling that Giselle and Jed would get on famously. Maybe if she played matchmaker, she could make both Jed and Giselle happy.

'I mean it, Roxy.' He kissed her lingeringly. 'And I want to say goodbye to you now, in the best possible way.'

'Don't you mean *au revoir*?'

'No, I mean goodbye – as a lover. And *à bientôt* as a friend.'

She grinned. 'Showoff. Just how many languages do you speak?'

'Just French and English. My German's very, very rusty, and my Latin's even worse.' He parted her labia, sliding his finger deep inside her. 'Oh, you could say that I also speak the language of love – if you want me to be *really* corny.'

Roxy licked her lower lip. Part of her had wanted to laugh at Jed's terrible joke, but the way he was moving his finger inside her simply pushed everything else out of her head. All she could think about was the way that he made her feel. 'Jed . . .'

'Yeah. Me too.' He leaned over then and kissed her hard, his lips parting hers and his tongue sliding into her mouth.

Roxy spread her legs and he moved on top of her, kneeling between her thighs and fitting the tip of his cock to her entrance. Roxy exhaled sharply as he pushed into her, his cock filling her, and wrapped her legs round his waist. He began to thrust, moving his body in small circles to increase the friction between their bodies, and Roxy buried her face in his shoulder, trying not to cry. She'd known the man for less than twenty-four hours, and she was already close to falling in love with him; yet both of them knew that it was unfair to Tim. And they were ending it, now.

Her orgasm splintered through her; she made a small whimpering sound in the back of her throat, and Jed kissed her fiercely, continuing to thrust and taking her up to a higher plateau. Then, at last, he came, his cock throbbing deep within her; Roxy wrapped her arms round him, holding him tight.

Eventually, he slipped from her; he kissed her lightly, and climbed out of bed. 'Roxana Winters, you're one incredible woman,' he said softly.

She swallowed, not trusting herself to speak; Jed leaned over, and licked the tears that spilled from her eyes. 'I could love you, Roxy – but it isn't fair to any of us. So take care, and, next time we meet, we'll be friends. Okay?'

She nodded, still not speaking, and reached up to touch his face. He turned his head, kissing her palm and curling her fingers over it. 'See you later, Mrs Fraser,' he said softly, picked up his clothes, and left the room.

Roxy was in a daze for the rest of the day; she couldn't work on the VRX program, because it made her think too much of Jed. In the end, she simply tapped into the security database, using Tim's ID, and looked up Jed's record. As she'd thought, he was two years older than she was. An only child who'd read psychology at Cambridge, had a PhD with a thesis on social behaviour, and a career as a forensic psychologist.

No wonder Ferris had picked Jed Mortimer to be in charge of the Houses of Correction. Who better to "re-educate" people who didn't fit into the system? The thing was, Ferris had miscalculated. Jed Mortimer, like Tim, didn't agree with most of the Traditional Values manifesto – and he was out to change things.

Some days later, Tim seemed distracted over breakfast; Roxy guessed immediately what was going on. 'Tim – you're planning to do something today, aren't you?'

'No.'

'Don't lie to me. We can't afford secrets between us.'

He sighed. 'I don't want you to worry.'

'Tim – be careful, won't you? Promise me.'

He pushed his chair back, walking over to her; she stood up, and he held her close. 'Of course I will. Roxy, it's going to be a bloodless coup. No violence, nothing like the last time. No one's going to get hurt.'

'What about Ferris?'

'We'll deal with him – and we'll do it without force. There's a meeting this morning. That's when we'll strike. We'll simply overpower him, and overturn all his edicts.'

'Tim, revolutions don't happen as quickly and easily as that.' Her eyes were filled with anguish. 'I don't want to lose you, Tim. I don't want you to die.' Or Jed, or Sheppard; she was fond of both of them.

'So what do you want to do?' Tim asked. 'Call it off, and live the rest of our lives as a lie – you as a woman called Chloe, who can't even wipe her nose without asking her husband's permission, and me doing a job I despise? Do you want Jess and Giselle to stay in the House of Correction forever, and Phil to marry some woman the party dictates, to make sure they have viable and genetically strong children?'

'No, of course not.' She grimaced.

'Well, then. Be brave.' He kissed her again. 'I'll see you later.'

'Tim – I love you.'

'And I love you.' He smiled at her. 'And when we're through all this mess, I might even agree to marry you – if you propose to me romantically enough.'

She laughed. 'Since when do we need a bit of paper?'

'Mm – I just like the idea of being married. And having lots of little Roxylets.'

'We'll see.' She sobered. 'Tim – last time you talked about marriage, we were split up.'

'No, we weren't – actually, the very last time we discussed me having a wife, Emma Lynn P. Hurst was sitting on my lap, bossing me around and tampering with the data in my program. She's been here ever since, in her new name of Chloe Fraser,' he reminded her. 'Don't worry. Everything's going to be fine.'

'Yes.' Roxy said the word with more conviction than she felt.

After Tim had gone, she spent the rest of the morning pacing up and down the flat, worrying, wondering what had happened to him. Supposing that the meeting went wrong?

She couldn't bear the sound of the television. It was too irritating, listening to facile male reporters droning on and on and on about unimportant events. She kept the set on teletext, flicking through the news pages and waiting for the moment that it all happened. Reeve wasn't one of them, so publicity would happen after the event, rather than preparing people before it. She and Giselle and Alice had already agreed who was going to do what, and when. Even so, she kept flicking through the news pages, willing there to be something to tell her that it had worked.

The phone rang; she ran over to it, picking it up. 'Yes?' She was unable to keep the panic from her voice.

'Chloe, it's me. Alice.'

'Hello, Al.' Roxy was normally pleased to hear from her best friend, but at that precise moment, she was just too on edge.

'I was just wondering how you were,' Alice said quietly.

'I'm okay.'

Alice coughed. 'Let me put this another way. I believe that Marcus has an important presentation this morning, with Tim. I thought it might be nice if we spent some time together.'

Roxy stiffened. 'Tim didn't tell me that Marcus was going to be in the meeting. I mean, he mentioned Marcus's name, as one of us, but he didn't tell me what Marcus's role was going to be.'

'Marcus didn't tell *me*, until the last minute. So, as I'm at a loose end all day, I'd rather spend today with you.'

'Al . . .'

'I know,' Alice said. 'I know everything. That's why I want to be with you now.'

'Just be careful.' Roxy said. 'Drive carefully.' She put the phone down, biting her lip. God, if this all went wrong, now . . . They'd come for her, they'd come for Alice, they'd kill little Eleanor.

Yet, as Tim had said, how could they not do it?

Roxy and Alice spent the rest of the day drinking coffee and glancing at the teletext. Alice had taken Eleanor to her mother's for safe-keeping the previous day; she made frequent phone calls to check that everything was all right. Neither of them could eat anything, or do anything; Alice suggested playing Scrabble or cards, to keep themselves occupied, but Roxy shook her head. 'I can't concentrate, Al. Not when I don't know what's happening to Tim.' She bit her lip. 'I don't know whether to destroy VRX again, or to leave it.'

'Leave it,' Alice said. 'We're going to fight them this time, every step of the way.'

'Why hasn't he phoned?' Roxy said. 'The longer it's been since I've heard from him, the more convinced I am that something's wrong.'

At that precise moment, the teletext screen went blank. Roxy and Alice looked at each other, fear flickering over their faces.

'It could be anything,' Alice said. 'It's a news blackout: we can't tell if Ferris won, or we did, until we hear from Tim.'

There was a loud bang outside; Roxy scowled and headed for the kitchen, returning with two carving knives. She handed one to Alice.

'It sounds like Ferris won, or Tim would have called us,' she said. 'You're right. This time, we're going to fight them. They won't catch us unprepared.' Her mouth tightened. 'I'll be avenged for Tim, for Monty, and everyone else who's had their lives ruined by Ferris's crew.'

The front door opened; Alice and Roxy both picked up their carving knives and stood, waiting, in silence. After what seemed like an age, the living room door opened . . . and Tim came into view. Roxy, who had been waiting with her knife poised, ready to stab anyone who came through the door, dropped the knife and leaned against the wall. 'Christ, Tim, you scared me! I nearly stabbed you!'

He grinned, and took her in his arms. 'I'm sorry. I know it wasn't funny, Rox, but I couldn't resist it.'

'So what happened?' Alice asked. 'Where's Marcus?'

'I'm here,' Marcus said, coming in with a bottle of champagne. 'And I have news for you, Alice, my darling. As from tomorrow, I'm going to be a house-husband and spend my time looking after Eleanor and developing a few ideas, and you are going back to work.'

'You mean – you did it?' Alice asked, delighted.

'Correction,' Tim said. '*We* did it – all of us.'

Roxy couldn't help the question. 'Is Jed all right?'

'Yes.' Tim rolled his eyes. 'And so is Sheppard. I told you, there was no violence.'

'So what happened?'

'We had a meeting with Ferris. Marcus, as my partner, was there; Jed, as the head of the department closest to mine, was there, too. Sheppard had to be there, to look at the finance; and Roper and Ellis joined us.' He shrugged. 'So. We opened the presentation – then I told Ferris that we were taking over. He threatened us with a gun, but Jed overpowered him before he could even try to aim it at one of us. He's in prison now, under armed guard.'

'Right.' Alice looked at Tim. 'I need your phone – I have to speak to Giselle.'

'And get the publicity under way,' Tim agreed. 'Sure.'

'Don't say any more, until I get back!' Alice warned.

'There isn't any more,' Tim said, with a smile. 'But I think we should open that champagne, now.'

'I'll get the glasses,' Roxy said.

By the time that she'd found the glasses, Marcus had opened the champagne, and he'd poured it into the four glasses, Alice was back. 'So, what happens now?'

'There's a lot of mess to clear up,' Marcus said. 'Most of the government will stay in power, until the elections can be sorted out – otherwise the country will be in chaos.'

'"Most" doesn't include Reeve, I hope,' Roxy said grimly.

'No. He's currently in solitary, waiting for us to decide what to do with him.'

'Just give her a spoon,' Alice said. 'She'll carve his heart out for you.'

'I'm afraid I can't,' Roxy said.

Alice was surprised. 'How do you mean?'

'He doesn't have a heart,' was the crisp rejoinder.

'Point taken. What else is planned?' Alice asked.

'The prisoners in the House of Correction will be freed. Sheppard's sorting out the financial side of it – we can't give compensation, but we'll give them all their property back. Any money that was moved from a woman's account will be moved back, plus interest,' Tim said. 'If the man who took control of it has used it at all, the government will make up the deficit, and he'll pay extra tax, over the next five years, to pay the government back.'

'What about employment?' Roxy asked. 'Do I go back to Visicom?'

'If you like.' Tim coughed. 'We think that all jobs should be on a half-share basis, provided that the original job-holder agrees.'

'Sounds fair enough to me,' Roxy said. 'Actually, though, I was considering going self-employed, and developing VRX properly.'

Alice grinned. 'About time, too!'

'Do we continue living here?' Roxy asked.

Tim shook his head. 'I get the Hampstead house back; but I don't think either of us could face it.'

'No. But I don't want to stay here, either.'

'How about Holland Park?' Tim suggested. 'If our decorators feel like staying on for a bit and finishing the place off – or, at least, make sure that the kitchen and bathroom are usable . . .'

'Sounds good to me.' Roxy paused. 'Where's Reeve?'

'I told you. In solitary,' Tim said.

'I mean, I want to know his location.'

'Rox, just leave it.'

'No. I'm not going to touch him; I just want to pay him a small visit.'

Tim sighed. 'All right. But leave it a couple of days, will you?'

A week later, Roxy walked into the prison. She handed the guard her card, for scanning. 'I'm here to see Reeve,' she said.

'He's in solitary. No visitors,' the guard said.

'Come on, Phil. Don't be mean.'

He grinned. 'Hello, sweetheart.' He kissed her lightly, then scanned her card, and whistled. 'I see, Madam, that you have special privileges. I'd better escort you to him.'

'Thank you.' She followed him down the long narrow corridor; it was fitting, she thought, that Reeve had been taken to the same place where she'd been held. A wry smile twitched the corners of her lips as she discovered that not only was it the same building, it was the same room.

'Remember this place?' Philip asked softly.

'Mm. But I don't think that Reeve will have the compensations that I did.'

'No, I doubt it.' He squeezed her hand. 'Rox, you're not going to do anything rash, are you?'

'Like what?'

'Killing the guy.' His face tightened. 'I stay away from his room, because I want to kill him for you.'

'I have something a little more subtle in mind than bloodshed,' Roxy said. 'And I need to see him alone.'

'Are you sure?'

'Sure,' she confirmed.

'If you need any help, just shout for me. I'll be at the end of the corridor.'

Roxy smiled at him. 'Thanks, but I can handle him.'

'Even so.' He winked at her. 'Good luck.'

He opened the door and she walked inside; she heard the lock click behind her.

Reeve looked up; he seemed to have aged since she saw him last. He didn't speak but cast his eyes down to the floor again.

'Don't you know me?' Roxy asked.

He lifted his head and frowned. 'No.'

She put her hands up to her eyes, removing the coloured lenses. 'Try again.'

His eyes narrowed, and then his face darkened as recognition hit him. 'Roxana Winters.'

'The very same. Just a different haircut – and colour, for the time being.' She looked coolly at him. 'You know why you're here, don't you?'

'Because I supported Ferris.'

'No. That wasn't a crime, in itself; everyone's entitled to their beliefs. But what they're not entitled to do is to violate other people. You're here for what you did to me.'

He said nothing, and her mouth tightened. 'Don't you even have the grace to apologize?'

'Why should I?'

'Because you treated me badly, Reeve. You used me as a whore. You didn't care about what was happening to me. You could have made things good for me, too – but you didn't. You abused your power. And I vowed, then, that I'd kill you, one day.' She smiled thinly. 'I could have killed you before I escaped, but I wanted to wait. I wanted you to know that I'd be out there, waiting for you.'

'Fraser said that you were neutralized.'

'Because we changed my record. I became Chloe Fraser, living a lie.'

'His wife?' Reeve hadn't been expecting that. 'How did you persuade him to help you?'

'He was right. You're slack. You didn't even check my record, and find out that I lived with Tim Fraser before Ferris's rule.' Her lip curled. 'You don't know how close you were to the edge, Reeve. But now, you're here – in the same room I was kept in. You're feeling how I felt, locked in here, not knowing what was going to happen to me or what was happening outside.'

'So what are you going to do? Order me to be a drudge for you?'

'No.'

He swallowed. 'You're going to kill me?'

She shook her head. 'I've thought about it – fantasized about it. What tipped the balance for me was the way you let me have a shower, then took me again, and wouldn't let me clean myself. You made me dry myself on your used towel. You were out to humiliate me.' She drummed her fingers against each other. 'I thought about killing you, very slowly. But now I realize that you're not worth it.' She looked at him with contempt. 'I'm just going to leave you here to rot. Because you're never, ever, coming out of here. If you escape, we'll pick you up in seconds – and you'll be taken to a more secure jail.' She smiled thinly. 'And if you try going out of solitary, you won't last a second in the jail.'

'Why?'

'Because,' she said quietly, 'my field's in computing. And I've made some very subtle alterations to your record. All I have to do is release details of those changes.'

'What changes?'

She spread her hands. 'That's for me to know, and for you to think about.' She rapped on the door, signalling her readiness to leave.

'What changes?' he repeated, standing up.

'I wouldn't try anything,' she said, looking at his threatening stance. 'The guard will be here any moment now.' And Philip would be more than happy to deal with Reeve for her, if he laid so much as a finger on her.

'*What changes?*'

'Ignorance is strength, remember,' she informed him tightly. 'I just wanted you to know that I'm the one responsible for it.'

The door opened, and she left; Reeve hammered on the door, and she could hear him all the way down the corridor. 'What changes? What have you done? What changes?'

Philip raised his eyebrows. 'I don't know if I dare ask what you said to him.'

She grinned. 'Jess gave me the idea – after a conversation with Jed. Speak to her about it.'

'I will, tonight.' He smiled at her. 'I don't think that I'd like to be in Reeve's shoes.'

'No. Well, you're not that sort of person,' she reminded him. 'And he deserves everything that's happening to him, right now ...'

EIGHTEEN

Some months later, Roxy was having lunch with Sheppard at his flat.

'It was a good meeting,' Sheppard said, filling their wine glasses.

'Yeah.' Roxy smiled at him. 'Thanks to you. Without your financial wizardry, I think I'd have been stuck.'

'Thank you.' He handed her a glass. 'Well – here's to us.'

Roxy didn't usually drink at lunchtime, but she made an exception this once. It wasn't every day you signed a million-pound contract to produce the program you'd worked on for years. She lifted her glass in a toast, and sipped the buttery Chardonnay. She smiled to herself. In common with many of the financial people she'd met, Alan Sheppard had a weakness for very good wine.

Things were good, she thought. Since Ferris had been deposed, the new government had done a lot of good. They'd been voted back into power when the elections had been called, although one or two of the ministers, like Sheppard, had bowed out, saying that they wanted to go back into business. The few positive aspects of Ferris's government had been retained, and life was looking good.

Except for one thing. Roxy tried to blank it from her mind; now wasn't the time to think about *that*.

'Roxy,' Sheppard said softly, 'you haven't heard a single word I've said to you.'

She flushed. 'Sorry, Alan. I was miles away.'

'Look, I may be speaking out of turn, but—' He sighed. 'I care about you, Roxy. You're unhappy, and I hate to see you like this.'

She bit her lip. 'I'm fine.'

'No, you're not. You have shadows under your eyes – and even though today means that your business is going from strength to strength, you're not smiling.'

'I'm fine,' she repeated.

He took her hand, stroking it. 'Roxy. I thought we were friends.'

'We are.'

'Then why don't you trust me?'

'I do.'

'With your business, yes.'

She sighed. 'All right. If you must know, it's Tim. We're not getting on very well at the moment.'

'Do you want to talk about it?'

'Not really; but I suppose that it would do me good.' She swallowed. 'We don't see each other very often; he's busy at work, and I'm busy with VRX. But when we do see each other, we end up rowing. We're probably both overdoing it, and need a break, but he refuses to take a holiday.' She shrugged. 'And he's just not interested in me any more. I can't remember the last time we made love. Probably the first week after he deposed Ferris.'

'Oh, Roxy.' Sheppard pushed his chair back, and came to put his arms round her shoulders. 'He's crazy. You're beautiful, soft and warm and lovely, and if I were ever privileged to have you in my bed, there's no way I'd be able to keep my hands off you.'

Gently, she removed his hands from her body. 'That's very sweet of you, Alan.'

'But no. I know – you only have eyes for Tim, even though you're not getting on too well with him.' Alan shrugged. 'Well, that doesn't change things between us. We're friends, as well as working together in business. If it ever gets to the stage where you don't think you can live with Tim any more, you're welcome to my spare room. No strings, and I'll even put a lock on the door, so it'll be more private for you.'

She smiled at him. 'Alan, that's very sweet of you, and I appreciate it. But if things do become that bad, I'll probably stay with Alice for a couple of days, until I find myself a flat or something.'

'Well, the offer's there.' He smiled at her. 'Now, shall we change the subject?'

A few weeks later, Roxy had to admit to herself that things had become bad enough for her to move out. She and Tim were barely speaking; she thought that they'd reached the point of no return. She decided to make one last effort and maybe seduce him, with the idea that the intimacy of making love might be what they needed to repair their relationship. But Tim pushed her away, saying that he was too tired.

The next day, she tackled Alice about it. 'Al – I need a favour.'

'Of course.' Alice was radiant, shining in her seventh month of pregnancy.

'You don't have to say yes.'

'I don't know what the question is yet,' Alice said with a grin.

'Okay.' Roxy took a deep breath. 'I'm leaving Tim. Can I borrow your spare room for a couple of days?'

'You didn't need to ask that. You know you can stay here,

any time you like.' Alice looked searchingly at her. 'Are you sure that you really want to leave Tim?'

Roxy nodded. 'It's changed between us, Al. He's become a workaholic, and I'm tired of being neglected. And before you say that I'm just as bad as he is – at least I've made the effort to reach him. He's just pushed me away, every time. It's not going to work.'

'Right.' Alice sighed. 'Well, as long as you're straight with him, and you tell him why you're leaving – if that doesn't bring him back to his senses, then you can stay as long as you like.'

Roxy rested her hand on Alice's stomach, feeling the baby kick. 'You need your space, Al. It'll be for a couple of days, and that's all – just until I find a flat.'

Alice took her hand and squeezed it. 'I'm sorry, Rox. I really thought that you and Tim . . .'

'Yeah, I know. So did I.' Roxy sighed. 'It just wasn't to be.'

When Roxy informed Tim that evening that she was leaving, he said nothing. Stung, she packed quickly and left, there and then. Within three days, she'd found herself a new flat and arranged for the contents of her study to be delivered to her new home. She deliberately left behind anything that made her think of Tim: though she didn't wipe his picture from VRX. Somehow, she couldn't bring herself to sever the last link.

She spent her time working on VRX, and the occasional evening with friends. Jess and Philip fussed over her, as did Alice and Marcus. Giselle, who'd moved back to her own flat, rather than moving in with Jess and Philip, plied her with wine and good conversation. Roxy's matchmaking between Giselle and Jed hadn't worked; they liked each other, but the sexual chemistry just wasn't there. Although Jed was part of Roxy's set of friends, she avoided him, thinking that she couldn't face him; she didn't want to fall into his arms on the rebound from Tim.

Then, one night, the phone rang. It was Jed. 'Roxy.'

'Hi. How's the new job?' At the elections, Jed had been voted in as Minister for Health, and he'd been busy ever since.

'Fine.' He paused. 'I spoke to Giselle last week.'

'Oh?' Roxy kept her voice light, but her heart was hammering.

'She told me that you and Tim had split up.'

'Yes.'

'And I just wanted you to know that, if you could do with some company, I'm here.'

'Thank you.'

'Thanks, but no thanks – because you're busy.' His voice held the ghost of a smile. 'Coward.'

'I'm not being a coward, Jed. I just want to make sure that I see you for the right reasons.'

'Then have dinner with me tomorrow night. My place.'

'No.'

'Yes,' he insisted. 'No strings. Just dinner.'

'Just dinner, then,' Roxy agreed. 'All right.'

'Good. You won't regret it. Eight o'clock.'

'See you then.'

The next night, although Roxy had promised herself that she was only seeing Jed as a friend, for dinner, she found herself dressing up. She wore a jade-green silk shift dress, teaming it with a black chiffon shirt, which she wore as a jacket, and a pair of black leather stilettos. Although her hair was still short, it was back to her natural fair colouring, and the colours she wore suited her. She added mascara and lipstick – another rarity, since she didn't usually wear it – and set off for Jed's flat.

She arrived at eight o'clock precisely, with a bottle of wine and a bunch of white roses. He answered the bell immediately, and smiled at her. 'Hi. Come in.' His eyebrows lifted as she gave him the roses. 'Since when do women buy men flowers?'

'Since when has there been a law saying that they can't?' she retorted.

He sniffed the bouquet. 'Beautiful.' His eyes held hers for a moment, and she flushed. He wasn't just talking about the roses: he was saying what he thought of her. The worst thing was, she felt the same: she couldn't help staring hungrily at him, remembering what it had been like when his body had fused with hers. The thought made her loins tingle and her sex moisten.

'Come and sit down, while I put these in water.' He ushered her through to the dining room, and returned a couple of minutes later with the bottle of champagne she'd brought him, open, and a vase containing the roses. He set the roses on the mantelpiece, then poured them both a glass of wine. 'Cheers,' he said softly.

'Cheers.'

'You remembered that I only drink one kind of wine.' He took a sip.

'I wasn't sure what you were cooking, but this goes with most things.'

'Indeed. It's salmon. I hope that's okay?'

She was surprised. 'But I thought you were vegetarian?'

'No, I just don't eat red meat. Whoever filled in my record in the National Database didn't realize the difference.'

'Right.'

The salmon *en croûte* was surprisingly good. She smiled at him, her eyes laughing. 'I bet you bought this from M&S.'

He was unabashed. 'I don't have time to cook, though I

used to enjoy it.' He reached out to take her hand. She looked so beautiful by candlelight, though she also looked incredibly unhappy. No doubt she'd been pushing herself too hard, since she'd split up with Tim.

He rubbed the back of her hand. 'Rox, do you want to talk about it?'

'What?'

'There are shadows under your eyes, and you look so unhappy.'

'I'm fine.'

His face was filled with concern. 'Well, you don't look it.' He sighed. 'I think it was a bad idea, having you over for dinner.'

'Meaning?'

'I promised you it would be just dinner. But drinking champagne, listening to this music—' he'd put on a CD of Rachmaninov's third piano concerto '—and the way you're looking at me: it makes me want to hold you and touch you.'

She licked her suddenly dry lips. 'Jed.'

'Oh, hell,' he said. 'I can't handle this, Rox.' He stood up and pulled her to her feet, wrapping his arms round her and jamming his mouth over hers. Roxy matched him kiss for kiss, bite for bite, her hunger rising as she felt his erection press against her pubis.

'Perhaps it was *à bientôt*, after all,' she said softly, when he finally broke the kiss.

His answer was to pick her up and carry her through to his bedroom.

'And since when did you develop macho tendencies?' she teased.

'I don't know. My body's just taken over from my brain,' was the equally teasing reply.

He set her on her feet, and went over to the mantelpiece, lighting the large beeswax candles that stood at each end. At Roxy's raised eyebrows, he said, 'No, they're not seduction aids. I just happen to like candlelight.'

'Right.'

He switched off the light, then walked back over to her, undressing her slowly and licking the skin of her inner elbow as he uncovered it, in a way that made her shiver. He helped her out of her dress, then pulled her back into his arms, kissing the side of her neck; she arched against him. Her nipples were hard; he could feel them through the thinness of his shirt and the lace of her bra. Groaning softly, he slid the straps of her bra over her shoulders and dropped to his knees in front of her, burying his face between her breasts, then turning his head slightly so that he could take one nipple into his mouth.

As he began to suck, she slid her fingers into his hair, urging him on, and he removed her half-slip, pulling her knickers down at the same time. She wasn't wearing stockings; he leaned back to look at her, loving the way the candlelight flickered over her skin. A dreamy smile crossed his face, and he stood up again. Roxy helped him undress, and they fell into bed, kissing and stroking and licking, their movements frenzied. Then, at last, Jed pulled her on top of him. She rested her quim against him so that he could feel how warm and wet she was; when she lifted herself slightly, he curled his fingers round hers and, together, they manoeuvred his cock so that it pressed against the entrance of her sex.

Slowly, slowly, she sank down onto him.

'Rox, you feel so good,' he said hoarsely.

She bent her head to kiss him; he kissed her hard in response, and she began to move over him. He slid one hand between their bodies, his fingers seeking her clitoris;

as he began to rub her, bringing her to a frenzy of need, she moaned and tipped back her head. She lost count of the number of times he brought her to a climax; then, at last, sated, she lay against him, curled into his arms, with one knee pushed between his legs and one hand resting lightly on his hip.

'Oh, Roxy.' He rubbed his cheek against hers. 'I was getting to the point when I was going to ask Sheppard for an advance copy of VRX, scan your face into it, and spend my nights making love with you again.'

'Jed.' She swallowed. 'Look, I was hoping that things would work out with you and Giselle. That's why I introduced you.'

He shook his head. 'I like her, but that's as far as it goes. There isn't the same chemistry.'

She cupped his face, making him look into her eyes. 'What I'm trying to say is that if anything happens between us, I don't want it to be on the rebound.'

He watched her for a moment. 'You're still in love with Tim, aren't you?'

She closed her eyes. 'I thought that maybe—'

'Maybe making love with me would exorcise his ghost?' Jed asked softly.

'No. I wasn't intending to make love with you. We said, "no strings".'

He smiled ruefully. 'If Tim lets you go, he's a bigger fool than I give him credit for.'

Roxy bit her lip. 'I don't know what's going to happen, Jed. But if my feelings for him ever do change . . .'

'I know.' He stroked her face. 'In the meantime, how about some more exorcism? I think it's something we both need . . .'

A week or so later, Roxy returned home from a meeting with Sheppard. He had become the financial director of her business, and Roxy thought that it was the best business decision she had ever made. Things were going well with the firm, and the first copy of VRX was scheduled for production in two months' time. Sheppard's management of the business side of things meant that Roxy was free to spend her time developing more programs. Nearly everything in her life was perfect.

But not quite, she thought, opening her front door. Maybe Alice was right, and a holiday would help. She'd been working hard. A couple of weeks spent lying in the sun, reading trashy novels, would do her the world of good. Maybe she'd ask Giselle to join her.

She closed the door behind her, and suddenly noticed that her study door was open and the light was on. She'd switched off all the lights before she'd left the house that morning: which meant that someone was in the house.

Cold fear settled in her stomach. Who was it? What did he want with her? Should she call the police? But then again, if she phoned the police, he'd hear her – so she had to tackle him head on. She had nothing to lose.

She pushed the door open, and stared in surprise as she saw Tim. 'What the hell . . . ?'

'Good evening.' He spun round from her desk, and smiled at her.

'What are you doing here?' she demanded roughly.

'You sent for me.'

'I did not.'

He gestured to her PC. 'Have a look at your e-mail. I think you'll find a message on there.'

'Have you been hacking into my system?' She marched over towards him, pushing him aside, and tapped into her electronic mailbox. There were two new messages. One was an incoming one, which the log said she'd selected that morning: *Data interchange with the man of your dreams? Then e-mail me.* There was a number below, one she didn't recognize. The message above it was one that had been sent from her mailbox, five minutes later: *Yes, tonight, eight o'clock, my flat.*

She glanced at her watch. It was quarter to nine. So he'd been there for forty-five minutes. Long enough to hack into her system. 'I didn't send this message, or read the other one.'

'Didn't you, now?'

'You've been hacking.'

He grinned. 'Okay, I have. But you're not whiter than white in that direction, are you?'

'Meaning?'

'Surely you remember, Miss Hurst?'

'Tim . . .' She sighed. 'Look, I'm tired, I've had a long day, and I want to go to bed.'

'Rox, I'd like to go to bed, too, but we need to talk.'

'It's past that. When I wanted to talk before, you weren't interested.'

'I was a fool, Rox.' He coughed. 'The Minister of Health was right about me.'

'Jed? What does he have to do with this?'

'He dropped in, for a social call.' Tim rubbed a hand over his face. 'He told me a few home truths. And he's right.' He sighed. 'Oh, Rox. I wish I could just turn back the clock.'

'I was thinking about trying an experiment with time travel,' Roxy quipped.

He grinned. 'That sounds more like something out of one of Alice's novels.'

'It is. She's doing a collaboration with Jess, and they've both been picking my brains, for an anorak's viewpoint.'

'Right.' He smiled at her. 'Rox, can you forgive me?'

'I'm not moving back in with you.'

'I'm not asking that. I just want to start again, right from the first night I met you. We'd been out to dinner, and I insisted on seeing you home. Then you asked me in for a coffee. I was going to behave myself, but then I caught the scent of your perfume, and everything else went out of my mind, except how much I wanted to make love with you. And I remember,' he said softly, 'doing this.' He dipped his head to kiss her, biting gently at her lower lip and then sliding his tongue along it until she opened her mouth to kiss him back.

His hands slid down to span her waist, resting on the curve of her hip; slowly, he eased his fingers under the hem of her top so that he could stroke her lower back. Roxy arched her back in pleasure, and he rubbed his nose against hers. 'God, I'd almost forgotten how good you feel.'

'Mm.' Roxy was wary.

'I want you, Rox. I want you so badly.' He slid his hands upwards until they cupped her breasts, then rubbed her already erect nipples with the pads of his thumbs. He nudged one thigh between hers. He nuzzled the sensitive spot at the side of her neck, opening his mouth over her skin; when she shivered, arching against him, he undid the clasp of her bra and shifted to cup her breasts properly in his hands.

'Roxy,' he said softly, 'that time, you said that we were too old to neck in the kitchen. I guess that we're too old to neck in your study, too.'

She swallowed hard. 'Tim ... I don't know if I'm ready for this.'

'It's the only way I know to break down the walls, Rox.' He kissed the end of her nose, then led her out of the study. He paused by the fridge, to collect the bottle of champagne he'd left there earlier and a punnet of tiny out-of-season straw-berries, and paused in the hall. 'I don't know my way around here. So take me to your bed, Roxy. Make love to me.'

Memories flooded back: their first time together, when he'd made the same appeal – and when she'd led him to her bed, made love with him all night.

'The woman of my dreams,' he said softly, rubbing his nose against hers; Roxy gave in, and took his hand, leading him to her bedroom.

He put the champagne and strawberries on her bedside table, switching on the light while Roxy drew the curtains; then he pulled her back into his arms, kissing her hard. The old passion flared between them, and they stripped each other swiftly, hungrily. Tim picked her up, pushing the duvet aside and laying her on top of the bed; he stood there for a moment, looking at her.

'God, you're so very beautiful,' he said huskily.

'And you talk too much,' she retorted.

He grinned and joined her on the bed, kneeling between her thighs. He rubbed the tip of his cock against her quim, testing her arousal; she felt warm, her flesh slippery, as he touched her. She tilted her hips, pushing against him, and he slid into her, up to the hilt. She gave a small sigh of pleasure and lifted her legs, wrapping them round his waist so that he penetrated her more deeply, and he began to thrust, using long slow steady strokes that made the tension in her grow stronger. Her fingers dug into his buttocks, urging him to push harder, deeper; he groaned. 'God, you feel fantastic. Like warm wet velvet. Like a bunch of dewy roses.'

'You're a lousy poet,' she murmured.

'Just as long as I'm not a lousy fuck,' he retorted, and pushed deeper. Roxy cried out, and her body went completely rigid for a second; he felt her internal muscles contract hard around him as she came. The feeling of her quim rippling round him was enough to tip him into his own release; he cried out, and came, his cock twitching deep inside her. He remained inside her, supporting his weight on his hands and knees, unwilling to break the closeness; he buried his face in her hair, breathing in her scent.

When he slipped from her, he rolled over onto his side, filling a glass with champagne and handing it to her. Roxy sipped it and passed the glass back to him; he turned it round so that he drank from the same place that her lips had touched. She pulled a face at him, and he grinned, feeding her a strawberry.

'I still don't believe that you hacked into my mailbox,' Roxy said.

'It wasn't hacking, exactly . . . I simply guessed your password.' He glanced sideways at the bottle.

She flushed. 'Champagne.'

'It was an easy guess – once I knew that you'd seen Jed the week before.'

Her colour deepened. 'What happened between Jed and me – did he tell you about it?'

'He didn't have to. I guessed. That's why he was so angry with me – because he said you were still in love with me, and I was too stupid to see it. He said that if he could trade places with me, he would; and at least he knew how to treat you properly.'

Roxy winced. 'I'm sorry.'

'So am I.' He smiled at her, and fed her another strawberry. 'You've done well with VRX. I read a glowing report in the press today. Congratulations.'

'You should start seeing some of the profits yourself, soon,'

Roxy said, 'as you were co-developer. Sheppard's my financial director, and I asked him to set it up.'

'Hey, I'm not the one who's taken it this far.' Tim shook his head. 'I can't accept any money.'

'Well.' She curled into his arms. 'How are things going at Comco?'

He wrinkled his nose. 'Routine.'

'I know a small up-and-coming company who could use a good creative programmer.'

'Oh?'

'I've been spending some time with Philip and Jess recently. Phil's going back to university to do his Masters degree. His thesis will be on technology and its influence on fiction.' She grinned. 'Apart from Jess and Alice, that is. Anyway, he persuaded me to read this novel, *Brave New World*. There was an idea in there about films – they called them "feelies" – where the people who sat in the cinema seats could feel everything that the characters felt.'

'I can see its appeal to you,' Tim said.

'Imagine, a whole cinema, with everyone tuned into the film and able to feel what was going on. Like VRX, but a couple of hundred headsets, all linked . . .' Her eyes glowed. 'We can do it, Tim.'

'Yes, we can.'

She looked at him. 'So how about it? Are you interested?'

'Yes.' He paused. 'But is our relationship going to be just work?'

'That depends. I don't want to rush back into anything.'

He nodded. 'I'll take it as slowly as you like. But I want you back, Rox, as more than just a co-worker. I want you as my partner.'

She spread her hands. 'I can't promise, Tim. You hurt me.'

'Yeah, I know. And I'm sorry.' He stroked her hair. 'I'll join you in development work at VRX, if you meant your offer.'

'I do.'

'Except this time,' he said softly, 'there will be no dangerous games involved – and this time, I'm not going to let work be the main thing in my life. You'll come first.'

'Except, of course,' Roxy said with a grin, sliding her hand down his body to curl round his erect cock, 'when we have to test certain films.'

'Indeed,' he agreed, moving swiftly so that she was lying on top of him, and his cock was sheathed within her once more. 'When we will, of course, have to work extremely hard to make sure that we can transfer this sort of feeling to the sensor pads . . .'